DYING DAY

Book 7

KORY M. SHRUM

This book is a work of fiction. Any references to historical events, real people, or real places have been used fictitiously. Other names, characters, places, and incidents are the product of the author's imagination. Any resemblance to actual persons, living or dead, business establishments, events, or locales is entirely coincidental.

No part of this book shall be reproduced or transmitted in any form or by any means without prior written permission of the publisher. Although every precaution has been taken in preparation of the book, the publisher and the author assume no responsibility for errors or omissions. Neither is any liability assumed for damages resulting from the use of information contained in this book or its misuse.

Dying Day (2nd edition)
ISBN 978-1-949577-06-8
Copyright © 2017 Kory M. Shrum
All rights reserved.

TIMBERLANE
PRESS

DYING DAY

AN EXCLUSIVE OFFER FOR YOU

Connecting with my readers is the best part of my job as a writer. One way that I like to connect is by sending 2-3 newsletters a month with a subscribers-only giveaway, free stories from your favorite series, and personal updates (read: pictures of my dog).

When you first sign up for the mailing list, I send you at least three free stories right away.

If giveaways and free stories sound like something you're interested in, please look for the special offer in the back of this book.

Happy reading,

Kory M. Shrum

AUTHOR'S NOTE

This is the seventh and final installment in the *Dying for a Living* series. Just writing that sentence makes my breath catch. For those of you who don't know, *Dying for a Living* was my first novel.

Jesse Sullivan was the first character who came to me, alive and in full-color, through the illuminated fog of my imagination. She was the first clear voice I heard in a mind full of such voices. So there is something incredibly, and surprisingly, bittersweet about ending her tale. Even though I knew how this series would end the moment I wrote *Chapter 1* on August 25, 2008, it's strange to finally arrive here.

I want to thank all of the readers who were here with me from page one. Thank you for reading. Thank you for listening. Thank you for making room for Jesse and Ally and their many friends in your hearts and minds. And while I plan to write many, *many* more stories over the coming years, Jesse will always be my first joy and heartbreak. Just as you will always be my first readers.

You're both more precious to me than I can say.

Daniel Phelps' fingers are so cold he thinks they'll fall off, snapping like icicles from the rain gutter. He positions his feet in the frosty grass, liking the way it crunches under his sneakers, even if the cold has weaseled its way through the canvas and his thick socks to nip at his toes. White breath billows in front of his face with each exhale, but he ignores all of this. He concentrates on the dusty baseball in his right hand. He throws it high. It pulls to the right. On the other side of the lawn, his uncle opens a battered brown glove and catches the ball with a grimace.

"That's your third wide pitch. You want to quit?" Uncle Paul calls out. His own breath is white smoke in front of his eyes. He lifts his John Deere cap from his head and scratches the scalp underneath. He rotates his shoulder clockwise in its socket, the Carhartt jacket lifting and falling with the movement.

"I'm fine," Danny insists. He isn't going to let something as stupid as a burning arm rob him of this chance. Baseball tryouts are Friday, and Danny intends to spend every free moment between now and the two o'clock meetup on the pitch, warming up for it. He's gotten up at 5:30 every day this week to throw with Uncle Paul.

His uncle looks at his watch. "We've got time for a few more. It's just past seven."

Time. Time before the school bus with a patched tire picks him up at the end of the driveway. Time before Uncle Paul takes his own truck into town and works ten hours at the cereal plant doing whatever it is a foreman does there. Time before Aunt Jody appears in the door smiling with their tin box lunches in hand.

That part of their morning routine always makes Danny a little sad. It makes him miss his mother, dead for almost two years now, and makes him miss his big sis Jesse, too. He hasn't talked to Jesse in months, and he isn't sure he's ever going to talk to her again.

Every time Jesse's face blasts across the evening news, Uncle Paul and Aunt Jody change the channel or send him on some needless errand out of the room. *Danny, will you check the mail, buddy? Danny, I think I left my car windows down, and it's supposed to rain. Danny, can you go make sure the shed is locked up good and tight?*

Once, he asked his aunt and uncle if they thought Jesse would be okay. They'd exchanged a look over their plates of roast beef and mashed potatoes before Aunt Jody said, "I'm sure it's all just a misunderstanding, sweetie. They'll sort it out."

This was pretty big of her, because Aunt Jody doesn't like what the TV calls "zombies." Those people like his sister who can die but come back to life. Some of them work as death replacement agents, saving people, actually *dying* for them— which Danny thinks is about the coolest job in the world— even if people are creeped out by it.

Danny was surprised to find that the kids at Lincoln Middle School didn't think his sister's job was cool. They'd reacted with sneers and cruel taunts when he first told them. One boy even shoved him into a locker and called him *zombie lover*, asking him, *so you like your cunts cold?* He knew what the c-word meant. Some of the older boys talked like that, and made fun of him because he didn't. *You sound like a librarian, Phelps.*

When he goes to Lincoln High next year for tenth grade, maybe it'll be different. That school is three times as big and serves two whole counties instead of just their small town, Richboro, population 2,828.

His uncle snaps back and releases the baseball. It sails past Danny and rolls down the hill behind him, toward the trees lining the driveway. Danny doesn't even see it go by.

His uncle barks a laugh. "What happened, Dan? Your brain short circuit?"

Danny doesn't answer.

His eyes are fixed on the black swarm on the horizon. A mass unlike any he's ever seen is rushing toward him, and with it a high-pitched whine that makes his flesh crawl along his bones.

He steps toward it, mouth falling open.

Birds. Danny realizes he's looking at birds—hundreds, maybe *thousands* of birds—diving and flying as if Hell itself is on their tail feathers. Some of the birds collide with one another, and when they do, their talons come out, swiping and screeching, and they fall to Earth in a feathery ball of terrified rage.

"Must be a storm," his uncle says. But he doesn't sound like he believes this himself. "Just a bad storm."

"What is that?" Danny murmurs. "Lightning?"

He points at the strange ripple of purple electricity rolling across the sky. It spiderwebs like heat lightning, but this is February, not July.

"Mother of God," Uncle Paul says. "Get in the house."

Danny doesn't move. He just stands there, neck craned back and staring.

The purple light covers everything. It shimmers like fish scales, blotting out the sun and the clouds, giving the world a twilight hue. The pond, the yard with all those baseballs in the grass glow purple now. The house looks possessed, like something out of a horror movie, with the violet light collecting in its window glass.

A *BOOM* cracking across the sky makes Danny turn and look back toward the horizon.

The purple is changing. It's turning orange. No. Not orange. It's *fire*.

The sky is on fire.

The sky is on fire, and all Danny can do is look at it.

He feels a rough hand seize the back of his neck and jerk him toward the house.

"We've got to get indoors!" Uncle Paul begins dragging Danny after him. His sneakers stumble up the steps and into the house, and the door is slammed behind them.

Aunt Jody screams. One hand goes over her heart, the other is clutching a knife coated with peanut butter poised over a slab of white bread. "Heaven's sake, Paul. Is that really necessary?" She pulls the earbuds from her ear and glares at her husband. "I could've cut my finger off, and you'd have found a surprise in your sandwich."

Uncle Paul says nothing. He only pulls back the kitchen curtain to reveal the flaming sky.

In the distance, an emergency siren begins to wail.

———

OFFICER JEFFERS STOPS HIS POLICE CAR IN THE CENTER OF 2nd Ave. He is a block from the Starbucks where his partner, Officer Gaul, waits with their coffee. Without thinking, he leans over and flips the switch that controls his flashing lights. The blue lights spring to life, splashing across the asphalt and brick-faced buildings lining the avenue. This does nothing to deter the looters. But if he is being honest with himself, Jeffers doesn't give a damn about the looters.

The swarms of ransackers crawl in and out of busted windows. Two men climb into the back of a battered red pickup with a sixty-inch flat screen between them. A gang of teenagers in denim jackets and hoodies run into the street laughing, arms full of iPads and Bose earphones. Even a petite woman in a pencil skirt and pristine white dress shirt wobbles to her car on unsteady red stilettos, holding a Keurig against her chest.

A *Keurig.*

None of them look at Jeffers or his patrol car in the center of the road. But several throw nervous glances up at the sky. Jeffers himself seems unable to look away from it. He doesn't see his partner Gaul step out onto the sidewalk without their coffee. He only notices him when four or five green-aproned employees dart out of the Starbucks, each throwing a panicked glance at the sky before ducking into the parking garage across the street.

Only then do the officers' eyes meet, and Gaul begins to run toward his partner as one might run from gunfire: eyes as large as saucers, head ducked and covered by shaking hands.

Some dull remnant of his training tells him to arm himself, tells him to prepare for the fight.

Jeffers' thumb reflexively unsnaps the leather strap holding his pistol in place at his side. But he doesn't draw his gun. He has no target. The looters, sure, but the looters are not the problem.

The sky is the problem.

There was no training for this. No practice scenario. No drill.

Officer Jeffers remains transfixed, staring at that sliver of sky between the tall buildings. It shimmers purple, warping and wavering as if the sky has turned from air to water, and impossibly, they are watching lavender waves slap against an invisible shore. *They* have become the shore.

An explosion rocks the street, and orange flames leap from a storefront half a block down. People scream. Panic erupts as black smoke billows into the sky.

"What is that? What the fuck is that?!" Gaul slaps the hood of the cruiser as if touching home base, as if a simple *olly olly oxen free* will save them all.

KIRK STANDS ON THE LARGEST HILL IN THE MT. OLIVET Cemetery and counts his blessings. At least it won't rain.

And it certainly won't snow. Their Nashville winter has been too mild this year for snow.

Kirk is grateful for this, because the only thing sadder than lowering an old friend into the earth is lowering an old friend into the earth while cold rain beats down. He is pleased with how the service has gone so far. Reverend Hanscomb has been solemn but kind, apparently sober for the occasion. Kirk detected no clue of the old man's drinking except for the tremor in his hands whenever he repositioned the Bible in his palm and turned the page. Kirk doubts anyone will notice this, or if they do, they'll mistake it for an old man's tremor, not a drunk's.

But who is Kirk to judge? He's getting quite close to "old man" himself these days. His stiff back, sore feet, and wandering mind tell him so.

Of course, perhaps he should be grateful for the opportunity to grow old at all.

Kirk turns and looks at a grave higher up on the hill, half hidden by the shade of the weeping willow that looms over it.

No, not all of his friends will have the privilege of becoming an old man.

A soft press on his arm makes him turn back. Mrs. Pamerson squeezes him again. "Morty looked real good, Mr. Kirk. Thank you so much for fixin' him up so nice."

Kirk takes the back of the widow's hand and kisses the knuckles. He does this gently, knowing that her arthritis has been unbearable for years now—so bad, in fact, that just looking at her twisted knuckles makes his own heart hurt. "It was my pleasure, Mrs. Pamerson. Morty was a good friend, and I try to do right by good friends."

Again, the urge to look over at the lone grave beneath the tree pulls at him. *Is that true? Do you always do right by your friends?*

Mrs. Pamerson's daughter Judy appears, and with a polite smile, separates her mother from the mortician and funeral director who helped lay her father to rest. The other mourners have already started down the hill, walking toward the palatial funeral home with its ionic columns and large, open black door. They'll sip punch and eat cookies. The caterer will bring out the food in thirty minutes, leaving enough time for everyone to get a drink or two into their hands before it comes.

But Kirk lingers despite the thinning crowd. He gives final instructions to the boys filling Morty's grave with soft, overturned earth, and then he walks up the hill toward the grave weighing heavy on his mind. Legs burning, he steps beneath the enormous weeping willow. Its large roots protrude from the earth all around, and he steps over these carefully in his polished loafers.

He kneels before the grave, daring to put one knee of his dress slacks on the cold earth. But what are dress slacks when compared to honoring a good friend? He places a hand on the frosty stone as one might place their hand on the head of a child.

James T. Brinkley. Veteran and friend.

We've got to help her, Brinkley had said. Lord, how many years ago was that? Brinkley had stood in Kirk's office right here at Mt. Olivet with that battered leather jacket slung over one shoulder.

I need your help, Randall. You know I wouldn't ask if I didn't. Since he left the military, he'd had a quiet life and liked it that way. When Brinkley walked into his office with a favor, it was like his old life had caught up to him, and he wasn't sure he was happy about that. But Brinkley had done right by him— more than once.

So even though Kirk had never worked on anyone with NRD before, he accepted the challenge. He went to the seminars and took the accreditation class. He shopped for the cosmetics made special for girls like Miss Jesse. He did it all, because he knew how much his friend cared about this girl, and he knew his friend must've had his reasons for helping her.

They're the most vulnerable when they're dead, Brinkley had told him, *and I can't just trust anyone with her. But I trust you.*

And was that trust worth it? Kirk wonders. He isn't sure. Part of him believes that he will always be the young, dumb kid who took a bullet in the thigh because he never knew where to look for the enemy.

"Did I help you?" Kirk asks, feeling his throat go tight. "Did I do enough?"

Because Brinkley is dead, and Jesse is gone.

But he is still here. He is *still* right here.

Kirk pinches his brow, and squeezes his eyes shut. And this is the truth of it.

It's hard to survive.

It is harder to be the last one standing, leave the people you love behind and somehow get up every morning, eat, sleep, and look in the mirror at his aging face without asking, *why not me? Why not* me?

With a sigh, Kirk stands from the grave, knees popping, and brushes one hand over his slacks. He starts down the hill toward the house. He can smell the food, even a good fifty feet from the funeral home's closed door.

Twenty feet from the black lacquered door, a *crack* resounds across the sky. If Kirk didn't know better, he would have guessed someone broke the sound barrier, and the *BOOM* echoing over his head was a sonic blast assaulting the Nashville atmosphere.

Kirk searches the sky, heart pounding, but sees no aircraft. No contrails in the sky.

He sees only fire. For an instant, it looks like purple lightning, but then the lightning gives way almost immediately to bright orange flame, separating them from the space above. He guesses the bright shimmering shield must be higher than the highest planes.

He *hopes* it is higher. For the sakes of the countless souls air-bound.

Before he can guess which enemy must've launched the attack, before he can even say a prayer for them all, the ground begins to quake.

———

Julia?" Regina calls. Her heart hammers in her throat as she runs along the beach, searching for her daughter. "Julia, where are you?"

She turns in every direction, her fingers pushing into her temples. She assumes the worst, of course. That her husband has found them or *Caldwell* has found them. That one or the other is here to kill her daughter and then Regina herself, but only after making her sorry that she disobeyed him. For all of their careful planning, somehow, they've been found, and Julia has been taken, and she will never see her again.

A woman in a red bikini spreads lotion across her bare, brown legs. A man in a wet suit shakes the water and sand out of his face before dragging his board back into the waves again. A black dog runs down the beach, barking and snapping at the gulls who take flight. Only the bravest remain, destroying a crumpled bag of Cheetos between their snapping beaks.

"Momma!" a voice cries. "Momma, look!"

Regina whirls and sees her daughter twenty feet away, yellow and white sundress twirling in the sea breeze, her feet sinking in the wet sand. One of her white hair ribbons has come undone, and it's flapping in the breeze.

Regina runs to her, scoops her up, and squeezes her so hard the girl cries out. "Don't you ever!" she hisses. "Don't you *ever!* I told you to wait for me! I told you to stay where I could see you!"

"But I—"

"I don't care! I don't care! You do what I tell you, do you understand me?" It isn't a real question. It's the kind of nervousness her own mother was prone to, and she hates herself for unleashing it on Julia now, even as relief rolls over her like a wave. But she can't bring her fear entirely under control. She can only run her hands over her daughter's bare, tanned arms and legs and pray under her breath.

"But Momma, *look!*"

Regina follows her daughter's pointing finger out over the bright horizon. Past the sailboats and jet skis and paddleboards littering the Caribbean waves. Julia is pointing too high for it to be something in the water.

Regina shields her eyes against the sun. First, it is only white clouds and sunshine rippling on the water. Then, as if on cue, the sun darkens. It is as if someone has thrown a sheer, purple scarf over a lampshade. The world dims. The dog, the people, and even the gulls fall silent. The waves still.

"What is that?" Regina whispers. She hears someone behind her murmur the word *eclipse*, and that sinking dread in her chest eases. An eclipse? Regina doesn't follow astronomy. Eclipses, Bastille Day, there will just always be some things in the world she'll never take note of, and she is okay with that —as long as Julia remains alive, safe.

"It's the clown, Momma," Julia says, wiggling down out of Regina's arms, her feet splashing in the surf. Regina has just a moment to wonder where her sandals have gone—the red Mickey Mouse ones she'd slipped onto her daughter's feet that morning.

"The clown?" Regina asks. "What clown?"

"She came to my birthday."

The blood in Regina Lovett's veins turns ice cold. Thinking of Jesse Sullivan will do that to a person. Regina lets her gaze slide lazily up and down the beach, at its disturbing stillness, but she doesn't see the death surrogate she hired years ago.

"What do you mean?" Regina asks. She hopes she sounds interested. Nonplussed. But all the spit has left her mouth, and her lips are suddenly, unexplainably dry enough to crack.

Julia places a hand over her chest. "I feel her. I feel her right here."

"You think this purple light has to do with Jesse Sullivan?" Regina asks calmly. Amazingly calm, given the fact that every-thing inside her is screaming *run! For god's sake, run!*

"Momma, right here." She taps her little fingers with their

peeling, pink nail polish against the front of her sundress again.

Does she feel something? Regina wonders. Some connection to the young girl who saved her life? And if so, she wouldn't be the only one. Surely it would be every person that Jesse Sullivan has replaced.

Regina imagines them as they sit in their cars, or behind their desks. As their eyes open in their beds, or their showers pound down on their heads. As they pause in lifting a hammer to nail on a shingle, or as they pull their cars into the garage at the end of a long day. Does every single one feel a strange current in their body as Julia is describing?

Her five-year-old asks, "What's happening, Mommy?" And Regina hears her daughter's fear for the first time.

Regina takes her hand, and they look out over the water together. All eyes on the horizon for what is to come.

"I don't know, baby," she whispers. "I don't know."

———

EVE HILDEBRAND TOSSES AND TURNS ON THE STIFF jailhouse mattress. A coil pushes defiantly through the lumpy cotton and discolored sheets. It jabs her in the hip whenever she seeks refuge on her right side, causing her to roll again onto her left side.

Dreams of her dead daughter keep her up most nights, the girl's voice inciting a flash of thick, cold sweat to form on the back of her neck and across her greasy scalp. This night is no exception.

Her daughter, chubby-cheeked and smiling, is running toward her open arms, giggling and laughing. Eve bends down to scoop her up the same moment a shadow rises high behind her. Eve's heart drops. The shadow advances, swooping in quick like a gaping, carnivorous mouth.

"No!" Eve is on her feet running, desperate to reach her daughter, certain she will throw her body over her daughter's, and somehow through the power of love alone, save them both.

But the shadow is too fast. And in this dream, like all the others that have come before it, the girl is snatched up by the darkness. She's dragged away, her face red and wet from wailing, as Eve runs helplessly after her.

She jolts upright in bed, her head scraping the bottom of the bunk above. The sudden burst of pain across her scalp only heightens her panic. Her body is cold and clammy with sweat. The hands she brings to her hair shake. Her pulse is so loud, it's like the thrash of an ocean between her ears.

Only a dream, it was only a dream, her mind chants, dragging her back from the precarious edge of hysteria. It surprises her that her mind is so ready to cling to sanity even after everything has been taken from her. But reality is worse than the dream. In reality, Nessa isn't in danger.

Nessa—sweet, *sweet* Nessa—is dead.

No, not carried off by the shadow monster of her guilt and grief, but taken as leverage, and murdered because Eve had failed to comply. Her baby *killed* because a bad man had tasked her with murdering Jesse Sullivan, and she'd failed.

She failed, and it cost her everything.

She'd love to make Jesse Sullivan know what it feels like. Maybe she could kill her little friend. What was her name?

A sharp pain stabs through her skull, cutting off all thought.

Eve shoves the heels of her hands into her eyes and cries out.

"Stop your fussin'. I'm tryin' to hear," her bunkmate says.

The black woman stands by the cell bars, staring out into the corridors. She's got her arms folded across her chest as she presses her right side into the bars as hard as she can. The beads at the end of her long braids clink together as she angles herself, trying to see something down the way.

"Somethin' be happening," Kenisha says. "The guards came 'round lookin' in on e'rbody. They were runnin' and carryin' on. Woke me up."

Eve tries to get out of the bunk, but her hair snarls on metal wires, yanking a yelp from her. She reaches up and carefully picks strands of her hair out of the wires, and when that proves too frustrating, Eve rips the last few strands free from the metal hatchwork, and a blond tuft comes away in her tight fist.

Kenisha doesn't make room for Eve as she comes up behind her. Just as well. Eve is four inches taller—supermodel tall, as her father would say—and Eve can see over the woman's shoulder just fine. Rubbing her throbbing head, she peers into the low light.

At the end of the hall, near the security station, all of the guards stand in a cluster. Shoulder to shoulder, their gazes are fixed on the television hanging over their heads. It's impossible to see what is on the screen, but their worried murmurings and wide eyes make Eve's heart speed up. The flashing television lights give each guard a ghostly pallor.

"I can't hear shit. Can you hear what they be sayin'?" Kenisha asks, uncrossing her arms and pressing herself harder into the bars.

"No," Eve says.

"What're they lookin' at?"

"The television."

"No shit. What station? The news? It's not like a titty show or somethin' is it?"

Eve doesn't see any tits. She sees Nessa's screaming face, flashing as clear as any emergency bulletin. *If only I'd been stronger. If only I hadn't hesitated when I had the chance to cut off that bitch's head, Nessa might still be alive. Alive.*

Not for the first time, or the hundredth, Eve wishes she'd been successful in killing Jesse Sullivan.

She isn't the only one.

What if I could grant that wish? A cold voice whispers in her mind.

The hair on the back of Eve's neck prickles. A cold sweat stands out on her skin.

"What did you say?" Eve asks.

The other woman clucks her tongue and rolls her eyes. "I ain't said nothing to your crazy ass."

What if I could help you achieve the revenge you seek against Jesse Sullivan? The voice coos. *What if you could make her suffer the way you have suffered? Make her hurt the way you hurt?*

Impossible, she thinks. Eve's locked up in jail, and who knows where that bitch is.

I can help with both.

The lock on their cell door clicks open, and the steel door slides an inch away from the latch.

"The fuck—" Kenisha jumps back from the door as if it's just sparked. "What the fuck you doin' girl?"

Eve looks across the walkway and sees a man standing there. He is tall, long hair blowing as if in a gentle breeze, and there's a glow about him. He *shines*, so bright that she can't clearly see his face.

"You're the devil," she whispers.

No, the man replies, speaking straight into her mind again. *I am your salvation.*

They'll shoot me. They'll kill me before I ever get one foot out of this cell.

I will remove every obstacle, the man assures her. *Believe in me, and I will avenge your daughter.*

Still, Eve hesitates. Leaving her cell, trying to escape jail and the authorities, that could earn her half a dozen bullets in the back at best.

What do you have to lose? the man asks.

Eve sees her daughter's face in her mind. The big grin. The freckles. The eyes that would never shine again.

"Nothing." Eve slides open the door.

CHAPTER ONE

Ally

3 days earlier

The hospital room is cold and dark like a cavern, but I barely notice. I'm obsessed with the sketchbook in front of me as I flip frantically through its pages. I see pencil drawing after pencil drawing, beautifully rendered, but I can't find what I'm looking for, and this seems to be the trend as of late.

For every inch we crawl forward, we slip a mile back. At least, it feels that way. Caldwell and his wife Georgia are finally dead, and we're free from his attacks. But Gloria is in a coma. Maisie is gravely wounded, nearly dead. And Jesse is gone.

My stomach flops, twisting itself like a rag in a furious fist. *Jesse is gone.*

I flip through the sketchbook faster and faster. It lays open on Gloria's motionless legs. The heart monitor attached to her finger beats a slow, steady rhythm. I'd have to be in a coma myself to remain that calm.

At the fourth or fifth pass through the sketchbook, the pencil sketches become completely illegible. Gray lead clings to my fingertips as I flip. The tears stream over my cheeks, plopping onto the page.

There's nothing here. Nothing I can use to turn this situation around.

No sign of how to save Jesse. No sign of how to stop her either.

There's not even a clue for where to look. Every picture I see is what's already come to pass.

Either Gloria was incapacitated before she could see this far into Jesse's future, or even Gloria couldn't possibly predict how this would end.

I slam the cover of the sketchbook closed and collapse into the hard plastic chair by her bed.

I put my face in my hands and cry. I don't know what else to do. I can't call Jesse. She has Caldwell's teleportation ability, so I can hardly chase her down. I think of Caldwell leaping from New York to San Diego in a single step. If she doesn't want to be near me, there is nothing I can do to make her.

She's also absorbed Caldwell's power of telepathy when she killed him, but I don't think she can hear me wherever she is now.

Jesse, I beg. *Please come back.*

Jesse, please.

Nothing. Nothing but panic making my limbs heavy and stomach sour.

Yet I can't stay still in the chair. So I stand again. I pace, hands on hips, and try to steady my breath. I need to clear my head. I can fix this if I can just have some time to think.

I keep glancing at the doorway, but it remains empty. She's gone, I tell myself. She's really gone.

I have to, she'd said. But what exactly is she going to do?

It gets so much worse, Al. More wars. More death. It's unbelievable. But it doesn't have to be that way.

I throw my head back and swear at the ceiling. "Damn it, Jess. Don't do this." Whatever *this* is.

I realize I'm listening for her response—that part of me still hoping that she can hear me. That somehow, I can talk some sense into her.

Nothing. No response. Not even a tingle in my gut.

I'm stuck in this freezing hospital room, cold sweat soaking my palms, until I have a better plan.

When Nikki returns from her call to Jeremiah, hopefully she'll have good news. She called him a prophet. Jeremiah himself told me in Chicago he's been having visions of Jesse ever since she was called to be a partis—one of the original twelve with a gift. He warned me that she shouldn't be the one to ascend, that she would kill us all. She would end the world.

But I can't accept that. I refuse to believe that the girl I know and love could do that.

With Gloria wounded, and her sketchbook useless, we'll have to keep our eyes open for other leads.

At the very least, I hope Maisie's alright.

If Jesse has all the partis powers, I don't know how it's possible. Taking Maisie's power from her was supposed to kill her.

Don't think about that now. That isn't something you can fix.

I wish I could talk to my brother, Elijah. He's supposed to be the older, wiser one.

Six impossible things before breakfast, Alice. That's what Eli would say, a reference to a favorite book from our childhood. To hear his voice now, even imaginary, is a comfort. Picturing him in Louisville with his pregnant wife, in his JC Penney suits and gator-skin shoes, running his law firm while the rest of us fight forces unseen—it's a comfort to know there are other good people in the world—

fighting the good fight—but also living normal lives.

That's what I want with Jesse. That's what I should've said when Jesse asked me what I wanted. I should've said utility bills and fights about loading the dishwasher. Innocent squabbles over which movie to watch and if it should be pizza or pad thai for dinner.

No more dying. No more picking up her corpse from the morgue or funeral home. No more hiding or running away from people who want to murder her for her power—either because they want it for themselves, or because they fear it.

Well, that one problem is solved I suppose—there are no other partis left. No one gunning to absorb her gifts. But I'm not sure the other dangers have passed. And I don't think I'll ever look at a pizza menu again, let alone have an argument about it.

Before Gideon took off to "handle a pressing matter," he told me to keep Gloria and Maisie close. I'm trying. With Maisie in tow, we left the desert, Nikki and I, and came to get Gloria in Nashville. Thank god, we found her alive. Dr. York has done what he can for her, but who knows if she'll fully recover? Who knows if she'll be able to see what comes next?

Georgia and Caldwell are dead. Rachel is dead and Jesse is on the loose. Why aren't we coordinating our efforts better? Why don't we have a direction? A plan?

I don't think a single one of us knows where to start.

I wipe my runny nose on my sleeve and look around for a tissue. When I don't see a box readily available, I stand and head for the private bath opposite Gloria's bed.

I only take two steps and freeze.

Against the opposite wall stands a man. Tall, slumped with his arms folded over his chest. He's dressed for the cover of *GQ Magazine*, clean lines hugging his perfect form. His eyes are brilliant green with a chin that you could break a board on. The only feature even approaching imperfection is his mouth, which sits full and a little too large for his face.

I've seen this man before, projected from Jesse's mind into my own.

"Gabriel?" I whisper, my voice cracking from either tears or utter surprise.

I'm frightened to look away or blink for fear he'll disappear. Again, I've only seen him through Jesse's eyes, through that strange telepathic connection, but Jesse isn't here now. For all I know, I'll never see her again.

"I chose well," he says. He flicks those emerald eyes up to meet mine. An unnatural light shines through them, illuminating him from the inside out, like there is a lamp deep in his chest, and I can see those flickering flames shining. "I stand by my decision."

"What decision?" I ask.

"She chose you. And I chose the one with the best heart," he says, and when he shifts in front of the hospital window, I see shadows over his shoulders. Black shadows the shape of sparrow wings, narrower at the tips. I blink, and they're gone.

He goes on. "The heart is the most important part of choosing the apex. Others disagree, but I am certain in this. The heart, it is essential. An apex without a good heart makes a poor channel. The heart must be steadfast and true. Only then is it undefeatable."

I bravely blink again, but he doesn't disappear. He remains fixed against the white cinder block wall, arms folded over his chest as if he has all the time in the world.

"Where is she?" I ask. On cue, my imagination produces an extensive list of all the terrible things that could've happened to Jesse since she's disappeared.

"You are her tether to this world. I will need your help."

He uncrosses his arms and walks toward me. He places one polished shoe deliberately in front of the other. "It's not too late to save her. To save you all."

Hope springs in my chest. "Tell me where she is, and I'll try." God help us, I'll try with everything I have.

Gabriel stops in front of me. He tilts his chin down and considers my face. He lifts a pale hand and extends one index finger. I can hear Jesse saying *E.T. phone home,* but I'm too afraid to let the laugh surface.

He places his finger against my temple. The second his smooth, cool skin makes contact with mine, I see Jesse's face.

She's so clear I can count her eyelashes. Her dark hair is spread over the snow. Her face is pale except for the red flush to her cheeks. With her eyes closed, she lays cocooned in her shield with her hands at her side. She looks like a cursed princess in a fairytale.

She's dreaming.

And I know exactly where she is. 63.5°S 138.0°E.

My eyes fly open to find him still standing there.

Hurry, he whispers through my mind. His eyes are dark blue. It reminds me of a summer sky at midnight, complete with a halo around his moon pupils. *If you are not there when the gate opens, all will be lost.*

Nikki's voice breaks the spell. "Good news: Maisie lives. The doctors insist she'll make it. Bad news: She's asking about Jesse. I wasn't sure how much you wanted to tell her. Jeremiah is right behind me. He's dealing with all this shit hitting the fan, but will meet us here once he's done making calls."

I spin twice, hoping to see him in the corner or behind a chair, but he's truly gone. It's only Nikki, Gloria, and me in the hospital room.

"What's happening?" Nikki arches an eyebrow. She stands in the doorway with two steaming Styrofoam cups. "And what's on your face? It looks like pencil smudges."

I don't answer her. I grab my coat off the back of the bedside chair and Gloria's sketchbook.

"I have to get to Antarctica. I have to get there now!"

Nikki arches an eyebrow. "*What?*"

I'm already running down the hospital hallway, dodging wheelchairs and staff. I'm determined not to waste the precious time we have left. I have to call Gideon. Or maybe I can get ahold of Jeremiah. Someone with an aircraft. I'll accept a ride from anyone.

I dodge nurses pushing wheelchairs and doctors with metal clipboards. I duck around a man with a bouquet of roses propped in the corner of one elbow as he asks the nurse behind the desk where the maternity ward is.

Someone yells for me to stop running. I don't.

I reach the elevator and mash the plastic button, five or six times even after the orange triangle pointing down illuminates.

The silver doors open and a flood of people step off, splintering off as they head for different hallways.

Jeremiah steps to the side to get out of the way. He arches an eyebrow at the sight of me.

"I know where Jesse is," I blurt, turning back as my name is called. Nikki is trying to navigate the chaotic corridor with the two coffees still in her hands. She holds them high over her head the way coeds hold red cups at a party.

I recite the coordinates that Gabriel planted so clearly in my mind. "63.5°S 138.0°E."

He tilts his head. "That's the South Magnetic Pole. How do you know that's where she is?"

I want to shove him back onto the elevator, mash more buttons and get onto the nearest plane. Who knows how long it will take us to reach the South Pole?

"She didn't tell me she was going there. Gabriel did."

Jeremiah's eyes widen behind his turtle shell spectacles. His fingers fly up to the collar of his shirt and he adjusts it as if it's choking him. "You *saw* Gabriel? With your own eyes? And he *spoke* to you?"

Nikki catches up to us. "Seriously, what is going on?"

She forces me to take one of the coffee cups.

I huff but take the cup. "I can explain on the way, but we need to get there as soon as possible. Do you understand?"

Jeremiah isn't even looking at me. His gaze is fixed on something opposite the elevator.

A collection of twenty or so eggshell plastic chairs sit off to the right of the service desk. Over the mostly empty seats, pinned to the far wall, is the flat screen television hovering over an unkempt magazine rack, with battered issues of *Good Housekeeping* and *Golf Pro* jutting from its wire embrace.

I'm a second away from throwing this coffee in his face.

"*Hello*? I need you to take me to her. I need to reach her before..." Before what exactly? Gabriel said *before the gate opens*...but I don't know what that means.

"Turn that up," Jeremiah calls, pointing at the television. The nurse looks up and glares at him. I don't blame her. I'm sure she has more important things to do than turn up a television for a man. She doesn't oblige him.

It's an old man leaning heavily on a cane who pushes the volume button dutifully.

A female announcer with bleached and coiffed hair says, "—at least three dead in the blaze. Because of the isolated location of this incident, we do not yet have all the details. More as this story develops."

The squat concrete building is in a landscape of snow flames, the black smoke looking all the blacker for its tundra surroundings. A sinking feeling overtakes my limbs.

"Shit," Jeremiah says. "We missed it. Tamsin."

"On it," Nikki says.

She's set her coffee cup on the nurse's station and is scrolling through her phone frantically. I'm already doing the math in my head. How long ago had I seen Jesse? How long ago did she come before Gabriel? Thirty minutes? An hour maybe. Tops.

I remember the tears in her eyes shining brightly under the hospital fluorescents. *I have to. Al, I have to.* Have to what? Surely Jesse couldn't cause too much damage in an hour, right?

My stomach only twists harder.

"Found it," Nikki says, after only thirty seconds of searching. She reads the news report aloud. "An explosion has rocked the South Pole research station today, killing five and injuring at least a dozen more."

My heart pounds so hard I feel woozy from it. I can hear the blood rushing in my ears.

"It is unclear if the explosion is the result of equipment malfunction or malintent. Shortly before the explosion, researcher Tom Duchovny tried to make contact with the proper authorities but was cut off before providing the clear details of the situation. It seems the explosion has damaged equipment and disrupted communication, severely limiting communication between the remote research facility and officials. Fortunately, research center staff is limited during winter from February to October, as the majority of occupants return to warmer climates. However, this also means the 45 remaining staff are without aid until assistance can arrive. This does not bode well for those injured in the blast."

"We have to hurry," I say again, finally seeing the dawning realization in their eyes. "I need to get to her before anything else happens."

Nikki looks up from her phone, her face pallid in its ghostly light. "We're too late for that."

CHAPTER TWO

Jesse

Nighttime waters, warm and enveloping, wash over me.

Given how much my stiff body aches, it feels nice. The last two days have been hell. Rachel died. Caldwell died. Georgia died. Maisie almost died. Even Gloria might be dead, though she seemed to be hanging on in that hospital bed, with all those cords and wires sticking out of her like puppet strings.

And here I am. I just don't get why.

The way we've been dropping like flies, it doesn't make any sense to me. I should be dead with the rest of them. I should've never been the last partis standing. Any one of the other partis would've made more sense.

Yet here I am.

Wait—where is here exactly?

"Gabriel?" I whisper, and even as I float through the spongy dark of this comforting black, my voice works fine.

Open your eyes, he says.

I open my eyes and see—white. White snow and a blue

sky as far as the eye can see. There's also a fuzzy, blinding orb just above the horizon. The sun?

"Where the hell are we?" I ask. "The North Pole? Is that the last partis test? To meet Santa?" Because I haven't believed in Santa for years, and even if I did, I'm sure he wouldn't give me anything but coal and a swift kick in the ass. Killing people, including one's own father, has probably etched my name on the naughty list, permanently.

"We are at the convergence point," Gabriel says.

I sure as hell don't see anything *converging*. There's only ice, snow, and that soft blue sky.

If I'd known this was a hurry-up-and-wait deal, I would've spent more time with Ally—more time saying goodbye. More time saying I'm sorry...

My breath hitches.

I don't even know what that apology would sound like. I'm sorry that I have a stupid neurological disease that makes me weird. I'm sorry that my father was a homicidal maniac who tried to take over the world. I'm sorry that I killed people to protect us —I'm sorry that I'm not as sorry about any of that as I should be.

It's probably for the best I didn't know I had more time. Who knows what pathetic things I might have said?

I look down at my hands. There's dried blood in the folds of my knuckles. My forearm has a big, ugly, black bruise on it, a defensive bruise from when I raised my arm to protect my head. A blow to the head is the one way to kill me. Or at least it was.

I say, "I'm cold, but not as cold as I should be here in Winter Wonderland."

"Your powers will protect you from the elements," Gabriel says. I turn to look at him then. His long black hair hangs around his face. His green eyes are as bright as ever. His long, slender hands are hidden in the front pockets of his dress pants, even the wrists covered by the long black lapel. The wind ruffles those locks and pulls black feathers from his wings. Angel problems.

"Which power? My shield? The inner fire?"

He considers this question thoughtfully. "All. Yet a coat would be a necessary precaution. I can never be quite sure how fragile your body is."

Fair enough. And why would he? I've gotten myself killed so many times, it would be hard for him to know how a little temperature damage might affect me.

"But we cannot leave the convergence point for long."

I look in all directions and see nada. "Uh, nearest coat?"

I'm not sure this even matters since I can teleport anywhere at any time with just a thought and a prayer—a prayer, because I'm still a bit clumsy about it.

He steps toward me, and as I open my eyes to receive him, I'm already feeling the world shift. That uneven tilt of it folding in half and plopping me down somewhere else. I take a step so I don't fall, and my heel comes down, not on a frozen ice shelf, but poured concrete.

The first noticeable difference is the temperature shift. I'm no longer outside and at the mercy of the elements. Now I stand in a cement hallway. A *heated* hallway. Ah, good ol' fashioned temperature regulation. Civilization at its finest.

I reach up and brush fallen hair from my face, and lights blink on. One after another as if they are instructing me to move forward. Motion sensors? That seems fancy.

I give Gabriel a wary look. "Where are we?"

The only response is the slow pivot of a metal hinge. I look up. Cameras rotate on their pedestals, craning their mechanical necks my way.

Heavy boots thump against the cement.

"Hide!" I hiss. I'm commanding Gabriel to hide me even though I know it's up to me to move heaven and Earth. I'm the one with the teleportation power now. I'm the one who murdered her own father to get it.

It's more than that, a wiser, more compassionate voice says. *You killed him to save the people you love.*

A man appears. And he has a gun.

"Who the hell are you?" he asks. He has a thick beard that's as white as the hair on the top of his head.

"Santa?" I don't think it's *really* Santa. After all, why would Santa have a gun? And maybe a gun isn't the right word for it. Harpoon? Does Santa hunt polar bears? That seems very *non-benevolent-jolly-good-fellow* of him.

The man's face pinches in confusion. Two shocked, snowy caterpillars, which I'm pretty sure are serving as his eyebrows, scrunch together. "Wait. Aren't you...?"

My heart kicks in my chest. Right. My face is plastered all over the news along with Rachel's, Gloria's, and Ally's, because we're being blamed for Maisie's kidnapping and the destruction of Chicago—which, by the way, was totally Caldwell's fault. He's the one that blew it up! And he's dead, so it's not like he can confess anytime soon.

I flash a nervous grin. "I'm not a terrorist. Look at me. Do I look like a terrorist?"

I wince. *Gee-zus. Way to go, Jess. Let's just make this racist while we're at it.*

"I mean, not that terrorists look a certain way or anything," I say. "White people can be terrorists. Women can be terrorists. So I guess I could look like a terrorist."

The disgruntled, white caterpillars only writhe in confusion.

"Rick, what's the problem?" someone calls. Over his shoulder, another guy appears. This one is young, maybe late twenties with a silver thermos in one hand and the other in the front pocket of his lab coat. This kid sees me, and his brunette eyebrows shoot up and his mouth rounds with surprise. "Whoa, it's her!"

Shit. My notoriety has reached the South Pole. I must be bigger than the Backstreet Boys now. I'm not sure if I should be flattered or super annoyed.

Santa's finger twitches on the trigger, and the harpoon releases with a *sklunk-spoosh*, whistling through the air toward me. Several things happen at once.

I stumble back, and in doing so, I disappear. The familiar squeeze of darkness as the world shifts forces the air out of me. When my foot comes down on concrete in a black room, more motion lights click on, responding to my arrival.

I suck in air only to spit it out again. "Can you believe that?!" I scoff, indignant. "He tried to harpoon me. *Harpoon* me! Never in my life has someone tried to harpoon me! And people try to kill me all the time!"

"Jesse," Gabriel says. He stands beside me, his face alight with a soft pulsing purple. As the light dances over the angles and planes of his face, I realize I've not only teleported from the harpoon's path, but I also erected my shield. I could have just done one or the other, but I guess both work in a panic.

"Seriously, who harpoons a lady? A lady!" Okay, I'm stretching the lady part here. I wouldn't even call myself a lady. But a harpoon! Really? *Really?*

"*Jesse*," Gabriel tries again.

The rising concern in his voice breaks the spell of my indignation and surprise. I put down my obsession over almost being harpooned to death. "What *now?*"

"Your shield is causing interference to this primitive equipment."

I look around. Floor to ceiling computers, a forest of blinking knobs and dials and touch screens don't look primitive to me. They looks fancy. And expensive. And if it breaks, no doubt that'll be added to the long list of things that I've done to piss someone off.

"Now, now, just because someone tried to *harpoon* me—" I kind of love this word, *harpoon* "—doesn't mean we should make fun of their toys," I say.

A strange, acrid smell stings my nose. I stick out my tongue and pinch my nose shut. "Blech! What is that?"

"Your shield—"

"My shield does *not* stink! It's never stunk before!"

One of the machines closest to me sparks. Thick plumes of gray smoke seep up between the panels. Oh, maybe not my shield itself, maybe where my shield is rubbing against the machines.

Another machine sparks fire, and more smoke leaps toward the ceiling.

"Oh," I say, the situation dawning on me. I turn and my shield turns with me. The purple field barely brushes the surface of the machine, but the metal hisses and crackles. Screws leap from their holes and zing across the room. "Oh, I see. They don't like that."

The door flies open, revealing harpoon-wielding Santa and his thermos-clutching elf. It looks like three others are right behind them.

This must be evil Santa. If good Santa is at the North Pole, here's his evil Santa twin at the South Pole. And he has a posse. That's fine. I have an angel.

"What did you do?" Santa asks. The caterpillars writhe.

"Look, I know this looks bad," I say. "But it was an accident. I didn't know it was gonna do that."

"The terrorist is destroying SOSHA!"

"I am not! I'm just standing here!" I yell. "I'm not destroying anyone!" I blink. Who the hell is Sasha?

A horrible sound crackles behind me, and I turn in time to see one of the panels rip off the face of the machine.

Without thinking, I jump. The world squeezes me through one of its tight and unseen places before spitting me out again on the snowy tundra.

"You still need a coat," Gabriel warns.

The elements. Death by snow. Right.

"Damn it. They distracted me with the harpooning! I'll jump, you steer, got it?" I groan and jump right back into the South Pole station. I'm trusting Gabriel to use his omniscient presence to steer me toward a coat.

When the darkness squeezes and spits me out again, I'm in what looks like a cafeteria. Ten tables with eight or nine seats each sit arranged in the open space. A silent TV is glued to the wall, its newsreel flashing. It's news all right, but not about me, not at this very second anyway. A Ken doll is going on about some bombing in Afghanistan, followed by an orphanage fire in Germany. I don't have time to stick around and see if I'm going to be the next exciting story.

I'm searching the room, surveying the tables littered with stuff.

Laptops sit open. Half-eaten meals are untouched, forks left on plates as if just put down. The room is bright because of a large window overlooking the tundra. It stretches as far as the eye can see.

The room looks strangely apocalyptic. As if all the people that were just here eating and laughing and perhaps bitching about work just disappeared. Of course, it's probably because everyone rushed to check on the machines that my shield messed up.

"Should I leave a note?" I ask. "A simple, 'I'm sorry that my shield rubbed your machine the wrong way?'"

I look around the tables for a pen. I don't see one. But maybe someone has one in a pocket?

Coats hang on the back of chairs.

Ah, coats. Right. It's really hard for me to stay focused

today. Is this how insanity starts? I mean, I knew taking all the powers was going to have its consequences but—

"Coat!" I pluck a puffy, army-green coat with a tawny fur lining from the back of a plastic chair. It's so fluffy I bet I could move into it. Oh, I'll have a nest of chocolate! And coffee.

"Take the backpack as well," Gabriel says, his green eyes sparkling. When he looks up to meet my gaze, I see orange and gold flecks dance around his pupils. "It has food."

His wings twitch. The light from the big window makes his feathers shine. They're sleek and black like crow feathers, as slick as oil.

"You mean I'm going to need to eat? I thought I was going to ascend through that gate or something. You seem awfully concerned for my physical well-being, given the fact that I'm pretty sure you're gonna blow me up by the end of the day."

"Take the pack," he says, unsmiling. No sense of humor, this guy. *I'm* the one that's gonna go boom. And yet *I* can find the time to make a joke. Geez.

Screams make the hair on the back of my neck rise up. The screams are followed by shouts. The building rocks. Plaster dust rains down from the ceiling onto my head. *Time to go!* I snatch the green pack and step back, shifting the world under me.

I'm squished by the darkness again, the air forced from my lungs the way toothpaste is pushed from a tube, and then *poof!* The bright white light of abundant snow again.

I survey the landscape of endless white and blue. The cold air stings my cheeks, so I pull on the coat and zip it up to my chin. It falls past my knees, but the soft, furred collar covers my cheeks from the wind. I flip up the hood and complete my cocoon of warmth.

I must be a mile away, but I can see the black smoke of

the burning research station. Really big, black plumes roll toward the sky like ink in water. I sigh and snuggle deeper into my coat. "It's like I got the reverse of Midas touch, you know? I've got Sadim's touch."

Gabriel frowns the way he always does when he isn't quite following.

"You know, Midas touched stuff and it turned to gold. I touch stuff and it blows up. So it's the opposite."

He says nothing. So I snuggle even deeper into the coat. It's amazing. Purple shield or no, this walking blanket is hella comfy. I actually feel bad stealing such an awesome coat from someone. If this was my coat, I'd totally miss it.

"Are they going to be okay?" I ask, eyes fixed on the rolling plume of smoke.

He doesn't answer, and somehow I know that someone died. Maybe more than someone.

I take a moment to let that sink in.

What horrifies me most isn't the idea that I might have accidentally killed more people. It's that I'm not sure I feel anything. Killing isn't one of those things that is supposed to get "normal" over time. I should be just as horrified now as ever.

But when I dig deep for those feelings, all I find is exhaustion—I'm so tired of it all. I'm tired of running. I'm tired of being hunted. I'm tired of being the bad guy. Just...tired.

"They have come to test the gate," Gabriel says. It's his tone: part fear part...excitement? Whatever the emotion, it makes me look up. I follow his gaze toward the horizon, the opposite direction of the smoldering research base behind us.

Something weird is happening.

The glacial horizon bleeds into a beach horizon. One minute, I'm looking out over a tundra, snow and ice toward the blue sky above.

Then it's not ice. It's ocean waves. Gray water ruffled with cresting white rolls beneath a turbulent, stormy sky. Ice and blue. Storms and ocean.

"Uh, Gabriel?"

"It will become harder for you now."

"Oh good! I was getting so bored. You know, watching one of my best friends die, murdering my last remaining parent, pulling my sister back from the brink of death, and saying goodbye to probably the only person I've ever loved. It's just been *so* uneventful, you know?"

He doesn't do the big-eyed blink I've come to expect in the face of my sarcasm. His eyes remain fixed on the darkening horizon. The horizon that keeps flipping back and forth between baby blue sky and storm clouds.

Shit. This is serious.

"Hard how?" I ask, unable to hide the quiver in my voice. I tuck myself deeper into my stolen coat.

"It will depend on how they move against us. Now you must be in two times at once. Possibly more."

So. Many. Questions. Starting with *they*.

Prepare yourself, he says. We shift from the icy barrens to the ocean again, the smell of salt and sand stinging my nose.

I stare at the approaching darkness and pull my stolen coat tighter around me. Prepare myself. Sure. Like darkness is ever something we can prepare for.

I lick my lips and take a deep breath. "Does this battle have to do with my choice? You said I had to make a choice, and now you're telling me I have to fight. Which is it?"

Gabriel's green eyes latch on mine. I see the tension in his shoulders. He is ready for this. At least one of us is.

"You must fight for the right to choose. You mustn't let them take that from you."

CHAPTER THREE

Ally

"We have a helicopter on the roof that can transport Captain Jackson. I can't make you, but I hope you'll come with us?" Nikki makes the statement turn up at the end in a question.

I glance down the hallway and see four nurses pushing Gloria's bed out of her room. They turn the bed this way and that way, maneuvering around an elderly woman with an unlit cigarette between her fingers and an IV drip overhead. One nurse, with a harsh grimace on her spray-tanned face, pulls the old woman backwards into an adjacent room so the bed can get by.

I wonder if I should stop them. Does Gloria even have family or friends? Someone to speak on her behalf and question the care she receives? I don't think so.

"What authority do you have to take her?" I ask Jeremiah. In my mind, the words are bitchy and accusatory. But on my lips, they're just tired.

"Al—" Nikki's shoulders slump. "We aren't kidnapping her, but we can't leave her here. Until we know who is still loyal to Caldwell and what kind of reaction we can expect to his death, she's still vulnerable. We need to keep her close for the same reason we want to keep you close. You're not out of danger yet."

My mind understands the truth in her assessment. It makes perfect sense that someone might want to kill Jesse, Gloria, or me, even more now that their leader has been murdered. Revenge can be more motivating than love or loyalty. But I'm not worried about me or Gloria, truth be told. I'm only worried about Jesse.

She didn't seem herself when she appeared in Gloria's room. Gabriel had showed her something, scared her, and I'm absolutely sure that whatever she's doing now, she isn't doing it with a clear head. God, what I wouldn't give to talk to her and find out what is going on.

"I'll come," I say, because until I can get my ride to Antarctica sorted, I plan to stick close to Maisie and Gloria. And Jesse isn't making it easy. The airspace over Antarctica is in temporary lock down for 24 hours pending investigation.

Her shoulders slide away from her ears. "Thank you. Let's get up to the roof."

She leans forward and mashes the elevator button just as Gloria's hospital bed rolls up to meet us. The nurses pushing her each have long, exhausted faces. Dark circles, deep lines. The clear symptoms of chronic stress. What must I look like? I can't remember the last time I wasn't taxed by one peril or another. And yet—what would I change?

What do you want, Al? I hear the question in Jesse's panicked voice. And I remember my response clearly: *You. Just you, Jess.*

I still want that. I want her safe. I want her out of all of this. I'd even take our old life of death replacing and my near-ulcer-causing frets about whether or not Jesse's death replacing might result in her demise. But truth be told, settling for the old life is still settling.

I'm done. Pure and simple. I'm tired, and I'm *done*.

But you don't have the luxury of being done, my mind says. *This isn't over yet.*

Nikki and I let Jeremiah and the nurses take the elevator to the roof first, then we ride up after. It isn't until the chime dings, announcing our arrival, that I realize Nik has taken my hand. She squeezes it and then lets it go.

"It'll be okay," she says. Her full lips tilt up at one side, a smile that's meant to encourage more than seduce.

You don't know that, my mind bleats.

I step out onto the roof and into the roaring wind. I push back the mass of blond hair covering my eyes, and there's Jeremiah, one finger in his ear and yelling into the cell phone over the roar of the helicopter blades slicing the air at the edge of the rooftop.

One of his black, polished shoes is propped on the lip of a low stone wall outlining the roof.

Nikki reaches the helicopter first, covering her ears and dipping her head before using the handle on the outside of the aircraft to haul herself up into its cabin. She turns back and offers me a hand.

Doubt washes over me again the moment before I reach out and take her hand. Again I think, *what am I doing?* I should be in Antarctica. I should be there *now*.

But I can't steal this helicopter. If Gloria was conscious, she could fly it, but I surely can't. And I can't simply charter one.

I'm an outlaw. A fugitive from the government. And even if I weren't being hunted for arrest, interrogation, or outright murder, I have no money on me. No car. And everyone I care about is right here.

Almost everyone. *Jess. Don't you dare die on me.*

Nikki helps me into the black leather seat and starts working on my seatbelt. When we first began dating, I used to yell at Nik for this—her insistence that she do up my buckles: belt buckles, seat belts, harnesses...then I realized she can't stop herself any more than I can stop fretting over Jesse.

It's strange, this role reversal. I've never had anyone who tried to take care of me except my mother and brother. And even now, I never know quite how to handle it.

"Where's Maisie?" I ask. I'm shouting. The back of my throat burns with the effort. Instead of answering, Nikki half turns from where she squats in front of me and inclines her head in that direction. I peer around her into the darkness and see Maisie, curled tight in a stiff white hospital blanket and scrubs. She gives me a small, weak wave.

Relief washes over me. She's okay. She's really okay.

She looks exhausted and run down. Of course, just hours ago she was dead, so this is an improvement. We're all run down, and not only because the last few days have been crisis after crisis.

Maisie deserves so much more. A steady, stable home for starters. And she's never going to get it with us. But where would we even send her now that Jesse's orphaned her?

I shouldn't think of it like that. But no matter how I frame it, Maisie's mother and father are dead, and she is a minor for another year. What in the world will we do about that? More questions that I don't have answers to.

Winston sits in the seat beside her. His pug eyes wide and worried. At first, I think he's shaking and that's why she's keeping him close to her side. Then I realize he's barking, his dark chin wobbling. I just can't hear him over the roaring blades.

Nikki offers me the black headset that will muffle the noise and make it possible for us all to speak.

I slip the earphones on.

"I want to get Gloria and Maisie somewhere safe," I say,

hearing my voice echo back to me through the black headset squeezing my head.

"That's our agenda, too," Nikki says, adjusting the microphone in front of her face. Her voice is mechanical and echoes like the voice on a CB radio.

I wave to get Maisie's attention and tap the side of my headset. She slips hers on and angles the microphone.

"How are you holding up back there?" I ask her.

Maisie turns from Gloria, whose hand she'd been stroking moments before, and laughs at me. It's such a Jesse laugh—a short, sarcastic snort—that it hurts my heart.

"My brains are still in my head," she says. "That's more than some can say right now."

The sad part is I don't know if she's referring to her parents or the boy who got murdered. I understand she befriended a boy, albeit briefly, when she was in the desert. Her mother had kidnapped her back from us and went on the run. Of course, Jesse tore apart a town and murdered her parents to get her back, but not without casualties.

"Maze?" I tilt my head in question. If she's anything like Jesse, this sarcasm is a front.

"I'm okay," she says. But her eyes are filling with tears that sparkle in the light. "Winnie Pug needs water. I think he's going to bark himself sick. I think he's traumatized from the last time he was in a helicopter."

Before I can issue a warning glare, Nikki already asks the dreaded question. "What happened last time?"

Maisie's mouth runs away with her before I can intervene. "Apparently Jesse and Ally jumped out of a helicopter into the city to look for you. And Winston saw it and tried to jump out after them. But Rachel caught him. She was still holding him when Caldwell took her and put her in that church with no doors."

Nikki's fingers freeze on the last of her buckles. "You jumped out of a helicopter?"

"Without parachutes!" Maisie adds, voice ringing with admiration. "I wish I could've seen it."

"Maisie." I flash my own tight smile. "How do you even know what happened? You weren't there." Because Caldwell had already stolen her back from us.

Our first of many failures, the frightened me says.

But it worked out. And this will work out too, the assured me says.

I wonder if it's too late to call up my therapist and have an emergency session. It might be nice to talk to someone who isn't involved in all of this—and someone who isn't *me*.

"You. Jumped. Out. Of. A. Helicopter," Nikki says. Her face is turning red and her jaw is working. "Was this before or after you let Jesse push you out of a window *thirty-four* stories up?"

"She didn't push me," I say. I cut Maisie a sharp look.

Maisie mouths, *sorry*.

"I don't think you have any right to be angry. I survived. And it isn't like I'm going to jump out of a helicopter *again*," I say, as if this will calm her. I should know better.

Nikki looks ready to explode.

"And I thought you were supposed to be the sensible one," Nikki says. She slides the headset down to rest around her neck and watches Jeremiah give instructions to three or four people crowded around him on the roof. A clear dismissal.

I don't insist that she put her headset on so that I can explain myself. There is nothing I can say that will make her happy. Anytime I endanger my life, it makes her furious. I understand. I feel the same way about Jesse, but just as my concern has never deterred Jesse, Nikki's will never deter me.

Jeremiah reaches in and hefts himself up into the helicopter with a hand from Nikki. Then it's the three of us strapped in and ready to go, with Maisie, Winston, and Gloria's bed in the back end.

Jeremiah's voice booms over the headset a moment later. "We're going to ground. Our closest base with full medical facilities is in Oklahoma. As soon as we situate Captain Jackson and Maisie, I'll need to send you back with the helicopter, Tamsin. We need to break down all the Nashville units and move the equipment to the Oklahoma base. Parish and Unit 546 are already packing up. It will be an oversight mission more than anything."

"Yes, sir," Nikki says.

I think we'll take off now. Instead, we only sit there until I ask, "What are we waiting for?"

"One more," Jeremiah says, and gestures to the open seat across from him.

The door beside the staff elevator opens. Slate gray metal swings back and slams against the brick either with the force of the man exiting the building, or with help from the wind. Regardless, he moves toward the helicopter, bent forward at the waist with a hoodie over his head to protect him from the relentless roar of the blades.

There is something in his walk that I recognize, though I can't see his face beneath the hair and hood and flapping military jacket.

Nikki reaches her hand out and offers it to the guy who hauls himself up into the black cabin with one pull. He slides into the empty seat across from Jeremiah and slips the black hood back from his face.

Lane.

Lane. Dark hair tossed in all directions. Blue eyes bright. For a moment, I just stare at him. The only thing my mind can gather and articulate beyond the surprise is, "You got a haircut."

He mouths something I don't understand. Then he casts a glance at Jeremiah who motions for him to put the headset on.

Lane does, adjusting the microphone in front of his wet lips.

"What did you say?" he asks. His voice holds that strange metallic echo that I've grown used to even after these few short journeys.

"You got a haircut," I say again, and I feel a little self-conscious now. Why talk about his hair at all? Who cares about his stupid hair?

"Yeah," he says with a nervous smile. He runs a hand over his hair. "I wear it shorter these days. It's how Audrey likes it."

"Audrey?" I arch an eyebrow.

"My girlfriend," he says, and if I'm not mistaken, there's a slight blush rising in his cheeks. Why would that embarrass him? Does he think I'll tell Jesse? Or does he think Jesse would care?

Would she? Probably. Not because she wants him, but because she'd be a little offended that he had the audacity to move on.

I'm not sure what else to say about the girlfriend or the haircut, so I ask, "What are you doing here?"

Lane looks to Jeremiah, who is tugging at the bottom of his sweater vest beneath his black wool coat and lacing his hands in his lap. Ah, so this is Jeremiah's doing.

"We needed someone with NRD who also had contacts with Caldwell's men. Someone who could infiltrate the Disciples' headquarters and discover their intentions now that their chain of command has been destroyed. The first three in their chain of command was Caldwell himself, Georgia, and a Lieutenant Perry."

I lurch forward as the helicopter lifts then banks right.

My hands wrap around the straps securing me. "You're hoping they'll recognize him and not be alarmed?"

"Yes."

"And you think they'll just let you in the know right away?" I ask, very skeptical. I'm surprised how easy it is to have a chat with Lane when I know Jesse isn't sharing his bed.

"No, especially not when I show up as a confused amnesiac."

I frown harder. "I'm not seeing how this will work."

Jeremiah turns toward me in his seat, adjusting his glasses on the bridge of his nose.

"Caldwell used his mind control on all of his men, not just Mr. Handel." He presses on, obviously encouraged by my growing skepticism. "Very few members didn't experience full mind control at least once. I'm certain that Lane will be one of several disciples confused and disoriented in the wake of his death."

"But no one has seen Lane in over a year. Won't it be surprising that he appears now?"

"Not really. Lane could have been doing any number of things under Caldwell's instruction for that period of time. And he will not be the only one with this story, which adds an additional layer of credibility."

I turn to Nikki, searching her face for clues to how she feels about all of this. But she's guarded against me, perhaps still angry to learn I've been jumping out of helicopters and not telling her.

"I have it on good authority from our informants in Chicago that numerous men have returned to Caldwell's headquarters over the last few days. Most have been confused and disoriented, and after short briefings have been given short assignments."

"If you already have an insider, why send Lane?"

"We have people in administration," Jeremiah counters. "We need someone inside who will be taking orders."

"Because you want to know what their next move is."

"Hopefully, Mr. Handel will go in and discover that they are only packing up, tying up loose ends and disbanding."

"If you thought that, you wouldn't send him."

Nikki and Jeremiah exchange a look. Everyone with their secrets.

"You're expecting some kind of retaliation attack against Jesse, because she killed him," I say. And I know the truth of the words immediately.

"We just want to be prepared," Nikki says, with tenderness.

"Or you want to recruit," I say, looking straight in Jeremiah's eyes. I hold his dark gaze, sparkling in the low cabin light. "It must be quite the haul. A whole army and no general? I can only imagine what generous offers you may make from your bottomless pockets."

Lane shifts nervously in his seat.

It isn't until the words are out of my mouth that I realize I'm still mad at Jeremiah. Furious, actually. He tried to keep Jesse in a coma so he could control and suppress her powers. That isn't something I can just forgive. And now he has Gloria and Maisie to use against me because I simply don't have the resources to go against him. If I didn't have Nikki, the only other person who could probably help me is Gideon, but I don't know where he is. As soon as Maisie stabilized, he took off.

I need to find Gideon. If I have any ally beside Nikki, Gloria, and Maisie—it's him. But after Rachel's death, he might not want to be found. His excuse about "urgent matters" may have been a front for getting far, far away from us.

"Al—" Nikki says. It's meant to deter me, but it also sounds like a warning.

Wind rushes in from the open doors and blows my hair about my face. Lane and Jeremiah start up the conversation again as if I haven't just laid accusations against them. They talk schematics. Drop off and pick up points. How and when Lane should make contact.

Nikki continues to watch my guarded face.

Maisie continues to rub Gloria's hand and keep Winston tucked close under her arm. None of us speak, and I start to get furious about this again—something about the women being quiet while the men talk shop—until I realize I'm going too far. I'm riling myself up for nothing. And I will be of no use to anyone, including myself, if I get too upset.

I need to find my calm in this storm. I need to take this moment to gather my wits so I can bring all of me to this fight.

And I am doing what I do best: waiting. I am sure someone somewhere would consider this a pathetic plan, waiting around while everyone scurries here and there. But there is a difference between surrender and waiting for the perfect moment to strike.

CHAPTER FOUR

Jesse

The fur collar is warm against the back of my neck and throat. It's a comfort, and I bury my chin deeper, feeling it tickle my cheeks. I don't think it's just the coat warming me, nor just my shield protecting me from the elements. As I gaze out over the endless tundra, I can feel the fire from inside me. Beneath my skin, it swells and rises, reminding me that my firebombing power is never far away. But if I can do all that, why bother with petty theft?

"Gabe," I say, twitching my fingers in deep pockets. "I still don't get the coat."

"Your powers will be intermittent once we begin to shift. I am only taking precautions."

Yeah, about that. "Can we talk about *them* and this *shifting* you speak of? I'm all for just going on the fly in dangerous situations, but maybe if I understood what was happening with "the gate" and the whole ascending thing, then I would do a better job, you know?"

"Knowledge is power," he says, blinking those indifferent feline eyes at me.

"Yes!" I cry, almost overwhelmed by his simple understanding. "So let's start with *them*. Who are *they*?"

As if the topic itself has caused the world to shift its focus, the tundra disappears, and I am no longer standing inside a purple shield in Antarctica admiring eternal planes of snow and sunlight.

I am on a beach, overlooking gray waters that lap at the sandy shore. The army green puffer coat is gone. I'm in jeans, a black hoodie and matching chucks now.

Oh, now I know I'm dreaming. Matching shoes? I haven't had those in forever!

And yet, if this is a dream, how can the sting of salt and wind pull tears from the corners of my eyes?

I blink against the change in light. The tenth circle of hell, known as the Winter Wonderland, is so bright that now I'm blinking back the spots dancing in my eyes.

It takes me a moment to realize where I am. At first, I can only note the salt and pepper sand that slopes down into soft blue-gray waves. The stormy clouds above, looking ready to spit out a tornado any minute now. The way the beach rises on an incline, cresting in a forest-capped dune. Nestled on top is an A-frame beach house with black windows and sand-polished wood, its front porch propped up on stilts.

I look right and see the shore disappear in an ethereal fog. I look left and see the other side of the shore disappear into lush jungle.

Wait a minute.

This isn't just any beach. I've been here before. Gabriel brought me here when he first started introducing the idea that I have to make this choice. In this beach house I saw two—what I assume were metaphoric—versions of the future. Future number one: Ally and I *married*. Future number two: Ally is with Nikki, and they have two kids, Jesse and

Natalie. Presumably, she named her firstborn after me, because I'm dead in that scenario.

Awesome.

This is also the place where my dead handler Brinkley visited me. It was either one of Gabriel's tricks at opening my mind to some larger spiritual understanding, or my dead handler really did meet me in this place somehow and asked me to help Rachel.

Well I sure as hell didn't manage that, did I? Rachel is dead. Hell, they're all dead.

No, Gabriel counters. *You saved Maisie.*

True. But for what? What did I save any of them for if it all comes down to this choice: use my shield to protect Earth, or let them keep going and watch them tear each other apart?

I think about Brinkley's visit again, and seeing him even in my mind's eye, with that crooked smirk and James Dean jacket, makes my heart clench.

"So what is this place? Where are we?"

"The gate is your mind. But your physical body remains at the convergence point."

"The South Pole?"

"Yes," Gabriel says. "Every world and every universe overlap. They converge in a single point without time or distance. If something were to cross from one world or universe to another, to invade or infect or enrich or inspire another place—it enters through the gate. And you have brought the gate to the convergence point, where all worlds are most closely linked."

The waves slam against the shore as the sky continues to darken. Those storm clouds look mighty ominous. I try to understand what I see, to comprehend what terrible enemy is headed my way.

"What are they?" I ask again, a slight variation on my first question of who. Given how weird Gabriel is, maybe they aren't *who*. "I'm guessing they aren't coming to enrich or inspire. So what do they want? To invade?"

"Yes."

"Are they like you?" I ask. "Are they angels—or as Rachel believed—ancient aliens?"

"Yes."

My heart skips a beat. "Yes, angels or yes, aliens."

He says nothing to this.

"So the angel-aliens want to destroy Earth?"

"Time," he says. "They would undo this time."

A sudden, brilliant memory resurfaces. Monroe, another partis and friend of Gloria's, used some kind of hoodoo to show me his own beach. Whatever this place is to me—this beach house I see—wasn't unique. The other partis had a similar "meeting place" in their own minds and dreams. In Monroe's all the partis were alive and holding hands in a circle around an enormous and terrible power. In his version, we shared the power. We'd learned how to channel it between us to keep the bad angels away. We hadn't killed each other for it.

"If the others had survived—Rachel or Monroe—would they be here to fight with me?" I ask, but it isn't a real question.

"If you brought them here, yes. But they must be willing to come. They must be willing to see what you see. And often that distance is far too much for others to consider crossing."

Loneliness wells inside me like cold water in the back of my throat. It becomes impossible to speak.

"You are strong enough to face them alone," Gabriel adds, perhaps mistaking my melancholy for fear or doubt. "I made sure of it."

This should comfort me, but it doesn't. There is something about this place, about the looming beach house, the stormy shore, and about Gabriel's brooding that makes it impossible for me to shake these feelings.

I glimpse leathery wings and talons poking out of the black storm clouds. They're getting that close. And let me just say that *leather* wings and *talons* aren't what I was hoping to see. Bunnies! Why couldn't my gate be overrun by long-eared, twitchy-nosed, swishy-tailed, little *bunnies?*

A gust of wind knocks Gabriel's black hair into his face and whips it around his head. He's pretty gorgeous. I want to slap him for it sometimes. There's something about a boy as pretty as me that just invites a good slapping.

"You are with me, Jesse, are you not?"

My heart kicks.

"Of course," I say, and cave to my sudden urge to wrap my hand in his. "We've come this far, haven't we?"

He smiles then. Beautiful. "Further than you can possibly know."

"Okay, okay," I say, untangling my fingers from his. "If you're going to get all sappy and cryptic again, I'm going to have to call a time out."

He seems unfazed by this. "We are the Resistance. We hold hope in our hearts when there is none. We are the light that never ends."

"That's pretty. Did you read it on a cereal box? Hmm, cereal. I'm sort of hungry. Aren't you hungry?" Where's that pack I stole?

"You would like her," he says. "The one who said those words."

"Gabe! You have friends?"

His face shifts back to seriousness just as the sky erupts with a tremulous screech. *They're here.* Whatever is in the storm clouds—they're finally here.

I brace myself for impact and widen my shield to give me more of a buffer.

"The shield will hold," Gabriel assures me in a tone that could be mistaken for benevolent calm, but he isn't wasting any of his precious, comforting smiles on me now. His eyes remain fixed on the swarm blotting out the sky.

Talons from both hands and feet sink into the side of my shield. A snarling face hisses at me from above, red hair like fire streaming around its face, black eyes dilated. This first angel is joined by another and another, until my whole shield is covered by snarling faces and scraping claws.

The shield will hold, Gabriel assures me again.

"Are you sure?" I ask. My flesh is starting to crawl, and I'm doing this nervous thing where I shift back and forth from foot to foot. "They're really digging in."

He raises only one hand. It's barely a gesture at all. And yet the attacking angels scatter like pigeons. Black, white, and gray feathers fly in all directions. They swarm and circle, creating a cyclone above our heads. And in some ways, this feels even more menacing than the first attack maneuver.

I look to Gabriel again, hoping for instructions, information, anything. *What do I do what do I do what do I do* is playing on a loop in my head.

"What do I do?" I blurt. It comes out high and tight.

But Gabriel isn't saying anything. He isn't really moving. He's just standing there with his hands in his pants' pockets. The only clue I have that the lights are on upstairs and anybody is home is the look in his eyes. His eyes are bright and feral beneath the milky-gray of storm clouds.

"Great. Good talk," I mumble. "I feel *100%* prepared for... whatever."

Without looking at me, he says, "There's only one we must fear."

The cyclone disperses. Their shadows pass over the beach. I keep looking up and behind me, waiting to see if they'll double back and try again.

Gabriel stiffens for an instant. It's such a slight gesture, I can't be sure he moved at all.

I follow his gaze and see the problem. There's a man walking across the water toward us. Walking *on* the water. I consider calling up the water, making it soak him like a dog.

"It won't work," Gabriel warns, plucking the thought from my mind.

Good point. If a dude can walk on water, he's probably got a waterproof suit, or something.

"So this is the one? The last baddy? The one we have to kill before we take the castle and save the princess?" I ask.

Wannabe Jesus walks casually toward us as feathers from the circling angels rain down like snow. I should be keeping my gaze wide for sneak attacks, but I can't look away from the guy approaching. There is something very disturbing in the way he walks. It reminds me of someone.

Caldwell. He moves like Caldwell.

My heart skips a beat. "I killed you!" I shout, assuming the worst.

The moment the man's foot touches the sand, gravity takes hold. We are firmly on the beach now, sand shifting underfoot. The smell of salt is sharp. The wind pulls tears from my eyes and cools my cheeks.

"No, you killed my host," he says. His voice is boyish, almost petulant. It invokes the urge to say *sorry*. Or spank him with a ruler... I'm honestly not sure which.

I bite down on my lip instead.

He stops at the edge of my shield. Wild, long, blond hair whips around him. His eyes are so blue that it almost hurts to look. "What a lovely dreamscape you have here."

He runs his fingers along the surface of my shield.

It seems as though he's trying to initiate small talk. However, I'm obsessing over what he said.

His host.

Caldwell. My late father who will never walk Earth again because I shoved a kitchen knife through his throat. But for good reason—I mean he wanted to kill me—again... Before that, he manipulated me, lied to me, and used me to help him off some of the other partis. Even if I'd taken the high road, he would've killed Maisie eventually—which I would have never in a million years allowed to happen.

Talk about daddy issues.

"You're Michael," I say, recalling the name my father used for his angel. At least, I'm *pretty* sure he said his angel was named Michael.

He smiles. "My reputation precedes me."

"Your arrogance precedes you," Gabriel says.

I turn and gape at him, surprised by the harsh tone. "Tell us how you really feel, Gabe!"

Michael smooths a hand over the lapel of his suit as if he's surprised to find himself wearing it. It's the same beautiful suit that Gabriel has on... Really, what is it with angels and Versace?

Michael starts to circle me with slow, deliberate steps, his fingers still trailing along its surface.

It reminds me so much of Caldwell. The way he walks—walked—hands in his pockets, one foot in front of the other—very *devil may care*.

The angels swarming all around us fall away suddenly. Their darting forms no longer darken the sand.

In a blink, they appear behind Michael, neatly lined up. But they aren't wearing Versace—or whatever the angel equivalent is. They're armored in light. A shimmery gold glow covers their chests and limbs. Maybe it's not armor at all. Maybe it's pure power.

The talons are gone from their bare feet and hands, and they look so normal that I wonder if Gabriel has a crazy talon form. I hope to never find out.

We stand in the sand, facing each other, battle ready. Well, they look very battle ready. I really have no idea what I'm doing. How do you even fight angels? I've got the shield and the firebombs and all that, but I suspect they have tricks for that sort of thing. And if they don't, what pathetic angels they are!

Michael continues to run those long, tapered fingers over the surface of my shield, causing violet ripples to flow around me.

"You did an excellent job of hiding her, Gabriel, I will give you that," Michael says. He fixes his brutal, blue eyes on the angel standing at my left shoulder. "Until she reclaimed her power, I didn't realize who she was. And Azrael has kept me from finding the other."

Azrael. Maisie's angel. I'm about to open my mouth and shout obscenities at him. If he thinks he's going after my sister. I'll tear him apart where he stands.

Gabriel's hand shoots out and seizes mine. He squeezes so hard I yelp.

"Geez," I whisper.

Make no mention of Maisie. Do not even speak her name. You'll put her in grave danger.

Because she's the only partis still alive? I ask.

Yes. And other reasons.

"I didn't even know what she was when Caldwell put her right in front of me. Of course, he was too emotional, but they often are about their offspring. An unfortunate biological imperative, I'm sure. But that was distracting enough to hide the truth of who she is."

"She, she, *she*," I say with a snort. "My name is Jesse, you know."

His smile widens. "Is it?"

No names, Gabriel reminds me.

"Well, you know, Madonna was taken."

He smirks. "Congratulations on reaching ascension," he says, flicking his blue eyes to me. "It is very noble that you are willing to sacrifice your own heart for the sake of your kind. You must have your reasons. Perhaps you've grown tired of her?"

Michael smiles, revealing his brilliant, wolfish teeth. Man, I can see why he and Caldwell got along. This guy doesn't look congratulatory at all. He looks like he wouldn't mind putting his fingers through my eye sockets.

Meanwhile, my stomach feels like there is a fist curled around it. Sacrifice my heart? No one mentioned anything about sacrificing my heart to ascend...did I miss the freaking memo?

That better be a metaphor he's using, Gabe. Like me being a cold-blooded killer sort of thing.

Michael clucks his tongue. "You haven't told her everything, Gabriel. No wonder she was so willing to slaughter her own family."

You must guard yourself, Gabriel says. But he's whispering through my mind instead of speaking aloud. *Some attacks can pass even the most steadfast of shields.*

"No doubt you're warning her not to believe a word I say," Michael says with a boyish pout. "But tell me, Gabriel. What lie have I told her?"

Gabriel says nothing.

"Tell me *one* lie I've spoken."

Still nothing.

Michael meets my eyes and they flash, feral, like fox eyes in the high beams of a car's headlights. "Maybe I'm not the one you should worry about, Jesse. I'm not the one who tricked you into sacrificing the woman you love."

My mouth opens, but Gabriel's hand is stone-hard on mine. A stream of swear words pours out of my mouth. Finally, when I'm sure I won't kill Gabriel, I blink back tears and yank my hand free. "I'm glad to know that my angel isn't the only cryptic one in the universe. It must be an angel thing."

Michael laughs.

"What's so damn funny?"

"*My* angel. I suppose it's true enough. He is yours, whatever form you take."

I default to the only weapon I've always had. My sarcasm. No matter how bad things get, it never leaves me. "Do we need to have the talk? A little how-to-communicate-with-humans 101? I've had to give Gabriel the talk about eight times now, but he's getting better."

Michael doesn't take my bait. He only gives me an amused grin. But there's no real humor in it. Again, I get this sense that this shield is the only reason he hasn't torn my eyes from my head yet.

"Your faith in her amazes me, Gabriel," Michael says. "Even after all the horrors, you still serve her."

Hey, what horrors is he speaking about? Killing people? "It's not like you left me a choice, buddy."

"I dare not believe I know better," Gabriel says.

Michael's grin widens. "Because your loyalty makes you a fool. That was always your problem. If only I could persuade you to be loyal to me."

Michael gives Gabriel a devilish wink. Then he disappears, leaving only the vast beach stretching out before us. And his whole army disappears with him.

We are on the tundra again—the convergence point as Gabe likes to call it—hunkered inside my shimmering purple field, and I'm more confused than I've ever been. I've always been confused by almost everything that has to do with the partis and angels and weird powers and stuff, but I thought I had an idea of what was going on. The gist: The angels are fighting over the fate of the world. Some of the angels want to keep it safe, others want to destroy it. And it's the choice of the planet's apex that tips the scale.

But none of that makes sense now. Michael suggested so much more...

I tuck my chin in the stolen coat and try to process what the hell just happened. But let's be honest here, thinking has never been my strong suit.

"So..." I say to the vast shelf of ice and snow before turning my gaze on Gabriel.

The tension has left his shoulders, but his face is stony as ever.

"You and Michael?"

Gabriel only blinks at me.

"I mean, that wink..."

No laugh. No smile. No mischievous grin. I guess my humor doesn't work on angels. Alternative? Stuck together in crappy sadness.

Best to just face this head on then. That's what Ally would do—but she's always been braver than me.

Ally.

My chest clenches.

If she were here, she would tell me to pick just one part of the problem, just one question. And from there, hack my way in.

You haven't told her everything, Gabriel. No wonder she was so willing to ascend.

"So tell me the truth," I ask, my skin turning as cold as the barren landscape around us. "What is going to happen to Ally?"

CHAPTER FIVE

Ally

The flight to Oklahoma is quicker than I thought it would be. Snow is falling in loose, non-committal flakes as we touch down in a wide-open runway. After the settling bump of landing, my door slides open and I'm greeted by a man wearing giant earmuffs. He offers me a hand and helps pull me from my seat out into the frigid air made colder by the merciless helicopter blades.

I pull my red coat tighter and look around, trying to get a sense of where I am and the time.

A strip of concrete extends to what can only be described as a sloping slab of concrete. It slants as a boat ramp might, disappearing beneath the horizon of my vision.

"That's the base," Nikki says, catching my gaze. "You enter there, and it takes you a mile underground." She turns and points in the opposite direction. The concrete roadway extends toward a gate, ending in a concrete barrier and presumably connecting to a road on the other side. "And there's a whole lot of nothing over there. Lawton is about forty miles east. Nothing but small towns from here to there."

I look at the base again, and a sense of foreboding washes over me.

Nik laughs. "Yeah, it's not much to look at, but it's safe. It's true it's a little clinical, but there are certain parts that are downright homey. Hopefully, we won't be here long."

Perhaps she is right, but all I can think about is that movie where a zombie infection originates from such an underground facility. And the idea of going so deep underground doesn't make me feel safe. It makes me feel trapped.

"Do you really think we'll be safe down there?" I ask. I fall into step beside her as Gloria's bed is pushed ahead. Maisie carries Winston on my left side. I take just a moment to reach out and squeeze her arm. It's a silent question that she seems to understand. *You okay?* She nods as if I've spoken.

"If Jesse goes nuclear, I don't think even five *hundred* miles underground would do any good. I think Jeremiah is hoping for some kind of minor catastrophe. A place to hide until the worst passes. Of course, you're right. There are limitations."

"Jesse won't hurt us," Maisie says. She glares at us, her eyes bright and sunken. The skin under her eyes is so dark. Too dark for a sixteen-year-old.

Nikki's jaw tightens. "I hope not, kiddo."

"Don't call me *kiddo.*"

Maisie marches ahead of us, her blond hair blowing in the wind. She's scrambling to keep pace with Gloria and the attendants who are pushing her bed down the ramp into the base.

"Sorry," Nikki murmurs. Maisie's already charged too far ahead. "I didn't mean anything by it."

"I know," I say, and squeeze her arm again. "But her parents are dead and her sister is..."

How do I finish that? Missing? On a rampage? Endangered?

"Right," Nik says, the lines around her mouth deepening. "I keep forgetting that those monsters were her parents."

"Monsters or not, I'm sure anyone would be confused if their parents were killed by their sister."

Nikki only nods. "She's going to need a lot of therapy."

I snort. "We're *all* going to need a lot of therapy."

Nikki turns and offers me a fist. I only frown at it.

"May we all live long enough to get the therapy we need," she says. It's a devilish smile that lights up her face. If I'm being honest with myself, she's cute.

I brush my knuckles against hers. "May we be so lucky."

We laugh, short, choked sounds. We sound like two people on the verge of losing it.

"Of course, I'm pretty sure that isn't how fist bumps work," I say. "So you've probably disqualified our luck by misuse alone."

Nikki only smiles bigger.

I add two more items to my to-do list, though. Two things I need to do when both Nikki and Jeremiah are out of earshot: contact Gideon, and talk to Lane. And maybe also pass a warning to Maisie, if the opportunity arises.

I'll have to keep my eyes open for the chance.

I cast a look over my shoulder and see Lane and Jeremiah in deep discussion. Lane's head is cocked so he can better hear whatever the man in the sweater vest and wool coat is saying.

He looks up and meets my eyes. I cut mine to the right—to nowhere in particular—with a slight incline to my head. I hope the message is clear. It's easier for two people to find a closet to talk in if both are aware they're looking for said closet.

His expression remains guarded and unmoving. I can't tell if this is a refusal to talk to me, or if this is his way of being discreet while Jeremiah continues to pour instructions into his ear. He used to care about Jesse once upon a time. I find myself praying that hasn't changed. The very fact that Jeremiah chose him out of everyone gives me hope.

When I turn back, I bump into Nikki, who has stopped walking. I yelp in surprise and she mumbles her apology. Then I see why she's stopped.

We are in an enormous holding area that reminds me of the DMV after hours for some bizarre reason. Empty and dark windows sit to the left, and it is easy to imagine a queue lining up there. But to the right are double doors.

A scrub-clad medical team has appeared and surrounded Gloria and Maisie. Maisie is being ushered into a wheelchair and a nurse is trying to remove Winston from her lap. Maisie isn't having it.

"Nik," I say, and fortunately that's all I have to say to initiate the chain of command.

"Jer—" Nikki says.

Jeremiah pauses in his instructions to Lane and looks up just long enough to assess the situation.

"The dog stays," he calls.

The nurse's cheeks blush and her jaw sets. She is clearly unhappy to make this accommodation, but she stops trying to take Winston from Maisie's arms, which is good for Winston. If Maisie had squeezed him any tighter, she might have popped his little eyes from his head.

"Where are they taking them exactly?" I ask. I know they need more medical care but I don't want to lose track of them in this enormous place.

"Gloria needs more surgery," Nikki says, flipping her ponytail over one shoulder. The orange streaks stand out against the black sweater she's wearing. "They did as many reconstructive surgeries on her bones as they could before moving her, but there are a few follow-ups that need to be addressed. She had countless pins added. She'll be lucky if she can ever walk again."

My heart aches. Oh, Gloria. Even if she wakes from the coma, a long, hard road to recovery lays before her.

"And her kidneys aren't doing so well either. They're failing. It's unclear if she'll need an actual transplant or perhaps just several rounds of dialysis until they can function on their own. Of course, this says nothing of the crushed muscles and damaged veins."

I place a hand over my heart.

"She should count herself lucky that it wasn't her head, and most of her vital organs seem all right. She's incredibly lucky."

"Crushed and possibly never able to walk again," I remind her. "Let's not go too far."

She concedes the point with a nod of her head.

"What about Maisie?"

"They're just monitoring her. I am sure you've had enough experience with Jesse upon resurrection to know that her body will heal, but she can use some TLC until it does."

I do remember. It seems like only yesterday that Jesse was almost decapitated by Eve and died of blood loss and spinal cord damage. For days, I fretted over her while her body worked its magic. Then she was up and moving, albeit stiffly and begrudgingly. She never felt well for the few days after. That could explain Maisie's haggard appearance—or the buckets of sadness that we've heaped on her.

"Let me give you a brief tour," she says. "And you too, if you're interested."

"Yeah, thanks." Lane sidles up to her right side as soon as Jeremiah disappears through an adjacent door, the blue phone light in his ear lit up to signify a call. Lane sees me watching. "He says his wife is on her way."

"Yeah, we're moving everyone here that we can," Nikki

says, pushing open the door which just swung shut behind Maisie's chair. "This base has the capacity to house over sixty thousand."

"Sixty thousand!" I balk. This place must be even bigger than I imagined. That creeping sense of descending into a pit where I'll never see the light of day overwhelms me again.

"We can sustain that population for about six months on the rations that have been stocked here over the years. But if a global event were to happen, we would have to establish a long-term solution."

"Let's hope it doesn't come to that," Lane says gravely.

I must agree with him.

Maisie, Gloria, and the team hook a right through a set of doors that say do not enter.

"This is the medical wing," Nikki says, gesturing at the swinging doors. "It sits here in the center, so it is accessible by all eight units, each with a different entrance."

It's not hard to imagine. The tiled floor and white walls have a very hospital look to them.

We keep moving on.

"The base is divided into eight units," Nikki says. She leads us down the hall away from the medical ward to an elevator and mashes the down button. "Think of them as octagonal shafts under the earth. We are in unit three, which has sixteen levels like every other octagon. Each unit is meant to accommodate eight thousand occupants. Levels one through eight are the living quarters. Levels nine through eleven are cafeterias. Levels twelve through fourteen are work stations. At full capacity, people will be assigned work to help maintain and supply their unit. Level fifteen is for recreation and level sixteen is the only joined level."

"Joined with what?" Lane asks as I continue to count the tiles under my feet and cast glances over my shoulder as if memorizing my way out.

"The other units," Nikki says. "It's a gathering place if we need to assemble for any reason. Important announcements. Rallies."

To hold each other, pray, and say goodbye to the world as we know it, I think.

Nikki mashes the button for the third floor.

I'm holding my breath as we descend. *Get ahold of yourself,* I groan. What is wrong with me? I act like I'm going to prison.

We step off the elevator onto level 3. It opens on an enormous common area. Lounging furniture of all kinds is scattered around the perimeter of the walkway. The way the walk and walls curve, I get the sense that I'm moving through an enormous hive, this octagonal shape like countless interlocking honeycombs.

We move past the lounges, past the rec area with ping-pong tables and fake plants. Past the dormitory-style bathrooms with their small mosaic tile and fluorescent lights, and then stop in front of a door marked 3.

Nikki taps a small, metal bracelet to the black box on the door. It flashes green and then opens.

Lights blink on when we enter.

"Fancy," I say.

"You'll hate them really quickly," she says with a snort. "Anytime I don't move, they turn off, and that's really annoying when you're doing anything calm like reading a book or lying in bed and considering the direction of your life."

Lane pities her with a polite laugh.

Two sets of bunk beds sit against opposite walls, a top and lower bunk on both sides. Behind them, against the far wall, are two desks side by side and two tall armoires, which when opened, reveal an upper and lower rack, presumably for clothes.

In front of the beds, in the small space between the foot of the bunks and the door, are lockers. Nikki taps the metal watch to the lower left locker and it opens.

"This is where you can put your stuff. Just don't accidently shut your watch inside, which is exactly what I did. It involves calling the technician, and he's notoriously slow about it. Imagine Eeyore on downers. I put you in 333 to make it easy to remember. Third unit, third floor, pod 3. Got it?"

"Do you think I have a bad memory?" I smile. I'm trying to look grateful despite the claustrophobic smallness pressing in on all sides. No idea if it's working.

"I could've put you in 666," she says with a quirk of the lips.

"Fair enough."

"All pods have to fill to max capacity. Maisie and Gloria are your bunkmates. I put myself down as the fourth, but I won't ever be here. I don't suspect I'll sleep for the next month at least."

"He'll keep you too busy," I say.

"It was the best I could do to offer you some space and privacy," Nikki says, glossing right over the topic of work.

Yet I can't help but notice we are skirting around the obvious here. Jesse wasn't an option for the fourth bunkmate.

My heart does a painful flop in my chest.

The clip in Nikki's ear lights up, a flash of blue. She cocks her head as if leaning into the sound. "Tamsin. Yeah. One minute. I'm on level three."

The blue disappears, leaving spots in my eyes and Nikki offering an apologetic smile. "I need to meet up with Jeremiah. Handel, I'll show you to your pod."

"You mean where I'll be if I make it back alive instead of being flayed as a traitor?"

We both turn and look at him. His face is too grave to be a joke. Nikki says, "Yes."

"I don't need a tour," he says and opens his hand, begging for the second black watch in her grip.

She hands it over. "347."

"Unit 3, level 4, pod 7?" Lane asks.

"That's the one."

She turns and gives me another look. "Jeremiah is going to start moving the refugees today. If you have anyone you want to add to the list, friends or family, you should contact them. There are computers and landlines in the rec room. It's best if you contact them before we just show up to collect them. They're less likely to panic that way."

"Oh, I can't imagine why the sudden appearance of soldiers forcing people from their homes would alarm them," I say.

Lane snorts. "You sound like Jesse."

Nikki tugs on her ponytail as if shrugging off Lane's comment. "Contact them so we can get them in before the lockdown, all right?"

Refugees. My god. Jesse is creating *refugees*.

"Lockdown?" I ask, heart pounding. I was right. This is a prison. "What exactly do you think Jesse is going to do?"

Nikki's jaw tightens. "You'll have to talk to Jeremiah about that."

I bark a laugh. "And when exactly is he going to have time to talk to me? Before or after he evacuates the refugees and launches his army?"

"He'll make time."

"I'm sure he will. He always makes time for what he wants, right?" I sound hateful and snide even to my own ears. What is wrong with me? I've never had a hard time being reasonable and diplomatic before.

You're terrified for her, my mind says. *And you don't like how this is shaping up. Underground bunkers. Evacuations. Your loved ones under lock and key, and Jesse—*

Nikki watches my face without comment. Maybe she's trying to read my thoughts. "I'm going up. Do you need anything else?"

"I'm okay for now," I say.

Nikki turns toward Lane expectantly but he doesn't follow her.

"I'd like to stop by the rec room," he says, hands in the front pockets of his jeans. "I need to notify some people, unless Jeremiah doesn't think I have anyone worth saving."

"I'll let him know," she says, her stare cold. She suspects him of something, but hopefully not something to do with *me*. "He'll want to finish your conversation I'm sure."

We stand outside of pod three and watch her go. Her slim, soldier build is tight with tension. She's as unhappy as I am—but I don't think it has to do with me, or even Lane. What did they say in that last phone call?

And of course, I am sure there is more going on here than what she's told me.

"Should we go up?" Lane asks. He's whispering, either because he thinks we're being watched or because he's afraid of making demands. Good. He should be.

"Yeah."

I wait until Nikki's elevator closes and the familiar groan of its ascending cables echoes through this cavernous place, then I head toward the elevators myself.

When I mash the button for up, Lane asks. "How are you holding up?"

"Is it me or does this place feel like a prison?" I ask.

"It's reminding you of the basement," he says. He looks up at me through his dark lashes, his blue eyes bright. I'm trying not to think about the fact that Jesse used to kiss him instead of me.

"What basement?"

"With Martin," he says. He sounds almost apologetic for bringing it up.

But as soon as he says it, I realize he's right. When Caldwell's lackey Martin kidnapped us in order to trap Jesse, he kept us in a basement. And though the basement was much smaller than this sprawling compound, it is unmistakably similar. That feeling of being trapped underground with no real way to escape.

"We were stabbed to death down there," he says as if I've somehow forgotten. "I'm sure that has left a lasting impression."

"You're probably right," I say, conceding the point, as I step into the elevator. Lane pushes the button fifteen, the doors close, and the elevator begins its ascent.

He's looking around the box for cameras. There's one in the top right corner.

"You're too obvious," I say, exhaling. It should be with irritation, but I just sound exhausted. I'm going to sound exhausted for the rest of my life, I think. However long that might be.

He leans toward me and I catch the scent of cologne and hair cream. Of course he styled his hair for this. Did he think he'd see Jesse? If I hadn't seen my ex in a while, and thought a chance encounter was imminent, would I spruce myself up with perfume and hair cream? Probably.

How many times had I changed my clothes that morning before I walked into Jesse's office and applied to be her assistant?

"I suppose it's stupid to think there's a place where we can talk without being monitored," he asks.

"Yeah," I say watching the numbers on the elevator change. *4, 5, 6, 7.* "Jeremiah is a big fan of technology. I'm sure every inch of this place is taped and bugged."

8, 9, 10, 11.

"How's Jesse?" Lane asks. His words come out in one rushed exhale.

I hesitate. "What did Jeremiah tell you?"

12, 13, 14, 15.

"That she's in trouble. And that if I want to help her, I need to go to Chicago and find out who her enemies are."

Who her enemies are. What I wouldn't pay to know that. We thought Rachel was a friend and ally, but she'd tried to kill Maisie. She did kill her friend, Niv, which Gideon told us later—and it looked like she was going to kill Jesse at the last minute, but didn't. And it's moments like this that make me realize maybe I can't trust anyone.

The elevator doors open, and we step out.

There's something about the rec room that's more comforting than the living pods. It reminds me of the rec room at the university center where I went to college, albeit briefly.

There are pool tables and lots of places to lounge. There's a library lining the largest wall with books in every size and color. Against another wall there are telephones. They remind me of old airports. There were phones on the wall like that before cellphones became all the rage and the phones were transformed into charging stations.

The world changes. It evolves.

And so does Jesse.

"I wish I knew who her enemies were," I say, and make a beeline for the nearest computer station. There are four rows with perhaps twenty computers per row, each tucked inside a shallow cubicle for privacy. I pull back a red chair on wheels and sink into it before pressing the power button. I want to contact Gideon first, and there won't be a number for that. But I know the email we promised to use if one of us was ever separated or in trouble—and I plan to use it now.

Lane sinks into the chair beside me, his body turned at a respectful angle as if to give me privacy while I log in and load the internet page.

"If you don't want to talk about Jesse, what did you want to talk about?" he asks. "You were the one who gave me the eyes in the lobby."

My fingers freeze halfway through my password. I finish and then turn to him. "I want you to be careful with Jeremiah."

His face pinches, that dark brow creasing. "Why?"

I aim for some unbiased version of the truth. "When we first went to Chicago to work for Jeremiah, he did some things that—" I search for the right words. "I'm just not sure he has Jesse's best interest at heart. It's pretty clear he has his own agenda."

He has his own agenda.

"Right, exactly. You could say that," I say.

"Say what?" Lane asks. The creases by his eyes only deepen.

"You could say he has his own agenda."

Careful, Alice. He can't hear me.

I freeze. The hair on the back of my neck rises and my skin crawls.

I pivot in my work chair but I see no one. Yet I recognized that voice.

Gabriel? I ask. Only now I ask in my head instead of aloud.

Yes.

I almost burst out laughing. For all the times I doubted Jess, picked on her or worried over her about her imaginary angel, and here I was the one hearing voices now.

To Lane I say, "He sent us on dangerous missions and provided little backup. At times, I felt like he deliberately tested Jesse's abilities. Then when her power grew too much for him to goad and control, he sedated her and kept her in a coma."

"Are you serious?" Lane's mouth falls open, looking appropriately horrified.

"Dead serious. Then one of the last things he said to me before we took off without him was his belief that Jesse will blow up the world. He clearly doesn't trust her."

"The footage..." he begins. "I mean, they're saying the stuff on the internet is a prank, doctored newsreels and all that. But it looked pretty damn real to me. And I saw her shield that night in at the farm house."

I'm waiting for the question.

"Did her... powers really evolve? Did she really hurt all those people?"

I look away from him and stare at the computer in front of me without seeing it. "The point is, how can Jeremiah be on her team when he seems to be preparing to launch against her rather than help her? I haven't heard any mention of a team going to Antarctica to get her. No one is saying, let's go check on her. Let's go see if she's okay."

Lane accepts my topic shift. "I see your point."

Jeremiah does not trust her, Gabriel adds. I nod and hope that Lane thinks it's in response to his remark.

"I'm not saying he has it out for her," I add. "But I have little doubt that he would eliminate her if he thought it necessary."

"I need to be careful what I tell him," Lane says. "Or he can use me against her."

"Yes," I say, with a sigh of relief. "And I hope you care enough about her not to let that happen."

His face pinches with his anger. "Of course I care!"

"Good. That's what I wanted to make sure of before you left for Chicago."

The red flush to his cheeks doesn't disappear. I sigh, feeling a little tactless.

"Look out for yourself too," I say, and flash a smile, hoping I seem concerned.

He huffs. "I'd better. If Tate is willing to sedate Jesse, why wouldn't he be willing to do worse to me? I'm nothing to him."

"Exactly. And you have to admit it is a little suspicious."

His brow pinches. "What do you mean? I did espionage for Brinkley. I have worked with these people in Chicago, if against my will. It isn't as though I don't make any sense as a choice."

Did espionage. I resist an eye roll. I'm not sure what Lane did for Brinkley exactly, but espionage seems like an exaggeration.

"You have no idea how massive Jeremiah's reach is. I worked for him for almost a year, and I feel like his resources must be limitless. Someone who *did espionage* and has worked with Caldwell's people in Chicago—I'm sure that description fits any number of people at Jeremiah's disposal. But he reached out to you. *Why?* It's something you better ask yourself."

Lane falls into his thoughts. I take this moment of silence as a chance to log in to my email and compose a letter to Blue Komodo.

"I'm going up," Lane says. He stands, pushing back his chair. "But I'll keep your advice in mind."

He starts to walk away but pauses and turns back. "But really, how is she?"

I pause in typing my email to Gideon and look up. "She's Jesse. Remember that."

Tough. Resilient. Reckless. Headstrong.

I force a smile. "Don't let anyone tell you otherwise."

Once the elevator closes behind him and I hear the cables vibrating above, I focus on finishing up my email. It requires a bit of concentration, since I'm using the code Gideon created. When I'm finished, I click *send* and close down the computer. I decide against emailing my brother and my friends. I have all of their phone numbers memorized for exactly this reason, should I be somewhere without a cell phone and programmed contacts.

As soon as I cross the room and lift the plastic phone off its metallic receiver, Gabriel shimmers into view beside me. I feel like I will vomit. It isn't just his disturbing beauty, something so otherworldly that under no circumstance could you mistake him for human, but it's also the immense fear that comes with his appearance—and the undeniable fact that Jesse is in certain danger. And not the kind of danger we can think our way out of.

His black hair is shaggy and wild about his face, those green eyes shocking.

I hold the phone and pretend to dial a number. How often has Jesse done this very thing—pretend to hide a conversation with—whatever Gabriel is.

"Is she all right?" I ask into the dead receiver as my stomach turns over and over itself.

"You must get to the convergence point." He shoves the image of Jesse in the land of ice and snow into my head again.

"I can't exactly drive to Antarctica," I hiss into the phone. "Could you take me?"

"No," he says. "She must remain at the convergence point and stand guard at the gate. There is another...evil trying to get in."

I have a feeling evil isn't exactly the word he wants, but he uses it so I'll understand the stakes.

I marvel at Gabriel's black wings. They look so soft. Without considering what I'm doing, I reach out and touch the feathers.

"You need to get to the gate," he says again. His eyes are green and luminescent.

A feather comes off in my hand, and I pin it between my thumb and index finger before I think better of it. Gabriel doesn't seem to mind my admiration of the soft, delicate down. "Reach her while there is still time."

Gabriel flickers and disappears then. The black feather is still between the fingers on my left hand.

My right cradles the phone to my ear in a sweaty grip.

I should be grateful that, Gloria or no Gloria, I know my next move: get to Antarctica, get to Jesse. I just don't know how to do that.

I absently smooth the feather over and over in the palm of my hand throughout all three phone calls that I make. I tell my loved ones what is happening and lay out their options. I cannot make their decisions for them, and I don't want them walking into this mess blind.

At the end of my third call, I tuck the feather into my pocket and try to ignore the obvious—that if Gabriel were only an illusion, I shouldn't be able to see this feather. I shouldn't be able to hold it in my hand and feel its soft down tickling the creases of my palm.

"Where are all the animals? I mean, I haven't watched Animal Planet in a while, but aren't there supposed to be penguins and polar bears and arctic foxes and stuff like that?"

Gabriel's feathers ruffle in the breeze. "They would flee from you."

"*Flee?*" I scoff. "From me? What did I do? How do you know they aren't fleeing from *you,* bird-man? You're pretty weird."

"They would sense your power and the convergence of worlds."

"Really now?"

Growing up as a child in the Midwest, I remember the big storms that would roll across the plains, the ones you could see for miles and miles. And I remember how enormous, dark, and swirling flocks of birds always preceded the clouds.

It makes sense that animals would move away from me, too. It's the shield. Or the electrical, invisible, crazy stuff flowing off of me. The animals are like *no thanks* and have migrated, I suppose, to the other edge of Antarctica to get away from me.

"Is Michael coming back?" I ask.

"He is looking for a way in."

"Into...?"

"You are the apex, and you control the gate. He must look for a way in."

"Because he wants..." I wave my hand, hoping it will prompt Gabriel to spit it out. Oh, believe me, solving the current problem is only the beginning. I intend to shake the whole truth out of Gabriel. Eventually. But this is Gabriel. I'm prepared for this to take a while.

"When the gate is open, and your power fully realized, he will try to seize it. He will wield you like a weapon to build the new world he envisions."

Scratch the record. "Wait, what? Surely, he doesn't think he's going to get me to do what he wants."

Come on. In no world has any man—or angel—been able to get me to do what they want.

Gabriel says, "He will try to defeat me first. Then he will try to take away your heart. When you are vulnerable, are you sure you will have the strength to stand up to him alone?"

Good point.

"But you called Ally my heart. What about that part about sacrificing my heart?"

No answer.

"Gabriel, don't you dare dodge my question again! If someone is going to hurt her, you better tell me!"

"It isn't safe to speak of her here. He is looking for your weakness. You will make it easier for him to discover who she is, where she is. Push her from your mind."

I snort. As if. As if there is a minute in the day when I don't worry about what she's doing or who she's doing. *When you're gone, who do you think will be there to pick up the pieces?*

Sasquatch said to me. Nicole-freaking-Tamsin. I wonder if she's already proposed to Al. Built her a house. Whittled her a rocker or built baby furniture or something. I can totally see it. She seems like one of those nesting lesbians…

"She is in danger of his attack. That is why I have not said more," Gabriel says.

"Then why are we here?" I should be with Ally. I should have a shield around her. A fortress. An army of ruthless butchers wielding bloody cleavers or something. And I should be taking a sledgehammer to any baby furniture that may or may not have been built in the last 48 hours.

"I'm protecting her in your stead."

"Oh really?" I ask, surprised.

"Yes, because you must focus on being here in this time, this place."

"Yeah, but why here? There's not even a Taco Bell."

"This is the intersection of worlds. This is our strongest position."

"So the place of convergence is where I use my powers—one way or another."

"Yes," he says.

"And the gate is the beach. And that's what? In my head?"

He doesn't answer. Per usual.

"Either way, I am what stands between Michael and Earth."

"Yes."

"But what Michael wants is to blow up the world and start over—and that's what I want."

Gabriel turns those feral eyes on me. What is it with the angels and glowing eyes today? "Why do you want to destroy Earth?"

"Because you showed me all the horrible things that will happen! You made it seem like the only way to save Earth is to take it to the beginning again, to give it a chance to right all its wrongs. And now you're telling me the psycho who whispered into Caldwell's ear for all those years wants that too, and so now I'm like, say *what*?"

Because if Mr. Nutty-McNutters wants what I want, I need to really think about this.

"I will not deny the truth. You have done irreparable damage to your planet. It suffers."

"Hey, now. Not me, personally—I mean, okay, I ordered a lot of pizza, but I recycled every single one of those cardboard boxes, thank *you*."

Ally made sure they got into the recycle bin, actually, but I pushed that thing out to the curb, thank you very much.

Gabriel continues on as if I haven't spoken. "Certain areas of your planet can no longer sustain their populations and those unstable areas will only grow in the coming years. Before equilibrium can be established, many lives will be lost. Millions will move, seeking lands with more resources. However, due to arbitrary social and political borders created by your nations, this will cause conflict. Those displaced nations will not simply remain and starve. They must migrate as your species has always migrated. And these migrations will not be without consequence. They will cause war, discord, and distress until compromise is reached and equilibrium restored. Conflict will breed conflict. War is inevitable."

I squeeze my head with my hands. "See, you used a lot of bad words there, Gabe. *Irreparable damage, war, conflict. Inevitable.* When you put them all together like that, it makes it sound *really* bad."

Gabriel blinks at me with the resting angel face I've come to expect. He says, "I cannot make the decision for your people. You must choose the direction of your own time."

"So funny story: in high school, I was voted Most Likely to Get Expelled for Burning Down the School Gym, not

Most Likely to Serve as Space-Time Ambassador of the Human Race."

His brow creases.

"Just saying I shouldn't be choosing the 'direction-of-my-own-time' either. You have terrible taste in apexes," I say, stuffing my hands in the thick pockets again. But seriously, we're screwed. No one in any universe should've put me in charge.

"You are the apex," Gabriel says, his voice sharp. "When the gate opens, you will ascend. And if your heart is with you at that moment, there will be hope and light. But if darkness stands in its place, darkness will prevail."

"No pressure."

"She is safe. For now. But we can go retrieve her, if you wish."

Ally. I can see her big brown eyes, wide and panicked when I said goodbye. I'm not going to do the goodbye thing twice. It was hard and horrible enough the first time.

"I told her bye because you said I was going to blow up. I'm not bringing her here so she can blow up with me! I thought you said I could remake the world. That I might die, but I could make it good for everyone else. And Michael wants to hurt her. Do you think bringing her down here and parading her in front of him is a good idea?"

I think of Michael's veiled threat. *What a sacrifice...*

"Is that how it's supposed to go down anyway? Was she supposed to burn up with me? Because if that's true, we're screwed. Kiss the planet and time and all of history goodbye, because it's not going to happen."

"What of her desires? What does she want?" he asks.

I jab a finger at him, ready to poke out one of his pretty eyes. "I don't know, but it's not to blow up! Nobody wants to blow up!"

I can make peace with the idea of dying for the people I

love because I've done it so many times now. So I'm more than willing to sacrifice myself if it means a better world for Ally, and Maisie, and Gloria. And of course, Winston. But asking Ally to go through that...

A faint sound catches my ear.

"What is that?" I ask, turning in all directions, surveying the tundra all around me.

The *whomp-whomp-whomp* grows louder. And because the tundra is vast and empty, I can see what is making the noise even though they are little more than tiny black dots on the horizon.

"Are those helicopters?"

"Yes," Gabriel says as he turns those green eyes in that direction, black hair hanging past his strong jaw.

"Oh, good. I was hoping someone would come check on the people at the station. I was worried about them. And someone is going to need a coat!"

I snuggle into mine.

"They are not coming to rescue those at the station. They are coming for you," Gabriel says.

Oh. Well, I don't even know why I'm surprised. I'm a wanted fugitive that just blew up a government facility—and it's like the second one this week. And they're probably still mad about the town in the desert that I *sort of* demolished. And as remote as the place may be, we have satellites all over Earth. Someone has seen my face I bet. If those scientists at the station were able to get wifi and news programs, then they've definitely told on me by now.

I sigh at the approaching helicopters. "And this is what I get for thinking I wouldn't have to kill anybody today."

Make your shield bigger, Gabriel whispers into my mind.

Of course, he doesn't have to tell me twice. I don't want those helicopters to get any closer than they already are. I exhale and expand my shield. It races across the snow, illuminating the iridescent white in a soft purple glow. I don't just go out, I go *up* at least thirty or forty feet over my head.

Who knows what they think of it? I'm sure I look like I'm in a glowing dome.

A voice booms over a loudspeaker. I'm not sure if it is coming from the helicopter or something like one of those handheld megaphones. I can't see from here. The six helicopters hovering above are little more than black smudges in the blue wintry sky overhead.

"Jesse Sullivan, you are surrounded. Surrender peaceably or you will be taken by force."

I snort. "Taken by force. Good luck with that."

Gabriel doesn't smile.

"Why do they always say that? '*You are surrounded.*'"

Gabriel's wings lift and settle. "Call your fire."

"I think that'll only provoke them. They look ready to shoot."

"Michael is close. Call your fire."

I flicker to the beach. Indeed, the angel is back, standing defiantly on the sandy shore and looking ready for an attack. And he has something in his hand. I can't tell what it is because there is so much light surrounding it, that the object itself is hidden. In fact, up to his elbow is gone in that pulsing ball of light. And it's crackling and spitting sparks.

"Um." I tug Gabriel's arm. "What is that?"

"It will disable your shield."

"*What?*"

"You must be prepared to fight with your other gifts. You have many."

"Okay, but what about the people with the helicopters and the real guns!"

"Dispatch them quickly," he says, flatly.

"*Dispatch* them. Freaking-A. You deal with Michael then.

This angel crap is your business." I flick back to my world, my problems.

"This is your final warning," the helicopter voice booms.

Well. Here goes nothing.

I call my fire. It blazes to life across my hands, licking up the air surrounding me in a bright blue flame. A gun goes off and the shield ripples. More gunfire, more purple rippling along the surface.

Hurry before the shield falls, Gabriel warns.

"Yeah, yeah. You're always in a hurry for me to murder someone. It's a little disturbing, you know."

"Billions will be lost if we fail."

I don't bother to point out that it looks like billions will be lost either way. Because I destroy the planet, or because the humans on Earth destroy themselves—or because some jerky angels showed up and decided to put us out of our misery. There doesn't look like a way to end this.

I suck in a breath, drawing my fire to its full height and swing my arm as one might if throwing a baseball. The flames leap from my arm and sail skyward. The helicopter I aimed for dips sharply right trying to get out of line of the fire blast, but not quick enough. The tail takes the blunt force of the impact and is blown off. Black sheets of burning metal rain down onto the snow. Then the tailless aircraft hits the snow, and the ice shelf under my feet rumbles. The blades hit the ice several times, bending and breaking with each impact until they lose momentum and stop.

My ears ache from the screech of crumpling metal and blades on ice.

The two people who parachuted—base jumped, really— out of the helicopter into the snow land several feet away, obscured by the red flames and black smoke of the helicopter's wreckage. If there were others in the helicopter, they went down with it. I hope they died swiftly, painlessly, on impact. I tell myself the high-pitched whine is only gasoline whistling in the fuel lines—not someone screaming as they burn alive.

The second and third helicopters try to attack from two different angles, no doubt trying to overwhelm me with their numbers. But it takes almost nothing for me to throw them the ol' one-two firebomb. The first takes the blast head on. The glass of the windshield shatters out in all directions. The nose dips and the helicopter dives toward the snow. No one jumps out before the black shell crumples against the ice shelf. So all occupants must be dead.

The third helicopter takes the hit to its underside, and the force of it blows it upward. When it comes down, the foot rail hits my shield, but my shield doesn't give. The helicopter is tipped backward, completely upside down and lands on its crumpled blades in the snow.

The remaining three helicopters regroup, forming a smaller version of the triangle formation they arrived in. And the one in front takes that moment to fire what can only be described as a missile at me.

A missile!

Never in my life did I expect to see a missile flying at my freaking head. What does one even *do* with that?

Jesse!

Gabriel's voice booms through my mind and the tundra flashes, replaced by that distant beach of the gate, of the in-between, whatever it is—at the precise moment the missile unlocks from its chamber and launches. I have just one moment to see it whistling toward me before my world disappears, along with all the snow and ice.

On the beach, something shoots from Michael's glowing-crackling orb and hits me square in the chest. A white torrent of pain rips through me. I'm screaming, my ears ringing with the sound. The sand shifts underneath and I stumble.

"Jump," Gabriel says. "Jump now."

Somehow, perhaps by willpower alone, I shuffle my right foot back, using the teleportation gift I inherited through patricide.

I'm in the dark place now, that place of no light, no sound, only endless compression. When my foot connects with the world again, it's the icy world. My hands hit the ice and snow, stinging on impact. I call the heat to warm my flesh and the ice melts, but better a little assault by the ice shelf than hypothermic hands that have to be cut off.

Bare hands.

No shield.

A wave of nausea mixes with the pain. Too much world shifting—and a jump to boot. I feel ready to puke my guts onto the snow.

I manage to get into a sitting position. My knees are folded under me like some Buddhist monk. I'm cussing up a storm. *Howling.*

I'm running my hands over my chest again and again, thinking it was the missile that hit me. It clipped me somehow or just seared off a boob or something, but it isn't the missile. It was whatever Michael shot from his freaking light orb.

"What happened?" I beg, running my hands over my burning chest. "Gabriel, what the hell happened?"

I look up to find the angel kneeling beside me.

No, not kneeling. Crumpled.

"Gabriel?" I ask, fear creeping in with the searing pain. "Oh shit, are you hurt?"

He lifts his head to reveal blood oozing from one ear and his nose. Considering I've never even seen so much as a wrinkle in his suit, I'm winded like a stiff punch to the gut—completely bewildered—which goes nicely with this horrible fire eating through my chest cavity.

"Oh my god, he hurt you!"

"You need to finish the helicopters," he says, lifting his hand to wipe his bloodied nose. It's such a human gesture that I'm stunned into silence.

"Jesse," he urges again. "You must finish what you started."

I turn and see the remaining helicopters regrouped in their triangle formation. I'm behind them, looking at their tails. I jumped myself out of the missile's path. They're hovering over the smoking wreckage, no doubt waiting for the smoke to clear to verify that I'm dead. What do they hope to see? An arm? A leg?

Without thinking, probably still in shock that my angel can be injured—a possibility I never in the world considered—I throw four firebombs without thinking.

Fresh pain rips through me, from the invisible wound that Michael tore in my chest. I sink to my knees, crying out.

The blue fire connects with the backs of the helicopters, sending them spiraling to the snow. All hit the ground. The ice shelf shakes with the impact. The black smoke blistering the sky intensifies, its billowing plumes thick.

Apart from the smoke and flames, nothing else seems to move.

And the pain in my chest spreads.

"You have to pull it out," Gabriel says, looking more like himself, which is good, because I'm on the verge of freaking out.

I run a hand down the front of my coat, but there's nothing. No wound. "Pull what out? I can't see anything."

"Not here," he says. "We must go back."

So we switch back to the beach. Back to Michael who stands alone on the shore, hands in pockets. He has one polished shoe planted on a rock in the sand. Man, I want to slap that grin off his face.

I tear open the front of my jacket and see blood pooling there. There was no wound at the Pole, but here, I'm torn open. A gaping, puckered hole oozes blood.

"What the hell?" I take a breath and plunge my finger into the wound. I see stars—a momentary flash of white-hot pain. I'm going to black out. Oh god, I'm totally going to black out. But I keep digging until my finger is pricked on something. But what's a little finger prick at this point. I grab onto whatever is lodged in my chest and pull. Sick chills rake my body.

Something rolls into the palm of my hand, beneath my bloody fingertips. I'm shaking, shivering, so it jumps in the crook of my palm.

Okay, not a bullet. It looks like a star plucked from the sky. I feel like I'm holding something small, no larger than a quarter, but the light it casts completely covers my hand. I can't even look at it fully without feeling the tears spring to my eyes.

Michael holds out his hand for it, for this strange star-like bullet, like I'm just going to hand it over. So he can shoot me again with it? No thanks.

I close my fist around it and feel its spurs bite into my hand. But again, compared to the fire ravaging my chest, it's nothing.

Michael smirks, his blond hair whipping around his head in the relentless sea breeze. He takes a moment to tuck it behind his ear and grins. "No matter. I have what I wanted."

"If you want to kill me, you're going to have to try harder than that," I say, full of piss and bravado as usual—except my words start to slur at the end. My eyelids are suddenly intensely heavy.

Michael grins. "Am I?"

I slump into Gabriel's arms.

Hold on, Gabriel pleads. His voice is sweet and soothing in my mind. *Hold on.*

To what? I think. Because there's nothing here anymore. I'm going to black out after all. And here I go, falling through an endless night, into Gabriel's soft wings as they envelop me.

CHAPTER SEVEN

Ally

*P*lane after plane arrives on Jeremiah's tarmac. Aircrafts bearing nearly every recognizable flag clutter the runway, having accepted Jeremiah's invitation to discuss Jesse—or as they're calling her—the greatest current threat to the world.

"Do you have more bunkers hidden in the world? Otherwise, the shower line will be very long." My heart thumps away in my throat. It's meant to be a light-hearted joke, but the words stick.

"They aren't here for shelter. Jeremiah only wants to inform them of the situation and gauge their intentions."

The fact that Nikki's reply is thoughtful, articulate, and completely serious only makes me more nervous.

"Any chance we can listen in on this conversation? I'd also like *to gauge their intentions*." I expect a flat-out refusal.

The crew and team members with armfuls of equipment wander past us. "Actually," she says and gives me a devilish wink. "Come on."

She pulls me away from the main entrance and tarmac, leading me toward a gray building on the left. A silver handle glints in the sun before she yanks it up. The door rolls skyward, much like a garage door, and we duck inside the darkness. White-blue fluorescents blink on overhead as we creep toward the back wall. It's a hangar of some kind, but whichever aircraft it's meant to hold is gone.

As far from the entrance as we can possibly get, we find an elevator large enough to hold at least twenty people. We step inside, and Nik pushes a button that will take us to level 17.

"I thought there were only sixteen levels," I ask.

"Did I say that?" she asks with a smirk. She adds a nose crinkle as if this is apology enough.

Of course, I'm not surprised. If anyone has nooks and crannies in his secret base, it would be Jeremiah. I do not pretend to know all the inner workings of this man, but I've worked with him enough to know he likes to be prepared, and he likes to play his cards close to the vest. So in no way would this base be all that it seems on the surface.

The elevator is so smooth that when it opens again, I'm surprised to see we've moved at all. I didn't feel the expected lurch or hiss of elevator cables humming and stretching somewhere out of sight. I step into a pristine and bright hallway. There are closed wooden doors on each side and one at the end.

We choose the door at the end.

It is an enormous conference room. Jeremiah sits on one side of the rounded conference table, speaking into a tabletop microphone resting in front of him—little more than a wisp of black foam hovering in front of his thin, moving lips.

Men—perhaps a hundred with the exception of twenty women at most—circle the table, each with their own microphones in front of them. Black suits and white shirts seem to be the order of the day, and I realize I must stick out like an eyesore with my wild, helicopter blown hair and my open, red coat and rumpled clothes.

Jeremiah was speaking when we entered. Upon seeing us, he pauses, takes a drink from the water shimmering in the clear glass at his left elbow, and proceeds. If he hadn't been staring me down the whole time, I would have thought this gesture was unintentional, not an obvious cover for his surprise.

We slide to a stop along the wall in a line of other spectators who seem to be part of, yet excluded from, the discussion.

I want to lean over and ask Nikki *why?* Why challenge Jeremiah? Why bring me here and let me listen in if it will get her into trouble?

But I think I know why. Jeremiah depends on Nikki. No one knows more of his secrets or does his bidding more willingly. He's relied on her for years as his second-in-command. What could he possibly say or do? And whatever that retaliation may be, it certainly wouldn't be here in the company of so many outsiders, even if he disapproves of his second-in-command's weakness. In this case: me.

And you have no qualms exploiting that weakness if it gives Jesse the upper hand, do you? My conscience chides.

"Therefore, sending a team to confront the suspect will only result in more casualties," Jeremiah says, obviously picking up and flawlessly finishing whatever thread we interrupted.

A man, perhaps sixty with thinning gray hair and glasses, laughs across the table. It's a sharp and bitter sound. "My apologies, Dr. Tate, but I have never met a *suspect* that did not succumb to enough firepower."

"There is a first for everything," Jeremiah says, calmly twining his fingers together on the tabletop and leveling the man with a steady gaze.

The man looks around at the others and laughs all the harder. "Please, do not tell me that every single one of you believes the story he is selling us? That one girl, a single *girl* has in her possession a bomb so great that she could detonate it and initiate an extinction event."

One of the women with a brightly colored orange sari leans forward and speaks into her microphone. "Even atomic bombs have their limitation," she says, eyeing Jeremiah with much more patience than the other man. "And you say there is only one bomb, not a hundred."

"I have tried to make it clear that the weapon she has is unlike any you've ever seen," Jeremiah says. "It is true that she is isolated in Antarctica, but her reach is great."

Isolated. Jesse isn't isolated. She has the ability to go anywhere she wants at a moment's notice. Why would Jeremiah deliberately mislead the diplomats?

"This begs the question of how she came by such a weapon, doesn't it?" says another.

A weapon. I reconsider what has been said so far and reexamine the words Jeremiah is using. Then I realize what is going on. He is sticking to the story fabricated by the press, the one in which Jesse is a terrorist. He hasn't said anything about her special abilities or the angels. Instead, he is using only real-world scenarios that they will accept and understand.

She is in possession of a weapon of mass destruction and intends to use it.

Only some do not seem convinced at all.

I lock eyes with a man at the table who starts to give me only a cursory glance, and then looks back for a double-take. My face heats.

"Isn't that one of the terrorists?" the wide-eyed man says from some country with a flag I don't recognize.

Nikki's hand closes over mine.

Jeremiah speaks in the same calm and perfectly inflected tone. "Yes, you may recognize Ms. Gallagher. She was a hostage for a time and is now under our protection. We need to remain focused on the problem at hand."

I open my mouth to contradict him. How dare he paint Jesse as some kidnapper? Does he want the whole world to go after her? Is he trying to get her killed?

Nikki's hand squeezes mine so hard that I yelp instead of launching my counterargument against Jeremiah's slander.

I rip my hand from her grip the same moment she bends down to whisper in my ear.

"He's protecting you."

"He's throwing her under the bus!" I hiss back and several members of the round table closest to me turn, casting curious and annoyed glances.

The sight of a man shouldering his way through the standing spectators lining the walls catches my attention. He's short, perhaps only reaching my shoulders, and so familiar. It isn't until he's almost upon me that I recognize who he is.

Agent Garrison. A squat man who almost threw Jesse in prison before we were able to prove her innocence. He later served as her temporary handler after Brinkley faked his own death. What in the world is he doing here?

"Ms. Gallagher," he says with a pert nod. "Can I speak with you?"

Nikki shifts uncomfortably beside me.

"Sure. Let's step into the hall." I slip away from Nikki, weaving past the others standing and watching the ongoing negotiations over what to do about Jesse.

Jesse. I want to stay. I want to argue and deliberate with these people, but what can I say? No, she isn't a terrorist, of course. But after that, they will want explanations for what they've seen on the television. They'll want to know what I saw with my own eyes. And there is the fact that Jesse *has* killed people. To protect us, true, but that may not be enough to justify the loss of life. Nor will any explanations of Caldwell's mind control hold sway.

Garrison holds open the door, and I step into the hallway first. As the door swings shut behind us, we step over to the side, to a little nook beside one of the closed doors.

"For the sake of time, let's state openly that I know Jesse is not a terrorist, and she does not have a bomb. I know that what she's doing, she's doing of her own—volition—and that it is not an isolated event."

My chest loosens. At least we can get to business now instead of using doublespeak.

"The FBRD has been made aware of the situation because it involves several of their agents. Liza Miller, Rachel Wright, Cindy St. Clair. You know these agents?"

"Yes."

He confirms with a sharp nod. "So let us say that these events have superseded our understanding of NRD as a neurological idea, and that perhaps something else is happening. Would you say the FBRD could expect this to happen to all agents or simply to a select few?"

"It's only Jesse now," I say, and I leave it at that.

Garrison searches my face and then nods again. "The FBRD is struggling to curtail this publicity. First the story about the murdered agents broke and now Jesse's...story. They are questioning whether or not the bureau should be disbanded and death replacing abolished, because an agent has radicalized—"

"She hasn't!" I hiss.

"I know," he says. His face folds with sympathy. "I know. But several people who've always looked for a way to shut down the FBRD are using her as the posterchild for their campaign. They claim this is why the agency should not exist and death replacing should not be an option. That repeat replacements only serve to create mentally unstable murderers, who are rather difficult to kill."

I look through the glass at all the people inside the room discussing Jesse and what to do about her. So many enemies. So many threats.

There is nowhere in the world Jesse could hide now—even if somehow we survived Gabriel's plan, where could she live and not be hunted? She would always be in danger.

If that was her life, I would follow her, without hesitation. But that is no life.

"You must be very worried for her safety," Garrison says.

I realize he's been watching my face very carefully.

"You have no idea," I admit. "But let me be clear, Agent Garrison, everything Jesse has done has only been done in self-defense. The casualties are the result of Caldwell's attempts to capture and kill her. And now he's dead."

Garrison's eyes widen ever so slightly, telling me all I need to know. So word hasn't reached all corners of Earth yet. Caldwell's death is still somewhat a secret.

"I pulled you out here, because I wanted you to know that the upper ranks within the FBRD are aware of the situation, and to learn how serious the situation with Jesse is. I cannot guarantee that they will present her side of the story fairly once the story fully breaks."

"I understand. But try not to paint her as the villain when you report back." The door behind me opens, and people begin filing out. A sea of black suits and nervous chatter. People are already lifting their phones from pockets and making calls. Orders are being issued all over the world and I need to know what's been decided. I'd better corner Jeremiah before he can escape.

Garrison looks ready to join the flood of people. "I'll try to keep you in the loop if you promise to do the same?" He recites my email from memory. "Is that still a working address?"

"Yes," I nod.

"I hope the next time we meet it's under better circumstances, Ms. Gallagher." He turns and hurries down the hall to catch the elevator before it closes on all the bodies huddled inside.

"Just do what you can!" I call after him.

"I promise," he calls back before the doors close.

I slip back into the conference room. It looks so much bigger now without all the people crammed inside. Jeremiah stands behind his seat while the people scurrying around him pester him for answers or make themselves busy rearranging the room: pushing in chairs, gathering up microphones, ducking under desks for forgotten pen caps and notes abandoned in haste.

Jeremiah has his hands on the hips of his brown dress slacks. He's arguing with Nikki whose face is red from the effort. I have a sinking feeling it is about me.

I make my way around the desks and join them, unable to suppress my own irritation.

"You're making this worse for her," I say, unclenching my teeth.

"She did this to herself," he says. He barely looks up.

I stop, stunned. I feel as if I've been slapped. "Excuse me?"

"The world views Jesse as a monster, because she's used her power recklessly. Do you know how much footage the world has of her burning people alive? Hours. *Hours* that we've had to confiscate, doctor, and reintroduce into the media circuit. If she were more careful—"

"Caldwell hunted her. Caldwell *killed* her," I say. Only I'm not saying it. I'm screaming it. And I can't remember the last time I've screamed at anyone. Except that this time I'm afraid for Jesse, and I have no way to get to her, no way to help her.

"Al—?" Nikki asks.

I take a breath. "Telling them that she is a terrorist is only going to make her a target. Do you want to get *more* people killed? Because it isn't like she is going to roll over and take it. Every person they send after her is going to die!"

"They already have," he says, flicking his eyes up to meet mine. "And they want to send another wave."

Another wave. My god, *another wave.* I take a breath.

"And what is going to happen when you tell them she killed Timothy Caldwell? He might have been her father, and it might have been self-defense, but they don't care about that. They're only going to say that she killed the leader of The Unified Church. A terrorist killed a respected religious leader."

Nikki and Jeremiah exchange a look.

A stone sinks in the pit of my stomach. "You've already told them."

"I said—" Jeremiah begins defensively, raising his palms toward me. "That Caldwell was killed in the attack, not that he was murdered. I said he entered the situation and was trying to help, but was caught in the crossfire. I painted as neutral a picture as possible."

"Not neutral. If you can paint me as a hostage, you could have painted her as one as well. But you didn't, because you want to keep her running. You want to force her to ask for your help when the whole world turns against her."

Something flashes in Jeremiah's eyes.

"But she won't," I say. "She'll *never* be some toy that you let out of a coma when you decide you're ready to use her."

I whirl, ready to run from the room. I have a sudden and desperate urge to check on Maisie and Gloria. Nikki may be one of the only allies I have left, but she's affiliated with this man with his dark machinations. Not evil, no. But people who want what they want and will hurt others to get it—they're dangerous all the same. I should have never let them bring Maisie and Gloria here. So what if I was outnumbered, I should have fought back.

Jeremiah reaches for me—to do what, I don't even know. Seize my arm? Shackle me? But his hand slams into a bright purple shield.

He pulls his hand back as if it's been burned. Nikki, too, looks shocked and surprised. When I see the dark shape take form in the corner of my eye, I expect to see Jesse there. It's always been Jesse who's thrown a protective shield around me.

But it isn't Jesse standing there. It's Gabriel.

He's forced me out. That large mouth moves out of sync with the words in my head. *Hurry.*

"How are you using the shield?" Jeremiah asks. He sounds both interested and hateful.

"I'm not." I stop short of saying *Gabriel is.*

Jeremiah is as good at reading people as I am. He knows I'm not lying. He looks around, but Jesse isn't here.

"She isn't here. She can't possibly be shielding you," he says. His voice thins to a high, strident tone. Is he jealous? If I didn't know better, I'd say Jeremiah Tate is *jealous* of this power.

"I need a ride to Antarctica."

Nikki gives him a furious glare before he even has a chance to respond.

In a very even tone he says, "No. I don't have the resources for that."

I laugh, bitterly. "Yes, you do. But you're steering clear of the gate, because you're afraid of what will happen when the gate opens."

I search his face, and see the recognition in his eyes. So he's heard of the gate.

He licks his lips and pushes his glasses up onto his nose again. "So the angels have told you that much, have they? Who told you about the gate?"

I neither confirm nor deny. Instead, I counter. "Who told *you* about the gate?"

Nikki's jaw is working again.

Jeremiah notes her discomfort and huffs. "Very well. I suppose we all have our secrets."

He tugs at the end of his sweater vest and steps around me. His exit from the room leaves me and Nikki alone.

As soon as the door closes shut behind him, the shield sputters and disappears. The shadow in the corner of my eye does, too. I turn anyway just to be sure, but no Gabriel. The white wall with its gray specks stands empty. *He's forced me out.* What did he mean? Another angel? Someone worse?

"Did you see Gabriel? Jesse's Gabriel?" Nikki demands. And it *is* a demand.

I arch my eyebrow at her.

Her tone softens. "It was Gabriel who erected the shield, wasn't it?"

"Yes. Because apparently Jeremiah can't be trusted."

"He won't lay a hand on you," she says.

My arched eyebrow only rises higher. "Not for lack of trying."

"He *won't*."

"And what will you do to stop him, Ms. Tamsin, the ever faithful second-in-command?"

I know what Jesse would say. *Break his hand. Blast his brains out his asshole.* But she is much more vulgar than Nikki is. Nikki only says, "He won't."

"He doesn't want to help her," I say. Let's see how open

and honest we are really being with each other. "He wants to pin all of this on her."

"No, he just doesn't prioritize her protection like you do," Nik says. "There are others worth saving, too."

That stings a little.

"What did the agent want?" Nikki asks. "I saw you step out with him."

"Garrison says the FBRD is in an uproar over Jesse. I suppose that can be blamed on her recklessness too?" I level her with a hard stare, daring her to echo Jeremiah's cruel words.

But her anger is gone and she seems to have control of herself again. Her endless patience has returned. "No, they lost it when their agents started getting murdered by Caldwell. This latest development is only making matters worse."

A diplomatic response.

"But you knew about the FBRD being under fire? And you didn't tell me."

She considers my face for a long moment, almost tenderly. Her jaw unclenches and her voice softens when she finally says, "That life is behind you now."

The finality with which she says it feels like a punch to the gut.

That life is behind you now. Death replacing. A cozy home in Nashville. Dog walking and Friday night pizza and too many soy lattes to count. Appointment books and cocktails with friends.

She reaches up and tucks a strand of fallen hair behind my ear. "Gloria is out of surgery, and Maisie is asking for you. Want to go see them?"

"Yes." Because Jeremiah may have refused to take me to Antarctica, but I'm not giving up so easily.

I'll find another way.

CHAPTER EIGHT

Jesse

My body burns. At first, I think I'm back in the barn, its rafters alight, its hay blackening in the crimson blaze. Somehow, time has reversed itself. I'm not twenty-six. I'm seventeen and dying.

No, Jesse, Gabriel whispers through my mind. Black feathers trail across my cheek. *Do not give up your Time.*

His voice is clear and bright in the encroaching darkness. Something inside me shifts, as if throwing itself out to break a fall—but feeling nothing.

Do not give up your Time, he says again as if this is supposed to mean something to me, but his voice is weaker. Farther away than ever before.

My feet find solid ground. I open my eyes, and I'm standing in a house, a small house that I'd know anywhere. The last time I saw it, it held my mother's coffin in the cramped living room where a television should have been. Now, it was as I remembered it when I was much younger. Six or seven. My father sits on a battered brown sofa with his head in his hands. He still wears his mechanic outfit, the navy-blue overalls with gold zippers and a white embossed name patch on the front that read *Eric.*

"You don't know that," my mother says. "Why do you need to work me up over something you can't possibly know?"

As soon as she speaks, she shimmers into view, bringing the rest of the liquid dream into sharp focus. Gabriel is somewhere behind me, begging me to come back. But I wouldn't know how to oblige him even if I could.

"Keep your voice down." My father tosses a look at the closed door just off the living room. That was my bedroom. Because of the position of the loveseat where my mother sits in her pajamas, a glass of water in one hand, they can't see what I see—the shadows of two twin feet beneath that bedroom door.

I must be awake in there. I must be listening with my ear to the door.

"They say it runs in families. If my brother has it, then I could have it. Jesse could have it."

My mother hisses. "Don't you dare put that on my head. She's fine. There's nothing wrong with her."

"I'm just saying we need to prepare for the possibility. If something were to happen, we don't want to handle it badly. We need to be aware."

My father knew about his NRD before he died? How could he? He woke up in a coffin underground. He liked to remind me he'd been an unlucky jack-in-the-box on more than one occasion.

I'm trying to place this conversation, but I can't. It's true that dying and resurrecting over one hundred times has made me forget a lot—and even more true that so few people remember everything from when they were six or seven—but this seems important. This seems like something I should have remembered.

"I don't want what happened to Dyson to happen to us. Promise me," my father says.

I look at my father's dark circles and greasy hands. I note my mother's red rimmed eyes. The swell of crickets pressing in on the windows from outside. The summer breeze wafting across my father's tanned skin.

Jesse—you must come back.

Gabriel's voice is stronger. And the world in which my parents sit in a dark house in the late evening while their little girl listens to secrets at the bedroom door wavers.

"Promise me," my father says again, his face shimmering.

"Goddammit, Eric. I promise," my mother echoes. "If either of you have NRD, I won't call them. I wouldn't even—"

Whatever she says to finish the promise is lost on the wind.

The scent of rain wafts up to greet me. A strong arm seizes me around the waist and pulls me back.

"You must not give up your Time." Gabriel's cheek is cold against mine. The vision breaks, and I'm on the sandy shore. I feel my body again.

"Stop saying that. I don't know what that means."

Whatever I'm about to say falls away. Gabriel is bleeding. His blood is on my hands. "What happened?"

"You must come back," he says through labored breaths. "I can't hold this for long."

I can't remember Gabriel getting hurt. I can't really remember where I was before I was in my childhood home, looking at my parents as they must've been...how many years ago?

Years ago...

There is somewhere I need to be...not the beach. But... where? I can't remember.

Gabriel's grip on my hips loosens. *Go back to your Time. Go back to the convergence.*

My mother's house shifts into focus again, hardening around me once more. But it isn't the early hours of a summer night. I'm standing there, eight or nine years old, looking between my mother and father with parted lips and a rabbity panic. My father is covered in dirt, still wearing the suit we buried him in, graveyard soil in his hair and flecks crusted in the sweat under his eyes.

My mother is holding the receiver to a cordless phone. She's crying.

"You promised," he says to her.

For a long time, nothing happens. No one moves.

Then she manages a nod and puts the receiver down.

My child double runs to him and throws her arms around his neck.

The world kicks forward again. My father remains alive. At seventeen, my double doesn't die in the barn trying to escape her abusive stepfather, because there is no stepfather. She dies in car crash leaving a party with a boy who'd had too much to drink and also kept trying to stick his hand up her skirt. The dark-haired boy wearing a flannel shirt swerves to miss a deer and sails off the road into a tree.

She—*I*—shove open the door and fall into the ditch beside the car. I bleed to death on the side of the road.

Jesse, you're going too far...

I wake up in a funeral home to the faces of my parents. I'm wearing a black dress. They aren't frightened that their corpse daughter has just opened her eyes. They know what I am, and they are okay with it. My father pulls me off the mortuary slab, worried, but relieved. My mother is crying and hugs me so hard the vertebrae in my back crack.

That fall I go to college. On graduation day, I stand with

them for a photo while a classmate, a red-headed girl I don't have a name for, takes a photo.

Jesse. I can't hold open the door.

I look at the smiling faces. I note the roaring cheer of all the people in the stadium, the swish of gowns, the blare of music. Confetti. I realize I'm looking for someone.

Someone is missing, some part of me insists. Someone isn't here. And her absence gives the whole vision a tainted glare that forms into pinpricks of pain in my mind.

The world shimmers again, crumpling like paper in a fist.

Then I see her face. A woman, blond and beautiful with warm brown eyes and a tiny diamond stud in her nose. I see her in her red coat. I hear her speak my name.

Only then does her name come to me in return.

Ally.

The last ounce of resistance leaves me. This world falls away, and when I open my eyes, I'm on an ice shelf shaking furiously. My eyes sweep the deep blue waters, the endless plateau of shimmering ice, the baby blue sky with puffy white clouds. In the distance something burns, weak black smoke of a cooling wreckage wafting up to the sky.

"What the hell was that?" Now I remember Michael's shooting star of pain. "What the hell did he do to me?"

"Michael used a disruptor. It severs your connection to your own time," he says.

And while I'm happy to know that shooting star of pain has a name, a disruptor, I can barely appreciate this information because Gabriel is not okay. He looks sick as hell and appears to be fading fast.

"Why do you keep saying Time like that—like with a capital T," I ask. "And what the hell did I just see? That's not how my life went. Was it an illusion? Like one of Caldwell's mind tricks?"

Gabriel waits until he's sure I'm done firing questions at him. "You saw a possibility."

"So if my mother hadn't had my father hauled away to a camp, that's how it would've gone?"

"It isn't that he disrupted your hold on this Time that concerns me," Gabriel says. "It is that he pushed you toward this possibility, of all the infinite possibilities."

He forces an image of Ally into my mind. I see her bright shining face again and know it was this image that he used earlier to help me see through Michael's trick.

"He showed me a world where I never met Ally? Why would he do that?"

"I don't know."

I blink twice. Wait, what? Back up. Did this angel really just say he didn't know? I was just starting to believe that they were angels. Wouldn't they be omniscient if that were true? They'd know everything.

Rachel's theory was that they were ancient aliens, come to shepherd us into a new era so that we could be a better, more awesome civilization. But then again, what aliens in their right mind would waste their time on us? Of course, people have pet rocks and sea monkeys, don't they? I guess it's possible some weirdo creature thought humans were entertaining enough.

What if we are the Tamagotchi craze of some angelic civilization?

Focus, Jesse. I remind myself. I've got bigger problems right now.

"Is the disruptor going to keep doing that?" I ask. "Knocking me out of my Time?"

"Yes. It will get stronger."

"And if it doesn't, what's he going to do? Go after my dog?" I hate it when the bad guys go after my dog. Or worse.

My heart flops. "Ally? Maisie? Gloria? Hell, even Gideon is growing on me."

"He cannot attack directly. He no longer has a corporeal host."

"So...*in*directly?" I hiss. I'm already plotting the invisible distance between me and Al. I'm summoning up my strength, ready to jump to her and kick Michael's angel butt.

Gabriel's hand clamps down on my arm. Hard. "He has barbed you."

I scoff. "Excuse me. No one *barbs* me without at least feeding me dinner and telling me how pretty I am."

Gabriel's eyes darken to that dangerous hue. No jokes then. "You're poisoned. You will be without a shield and will continue to grow more unstable as long as it is in your system. You must be more careful."

This coming from the guy who is bleeding all over himself.

"And what about you?" I ask, hissing at the sight of his fingers probing the wound. "What does the disruptor barb do to you?"

His jaw clenches and he withdraws his hand with a ragged breath.

He flickers. He flickers the way he used to flicker when the other partis were around me. But in every direction, there is only this ice desert. Not a single soul. I'm not even sure there's anyone left in the weakening black smoke fuming from the smoldering helicopters.

"Is he trying to take you away from me?" I ask. A stiff panic starts to take hold of my spine. "Because I don't know how to do what you're asking me."

"When the charge is complete, the gate will open."

"Yeah, you keep saying that."

"You cannot get lost in Possibility again. You must be

here. Now. And you must know what you want. If I am not with you—"

He says *Possibility* like it's capitalized, too. Like it's a place where everything lives between the immaterial and reality.

"If you're not with me!" I interrupt. I'm shouting, and the sound of it echoes vast over the frozen tundra. "What about all the partis and angel merging at the moment of ascension crap?"

"He will take my place if he can," Gabriel warns, and his words send a shiver up the back of my neck. I curl deeper into my puffy, stolen, coat. "We survived this attack, but there will be others."

He flickers again.

"Hey—" I grab his hands and squeeze hard. "Don't disappear on me. You know I can't fight Michael alone."

You are stronger than you think.

He squeezes my hand in return. Then he is gone.

CHAPTER NINE

Ally

I stagger out of the elevator, my hand gropes blindly for anything to steady me. My right fingertips brush textured plaster. My left hand goes over my heart as if to keep it in. Cold chills run from head to toe, cramping then releasing the muscles along my spine. By the time my shoulder connects with the wall, I'm trembling.

"What's wrong?" Nikki asks. Her hand is steady on my back.

"I don't know," I say, my heart galloping in my chest. "I feel...strange."

And I can't seem to articulate it any better than that. The sensation creeping along my skin *is* strange. Unsettling.

It's two layers, I realize. There's what's happening in my mind: like I forgot something important. An appointment. Or that I need to be somewhere. A certain panicky shock blanketing my mind. And then there is the physical experience—the hint of a flu, or an illness that is threatening to put me under for days.

"Can I—?" Nikki begins.

"Just give me a minute." I force the words out. A minute to lean against the wall and breathe.

Breathe, I tell myself. And I'm reminded of the therapist I saw so many years ago who taught me how to deal with my anxiety, and stress, and mounting anger in the wake of losing Jesse. I feel like all we did for the first month were breathing exercises.

Breathe.

My shoulder presses into the cold, hard plaster until the bone aches. But eventually the feeling does recede. The weight in my arms lightens. The hallway comes into focus. The sounds of sneakers squeaking on tiles. The soft *whoosh* of a door sliding open or shut.

But even as my body seems to weather the passing storm that nagging fear darkening my mind doesn't leave me.

"Do you," Nikki begins, but lowers her voice. She licks her lip as she casts a furtive look up and down the hallway. She leans in to whisper. Her breath is hot on my ear. "Do you see anything? Gabriel? Jesse?"

I look up at the ceiling's white tile with gray specks. The hallway is wide and empty except for the two of us.

"No. I just feel..." *like I'm dying. No, don't say that! She'll have a conniption.* "...off. Maybe I'm coming down with something."

The intercom in Nikki's ear lights blue. "Tamsin," she says, by way of introduction. But her eyes are fixed on mine, searching my face.

I feel guilty under that assessing stare so I push myself off the wall and step around her. On unsteady legs, I walk toward the red and white sign saying Patients Only. She reaches out and seizes my arm, stopping me from entering the hospital wing.

"Repeat that," Tamsin says, her face coloring red. Her eyes widen.

"Are you sure?" she asks the person in the earpiece but

she's pressing her fingers to the side of my throat, searching for the artery. She checks my pulse. Her shoulders relax.

Her gaze slides away from my face. "No, just monitor the situation and notify me immediately if it happens again."

The intercom goes dark and her crushing hold on my arm loosens.

"What's happened?"

"Two of Jesse's replacements just collapsed," she says, scowling. "Parish says they went into some kind of convulsive fit. One crumpled outside the office building where he works. The other went into cardiac arrest while riding her bicycle along the St. Louis riverbank."

She tries to meet my gaze, but I turn away.

"Come on, I want someone to look at you."

"Nick—"

"Two people she replaced. *You're* someone she's replaced."

You are so much more than that, Gabriel whispers. I hear the crackle of lightning and smell the rain on wet pavement—but the entrance to the hospital remains unchanged. Gleaming white doors beckon me.

"Is Jesse okay?"

"She's throwing off huge clouds of gamma radiation, but otherwise, no anomalies."

"But is she alive?" I ask.

Nikki licks her lips and holds the swinging door open so that I can pass through. I hardly note the hospital wing we step into except that it's brighter than the dim hallway where we stood moments before.

Nikki is obviously preparing herself to deliver news that will upset me. It's her tell really—licking her lips, followed by a sigh.

"A team was sent to apprehend her," she says.

"I'm sure that went well."

"The situation escalated."

"Of course it did."

"All of the helicopters were brought down and no one survived."

"Was she hurt?" I ask. I can barely hear my own words over the blood pounding in my ears.

"We don't know," Nikki says, her words full of apology. "Parish can't find her on the satellite. It's possible that she jumped and escaped without a scratch. She wouldn't still be putting off so much gamma radiation if she were dead, would she?"

"I don't know. I don't know how this all works," I say. *Breathe.* "But she could be seriously hurt." Hurt in a way that her healing ability can't help her.

Nikki licks her lips again. She sighs and says, "They fired Hellfire missiles. Two of them. Parish says..." Her voice falters.

"Just say it. I haven't run screaming yet, have I?"

Her eyebrow twitches as if to say *not yet but*... "Parish says that her shield disappeared a second before the missile launched."

I feel like someone is holding my head underwater. "It could have hit her."

A missile could have hit Jesse and blown her apart. Her healing ability could never put her back together again. That gamma radiation might not mean she survived. It could have something to do with the convergence point that Gabriel was talking about.

A woman in blue scrubs passes by, flashing us a curious look before she disappears through a second set of double doors.

"Or she saw it and jumped away," Nikki says, her voice lower now that she's been reminded we aren't alone. How could she forget it?

Please tell me she's okay. Tell me she isn't laying in pieces on some half destroyed ice shelf.

Gabriel says nothing.

"But we know that two people fell ill," I say, trying to quell my terror with what few facts and information I have. "Two of her replacements. Did this happen at the same moment as the fire fight?"

"No. It happened right after. Is it possible she drained them to heal herself or something?"

"She's not a vampire!" I hiss.

She holds her palms out in surrender. "I'm not saying that she is. But two people just fell over dead and you..." She sighs. "Something happened to you outside the elevator and I'm just trying to understand what is going on!"

"Can I help you?" A brunette asks. Her golden eagle eyes survey us with slight annoyance.

She's in scrubs too, her hair dark hair hanging in soft waves around her face. One hand grips her hip where a plastic badge hangs clipped at the bottom of her shirt. I didn't see her come in.

Nikki casts a look at the woman in the scrubs. "She needs to be checked out. She's sick."

"I'm fine," I say. "We want to see Gloria Jackson, please."

Nikki's earpiece lights up blue again. "Tamsin."

The woman and I exchange awkward glances as Nikki takes her call. When the blue light disappears she says, "I have to go up."

"Did—" I begin, but Nikki's hard stare silences me.

"No," she says. "This is something else." Then to the woman guarding the medical bay she says, "She has clearance to visit Gloria Jackson and Maisie Caldwell whenever she wants. And it wouldn't hurt if you could check her out while she's here."

"Against my will?" I say, and I hear the accusation in my own voice.

Her jaw tightens. "I find it hypocritical that you never stop Jesse from doing whatever it takes to protect you—and yet you won't let me do the same."

I laugh. It dispels the last of the dizziness, and I finally catch my breath. "I try to stop Jesse all the time. She just never listens to me."

The woman in scrubs has no interest in our squabble. She breaks in. "Okay. Shall I show you to Captain Jackson's room?"

"Yes, please," I say, embarrassed that we've just been standing here arguing.

"I'll walk you there. Jeremiah will want to know how she's doing," Nikki grumbles.

As we fall into step behind the woman in scrubs, the room comes into focus for the first time. It's a working emergency room, or at least it looks like one. Top of the line hospital beds and monitors line the wall. All of them are empty, but nurses and staff hurry around, checking machines, prepping stations, restocking supplies.

They look like they are preparing for something.

They're preparing for Jesse, I realize. For the casualties that she might cause.

Several of the hard-working men and women in scrubs look up, scowling at me for being there. That is until they see Nikki beside me. Their faces soften with recognition. Several come to attention as we pass. I wonder if she ever tires of it, being treated like a general, with such respect and deference. I'm sure she doesn't.

If Jesse were here, Nikki would never hear the end of it.

I think that one wants to lick your boots, Sasquatch. And that one wants to braid your hair.

A sudden swelling of homesickness and longing makes my stomach clench. *Where are you, Jesse?*

I want Jesse to appear before me, wrap her arms around me and take me with her—wherever she has to go, whatever she has to do.

But if she can't do that right now, for whatever reason, then I wish she would just tell me she's okay. That she isn't laying in pieces somewhere.

I try to push the image of blood on snow—so much blood—out of my mind.

Down a bright hallway, we find a room on the right with Gloria and Maisie inside. Maisie is in scrubs too, her hair still wet from a shower and her cheeks pink from steam. She smells like bar soap. Winston is on the foot of Gloria's bed where she lies supine and unmoving. Her eyes are closed. The monitor attached to her finger with a series of wires, beeps its slow, steady rhythm.

Maisie has her fingers intertwined with Gloria's.

Nikki looks Maisie over. "Are you all healed up?"

"Yeah," Maisie says. Her voice is tired and distant. "They said I could go, but I didn't want to leave her. There's this one nurse who keeps trying to throw me out because of Winston."

Nikki asks for a description and Maisie provides it.

"That's Helen," the woman in the scrubs says. "I'll talk to her."

"Thank you," Maisie and I say in unison.

Then eagle eyes disappears, leaving us alone.

Nikki reaches into her pocket and fishes out an intercom like the one nestled in her ear. It's black with a snail-shaped coil on its back. I haven't used one in a while. "Keep this. And you better call me if...anything happens."

I nod and accept the intercom, knowing it's the only way

she'll leave. And I suddenly want her gone so I can talk to Maisie—*really* talk to her.

Nikki's fingers linger on my hand for a moment longer than they should before she's out the door, her boots squeaking along the tile.

"Have you heard from Jesse?" Maisie asks. Her voice is hopeful if still subdued.

It tears my attention away from the empty doorway and bright hallway beyond. "No, sorry."

Maisie nods as if this no surprise.

I settle into the hard plastic chair, cold and unforgiving beside hers, and give Winston a scratch on the head. His cinnamon bun tail thumps against the crumpled bedding.

At this angle, I can see the puffy circles under Maisie's eyes. What I mistook for steamed cheeks is probably redness from crying.

I put an arm around the girl's shoulder, and that's all it takes. She falls into sobs immediately and with abandon. And why shouldn't she? In the last 24 hours, both her parents were murdered, and her sister is missing. Possibly dead for all she knows.

I pull her tighter against me. "You're okay. You're going to be okay."

Such pathetic platitudes. I almost hate myself for saying them.

"Nothing is okay! Nothing will ever be okay!" She sobs into my arm. I hold her and stroke her hair even though the plastic chair isn't conducive to such an embrace. She cries like this for a long time. The people in scrubs—doctors? Nurses? Certainly clinicians of some kind, continue to pass by the door without stopping in.

Finally her crying quiets. She asks, "Where's Jesse?"

I settle on the truth, at least *mostly* truth. "The last time they saw her was near the South Pole."

"What's she doing there?"

"We're not sure." I don't dare bring up "convergence points" or "gates" just yet.

"I've been talking to—" She peers over my shoulder at the door. "I've been talking to Azrael, but she sounds so far away. And distracted, you know? I think she's fighting other angels. The bad ones."

My heart kicks. "There are still people who think she is dangerous and they're trying to stop her." I don't make any mention of missiles or exploding scientific facilities either.

"But she isn't!" Maisie says, all wide eyes and insistence. "She could've killed me, but she didn't! She saved me."

"I know," I say, pushing the hair back from her face. *But she's killed so many others.*

"We have to help her. We have to get to Antarctica," she says. And it sounds more ridiculous coming out of her mouth than it does in my own head, even though I've been saying the same thing on a refrain since Gabriel first appeared to me and showed me where she was.

I run my fingers through her long, blond hair. Her face is still red, her blue eyes bright and cheeks tear-stained.

"I don't see how we can get there," I say. "We don't have a plane. I thought Gideon might be able to get us one, but I haven't heard from him." I make a mental note to check my email again. My cell phone may not work in this underground bunker, but it's been hours since I sent that email. Maybe he's written back. Hell, maybe he is on his way with a jet now, and I don't even know it.

I've also considered flat out asking Nikki to steal a plane for me, but given how she wants to seal me in this medical ward for my own safety, I can only imagine how that convo will go.

I pull the intercom earpiece from my pocket and turn it over wistfully in the palm of my hand, my thumb scratching at the red emergency button protruding from the back and the coiled call button, looking like a snail's shell imprinted on the front.

"He was there when I woke up," Maisie says, pulling me from my thoughts. "After Jesse saved me, I woke up and he was the first person I saw."

There's a strange cadence to her voice. She sounds older suddenly. But why shouldn't she, after all that she's been through. I realize she's talking about Gideon.

She lowers her voice and casts a furtive glance at the doorway one more time. She whispers, "He said he doesn't trust Jeremiah and that he's going to find someone else to help us."

I'm not surprised to hear this. Jeremiah's actions do not always inspire confidence.

"We'll find a way to help Jesse. I promise," I say, slipping the earpiece back into my pocket. It sounds like a promise bound to be broken. "In the meantime, we need to take care of each other. You, me, and Gloria."

Maisie squeezes Gloria's hand again. The woman on the bed doesn't react. The steady rhythm of her heart remains unchanged on the monitor beside her bed.

Here is the hard part, I think. No point in delaying it.

"I need to tell you something," I say and as soon as I say it, I realize that perhaps I've already made it worse. I can hear Jesse in my head—*oh gee-zus. What? No one says they need to tell me something and it's good news.*

Maisie's back stiffens. "Dad's not dead? He's going to show up and—"

"No, no. That's not what I meant. Caldwell's dead. He's never going to hurt you again."

"And my mother, too?" Maisie asks. And it doesn't really sound like a question. The tears well again and I doubt that I should have brought this up so soon.

"I'm sorry."

I expect more tears, but she is silent, replaying something in her mind.

I gently urge her back on track. "That's not what I needed to tell you."

Maisie nods, stilling herself. I can't help but admire her strength. I don't think I was half as capable at sixteen.

"I reached out to my brother and asked him to come here. I want you to meet him. He's a lawyer. A good lawyer. Very smart and very kind. And I think he can help you."

Her lower lip quivers.

"Or I can contact the Michaelsons. They are still technically your adoptive parents. You could—"

"No," she says. "No."

Her trembling lip breaks my heart. I thought this would be a source of comfort for her, to know she wouldn't be alone. That she wouldn't end up in some strange place. But I can see now that as well-intentioned as this talk may have been, perhaps it could've been better-timed.

But when else could I have taken care of this? I couldn't. Not when I'm planning to hop the first plane out of here.

"I'm not trying to frighten or hurt you," I say, pushing the hair back from her face. "I just believe you should have a say in where you live now. I wanted you to know that you wouldn't end up in foster care or anything like that. You're old enough to make this decision for yourself."

"My parents are dead. And the Michaelsons have moved on. Going back to them will be horrible for all of us. Missing daughter returns thirteen years after being kidnapped? If that gets out in the newspaper, it'll be huge. My face will be everywhere. How long before someone realizes that I look just like the infamous 'Maisie Caldwell.' It would be a total clusterfuck."

I flinch at her vulgarity, but she has an excellent point.

"I can't do that to them," Maisie says.

"Okay. But I hope you'll speak to my brother. If you want to be emancipated, if you want to get ahold of your parents' money so you'll always be financially secure, or if you want to stay with him until you're eighteen—whatever you want, he is willing to help."

The tears threaten to spill over again. They shimmer in her blonde eyelashes. "I guess living with you and Jesse isn't an option."

My own throat tightens. "Even if Jesse survives— whatever all this partis, end of the world stuff is—I don't think she will have a normal life. Too many people have questions. The best she can hope for is a life on the run until her name is cleared, and who knows how long that will take. You deserve a quiet, stable life."

When Maisie nods in agreement, the tightness in my chest loosens a bit.

"You don't have to decide today," I tell her. "But I just wanted you to know that my brother is coming to talk to you, and to vouch that he really is a wonderful human being. I hope you'll let him help you."

"Okay," she says.

We lapse into silence. A long, comfortable silence. After ten or fifteen minutes, I get up and untangle myself from the dozing girl beside me. I want to get to the rec room to check my email again. Fingers crossed I'll find good news from Gideon.

Maisie turns and looks at the sleeping Gloria, at their clasped hands. "I remember her."

I scratch Winston's head. "Who?"

"Captain Jackson. I remember her and this guy in a leather jacket with a crooked smile."

My heart skips a beat. "That was Brinkley."

"When my dad took me from the Michaelsons, we were

on the move a lot in the beginning. Lots of empty houses, and when I'd start to cry, he'd bring me toys. But then people would always catch up to us, and we'd have to move again. I didn't really know what was going on or why we were moving around so much."

"—you were very young," I interject.

She continues as if I hadn't. "But I remember that one time he left me with her."

"Your dad left you with Gloria?"

"Yeah. Something happened to my mom. I think she got shot, but I can't be sure. I just remember her screaming, and all the blood. Then the next thing I know, Dad is bundling me up, in the middle of the night. He still had blood on his hands. When he handed me over to Gloria, I was in this thick flannel blanket with my bear. I remember seeing my father's bloody handprint on my PJs, and I started to cry."

I try to remember what Brinkley said about this in his journal—about Caldwell knowing Gloria loved Maisie too much to hurt her. But it's been so long since I read it. And we stashed those notebooks in a safety deposit box somewhere in Pennsylvania, on the road to New York.

"I tried to ask Gloria about it once," Maisie went on. "I think all I said was something dumb like 'I remember you.'"

"What did she say?"

"She said that we'd met before when I was little, but that's all she'd say. When I tried to ask more, she shook her head and walked away. I think it hurt her feelings. I don't know what happened—I don't remember anything bad happening —but I wasn't able to get her to talk to me about it either."

"What do you remember about her?" I ask, my curiosity too strong to ignore.

"She was nice," Maisie says, with a sad smile. "She smelled like lemon drops and Coca-Cola." She shakes her head. "It's more than that. You know how sometimes being around certain people just makes you happy? It just feels good to be around them. Like going to Grandma's house for cookies or something. Except this grandma is an old psychic lady who carries a gun and drinks too much soda, you know?"

A surprised laugh escapes her.

"I know what you mean." I do. Jesse is one of those people for me—*the* person for me.

"It was like that," she says. "I don't have a reason why, it's just how I feel. She makes me feel safe."

"I'm sure she'll be thrilled to hear that, sweetie."

Her lip trembles again. "If she doesn't die before I can tell her."

CHAPTER TEN

Jesse

The water slams against the shore. Angry waves pound their frustrations on the sand. Or maybe I'm projecting here. Where is Gabriel? Holy hell, *where* is Gabriel?

The sound of shifting sand sends me whirling around to face whatever is coming. My heart is half hopeful, half fearful. Hope that it's Gabriel, full of excuses and apologies—fear that it's not.

It's not.

Michael stands alone on the beach, barefoot in the sand. He's wearing black capris and an open white shirt, exposing a bare chest. He sees me looking, and his grin spreads.

"What did you do with him?" I call up my fire without thinking. The blue flames whip in the wind along my arms.

"Oh, he's still around," he flashes me a fox-like smile, with rows of perfect teeth. "Unfortunately, he's very hard to get rid of. Believe me, I've been trying for a long, *long* time."

"Why did you change your clothes?"

He doesn't look down like most people would at such a question, he only raises an eyebrow. "I thought you'd like the change. Something a little more casual. Intimate. It's just us now."

My heart starts rocketing in my chest. "There will be no intimacy here. Got that?"

He grins, pulling on his bottom lip with his teeth. "I could take you by force, of course. But given your history, I think that will escalate this a little too quickly. The timing must be perfect. So we'll save that for the proper moment."

My mouth goes dry.

"Meanwhile, relax and enjoy the seduction."

The hair on my arms and back of my neck stiffen.

"Is it the form I chose? I don't know why you wouldn't like it." Now he glances down at his body. "It has symmetry. Strong, but a touch feminine."

"Listen, I don't care if you turn into Idris Elba. Touch me, and it'll be the last thing you'll do."

He considers me with those large, wet eyes for a moment. It's like a face-off—very western. Behind him, the beach stretches on until it's swallowed up by silvery fog. Behind me, it ends in a lush tropical forest. To my right, opposite the endless thrashing sea and shore to my left, is the beautiful beach house on its sandy dune.

"Are you sure about that?" he asks.

I watch his features shift and shimmer. The blond hair thickens, tangling into loose windswept waves. The face widens. The jaw softens and skin plumps. The eyes are bigger, lips poutier...It's Ally.

Ally stands on the shore, big brown eyes bright in the low light.

Her nipples poke through the thin white shirt, and her legs are bare beneath the capris.

I take a step toward her before I get ahold of myself. That isn't Ally. She hasn't been transported here by some angel mojo. That is Michael wearing her face.

When I look more closely, I realize he isn't wearing it quite right either. Ally is all innocence and steadfast perseverance. There has never been that much mischief in her eyes.

"Come here," she says. *He* says. And even though I know it isn't her, just hearing her voice makes my limbs go weak.

"No means *no*, sir."

"Don't you miss me?" Ally asks, and despite the flaws in her face—his face—that voice *is* perfect. "I've missed you so much."

Fire leaps along my skin. I'd called my power without thinking, and now it rages along my skin the way the waves rage against the shore.

"I'm so tired, Jesse. I want it to be over. Don't you want it to be over?"

I notice the shadows deepening along the sand. Thunder rolls. I dare a glance away from the Ally imposter in time to see the lightning spiderweb overhead. In that momentary flash, I glimpse the distinct form of angels flittering back and forth in the clouds, close, like sharks circling. They're waiting for the moment to seize my leg and drag me under.

"Don't you want it to end?" the Ally imposter asks. Her eyes glow like amber fire. It's beautiful, but it isn't natural. Not unless she has a candle inside her head.

Yes, every bone and thread of my body begs for it. *Yes. I'm tired. I'm so tired.*

"We can stop running, Jesse. We can be happy now. Nothing will hurt us."

Stop running. God, what I wouldn't give to stop running? It's been so long now I don't know if I could stop even if I wanted to.

My eyes fly open. I hadn't even realized they were closed, or rather, were lured shut by that melodic voice.

Imposter Ally is dangerously close. Our eyes meet and I see those dancing twin amber flames.

I encase myself in blue fire, letting it make up for the shield that won't come. Then I call Georgia's black smoke.

Ally's face emphasizes a pout, while batting those long lashes. "You wouldn't kill me, Jesse."

My soul aches. "I wouldn't kill *her*."

"*Her* who?" Michael asks with Ally's voice.

I widen the arc of the fire until Michael is forced to stop advancing. Blue light dances off his skin.

"Whose face am I wearing?" she asks.

Gabriel's warning returns. *I cannot protect the others the same way I can protect you.*

"I just need a name."

"A name?" I whisper, my voice tight in my throat.

Imposter Ally's grin only widens. Warning bells go off in my head.

No names. No names.

"No names," I murmur, feeling drunk and unsteady on my feet. "No names, Michael."

Her jaw hardens, eyes shift from glowing embers to a rich blue. In her place is the Michael I recognize, blond hair still blowing in the wind.

"You'll wish we'd done it that way," Michael says and he calls up the starlight again. His palm disappears in the starburst of light. The black smoke I'm using as a layer to my shield is forced back, withering in the light. Hadn't I seen a light like that before? In a church with no doors...

The angel creatures above screech like birds of prey. My mistake is looking up, trying to anticipate an attack from above. It is the man with a universe in his hand who is the real problem.

Sensing the impending attack, I try to call my shield, but the purple light only sputters and sparks. It's still too weak.

He blasts me. And no matter what I call up—blue fire,

shadow, Rachel's telekinesis, or Cindy's water—nothing stops the starblade from striking me in the chest.

Cold fire slices through me. I cry out. But my voice is lost in the wind and sea.

I'm falling.

I'm falling...

"GOOD MORNING, MR. REYNOLDS!" ALLY CHIRPS. I'M NOT sure how she sounds so damn chipper before the sun is even up. I'd rather stab myself in the hand with a fork than speak to people. "Are you ready for the *most* pleasant replacement experience today?"

"I don't think we should stand so close to him," I say, pulling her away from the bed. She's so pretty, but she can also be so gross sometimes. This guy's sheets smell. Or it's his pits. I don't know. But we don't need to make physical contact first thing, do we?

I suppose this unattractive friendliness is meant to offset her gorgeousness. How can the rest of us endure without such a mercy?

Mr. Reynolds still doesn't respond when I turn on the bedside lamp, illuminating his bedroom in a butter-yellow glow. I nudge him. "Dude, she's talking to you."

His eyes fly open as he jolts upright and presses his back against the wooden headboard. Crushing the comforter to his chest, he fumbles an earplug from each ear. His darting eyes search our faces. "Who the hell are you?" he asks.

"A real charmer," I say, and we're off.

He doesn't get any more charming as the day rushes on. By 7:45 A.M., Reynolds has accepted that Ally is his death replacement agent and that she is going to spend the day shadowing him. He seems fine with this arrangement—probably given her big boobs and endless smile. However, as her glorified bodyguard, I have sucked down about six cups of coffee at this point. And while I'm feeling a little less murderous with each cup, I don't really feel like I have a handle on this day yet.

There is something weird about it. I can't quite put my finger on what's wrong...but it's something. Something big. And my intuition is always spot-on, so...

Franklin Street is busy, the honking horns conveying that not everyone is happy to be alive on this fine Monday. So nothing suspicious there. In fact, I'm totally down with these people, though I do like the September chill icing my cheeks as we march down the street. But seriously, I can't shake this feeling.

I've got two arms, two legs, two eyes, two boobs. Everything appears to be in working order. Phone? Check. Wallet? Check. Did I leave the stove on? Considering I can't tell you the last time I cooked a meal, I'm going to go with *no*.

I'm wearing my favorite Three Stiffs with Picks T-shirt, and what's not to like about a soft cotton t-shirt? The local band's members are necronites like Ally, which means they have the same neurological disorder, but they aren't death-replacement agents and have no government contract like she does. What's wrong with showing a little pride for my #1 compadre?

"You have a very interesting job," Mr. Reynolds says, flashing Ally a smile. I've seen this "let's-get-to-know-the-cute-girl" bit before. Like, a lot. He turns to me. "Do you die, too? Are you the backup?"

Ugh. Conversation is the *worst*. "I'm here to put a foot up your ass if you step out of line."

He flinches.

"Or a fist, if you prefer. I'm not picky."

Ally shoots me a pleading look behind his back. Brinkley, her government-assigned handler, pops into my head. *One more bad review, Jesse, and I'll have to find someone else to oversee her replacements.* A real buzzkill, that guy.

And I guess they could get anyone to do this job. Anyone who can dial a phone or wrangle people who get out of line is basically qualified.

"Dear Sir or Madam, I am sorry for this inconvenience. In the light of your impending death, this must be a stressful time for you. Please accept my apologies for this situation and let me offer my reassurance that no matter what happens, you can count on the fabulous Alice Gallagher to save your ass."

Brinkley made me memorize this verbatim, and to be spiteful, I haven't changed a word. Not even the Sir or Madam part. Okay, maybe I changed save you to save your ass, but what's the difference really?

Reynolds office is laid out like a bi-level, encased in glass. The entrance has two glass doors that push open. The outer wall is a full window overlooking downtown Nashville. The floor is pale hardwood, shining in the slanted autumn light. A spiraling staircase with see-through steps coil off to the right, very modern.

His desk and bookcase are as transparent as the window behind him. So much glass! Oh, think of how many smudges I could make in one day here! This guy is gonna love me!

I've only managed to draw a very *dynamic* interpretive portrait of mankind harnessing the power of fire on one of the windows when Ally calls out my name. There's a tone to it that turns my stomach.

"Jesse..."

I turn, heart hammering in time to see Mr. Reynolds freeze in mid-motion. It looks like he was unravelling a laptop cord. Ally says something to him, but too softly for me to hear.

Reynolds hesitates, and I recognize it for what it is.

Clients often freeze up when Ally starts to react. No one wants to die. To the clients, in this moment before it happens, it seems as if any movement could be the wrong one. She steps forward and he steps back.

This is where everything goes wrong.

He hits the rail of his upper office and slips right over the edge. Ally rushes to his side. From where I stand, it looks like she tries to grab his lapel and pull him back to safety. But there's simply too much of him. Instead, she rolls over the rail with his momentum, a small yelp of surprise escaping her.

They crash into a glass desk, which shatters on impact. Shards of glass spray my face like water. I try to block the spray with an open hand and by turning my face away. I may or may not have a stream of choice words pouring from my mouth, the least of which: "Who designed this shit!"

I collapse on my hands and knees beside the wreckage. I'm trying to push all this glass off of Ally and make sure she is okay.

"Hurry, Jesse," she whispers as blood pools in the corner of her mouth.

Seeing the blood, something in my brain clicks. Some reality shifts at the sight of Ally bleeding on top of a man.

She isn't the agent.

She isn't supposed to die. She can't die.

I grab her and haul her into my lap, reality crashing down on me as this strange dream twists itself into a nightmare.

"No, no, no, no!" I say, shaking her a little as if death can be brushed off or scared away.

Her brown eyes flutter. She coughs, more blood bubbling out between her white teeth.

Then I see the shard of glass in her throat, crystalline from the light coming through the window.

I take a cell phone out of my pocket. I'm babbling to the

authorities to meet me here, to bring medical help, that Alice Gallagher is dying...

But they will never make it in time. Her eyes flutter closed.

"No! No!"

I scream until my throat burns. I scream and stumble out onto the sand. The impact jars me out of that long-ago memory—not a memory. And not a dream. A trick. A nasty trick.

I open my eyes to see Michael's face. He's grinning, triumphant. He twists the blade and wrenches it free from my body. Blood spurts out of me onto the beach, darkening the sand.

I press my hand over my wound. I roll over onto my back, trying to breathe. Can I die in this dreamscape? This mental gate as Gabriel called it?

Michael looms over me, his profile blotting out the light from the storm clouds above.

"Alice Gallagher?" he asks with a devilish smirk.

I taste blood in the back of my throat.

His smile only widens. "Now we're getting somewhere."

CHAPTER ELEVEN

Ally

I sit down at one of the computer terminals in the rec room and log on. While I watch the pinwheel whirl and click to life, I worry about Maisie. I convinced her to leave Gloria's side long enough to eat and get some sleep in our pod. But the look on her face when I pulled back the covers and urged her and Winston to crawl into the lower right bunk said it all: She's as miserable and heartbroken by our circumstances as I am. True, I haven't buried both my parents this week, but I am facing the loss of the person I love most in this world.

And it *is* the losses that are tearing us down. The sad, defeated expression on Maisie's face—an expression that no child should ever wear—echoes my own worst fear: *we will never all be together again. We will never be whole again. Because even more loss is coming.*

After I'd closed the pod door behind me, I had waited just in case she cried out or called me back. She did neither. Moments passed and I heard her soft crying, muffled as if into a pillow. I didn't go in and comfort her. If she waited until I left to cry, she wanted to do it alone.

And I respect that.

I bring my attention to the computer flashing in front of me. A few more strokes of the keys and the terminal finally grants me access. I launch a browser, go to my email, and type in my password. I see the familiar *Four Unread Messages* notification. Three of the messages are spam, one alerting me to a sale at Ann Taylor Loft as if I'm ever going to have time to go buy some sweaters. One is informing me that I've won a free cruise—oh how I wish that were true—I'd even take an Antarctica cruise, if it'd drop me off at a certain South Pole.

And the last email is telling me that Viagra will be 40% off if I just open the email and download the "exclusive" coupon.

I delete all of these emails and open the last. It's from someone called Blue Komodo. If anyone else read the email, they would see this:

1*161312$419229@@819@@18*1*161312$419229@@21
2^269@@111824!^6!!DB B25@@9222623@231213&426724!
(719@@72215@@

But as I'm reading, I see this:

I know where she is. I know where you are. Pick up: 23:00. Be ready. Don't watch the telly.

This is Gideon's cipher. One of three that he made all of us memorize not long after he came to our aid on Brinkley's order. He'd been very tight-lipped about what he'd learned and from where. I'd only learned that he was Brinkley's surrogate son, and a sort of apprentice through Brinkley's own journals. That he used to be the second son in a family of goat herders in Afghanistan, that it was Brinkley himself that killed his brother when he was forced to pose as a suicide bomber outside the military base where he was stationed. Brinkley was the sniper ordered to shoot the boy down. When Brinkley returned the boy's body to his family, offering his life in exchange for his guilt, they gave him Gideon instead—begging him to smuggle their only surviving son out of the country before terrorist factions recruited him by force as they were doing to so many boys in their village—as they had done with their firstborn.

I never even started to crack the code on the tangled history between those two: Brinkley and Gideon. And all those years they spent together after Gideon's adoption. I know he went from Afghanistan to India. India to London... that he has many shady, unscrupulous connections. That he is a flirt.

And that's all I'll probably ever know about him.

I read the message again, frowning harder. This last bit of the message is curious because I can hear it being said in Gideon's chiding, British accent. He would say it like a dare. Not don't watch the television but rather *I dare you not to watch the tele*. I check the timestamp and see the message was sent less than an hour ago. Has something else happened? Already?

Or does he think I haven't heard about Jesse in Antarctica? Or is this a different kind of warning altogether?

My curiosity gets the best of me, so after I delete the email, treating it like trash for anyone who might be reading over my metaphorical shoulder, I turn on the television.

The remote was on the armchair of one of those industrial, bland pieces of furniture, all stiff fabric and wooden arms.

It takes me several buttons to find a clear news channel with no static. I turn up the volume until a row of green bars show across the bottom of the screen. But no one is talking.

There's only the swell of thousands of voices rising from the crowd and the whir of helicopter blades.

I watch the flashing fragments of a story, trying to piece together whatever I've stumbled in on.

Whatever has happened, it must be horrible. Thousands are marching in the streets of Chicago, a wall of bodies so massive that the police stand on top of their vehicles and shout orders over the crowds with their red and white megaphones. It's unclear if the orders are being followed.

When the footage isn't being fed from circling helicopters, offering the widest view of the sheer numbers of people, it shows close-ups of men and women and children. Some are crying. Others are shouting, furious.

My stomach sours as suspicion creeps in.

Finally, the aerial montage of the swarm ends and a reporter is holding the microphone close to the mouth of a man in a suit. The interviewee looks pristine but solemn. I turn up the volume in time to hear him say, "These folks have peaceably assembled here today to mourn the loss of our great leader, Timothy Caldwell, and his cherished wife, Georgia Caldwell. These are dark times, when terrorists can get close enough to our beacons of hope and life and extinguish them."

The reporter, a woman in a white dress shirt and beige pencil skirt, asks, "What of Maisie Caldwell, their daughter?"

My heart speeds up.

"We have been told she is safe and is being cared for. Her whereabouts will remain undisclosed at this time in order to prevent the attackers from locating her."

"Understandable," the reporter replies. "And what do we know about these terrorists? What are their demands?"

"Our sources have informed us that the death of the Caldwells was the primary objective of this anti-religious cell, and now that it has been accomplished, they have gone underground. But we do not intend to let them get away that easily."

A wave of nausea sweeps over me. Without thinking, I sit down. I don't even know what I'm sitting on, but it's sturdy and it holds.

"We will find them, and we will bring them to justice," the man says, staring straight into the camera. "There is nowhere on this earth they can hide from our vast resources. We *will* find them."

"And do you currently know the location of the terrorists?" the reporter urges.

"We have a lead on Jesse Sullivan, the mastermind. She will lead us to the others."

"Do we have a sense of how large this cell is or how many are involved? Previous reports named five suspects."

"One of those named is confirmed dead: Rachel Wright. Captain Gloria Jackson and Alice Gallagher have been cleared of all charges. It has been revealed that they were hostages, like Miss Caldwell, rather than suspects. Jesse Sullivan and the unnamed British citizen are our primary targets."

"Is this connected to the attack in Antarctica? Is the same group responsible?"

"I'm sorry, but I cannot answer any more questions at this time," the pristine man says, and with a tight smile dismisses the reporter, throws one last wave at the crowd, and disappears through the grand archway and heavy doors of the government building behind him.

The news report starts over from the top again, as news is wont to do, and begins with the mourners, the announcement of Caldwell's and Georgia's deaths and the vow to hunt down those responsible.

Jesse Sullivan. Mastermind.

I laugh. It's a hard, bitter sound. Mastermind? How ridiculous!

I turn off the television.

I replay the news in my mind, being as repetitious as the news channels themselves. But I'm scouring for clues, trying to piece together what they *didn't* say as much as what they did.

They blame Jesse for everything. I suspected this is where it was heading when a diplomat from every nation came to speak to Jeremiah. But I had no idea...the fury on their faces. The utter hate.

They want to string her up. They want to burn her at the stake.

She's the only name they have. They cleared us—why? Was that Jeremiah's doing? Nikki's? And if it is true, then isn't Jeremiah also to blame for her guilt? Because if he could clear our names, then why wouldn't he clear Jesse too?

And Gideon was never named. Why? If Jeremiah is protecting Gloria, Maisie, and I, who is protecting him?

Maybe he is protecting himself. Maybe the *urgent business* he rushed off to *handle* was blackmailing or strong-arming someone into keeping his name out of it.

I fall back against the chair and put my face in my hands. I massage my temples until the pounding tension releases a little, but my heart and stomach remain in turmoil. I'm seized by the horrible foreboding that one has when they are in a bad, bad situation. My limbs feel heavy. I'm more than a little nauseous. I'm exhausted but also feel like I will never sleep again.

Any lingering hope that I had about clearing Jesse's name or resuming some kind of quiet life with her somewhere vanishes. I saw the masses myself. They will want someone to blame. They will never accept her name being cleared, not now that she is a target.

I'm glad that someone—anyone—is working to keep Maisie out of it. It's a small blessing.

"And it isn't just Jesse," I whisper, to no one in particular. I'm alone in the vast, empty rec room. Garrison gave me the impression they were trying to keep the public from making the connection between Jesse's job as a death replacement agent and the attack. But how can they? Surely one of her replacements will come forward, or a reporter will resurface the story from Eve's attack. It wasn't that long ago. And when they make the connections, it will certainly be enough to reignite the inflamed tensions between the Church and the Necronites.

What will happen when they discover a Necronite killed their beloved Church leader? I'm almost certain there will be a spike in hate crimes against them. If their condition isn't public, they may be safe. But others won't be so lucky. I'm suddenly so grateful that the bill forcing mandatory registration of all persons with NRD never passed.

I shudder and rise from my seat.

I need to speak to Maisie. But I don't want to arrive empty-handed, with no way to break into this awkward news. So I wander the rec room, tracing its outermost walls. They're lined with bookshelves. No real organization that I can tell, so I survey them in order.

I select five that I recognize, including one of our favorites—Jesse's and mine—from high school.

With the stack of books cradled across my chest, I take the elevator down. I feel like a ghost, sick and hollowed out with worry as I walk to our closed chamber. I balance the books on one arm and knock before entering. I could use the bracelet in my pocket, but this is better just in case Maisie isn't ready for company.

"Come in," she says, with a voice thick from crying.

I step into the cramped room and the lights come on with

my movement. Winston raises his head and thumps his tail against the blanket upon seeing me. He's under her legs, using her bent knees like a tent as they snuggle into the blankets.

Maisie sniffs, looking up from her pillow. Blond strands of hair are plastered to her face, and her eyes are puffy and red.

"Books," I say. "If you want to go to school next year, you'll need to catch up."

She blinks at me, sniffling again. "No school will ever take me. And if they did, I'm not sure a few books is all it will take to get me in."

"A public school would," I say. "They have to. And it isn't like you can't read or write. You just don't have any transcripts. But stories can be made up for that. Schools burn down. Parents divorce. People are moved around. You're smart enough to test into junior year at least, if not senior. I thought you wanted to go to school?"

It occurs to me that maybe I got that wrong. Maybe my desperate attempt to force some stability on her in order to lessen my own sense of helplessness and grief may have found the wrong target.

"You don't have to go," I add quickly.

"I want to," Maisie says, sitting up and rubbing her eyes with her hands. "I just never thought it'd be possible. I figured I'd get my GED or something. Then go to a community college or something."

"And miss prom and bullies, and smelly lockers and gym class? No way!" I smile. It's tight and forced on my face.

But she mirrors it with her own weak smile. She takes the books and shuffles through the titles. She settles on a red hardback with gold embossing. "The Way Home," she reads aloud. She looks up at me expectantly.

My heart clenches. "That was Jesse's favorite book when she was your age." A million years ago, it feels like. Of course it hasn't been a million—just ten.

Maisie waits for my explanation.

"I don't want to spoil it!" I say.

"Just give me the teaser," she says through her thick, clogged voice. "Like the back-cover version."

Fair enough, since this hardback has no back-cover synopsis to speak of. "Okay, well. A boy named Andrew and a girl named Gipsy fall in love when they're very young. An accident happens and one of them thinks the other is dead. Only they discover later that they survived. They reunite, but her head injury means she doesn't remember him. So he has to win her back."

I'm struck by the parallel.

Maisie puts a hand on her heart. "So romantic. Please tell me nothing horrible happens."

"Plenty of horrible things happen," I say. "But neither of them die, if that's what you mean."

"Do they end up together?"

My heart hitches. "War breaks out in the '20s and that tears them apart for a while. But yes, they reunite in the end. They have a beautiful house on the seaside, on an island just for the two of them—far away from the war and everything that happened. They're able to live in peace for the rest of their lives. We have to assume they were happy because the author never wrote a sequel."

Maisie pulls the book to her chest. "I'll start with this one. I could use a happy ending."

I force a smile. "Me too."

"What did Jesse like about it?" Maisie asks, fingering the pages. "She doesn't seem like the soppy romantic type?"

I scratch at the chipped gold letters with my fingernail. "I think she liked the woman's foul mouth, actually. She was a bit of a handful."

Maisie grins. The first genuine smile I've seen on her face in days. "She would. What did you like about it?"

"It's been ten years since I read it," I say.

This doesn't seem to matter to Maisie. She waits for a real answer.

I can remember one scene very clearly. There are certain scenes that just stay with you, even if it's been years since you've read a book you love. For me, I can smell the ocean and practically see the gray waves lapping at a soft shore, white foam rising over Gipsy's ankles and calves as she looks out over the sea. I can see the beautiful A-frame house with its glorious windows up on its stilts, tucked on the grassy dune. Two Adirondack chairs that Andrew, the hero, had built for her on the porch so they can sit in the evenings and watch the sun go down over the water. And that's how the book ends. The two of them on the porch of their house, together at last, watching the sun go down with only peace and gratitude in their hearts.

"The ending," I say finally feeling tears rise up in the corners of my eyes. "I love the ending. They paid the price for their happiness—but they got it in the end."

Maisie takes my hand and squeezes it. "I hope you and Jesse get your happy ending."

Me too, I think. But I know that it doesn't always work out that way. After all, there are always tragedies aren't there? Didn't Shakespeare write tragedies as well as comedies? Why should I get a happy ending, but not someone else? What have I ever done to deserve to be happy?

Maisie's lip trembles and fresh tears stand out in her bright blue eyes.

"I just feel so guilty," she says, finally lifting her head and dragging her nose across the sleeve of her shirt.

"What in the world for?"

"For letting them die! I'm the worst daughter in the world! Yes, Dad was evil, and no one could've changed that. But I feel like I should have said something, done something, anything different, and Mom would've changed her mind. She would've come around eventually. They would've stopped fighting, and the three of us could work together rather than fight. I screwed up!"

I reach out to stroke her hair, but she shies away from me. I let my hand fall to the coverlet. "Your mother loved your father. Because she loved him, she would choose him, no matter what you said, Maze. Her death was her choice. It wasn't your fault."

And Jesse's death will be her choice—that cold voice mimics. *Will you be so enlightened and reasonable when you lose her for the second time?*

I feel as though someone has kicked me in the throat. I swallow.

"I know you're right." She taps the side of her head. "Up here, I get it." She taps her heart. "But in here, I'm just all torn up."

I nod, still unable to find the words. I think of when Jesse died the first time. I was supposed to help her escape, and when I didn't show, she took her own life rather than go another day facing Eddie, her step-father.

I hadn't been there to help her out of it like I promised I would be, and she thought killing herself was her only other option.

For many long, terrible years I lived with the pain of believing that if I'd only been there, if I hadn't blown a tire and hit a mailbox. If the owner hadn't called the police, and if my parents hadn't come, discovered my plan and forced me home under lock and key. If only I'd recognized what danger Jesse was in—and how much harder I needed to try to save her—that I could have prevented it.

And when I heard she was alive by rumor and chance, I spent another year or so searching for her, and at last my search was rewarded—I found her alive and well. Even better, not the haunted, hollow girl I'd known in her last year, when things were the worst.

She was happy. She was smiling. And she didn't recognize me at all.

It isn't so different from Gipsy's story after all, I guess.

I took her forgetting as my punishment. I deserved this pain because I had failed her. She'd been in pain for a long time and so now it was my turn—and the hurt at being forgotten wouldn't even compare, would it? It would never come close to what she endured.

My brain knows better, of course. Through years of therapy I've come to terms with the fact that I couldn't have done anything differently. That so much of what happened was well out of my control. But on the hard days, when I wake up in darkness and cold, the voice of reason is far, far away.

I squeeze Maisie's hand. "I hope, one day, you'll learn to forgive yourself for what's happened."

"Why should I?" she asks, in her small tremulous voice.

"Because it's no way to live."

CHAPTER TWELVE

Jesse

....

ime slips again. The only blessing is that this time at least I recognize the shift for what it is. I lean against a bedroom doorway and watch two girls giggling on the bed. The wood frame pressing into my upper arm feels so real that I am sure I can convince myself that I smell the paint on the wall, and feel the bass from the stereo on my chest. The laughter, high and tinny, vibrates in my ears.

Ally, fifteen or sixteen, lays on top of her pink quilt with blue stars sewn in alternating patterns. She's furiously twirling a piece of hair around and around her finger, winding it up only to release it again. I'd forgotten she did that.

Jesse—me—lays on her stomach beside her, flipping through a copy of *Teen Vogue* and drawing devil horns on this person, a mustache on another. She gives a third a dragon tail. *I* give the boy in denim and cross trainers, holding a basketball under one arm, a dragon tail.

I recognize the room. It's Ally's, looking just the way I last remember it. Neither of our younger counterparts seem to know I'm here.

And as much as my mind struggles with the duality, the scene itself keeps drawing me in. I don't know if it's the intimacy of the bedroom, the fading afternoon light coming through the window, or the quiet house that tells me they're alone. Or maybe even the way Ally keeps watching me—teen me—without my realizing it. And when I lift my gaze, her eyes flick quickly away.

Or is it simply the fact I can't remember this? I'd forgotten almost everything from my life before my suicide because of the damage NRD causes to the brain with each death. Gabriel restored part of those lost memories shortly after he started appearing to me, but he never showed me this.

And there's the question: Did Gabriel keep this memory secret because it didn't matter? Or is this not a memory at all, but another of one those time-slipping possibilities?

"Why did Mrs. Poltaski call you to her office?" Ally asks, her finger twirling and twirling around her hair. She's nervous, I realize, and she's been working herself up to ask whatever she's about to ask.

The Jesse scribbling in the magazine turns the word *HELP* to *HELL* with a few strokes of her felt tip marker. Her marker hovers for a moment. "She just likes to talk to me about my dad sometimes. More are-you-sad-your-dad-is-dead bullshit. I hate it. So what if he died? People lose parents all the time."

She sounds careless, but I see the tremor in her jaw before it clenches.

Ally bites her lip. I think she knows the other Jesse is lying as well as I do. "I thought she talked to you about that on Thursdays."

Jesse pauses again.

"Would you tell me if something was going on?"

"Nothing is going on," Jesse whispers. But her eyes

brighten and tears rise beneath the lashes. "Why were you at Mrs. Poltaski's office?"

"If I tell you my secret, will you tell me what's going on?"

Jesse stops disfiguring the Vogue models and regards Ally for the first time. It is probably the word *secret*. I have to admit that it has my ears pricked.

"Maybe," Jesse says, sitting up on her knees to gaze into her friend's face. "If this isn't some trick like 'I talk to her about my periods. Or 'I think I want to be a nun' or something.' It better be a *real* secret."

Ally looks more than a little offended. "*I* think it's a pretty big secret. My mother would definitely murder me if she found out. You might stop being my friend over it."

Jesse snorts. "That isn't saying much. Your mother would murder you if she found out about the toffee chocolates you eat before dinner."

Teen Jesse's making jokes, but I see the curiosity written all over her face. She's hooked now, and so am I. I catch myself listening to the house again, just to make sure we— they—are truly alone. But when I lean out of the doorway, I see only an empty house.

Ally doesn't look like she's in the mood for jokes though. Her face is pale.

"Oh my god, you murdered someone," both I and my younger counterpart say in unison.

"There's a dead body under the house right now," younger Jesse adds.

"No," Ally says. "I wouldn't be talking to a guidance counselor about it! Not unless I wanted to go to jail."

Younger Jesse nods, conceding the point. "Good point. Then what is it?"

Ally hesitates. Color rises in her face and I'm almost certain I can hear her pounding heart from here.

"I'm gay," she whispers.

Jesse only blinks.

"I'm a lesbian," Ally adds, flicking her eyes up to search Jesse's face.

Jesse keeps blinking.

Ally's face flushes red. "I-I don't like boys. I don't feel about them the way you do."

"Are you trying to say it as many ways as you can?" Jesse snorts. "I know what a lesbian is."

"Oh god, don't screw this up," I groan. "Say something. Say something *nice*!"

Ally's face can't get any redder.

"So, like you want to kiss girls, not dudes," younger me says, pursing her lips.

Ally nods. Her eyes are fixed on her lap now, cheeks still bright with color, hands cupping her knees furiously. She won't meet my eyes, worse, she looks like she's braced for whatever horrible thing younger Jesse might say in return.

She's expecting rejection, I think. My heart clenches.

"Do you have a girlfriend?" Jesse asks.

Ally shakes her head, but she still won't look up.

"Have you ever had a girlfriend?"

"No," Ally says.

"Ever kissed a girl?" Jesse asks with her head tilted.

"No."

"Then how do you know you're gay?" Jesse asks and thankfully, she sounds curious rather than disgusted. Ally notices this too, and her face starts to soften with hope.

"How did you know you're straight?" Ally fires back.

Jesse shrugs. "I *don't* know that I'm straight."

Ally finally looks up and searches her face.

Jesse nudges her knee. "Seriously, how do you know you're gay?"

"It's just how I feel about them. I don't think about boys

that way. When I imagine kissing someone or holding their hand—it's never a boy."

"Does anyone else know?" Jesse asks.

"Well, Mrs. Poltaski. She's trying to help me work up the nerve to come out. She thinks I should wait until college, but I can tell my friends and family now."

"Come out of what?"

"That's just what it's called when you tell people – coming out. Like coming out of the closet."

"Why the hell are gay people in a closet?"

Ally's fear is quickly morphing into irritation. "I don't know. Because people put them there."

Jesse's indignation flares. "Assholes! You tell me who put you in a closet, and I'll beat their ass! Let's see how they like being shoved into tight places."

Her reaction is so genuine, I smile.

Ally laughs, but there are tears in the corners of her eyes. "And my brother knows. And now you."

"Third," Jesse harrumphs, pressing her back into the wall where the bed meets it. "Glad to know where I rank. Third behind some polo shirt-wearing prepster and a woman who thinks bedazzling is a thing."

"Promise you're not going to tell anyone. I'm not ready," Ally says.

"Who would I tell?" Jesse snorts. "You're my only friend."

Ally nods, but the tears that were building in the corners of her eyes finally spill over, and the crying begins. Jesse looks so alarmed—as alarmed as one might look if a velociraptor were to come crashing through the wall suddenly.

"I'm sorry!" Ally sobs. "I'm just so relieved."

Jesse's face pinches in offense. "What did you think I was going to say?"

"I don't know." Ally wipes her nose on her sleeve. "That

you think I'm sick, that I'm gross or that I deserve to die. That you never want to talk to me again."

Jesse looks like someone just spit in her face. "Do you think I'm one of those bigoted bitches?"

"No, but people get scared. People...people react badly."

Jesse opens her mouth to say something, but Ally's crying is so loud now that she just shuts it. Ally runs a hand through her hair, separating a chunk with her fingers. She begins twirling it around her fingers again.

"I would never *ever* stop being your friend. Unless you start holding out on the toffee chocolates. That's a deal breaker."

Ally cracks a weak smile.

I'm trying to desperately remember what these toffee chocolates are. They sound amazing.

"I was kind of hoping you'd confess to being a Russian spy. I'd make you teach me Russian. It's *so* sexy."

Ally laughs again, wiping at her eyes.

"I just wish you would've told me sooner, and I wouldn't have teased you so much about Chad Wrecker. I thought you liked him."

"God, no. He's a bully and a moron."

"Yes, but he's so *pretty*. I would understand your lapse in judgment."

Ally rolls her eyes. "I suppose one could lose their virginity to worse."

And just like that the mood darkens.

This is a long time ago... someone whispers. A familiar, if distant voice. *This cannot hurt you any longer. Don't let it hurt you any longer.*

The room shifts in both light and color, like a television losing signal for a moment, when the picture goes all static-y. This shift brings me back to myself again, reminds me that

I'm Jesse and a visitor in this place. And I'm not really sure how I got here. Or how to get out of here.

"Yes, they can," the other Jesse says and her otherness rushes up, separating me from the scene I was falling so thoroughly into. I feel weight in my limbs again. The door frame is cool against my arm.

"I told you my secret," Ally says. "Now tell me what's going on."

Tell me what's going on. Tell me what's going on. Tell me what's going on... It's such a monstrous phrase to be so simplistic. It weighs a ton on my chest—no, her chest—as if the gravity of the room has suddenly ratcheted up ten notches.

"I don't get along with my stepfather," young Jesse says. And I can tell by watching her that this is the gateway. She is testing the words on her tongue, her lips. Then she shakes her head as if it doesn't say enough, as if that isn't the way she wants to start.

Instead, she uncuffs the sleeves of her flannel shirt and begins to roll the fabric up toward the elbow.

She reveals enormous bruises on both forearms.

"Oh god," Ally says. She sits up on her knees. Her hand goes over her mouth as she takes in the bruises. "Oh my god, Jess. He beats you?"

"Sometimes," she says. And all of Jesse's brave façade crumbles. "If I don't...If I don't..." Her lips tremble and the words fall away.

You played the victim, a cold voice whispers in my ear. *You manipulated her feelings for you.*

"No." I whirl away from the two girls trying to see who the voice belongs to. But I only see engulfing darkness, swirling shadows, beyond the bedroom, nothing exists but an endless abyss.

You used her to survive, and you're still *using her to survive.*

"What? No."

See for yourself.

I turn back to the doorway, and there's Ally and Jesse, kissing—lips hot on one another—while Ally fills my ear—her ear with so many promises. Promises of safety. Promises of a better life.

She's always loved you more than you've loved her, and you played that love against her.

"No, *no*," I say, but doubt has its hooks in me. Doubt twists my fear on itself until I see only dark at the edge of even the good memories.

You forgot her. Forced her to find you again, to prove her loyalty again. Once, she asked for your loyalty, and you refused. You chose Lane over her. She became your personal assistant just so she could stay with you. She left university, her future, and molded herself to you, and you refused to give her the one thing she wanted.

"Stop it."

She finally stood up for herself, demanded a commitment after months of your indecision, and you let her go, knowing she wouldn't go anywhere. You ran to Lane, even though you knew he only loved you because of what you are, not who you are.

I want to protest. I want to beat back the dark encroaching on me, suffocating me, but I can't deny the truth of these words. Because it's true. All of it is true. I'd been too immature and stupid to realize how amazing and beautiful she was, how priceless her love and loyalty was. But Nikki knew, knew immediately, and I hated her for it.

You only took her to spite a woman you didn't like. You took her because you could.

"No!" I shout at the darkness.

You don't care about her safety. You don't care about her happiness.

"That's not true."

If given enough time, you'll only betray her, replace her with the next person who adores you for what you are—after everything she's done for you—you'll move on without a backward glance.

"Shut up already!" My screams pierce the swarming darkness until it shatters. I'm on the beach, on my hands and knees. The wind from that place tears at my hair and face, but the cold is sobering. The cold sharpens my reality. And part of me knows it isn't the cold of the beach I'm feeling, but the tundra. But I don't see the tundra. I see only this stormy beachscape.

Gabriel had warned me about Michael's tricks. And here I am, falling for every single one of them.

Gabriel? Where are you?

Michael stands a respectable distance away, looking like an English gentleman, one hand on the head of a cane—no, not the head of a cane, but the hilt of his sword, the tip buried in the sand.

"I'm slowly discovering why he is so loyal to you," Michael says, those words melodic. "You certainly have a strong will, a stubbornness I should despise, and yet—it's admirable, isn't it?"

I snort to hide my uneasiness. "You sure know how to make a girl feel special."

I can't seem to get off my knees just yet. I sound normal at least, or almost normal. My voice is a little dry, and there is a tremor in my limbs that wasn't there before he ran me through.

"What are you doing to me?"

"Unraveling you. Piece by piece. Softening you for the main event."

With a shaking hand, I probe the cut in my clothes until I find the skin underneath. Flaking blood crusts the surface, but there is no wound. Tenderness, absolutely. But no wound. Jason's healing gift must work even in this place—the gateway.

"Do you even know why you are opposing me? You're determined to guard against me, but you don't even know why," Michael says with derision. "Now that Gabriel isn't here to whisper lies in your ear, you have a chance to see the truth."

"The fact that you were leading Caldwell around by the collar is reason enough. I'm sure you were more than a little influential in his genocidal plans."

Michael's face screws up. "You think I am worse than Gabriel? I gave Caldwell truth. I helped him rise from the ashes of his oppressors then gave him my aid, *freely*. I did not blame him for what Gabriel did."

I should know better, but I can't resist. "What did Gabriel do?"

Michael's lips twitch with a suppressed smile. "He killed his own kind. Took their power and gave it to you."

"Your kind?"

He laughs, real amusement. "As if you could understand. Even now, your little mind is polishing me up and putting wings on me."

"You're not angels." Of course, I don't need him to confirm this. How many times have I seen the reality of Gabriel shift? How many times have I felt like I saw something... *monstrous*... *otherworldly*... lurking just under his skin?

"Please," Michael sighs, exasperated. He reaches up to pull away a strand of hair stuck to his lips. "You humans still believe that you're the best thing to emerge from all of creation in the billions of years it's existed? Sun still moving around the Earth, is it?"

"We haven't found any life."

"You haven't seen us because most of us regard you as ants on the pavement, or gnats on the trash heap—do you have conversations with these creatures? That is, if you notice them at all? No. You only notice them when they begin to be a problem."

"We've become a problem."

He gestures at the beach, at the sky, at the house. "Obviously."

I don't look around, despite this invitation. I have a feeling taking my eyes off him now would be more than stupid.

"Some would save you from being annihilated like the pests you are. Idiots." Michael pauses to emphasize the word *idiots* with bared teeth. "Fools decided that the ants were worth protecting, that you are as worthy of the Power to Create as we are. And so he drags us—his own brethren—into a battle for your salvation. But you aren't ready for this power. Nor do you deserve this gift."

I'm following most of this, but I'm stuck on the idea that the powers surging through me are stolen from someone like Gabriel. Or Michael. But the rest isn't new. Gabriel has hinted enough, hasn't he? I saw the visions he shoved into my mind months ago. Different civilizations evolving to a certain level of consciousness, and once they arrive at the moment—this moment—this is what happens.

"Ask yourself who murders their own kind and if you would call that creature *good?*" Michael presses on. "Or if you would call a human *evil* for carelessly crushing an insect colony. You think you understand all of this, that you see it clearly, but I assure you that you do not. Do you think creatures such as yourselves, as petty and oppressive and demented as you are—that you deserve access to the infinite?"

"So you want to destroy the ant colony—us—before we..." I feel a question in there somewhere, but I can't quite articulate it. I'm searching for clarity, but I'm also buying time until my limbs stop shaking. "And Gabriel wants to save it."

"Don't make him the hero. He's no Prometheus." Michael clucks his tongue. "He betrayed his people. He stole from them. Everything he's ever done has been for his selfish, misguided reasons. He's very much like you in that regard. No wonder he puts all his faith in you."

I don't even have a comeback for that.

Could Michael be right? Could Gabriel be as horrible as I am? Because let's be clear here. I'm no hero. If someone made a list of redeemable humans, I don't even know if I'd make it in the first four or five billion names—if I made the list at all.

Every time someone stands by me, Brinkley, Gabriel, or Ally—I'm bewildered all over again.

Michael smiles, his eyes burning like fire. "You will get her killed."

And I can hear the truth in his words.

Maisie and I stand in the rec room, our fingers combing shelves for other possible books to fall in love with. I got her up here because that cell of a room is too depressing. She needs light and high ceilings, and not to mention room to pace out her anxiety and grief. And in all reality, the smell of book pages and the feel of a well-worn cover under fingertips are better medicine for a broken heart than anything else I could offer her.

She slides a book from the shelf and turns the spine in the light to read the engraved gold letters. "*Rebecca* by Daphne du Maurier."

"That's a good one," I say.

She opens the cover and turns a full page. She pauses to read, "The classic tale of romantic suspense." She snaps the book closed and puts it back on the shelf. "Nope. I'm not really interested in romance or suspense at the moment. I'm a little tired of both."

I look at her over the rim of *War and Peace.* "When did the romance happen?" I can't hide my surprise. As far as I know, Caldwell had her locked in a tower for a long time, and then she was with us. Unless she is in love with Gideon, and her crush was clear to everyone, she didn't find love then. But there was that boy we found dead in the desert.

She laughs bitterly.

"I guess it isn't really romance," she says. "But I had a really good kiss."

"Really?" I say, unable to hide my curiosity.

She smiles. "Sam was...he was..."

Her eyes fill with tears and her lip trembles. And now I know exactly where this is going.

"He shouldn't have died. Why did Perry have to kill him?"

She puts her head on the bookshelf and begins to cry.

I close *War and Peace* and put it back on the shelf. "Some people are just cruel."

I place a hand on her back and rub gently as she catches her breath. I try to imagine what it must be like for her to lose so many people in such a short time. True, she couldn't have known this boy, Sam, for more than a day, but he'd obviously made an impression.

And did she need to be completely in love with him to feel a loss? To feel shocked and horrified at seeing him murdered?

"I don't know what's wrong with me. I'm crying like every five minutes."

"I think you have plenty to cry about," I say, saddened that she feels like she should apologize for showing her feelings.

"It's been a hard week for all of us. And no one else seems to be falling apart," she says, wiping her nose on her sleeve.

A long moment passes and I don't rush it. Finally she says, "We only kissed, but he was such a nice guy. I know I sound stupid because I knew him for like hours, but...but..." her voice breaks.

"I know," I say and I pull her into my arms and hold her. "Losing someone never leaves you."

Was it Eli who first told me that?

It happened the day after I'd stolen my mother's blue Buick and had planned to drive it over to Jesse's house and pick her up in the dead of night. We were going to drive the Buick to my brother's house in Louisville. Elijah knew all about Jesse's stepfather situation. When I first told him, he was so angry that he filed the report and launched the investigation himself. First, her mother interfered, defending her husband unwaveringly. Then as things heated up, Jesse retracted her own testimony.

He told me that they'd never believe me. My mom said she would never talk to me again if I didn't shut up about it.

So the only option we saw was escape. Run away. Get the car, get to Louisville, and with our help—mine and Eli's—Jesse could rebuild a life.

Only I never made it.

I swerved to miss an animal in the road—a fox? A raccoon? I can't even remember. And I hit a mailbox. The tire blew. The cops were called. I was sent home and thoroughly grounded. Not that I was getting on well with my mother anyway, given my recent confession about my sexuality.

When I told her I was a lesbian, she was so mad that she grabbed a fistful of my hair and cut it off with her sewing scissors.

If you want to be like one of them, *let's make you look like one,* she'd said.

But as soon as the handful of hair came away in her hand, she seemed to realize what she was doing and froze. She screamed like she'd seen a spider and shook her hand until my hair tumbled down to the floor. Then she ran from the room. She left me standing in my bedroom, scissors at my feet, clutching my mutilated hair.

I never told Jesse about that.

Or about how I had to shore it up to an uneven bob. Or about how my mother stopped talking to me for days at a time, and if she had to, it was only short instructions delivered without any emotion.

Alice, take out the trash.

Alice, your father wants to talk to you.

Alice, set the table.

As much as it hurt that Jesse had forgotten me—and everything we went through together—I considered her forgetting a blessing. Her death replacement had allowed her to forget everything that bastard had done to her. And he died the night Jesse died—eliminating any chance that he could turn on his son without Jesse to abuse. And because she'd totally and completely forgotten, in a way, I could almost forget everything that happened to me, too.

I pretended that my years without her, hollowed and raw, were a bad dream. It was just something that had passed and would never come again.

Only I've never believed that, have I? I keep waiting for it to come back. I keep waiting for that moment when she leaves me behind. Forever.

I realize Maisie is talking again. "And if it isn't that, then it's just wrong."

"What is?" I ask, finding my way back to this moment. Pain, I think. Pain anchors us to a time or place, like placing a bookmark between pages, so that at any moment we can fall right through again—find ourselves in those dark moments by surprise.

"I mean, he's like five or six years older than me, and he's still hung up on her. Even if it wasn't an age thing, he's all wrong for so many reasons."

"Who?"

She blinks at me, her eyes still bright from crying, voice thick with those tears. "Gideon."

"Right," I say, forcing myself to be here, now. "I can see why you would be reluctant to get wrapped up with Gideon."

"But he's all tall, dark, and mysterious," she says.

"And Gideon encourages it," I say. He flirts with her even though she's sixteen. She is still too young. Of course, I was even younger than her when I first realized I was in love with Jesse, that she was *the one*, and I would follow her anywhere.

I just hadn't realized how far *anywhere* would be.

"He wears her hospital bracelet around his wrist. This one side is burnt where he melted the plastic back together so it'd stay. He'll have to cut it to get it off. You just don't go falling in love with a man who has another woman's mental asylum bracelet on his wrist, you know?"

"Excellent point." There is a host of other reasons why Gideon isn't ideal. His worldliness. His rogue tendency to chase adventure. That isn't what Maisie needs now. She needs peace and quiet. And a chance to heal.

I am not her mother so I don't say any of this.

The elevator opens, and we both turn to see Nikki stepping into the rec room. "The refugees are arriving. Want to see your brother?"

We stand on the tarmac, Nikki and I, and watch the people deplane. Workers with clipboards give directions about how to enter the facility, where to get their dormitory watches and where they will find their luggage. I search the crowd for familiar faces. Most people I've never seen before, but a few I recognize. People I know Jesse has replaced. Several give me a double take as they pass by, surprise parting their lips. I force tight smiles each time our eyes meet.

"There he is," Nikki says.

My gaze falls on the man stepping off the plane. His scarf whips around him in the breeze. He pauses to knot it more tightly around his neck and to do up the button on his dark blue suit jacket. His hair is shorter than when I saw it last, and he's lost weight. But he still looks like a young Brad Pitt with thick blond hair. A leather suitcase swings in his left hand, a leather knapsack over his right shoulder. He pauses at the end of the exit ramp to help an elderly woman step down onto the tarmac.

My heart swells.

I cup my hands over my mouth and scream his name. "Elijah!"

He turns at the sound of his name and grins. I realize why Maisie's decision to stay in the rec room, perusing the shelves, might have been a small blessing.

It would be hard for her to see this—me reunited with my brother. It's been so long, years since I've seen him. I can't contain my happiness.

We're hurrying toward one another, our enormous smiles splitting up our faces. He drops his bags the second before I throw my arms around his neck.

"Al," he says. "It's damn good to see you."

It's true that it feels good. I can't quite seem to let go of him.

"Mother isn't here," I remind him. "No need to swear just to infuriate her."

He laughs. It's the rich baritone I remember and haven't realized I've missed so badly until now. "Don't tell me you've become sensitive to bad language. I remember the things that used to come out of Jesse's mouth."

I must have made a face, given away some clue.

His grin falters. I can see the questions dancing in his eyes. Instead, he forces a smile at Nikki and says, "Sorry, how rude. I'm Elijah."

"Nikki," she says and offers her hand for a shake. "Come on inside, and I'll show you where you're staying. I put you beside Ally."

Elijah nods, sunlight catching his eyes. "How thoughtful. Thank you."

I search his face for a hint of sarcasm, which would have come so easily from Jesse's lips. But his smile remains genuine, if a little more reserved from before.

But that is just Eli for you—endlessly cheerful. Except in the face of injustice, of course.

I never realized my brother was brave until he took a volunteer position at an immigrant rights advocacy clinic. He showed up at airports to help keep people from being deported unlawfully and families from being broken apart by cruel legislation. He's fought for—and freed—three black men who were wrongly convicted of crimes—one who had been in prison for nearly forty years.

And before his wife Kelly got pregnant, he talked about going abroad to fight for political prisoners. He used to terrify me with his half-baked plans to sneak into North Korea.

When he informed me that these plans would be postponed until my niece or nephew was in school, I couldn't have been more relieved.

I'm a little embarrassed that I had never realized how passionate and determined he was until I was older. I couldn't be prouder of him.

The blue light on Nikki's earpiece lights up. "Tamsin."

She stops walking.

We shuffle to a stop, too.

Her eyes cut to me. "Are you sure?"

My heart kicks up. Unable to stop myself, I mouth the word, *Jesse?*

Did they find her? Is she dead? The hammering in my rib cage makes my arms feel weak and heavy.

Nikki shakes her head. "I'm coming. Give me five minutes."

The blue light disappears, and her eyes refocus on mine. She pulls the pod watch from her pocket and hands it to my brother. "Ally will have to show you how to use this. I'm sorry, but I'm needed in the control room."

"It's okay," I say.

Quietly I'm relieved, as it means that I'll get to talk to him without having to find an excuse to dismiss her.

"I hope you'll be comfortable," Nikki says. "If you need anything, just let us know."

"I'm sure it's more than adequate," he says. "Anything will be better than the goat cart I slept in in Baghdad. That was hell on the back."

They exchange polite smiles before we watch her duck into the shelter and disappear through the door on the left of the service desk. I've only seen Jeremiah go that way.

I point at the door. "That must be the way to the control room. The medical ward is through that door on the right." We pass the queue of people lined up at the service desk. The elevator opens, and we step on.

He turns to me then and opens his mouth to speak.

"Not yet," I say. "This whole place is under surveillance. I'm not sure that I can find a place where we won't be on camera or recorded, but I can at least make it harder to eavesdrop."

He shuts his mouth and nods. "Can we talk about Jesse? She's far from secret."

I give a tight nod as the elevator descends.

"Is she okay?" he asks. His voice is heartbreakingly tender., and I feel the tears well up immediately.

"I have no idea," I say, my voice tight.

"Will she be okay?" he asks again, in that same low, steady voice.

I shake my head. "I don't think so."

"Are *you* okay?" he asks.

"No." I don't realize how desperate my own need to cry is until my brother has his arms around my shoulders, and I'm sobbing into his blue suit jacket. "No, I'm not."

"I'm sorry," he says. Nothing else. No patronizing *there, there...*

"Even if she survives whatever—*supernatural* thing is happening to her—the world wants to tear her apart. I've seen them with my own eyes, Eli. Almost everyone wants to hunt her down and kill her."

He just listens to me. He doesn't give me advice or offer platitudes. He just listens. Once my crying settles down, we step off the elevator into the third floor sleeping chambers.

With a thick voice and blurry vision, I show him how to use the watch to open the pod. First, I tried the pod to the left of mine, and it didn't work. So I try the one on the right.

We step in, and the lights come on. The small, stuffy room lights up, looking exactly like the one I'm to share with Maisie and Gloria—should she ever get out of the medical ward.

He barks a laugh. "Maybe I shouldn't have made the joke about the goat cart so soon."

"Small, I know," I say, sitting down on one of the lower cots.

He sets his briefcase down on the floor and presses the mattress with his hand.

Once he's sitting across from me, staring into my eyes, searching my face for some kind of instruction, I say, "Did you bring the recording I asked you to bring?"

He nods and pulls his briefcase into his lap. He opens it,

rummages through it for a moment before pulling out an old-fashioned tape recorder.

He pushes play, and a strange static comes through the speakers. He places this on the mattress beside him. I'm hoping the white noise is enough to distort our voices on any recording devices that may be hidden in the room.

I'm not even sure where to start. So much has happened since I saw him last—when he came to Nashville to help me get Jesse out of jail for a murder she wasn't guilty of—god, that was a lifetime ago.

"I haven't told Maisie that I've enlisted your help yet. I don't want her to panic at the idea of a lawyer digging around in her past."

"A very nice lawyer," he says with a genuine smile. "Did you know that the word lawyer in French is 'avocat'? As in 'je suis avocat.' It also means avocado, so I suspect it depends on one's mood if they are a lawyer or an avocado."

I spare him a smile because he's trying so hard to cheer me up.

"She'll need help getting access to her finances and keeping her identity secret. Objective number one is to make absolutely sure she isn't found and dragged through the press."

"Yes, because that kid has been through hell already," he agrees.

"Objective two is to transfer custody to Gloria Jackson."

My brother's face screws up in thought. "They'll both require heaps of cleverness."

I squeeze his knee. "You're the cleverest man I know. And more importantly, I trust you."

My brother shakes his head. "If you don't trust these people, why are you here? It's never a good idea to surround yourself with foes."

"Foes," I laugh.

When we were children, we played a game: *friend or foe*. It was just one of those games that siblings have when they're young. We would classify nearly everyone we saw as either friend or foe. The mail carrier. Cashiers at the grocery. A teacher. It didn't matter if they'd actually done anything, or if they were just the object of speculation. It was guaranteed to add humor to almost any situation.

If he asked me to classify Jeremiah, what would I say? Nikki? *Friend.* Gideon? *Friend.* Maisie and Gloria? *Friend.* Jesse...Gabriel... Others just aren't so clear cut.

"I ask myself that all the time," I confess, tugging myself out of my thoughts. "I trust Nikki, and I couldn't physically stop them from taking Gloria or Maisie, and I didn't want to leave them behind either. Nor do I honestly think they'd be safe with anyone outside of the compound. Jeremiah cleared their names at least."

I brace myself for my brother's judgment. This is where he'll say something about settling or taking scraps.

Instead he says, "These objectives signify your plan for Gloria and Maisie. But what about you?"

A lump forms in my throat. I can't look at him when I say, "Jesse is in Antarctica. As soon as I can, I'm going there."

His face is remarkably calm. Too intentionally calm. "You don't think you'll be coming back."

I search his face, looking for the right thing to say. A simple "no" would do, I guess. Or even, *if we survive at all, we'll have to go so deep undercover that I can never chance seeing you again, or at least not for a long, long time.* I think of the niece or nephew yet to be born. Of never meeting my brother's children.

Finally, I settle on, "You told me once that Jesse was a target, that there was something about her that invited trouble. And it's obvious that you were correct. But you said something else."

"Al—"

"You said that if I was going to be her friend, that I would be a target, too."

I search his face. I see his fear, his worry.

The lights click off. And Eli curses.

I wave my hand and the lights return.

Eli doesn't let any of this distract him. I know he's building his argument against me.

Before he can launch said counterargument, and heaven help me, my brother has always had a counterargument, every day of his *life*, I say, "I love her, Eli."

I can see him swallowing all the words he wants to throw at me. He runs a hand through his blond hair and lets out a long, controlled breath.

"What would you have me do?" I ask him. "Because if you can see some miraculous escape route out of here, some hidden trap door that I've overlooked, I'm open to suggestions. I'd give anything if someone could tell me the way out that keeps Jesse alive, and free, and happy, and with me."

And with me, a little voice whispers. My marvelously hopeful self.

He grips his knees through his jeans. "You still love her."

"Yes."

He shrugs. "Then it doesn't matter what I would have you do, does it?"

I smile. "No, not really."

He sighs again, a weary, resigned sound. He offers his hand, palm up across the small stretch of aisle between the bunks. I slip my hand into his. "I won't pretend to understand what is going on with the weird superpower shit. We didn't cover that in law school."

I crack a smile.

"But I won't lie, Al, I'm scared shitless for you."

"Me too," I say. I've never hidden my feelings from my brother, and I'm not about to start now. "Do you remember what you said to me when you went to Baghdad?"

His lips quirk a smile. "Don't be surprised if I come back with three wives?"

"No!" I twist his hand in mine and rap on the knuckles until he pulls back wailing. He probably regrets teaching his little sister that. "When I told you that if you came back in a box, I'd never forgive you, you told me: 'Al, if I come back in a box, then it means that I died for something I believe in, something I love.' You said I shouldn't be mad about that. That I should be proud of you."

His face tightens with emotion.

"If I don't come back, Eli, it's because I love her, and I believe in her. And I couldn't leave her behind."

His lip trembles for just a second, then it's stone hard again. He picks at a thread fraying from his pants. If I hadn't been watching him so closely, I probably wouldn't have seen that tremor of emotion at all.

The lights click off, and my brother swears again. I wave my hand, and they blink back on.

"The flaws of energy conservation," I mumble.

My brother couldn't care less. He stands from the bunk and pulls me into a hard embrace. It's fierce and a little desperate, but I don't mind. I don't know the next time I'll see him. The next time I'll smell that scent of Winterfresh gum and Dove soap. I find myself whispering prayers for him. Prayers for his coming children and wife. Prayers for Gloria and Maisie and, above all, Jesse. Prayers for all of us.

The door beeps, signaling that moment before it slides open and allows someone to come in.

Of course, I'm expecting Nikki, as no one else knows we're here, but it isn't Nikki who steps into the room.

It's Eve who blocks out the light from the hallway. Her

hair is dyed bright red. She wears a black and white striped sweater over dark jeans. A plastic tag sits fixed to one hip, the kind that explodes with ink if it is pried off.

She stole those pants, I think. But that thought dies away instantly. A slight rotation of her wrist catches the overhead light, and something flashes across my vision.

"There you are," she says, and I look from her face to the knife in her hand.

I turn slowly.

"Al—" my brother begins.

"Foe," I whisper. I angle my shoulder forward so that I am closer to Eve than he is.

As soon as Eve sees me do this, she raises her knife and points it at me. The blade is level with my eyes.

"Whoa!" My brother says. His hands lift in my periphery, but I don't turn my head. I don't dare look away from Eve. "Everyone take a breath."

I don't know who *everyone* is supposed to be. The only one making threats is Eve.

She turns the knife on him. "I'm here for her. She's the one that lied to me. *She's* the one who betrayed me. *She* got my daughter k-killed."

Her voice cracks.

I open my mouth, and Eve jabs the knife at me. "I know what you'll say. I already know what you'll fucking say!"

I don't dare contradict her.

"You think my Nessa deserved to die because I hurt your friend."

"I'd never say a child deserved to die."

"They sent me a picture of what they'd done to her," Eve says. Tears spill from the corners of her eyes. "What they did to my sweet baby's face. If I could kill a hundred of those monsters to bring her back, I would."

"Killing my sister won't bring your daughter back," Eli says softly.

"That's where you're wrong. He says he'll bring her back if I do this."

"Don't fall for that again," I say. "Someone already used your daughter to manipulate you. Don't let that happen again."

"This is different. This is an angel."

My stomach turns. An angel who wants to kill Jesse. Does this have to do with the gate? With the point of convergence that Gabriel mentioned?

Gabriel?

"He has the power to bring her back to me."

My brother stiffens beside me. "No one has that power."

"He does!" she screams. She points the blade at him. "He does!"

Gabriel. A little intervention, please.

None of us move. We stand there, frozen in place, waiting for someone to make the first move.

The overhead light clicks off.

We're thrown into complete darkness. Instinctually, I step back and the light clicks on to reveal Eve's face, screaming and hideous. She brings the knife down as a purple flash of light engulfs me.

Instead of burying the blade in my neck, it slides along the surface of the purple shield and scrapes the metal bunk overhead. Sparks fly, sputtering, but I manage to bring my knee up and kick her squarely in her chest. She falls back, arms going out comically to catch herself.

Eli yells and charges like a football player, knocking Eve full into the door.

She cries out, but manages to bring the knife around, slashing Eli's upper right arm. He screams. I dart forward, ready to pull her off of him. But the door opens, sliding up and away.

Both Eli and Eve spill into the hallway. Eve's head hits hard, and she goes limp on impact. That cracking sound couldn't have been good.

"What the hell?" Nikki says.

She takes in Eve, Eli, and then finally me, with my purple shield shimmering.

"He's been stabbed," I shout at her, anything to get her moving instead of just standing there trying to piece together the scene.

She pokes the intercom in her ear. "Man down. Send aid to pod 334 immediately. Prep medical bay."

I kneel beside Eli, rolling him off the unconscious woman, the knife only inches from her fingertips.

"Get that away from her," I say to Nikki. She kicks the blade further down the hallway. It skids along the white tile, blood droplets stark against the gleaming surface.

That's Eli's blood. My god, Eli could have been killed.

Eli hisses. "Easy now."

I'm ripping off the bottom of his dress shirt and pressing it hard against the wound. It soaks through with blood almost instantly. I curse and tear another strip.

"Kelly loves this shirt."

"This isn't funny."

When I tear off the third strip, Eli seizes my hand, crushing the fabric inside it. "Leave me some dignity. My belly button is showing!"

"Let me see," Nikki begs.

He scowls at her.

"Your *arm*," she clarifies.

While Eli and I tussle with the shirt, Nikki peels back the slit and inspects the wound inside. "This will need stitches," she proclaims.

So close. My god, that was so close. He could've died.

Tears hit the back of his hand. My tears. I look up to see their faces swimming in droplets of water and light. I blink to reveal their worried faces.

The elevator dings, and rushing feet pound down the hallway.

Nikki is trying to peel the fabric out of my hand. "It's okay. You can let go. They'll get him to medical and stitch him up."

"I shouldn't have brought you here," I say. My throat is thick with emotion.

"I came because I wanted to," Eli says. He's still trying to wrap his tattered shirt around his belly, but there isn't enough of it anymore.

"It was a mistake."

"No."

Two people in scrubs haul him up off the floor and into the black wheel chair. They leave me there with bloodied scraps of fabric at my feet and all those smears of blood.

I look up and meet Jeremiah's eyes.

"You brought her here," I say. Suddenly I'm shouting. "It was *your* plane."

Foe, my brain says. *Foe.*

"Alice—

"You did this!"

He opens his palms in surrender. "Al—"

But he doesn't get my name past his lips a second time. I'm already running.

A hand catches me around the waist and hauls me up.

"He's going to be okay," Nikki groans in my ear.

"It was his plane! He let her on! He brought her here, knowing she wanted to kill me."

Jeremiah doesn't even defend himself. He's already backing away toward the elevator.

"Let me go!" I scream.

But she doesn't let go. She holds me tighter until the elevator closes and Jeremiah is out of sight. Only then does she set me on my feet.

I push off of her. "He did this! He's responsible!"

"No," Nikki says, bringing her eyes up to meet mine with tremendous effort. "That was me."

Michael hurls another beam of light. I use the teleportation power to appear behind him, facing the opposite side of the shore. My feet dig into the sand, making too much sound. I manage to unfurl the death ribbons while his back is still turned. Smoke-like striking vipers shoot forward, gunning for his back. I have time to spare just one thought: I stole this power from Maisie's mother by killing her.

More proof that you are the monster you fear, a voice cackles through my mind. *You killed your sister's mother. How do you think she feels now? You took the only family she had and abandoned her. Like Danny—you left her with no one.*

I whirl to face the voice, expecting another attack from Michael, but he isn't there.

The smoke rolls along the sand and water, fizzing in the surf. I hear a sound behind me and turn just before something cuts through the air where my shoulder was a moment before.

"You're not very good at moving, are you," he says. It isn't really a question. One of his barbs of lightning strikes the sand and fizzles.

I struggle to keep myself upright. Mindscape or not, I still seem as slow and clumsy on this beach as any in the real world.

He sneers. "That's my power you're abusing."

"Yeah well, you've probably had it for centuries or millennia. I just got it." *God, really?* I think, stumbling on the thought. But it's true. Caldwell just died in the desert days ago, and now here I am—doing whatever the hell dance this is.

"Why use it against me at all?" he asks, sticking the tip of his sword in the sand again and huffing at me. "I will come through this gate, and when that happens, I will take this world."

"Keep telling yourself that," I say.

This is all bravado because I am not sure how many more time slips I can take. How much more guilt, or confusion, before I lose my foothold.

What happens if Michael forces me out? If he takes the gate for himself? Can he do that?

I wish Gabriel would tell me. Hell, I wish he'd say anything at all. Damn him and his poor communication skills!

Where the hell are you?

Michael laughs, circling me on the beach. I try to keep my position with the cold water rushing up the back of my thighs.

The full-bodied maliciousness of his laughter makes my stomach hitch. "Do you really think this is my only plan of attack? Sparring with you while the gate readies itself for me?

I roll my eyes upward, but only for a second. That's all I need—a shaft of light shoved up my ass while I give my opponent sass. "Is this the part where you tell me how powerful you are? How you've been holding back, and if I don't hurry up and comply, you're really going to give it to me?"

Michael's expression darkens. Without saying anything he lunges. "It isn't enough to unmoor you. I must strike you in the heart."

"Poetic."

"Would you really like to see?" he asks.

Gabriel flickers on the beach behind Michael. Whatever I'm about to say dies on my lips. I'm so happy to see him— my friend and ally—that I move forward, a cry on the tip of my tongue.

Something slams into my chest, knocking me back. My knees fold, and I hit the sand.

I'm trying to breathe, despite the sharp pain in my chest.

"You have to pull it out!" Gabriel shouts over the waves.

I know he's talking to me, but I can't lift my head. I'm staring at my hands in the surf. They are opening and closing on wet sand as white foam washes over my knuckles.

There are great flashes of light and roars like a hundred snarling animals trying to devour one another. But I can't lift my head. Feverish hot-cold chills crawl along my skin.

You have to pull it out.

That's what she said. I'm not even sure I'm talking aloud.

My teeth chatter. My shoulders shake.

I run a hand down the front of my shirt and find something protruding from my chest. I pull, feel my flesh pucker but not give. Whatever is stuck in me is in the meat. Oh man, this is going to hurt.

I suck in a deep breath and yank hard and fast.

An explosion of pain erupts through me.

I squint at the object in my hand, lifting it close to my eyes to inspect it. My fingers are soaked in blood. But before I can understand what I'm looking at, my vision clouds over, leaving me with only an angry smear of gray and black and white.

I have to blink several times before my wet palm comes into focus again.

A small arrow of light rolls along the creases. It has a silver tip of starlight at one end. No, not a star. A whole universe rolling like a marble in the palm of my hand.

Poison, I think nonsensically. *He's poisoned me again. And just when I was starting to feel okay.*

I try to stand, to get further onto shore before any more sand is washed out from under me, but I collapse onto my hands and knees.

The salt water—if this is even a real ocean—will burn like hell in my wound, too.

I only crawl a few feet toward the house before my elbows fold.

I roll onto my back, feeling the cool water wash through my hair. I stare up at the stormy sky. When the lightning crashes, I see a thousand angel-shaped shadows descend.

I step off a plane onto a dusty tarmac. Grit scrapes beneath my sneakers as I shuffle forward so the person behind me can pass. I look around, trying to figure out where I am. I note all the planes, all the people shuffling toward the concrete building, descending its ramp into the building itself. In the other direction is more endless, dusty earth. It isn't the desert, but it sure isn't lush either.

Someone squeals. A sound of irrepressible joy, and I turn, thinking I recognize the voice.

And there she is. Ally stands on the tarmac, her arms wrapped about her brother Eli's neck and squeezing.

I'm so relieved to see her smiling and happy that I don't

even care that she's standing beside Nikki—whom I could do without.

Before I consider what I'm doing, I'm running across the tarmac toward her. My sneakers slap against the concrete, echoing loudly as I navigate the pressing crowd.

When I arrive in front of her, she only blinks at me.

For one horrible second, I think this is a bad dream. She's forgotten who I am.

One hand goes to her chest. "Jesse."

I throw my arms around her. I'm hugging her so hard she probably can't breathe.

"I've missed you so much," she murmurs into my hair. "I'm so glad you're finally here. I have something to tell you."

"What?" I ask. My mind trips on this. Where is here? I don't even know. I can't even remember where I was before now—the presumptive *before* place that I must have left in order to arrive somewhere new at all.

I'm trying to puzzle it out, trying to remember where I was or what I was doing before I got on a plane. It was a plane, right?

"What do you want to tell me?" I ask.

"I got married!" she exclaims with all the fervor of a new bride. "Oh, Jess! It was wonderful!"

"What?"

"I got married!"

"Are you freaking kidding? To who?"

Nikki is standing right there, and her smile is vicious, triumphant. The next thing I know, there's a knife in my hand. I feel the cold weight of it settle into my palm only a moment before I thrust it forward.

Gut her, I think. *I'm going to gut her for this.*

I grab Ally, planning to shove her out of the way, but she wedges herself between us.

And the blade goes right through. Her flesh offers little

resistance due to the size of the blade.

Her mouth falls open in surprise. She coughs, blood splattering over her lower lip. Her brother tackles me, but I push him off easily.

Nikki watches all of this with a murderous grin.

"It was supposed to be you!" I scream at her. "It was supposed to be you!"

He grabs me from behind and lifts me off my feet. I kick the air, wildly screaming as several more guards appear from nowhere, to subdue me.

Ally and Nikki sink to the concrete. Blood is pouring over Nikki's hands and over Ally's lips, staining her teeth red.

"Oh my god, no," I say. No, no, no.

"You can't replace her," Nikki says, in a hollow voice. "You already did that."

I look at her, shocked at the steady drone of her voice. Instead of seeing her usual fiery expression, she has flat black eyes. Demon eyes void of emotion.

"You killed her."

"No," I say. "She won't die. She can't die."

"I don't know why you're so surprised. You always use her like this. You don't care if she gets hurt as long as you live to fight another day."

"That's not true!" I scream.

But Ally is coughing blood. She's moaning my name. She's crying.

"That's not true." I don't even know who I am trying to convince. Eli starts dragging me away.

The unthinkable happens.

The light fades from Ally's eyes. They stay open, unblinking. Her trembling lips stop moving.

Someone is screaming at the top of their lungs. Someone is howling like they're being skinned alive. It isn't until my entire body ignites in purple fire, that I realize it's me.

CHAPTER FIFTEEN

Ally

Nikki apologizes for the hundredth time. She explains how she was responsible for vetting the passengers onto the aircraft. How she should have caught Eve before she ever touched down. How she had made sure the cameras in both our POD and my brother's were disabled because of a fight that we'd had a long time ago about privacy in living quarters—back when we shared an apartment in Tate Tower – Chicago.

She keeps trying to assure me again and again that she takes full responsibility. I believe that *she* believes that, but I am not sure it's the whole story.

I'm only half listening to her as excuses pour from her lips. I'm preoccupied replaying the attack in my mind, trying to understand what just happened, what was said and what it means.

When the sharp burst of purple light exploded in front of my eyes, for a moment I was blind. Then when the color receded, I saw only sparks of light until my vision cleared. So for a full minute, I honestly wasn't sure if Eve had stabbed me or not.

The appearance of the shield was as surprising as it had been when Gabriel appeared in front of Jeremiah. And I saw him this time, too. Even if all he said was a hurried apology. *I cannot stay. Jesse is in danger.*

But Eve's words feel ominous. *He said he would avenge Nessa.*

The fact Gabriel had come at all...that Eve had talked about angels helping her and a promise to restore Nessa's life...What is going on with the angels?

True, my first instinct was to blame Jeremiah, but I've since revised that belief, now that the adrenaline has fallen and the danger has passed—that this might be a different threat altogether.

The bad angels, Jesse had said once. I think even Cindy made mention of them.

Is it possible that one is still in the game? Is this *he* Eve mentioned a threat I haven't accounted for?

It would serve me right to be so focused on the dangers of this world—the people with pitchforks—to overlook a worse threat to Jesse's life.

I need to widen my gaze or more surprise attacks will be inevitable.

"Did you see that?" Eli hisses proudly as the nurse wipes at his arm with an antiseptic-soaked swath of gauze. He is practically crowing. "Cat-like reflexes. Maybe I've got a little extra something in my veins too, eh?"

"Kelly is going to kill you," I remind him from my place on the opposite hospital bed.

"No, she's going to kill *you*. She loved that shirt, and you ripped it to shreds. I think she gave it to me for Christmas."

His enthusiasm for being stabbed doesn't recede in the slightest. Probably because his wife isn't actually here to give him a sharp lecture about not dying before their child has a chance to meet their father.

Nikki stands in front of me, hands on her hips. "I want you to check her again."

"It wasn't her blood," the nurse says and gives Nikki a weary look.

Nikki tries to death glare the nurse into checking me over again as I sit on the gurney with my feet hanging over one side. The nurse holds Nikki's gaze without so much as blinking. To my surprise, Nikki folds first, looking away with a sigh.

Then Nikki stabs the earpiece in her ear with her finger. It ignites blue. "I want you to replay the tape again. I want all the arrivals on the tarmac to be rescreened. I want to make extra sure we haven't let any other threats onto the base."

"Dr. Gray, can you *please* just look her over one more time?" Nikki begs.

Doctor, not nurse. My apologies for assuming it takes a lab coat to make a doctor.

Something softens in the doctor's face. She shrugs her dark brown braid over one shoulder and turns to me, looking ready to do as she's asked.

"Where is she?" a high girlish voice screams. "Where is she?"

Dr. Gray looks at the ceiling and sighs.

"Let her through," Nikki says and the guard at the door stops trying to push Maisie through the double doors.

Maisie tears her elbow out of the guard's grip. "*Excuse* me."

Then she's in front of me, face beet red with anger and screaming at the top of her lungs.

"She tried to kill you. Az—" she bites down on that last word so hard she bears her teeth in a grimace. "I heard she tried to kill you."

"It's okay," I tell her. I make it a point to keep my voice low and steady.

"Is it?" Maisie says. Her voice is still too high and too tight. "We are supposed to be safe here, and you were attacked—almost stabbed."

"She didn't even get close to me," I say.

"About that," my brother says from the opposite gurney.

I flash him a desperate look. His mouth snaps shut immediately. Then he says, "Are there vending machines or a cafeteria around here? I could use something to eat. We didn't even get peanuts on the plane."

Bless him.

"Fuck the peanuts!" Maisie screams.

"Maisie!" I can't hide my astonishment. I didn't even know she cursed.

"You were almost killed!" Her eyes fill up with tears, those bright blue irises shimmering.

I politely nudge Dr. Gray aside and pull Maisie forward.

"Look at me." I place a hand on each of her shoulders. "Maisie, look at me."

I squeeze her shoulders until she reluctantly meets my eyes.

I run one of her hands over my arm. "Not even a scratch."

The anger leaves her in ragged breaths. Her shoulders sag.

"I can't—" she says, pinching her eyes closed. Her foot stamps the tiled floor once. "Everyone keeps dying, and I can't—"

"Give us the room please," Nikki says. Dr. Gray and the guard step out, leaving Eli, Nikki, Maisie, and I alone beneath the harsh fluorescents of the medical bay.

I watch the tears stream down Maisie's cheeks, her eyes still pinched closed.

I take both her hands in mine, and she collapses against me. I wrap my arms around her and catch my brother staring. He wants to be introduced, of course. But now is hardly the time.

"If one more person dies, I'm going to lose it," Maisie whispers into my hair. "I'm just going to *freaking* lose it."

I yearn to tell her it will be okay. I want to assure her that she won't lose me. Or Gloria. And that Eli will be the most practical ally she could hope for. But I can't bring myself to lie to her.

You don't expect to come back, my brother had said. And it looks like I don't have to make her false promises. Nikki leaps at the chance to do it for me.

"Nothing is going to happen to Ally," Nikki says. "I promise."

Her face is hard with her determination. Maisie either doesn't hear her or doesn't care. Her arms stay clasped around my neck.

"I know Jesse—" Maisie begins. Her voice is so low that I'm not sure Eli or Nikki can hear her. "Az—*someone* told me that Jesse might—"

My heart clenches in my chest.

"So I'm, like, prepared for that, you know? But then I hear that you were attacked. And right outside our pod?"

She lets go of me and covers her face with her hands. She drops them to say, "Man, I'm so tired of crying."

"I'm sorry," I say. Because I don't know what else I can say. How many tears have I shed over Jesse?

"It seems like someone wants to stab you like every other day. How do you stand it?" Maisie asks. She glances at Nikki and Eli, who both remain silent with solemn faces. I realize that both Nikki and Eli are watching me carefully. It seems that Maisie isn't the only one who wants my answer.

I want to argue that I've never been stabbed. That being attacked is as much of a novelty for me as it is for them. But then I remember the basement. Martin thrusting a blade into my abdomen, rupturing my spleen.

"Seriously, I've lost all faith in humanity," Maisie says.

"Don't say that," I say.

"Why? Because we're surrounded by so many *awesome* people?" Her jaw clenches, the vein in her temple jumping.

"You have to look for the helpers," Eli says, voice steady. "That's what Mr. Rogers says."

"Who?" Maisie asks.

"Oh god, am I that old?" He asks me, looking genuinely horrified.

"For every horrible thing that happens, Maisie, you have to find the good people, too. People get murdered, and people hunt their killer and deliver justice. A hurricane destroys a home, and someone is there to pull them from the wreckage. Hateful people bully and threaten, and then someone stands up to them. Someone fights back. That's what Elijah means."

"It's not enough," Maisie says.

"Be the change you want to see in the world," Eli adds, helpfully. "That's what Gandhi says."

"What are you, a walking encyclopedia?" Maisie asks him.

"No, he's your lawyer," I say. "This is my brother Eli. I asked him to come."

"She doesn't need a lawyer," a man says. I turn and see Jeremiah enter the medical ward.

"Well, she has one anyway," my brother says, his voice hard.

Jeremiah's gaze falls on my brother, and something inside me tenses. My brother has stood up to corporate giants before without flinching, and he'll need that courage now that Jeremiah has him in his sights. But that's why I called him. I trust him with this. I know he won't fold under Jeremiah's pressure.

"Fast-acting there, Mr. Gallagher."

My brother gives his best *oh shucks* smile. "You didn't expect me to let that woman slit my sister's throat, did you?"

Both Nikki and Jeremiah flush.

I glower at Eli.

"Honestly, given how much surveillance you have in this building, I'm more than a little surprised by your slow reaction." My brother forces an apologetic pout. "I'm sure you tried your best."

Jeremiah adjusts the glasses on the bridge of his nose before looking over his shoulder at Nikki. "Tamsin, would you return Mr. Gallagher to his pod. I want to speak to Ally alone for a moment."

"As her attorney, I think whatever you want to say to her, you can say it to me."

"It's okay," I tell him. "You and Maisie have a lot to talk about."

He gives me a long, steady look before sliding off the hospital bed. "I won't be far away."

And even though my brother and Maisie leave without much of a fight, Nikki doesn't budge.

"What do you need to talk to her about?" Her voice hardens.

Nik never loses her patience with Jeremiah. I wonder again what they might have been fighting about in the conference room after meeting with the nation leaders.

"I have news about Jesse that Alice will want to know. And I believe she will likely want to hear this alone."

My heart stumbles. I swallow down flat out panic.

I manage to keep my mouth shut and only tilt my head to convey my curiosity. At least, I hope I look curious and not like I'm riding the edge of fear with white knuckles.

"I'm not going far either," Nikki says, sparing me a smile. It doesn't reach her eyes.

Once she leaves, and the hospital doors swing shut, Jeremiah sits on the opposite bed my brother just vacated. The intimacy of the situation is disturbing. The dimly lit room and just the two of us. The adjacent hall is unnaturally quiet as well as that area just on the other side of the swinging doors that lead to the lobby. I wonder if he decides to leap across this bed and suffocate me now if he would get away with it.

Undoubtedly.

Unless that helpful shield were to spring up spontaneously again.

"As you may have heard from Nicole, Jesse has disappeared from our satellite surveillance."

"I'm aware." *Tell me something I don't know.*

"I placed the order to search the earth for her, of course, but she didn't turn up. So I asked them to run the GRO program."

"G—"

"—it searches for gamma radiation."

"You found her?" I ask, unable to contain myself. I wrap my hand around the cold metal bar of the hospital bed.

"The location where Jesse was last seen, very close to the coordinates you provided in the hospital, are where we looked first. That area is still radiating an enormous energy signature."

"You can't possibly believe she is invisible," I say.

"That's exactly what I think," he says. "At least invisible to us."

"It certainly makes her safer," I muse aloud. "If they send any more agents to execute her, they won't have a target."

"Won't they?" he asks, eyebrows raise.

I only blink at him.

"The technology that I've utilized isn't private. Any of the government agencies who decide to dedicate manpower to investigating this situation can do exactly as I have done."

This situation. My god.

"I was intentionally vague, giving only the station that she attacked—"

"She didn't attack it!" I burst. "We don't know what happened there."

He nods in acquiescence. "Even if she hides herself, they could find her. If they sweep the area, they could mistake her for a device that's been buried. They may try to detonate *it* from above."

"They wouldn't mistake her for a device if you hadn't suggested it!" My anger rises in a scalding wave. I look down at my hands, hoping this will calm me and bring me back into myself. Except I see my hands shaking with fury.

"You forget that I have a wider view of this situation than you do. Your feelings for Jesse don't allow you to see a threat that could cost billions of lives. Are you saying that her life is more important than Maisie's? Your brother's?"

I unclench my fists and try to focus on the words.

Of course, if I had a dollar for every time a man told me I didn't understand a situation because my feelings were in the way—I'd be quite rich indeed. And while they are almost always wrong, I am less confident that is true now. I wouldn't deny to anyone that my feelings for Jesse make it hard for me to think most of the time.

Is it your love for her? Or your fear of losing her? a cold voice teases. It's my voice. One that I started hearing shortly after Jesse died the first time.

"I want to reunite you with Jesse," Jeremiah says.

My head snaps up, disentangling itself from its ruminations.

"If anyone can safely approach Jesse, it's you," he adds. "I want to send you in with a small team. I think it is the best way that will cost us the least lives."

This sounds too good to be true. Never in the time I have known him has Jeremiah just handed me what I wanted.

"Don't look so surprised, Alice. You gave me the idea."

"What is the catch?" I ask.

"No catch. Someone needs to speak with her and convince her to stand down. There is only one person on this planet that has a chance of succeeding. I want you to succeed, and you want to see her. In this arrangement, we will both get what we want."

"Do you understand what is happening to her?" I ask. I don't believe for a second that he does, but I'd welcome any theory at this point.

"I only know that she is transforming into something that will either kill us or save us."

"Is this what your visions tell you?"

"Do you taunt Captain Jackson for her visions?" He adjusts his glasses. "It doesn't matter. It only matters that you stop her."

Not *save her*. Not *bring her back*. He threw her under the bus to all the other nations because he knows and understands what I keep struggling to comprehend: Jesse isn't coming back from this. Whatever *this* is—it's the end of the line.

"And what if I can't stop her?" I ask. My fear is so pure and raw that tears pool in the corners of my eyes. I'm sure I look exactly like what he thinks I am. A foolish girl who can't focus on what needs to be done.

"If you can't..." he says, his voice trailing off. "Then we will do our best to survive it."

I think of his wife and daughter who are supposedly somewhere on this base. But I have not seen them in the living quarters or rec rooms. Perhaps Jeremiah has separate quarters and that is where they are. Yet the idea that he separates himself from everyone else, even here, makes me wonder if this place is really as safe as he claims.

And this sudden change of heart—his desire to send me

to Jesse now at the last moment—there is something off about it. I can't suppress my suspicions that no matter what he says, there *is* a trick.

But what can I say? *How dare you give me what I want? You're wrong—I can't possibly talk to her.* Refuse to go to Antarctica.

Then he says something that makes the world stop spinning. "I am aware that you've been in contact with Gideon."

I stop breathing.

"And that it is your intention to fly with him to Antarctica this evening."

I open my mouth to deny it. He could be guessing, trying to force my hand.

"Don't waste a lie on this," he says. "I have excellent code breakers in my employ, and if they say he will be arriving at 11:00 tonight, I believe them."

I look at the clock on the wall. If correct, it is almost six in the evening. I gaze at the ticking black and white face deliberately.

"I will allow him to enter the base if you promise to take one of my own planes. I am sure you can understand why I want to monitor the situation."

"Is that your price for your help? Surveillance?"

"And I will ask you to wait until 11:30 to depart. That is when I can spare the aircraft you need."

Spare it. Even in his generosity, he isn't prioritizing this rescue mission—because this isn't a rescue to him. This is a one-way trip.

But in my mind, I'm already doing the math.

"Will Nikki be coming?"

"Nicole doesn't want you to go. In fact, I suspect that if you would like to make it to Antarctica as soon as possible, don't tell her you're going."

My heart hammers. I can feel the pulse in the tips of my

fingers and temples. I think of the two of them in the confer-ence room again, fighting. Was that what this was about?

"She believes it is too dangerous and wants you to stay. I think the sacrifice is worth it, if it saves lives," he says. He removes his glasses and cleans them with the end of his shirt. "What do you think?"

"I think you expect me to die on this mission."

"It is likely," he says. He slips the glasses back onto his nose and meets my gaze with dark, unflinching eyes. "Does that change how you feel about going?"

"No," I say, without hesitation. "I'll go anyway."

"Then it's settled. I would use the last few hours wisely, Ms. Gallagher," he says. He slips from the bed, tugs at the end of his sweater vest, and gazes down at me over the long line of his nose.

My last few hours.

I barely have time to process this idea when Dr. Gray appears in the doorway, breathless.

"What is it?" Jeremiah asks, turning toward the commotion.

"It's Captain Jackson, sir. She's awake."

CHAPTER SIXTEEN

Jesse

*A*utumn is crisp and bright. The light soft and slanted of a late afternoon.

People in black huddle in the middle of the cemetery. I walk toward them, brown, burnt leaves crunching under my black rubber boots.

The whispering grows louder. "Two at once, how horrible."

"What were they doing out there that night?"

"There's to be an investigation?"

"No, didn't you hear? The authorities swept in and hushed all that up."

"Kyle says she was seeing the counselor at school."

"Why didn't Danica have an open casket?"

"Because the body must've been damn ghastly, Mary. Let it be."

"Go ask. It isn't like poor Dani hasn't hurt enough already."

"I would've still liked to see. I've never seen a burnt body."

"You would, you old bat."

I cut through the women I don't recognize, walking toward the one standing closest to the empty grave. Her blond hair whips in the wind. A black rain coat pulled around her. She can't be more than seventeen. Maisie's age.

Her shoulders shake with her crying. When she turns, her eyes lock with me.

Ally.

Recognition flashes in those amber eyes. She says my name. I don't answer. She says it a second time, a third, and the taller boy beside her tries to hush her, pulling her elbow back as she strains forward. This doesn't work.

Ally screams.

She steps forward, but the boy beside her—Eli, I realize, maybe in his early 20s—pulls her back.

My eyes fall on the etched tombstone.

Here Lies Jesse Sullivan

Beloved Daughter

No.

No, I—

A sudden hand shoves me in the back, and I'm pitched forward into the grave, into the endless black.

My hands hit something hard. A casket, I think. Oh my god, I'm laying on my casket.

But I open my eyes to see it isn't a casket, and I'm not in a hole. I'm on my hands and knees on a wood floor. I sit up. Touch my arms and chest tentatively, as if expecting to find myself incorporeal. A ghost. But I feel real enough.

A soft rolling sound catches my attention, and at last the room shifts into view.

It's a small apartment, consisting only of this room and a bathroom so small, I think someone would have to close the door just to sit on the toilet.

A mattress sits on a low IKEA frame. A girl lays in the bed, eyes open, fixed on the ceiling.

She's wearing a t-shirt that falls across her mid-thigh.

Still crouched on the floor, I watch her sit up on the mattress and cast off the bedding. She walks right past me as if she doesn't see me and heads into the kitchen area. She makes a bowl of cereal from a bowl on top of a mini fridge and a small half gallon of milk. The spoon is one of the plastic ones that comes from takeout, and she eats the cereal without speaking, leaning against the counter as she chews. Silent. Then she rinses the bowl in the sink and puts the plastic jug in the white fridge. She goes into the bathroom.

She does all of this without looking at me.

I pull myself up and go to the bathroom. I push open the door and see Ally's wet, slicked-back hair.

The room is full of steam from the hot tap. She sinks to her knees and lets it pound her skin until it's red.

"Ally?" I ask. I feel like this is a dream.

No answer.

"Al, can you hear me?"

Her back stays wedged into the corner of the stall. She just sits there, crouched as the water pelts her head and shoulders. It's a long time before she makes a feeble attempt to run some shampoo through her hair, and soap on her body. I stand frozen in the doorway, steam wafting past me.

She is so thin I can see her ribs expand, gaunt, with every breath. She shuts off the water. She is shivering before she makes any attempt to get out of the stall.

Her clothes are in a pile on the floor beside her bed. She grabs the first shirt and pair of jeans that she sees and pulls them on. She runs a red comb through her hair before buttoning up a coat.

Then she's down the stairs, out the door, and walking up the street.

At least I know where we are. St. Louis. I recognize this district near the root beer distillery.

I follow her. I call her name, and she pauses on the street. People part around her like water around a rock. She turns, very slowly, as if expecting to find a ghost there.

Maybe I *am* a ghost.

Is this the future? Ally's future after I die? Or her past? I can't tell.

But before she fully turns, she seems to change her mind. She starts walking again, taking a moment to tuck her wet hair under the hood of her coat. She's walking faster.

At any moment, I feel like she's going to break into a run.

Then she steps off the street into a building. A sign reads Trinity Counseling. I don't see myself reflected in the glass of the door. And I don't have to touch the door to pass through. One moment, I'm on the street. The next, I'm in the reception area, looking at a blue water cooler and a male receptionist who is humming a Justin Bieber song.

I must be dead. I saw my funeral, and now I'm a ghost. That must be what happened.

Time skips. Ally isn't in the waiting room of the counseling center.

And from the shifty way the receptionist looks at the closed door, I suspect I know where she's gone.

I enter the office building, and no one even tries to stop me. I follow Ally through the reception area and into a smaller office.

She takes a seat on a rose-colored couch, her hands coming to rest on her knees. Her back is rigid against the sofa. A woman in her late forties or early fifties is holding a Starbucks latte and smiling, nodding along to whatever Ally just said.

"I think that's wonderful," the woman says, her voice melodic and soothing.

"I wouldn't call a 'C' wonderful," Ally says. "I need at least a 3.5 to get into a decent law school."

"You have to give yourself credit for small victories, Ally," the therapist says, twisting the cardboard cup in her hands. "Last semester you failed half your courses and withdrew from the rest. This semester, you're passing everything. You've found an apartment in a better part of town. You're going to class. You're doing the work."

"Barely."

"You've had your job for three months. You're paying your bills on time."

"I was five days late for my car insurance, actually."

"Alice. You *have* a car," the woman says, with a gentle laugh. "Progress is progress. When you first came in here, you were contemplating suicide. You were fired from two jobs. You were a stone's throw from being homeless."

"I wouldn't have been homeless. Eli would have forced me to move to Louisville before he'd let me sleep on the street."

Ally wraps her finger around a thread coming from the rose-colored cushion beneath her. I think she'll tear the thread free, but she keeps twisting it around and around.

The woman seems okay with the silence. She watches Ally, but says nothing.

"But I'm not okay," Ally whispers finally. She looks up and meets the woman's eyes. Tears stand out in the lashes and shimmer in the light of the lamps. "On the street, just now, I heard her voice. I heard her calling my name."

My throat tightens.

The woman in the chair doesn't interrupt. But she stops turning the cardboard cup in her hands. When it's clear Ally isn't going to add anything else, the woman says, "You're grieving. When someone loses a person they love, they often grieve for years. You may never get over her death, but you can learn to live with it."

"It's been two years," Ally says, wiping at her eyes.

"You were best friends for almost six years."

"And I was in love with her."

"Exactly," the therapist adds, her thumb picking at the cardboard cozy surrounding her paper coffee cup. "It isn't unreasonable to think you'll need at least that long to move on. Even that may not be enough."

Silence fills up the room again. Finally, Ally breaks it.

"She died thinking I'd abandoned her," Ally whispers, the tears spilling over her cheeks. "I was supposed to come, and I didn't, and I never got to tell her why, and then she was dead."

"Misplaced guilt is dangerous and it impedes progress."

Ally falls back against the sofa and covers her eyes with the heels of her hands.

"You just have to keep trying. There is no better way to honor her memory than to keep trying and do what you can to make the world better. We all live with regret. You *can* live with it."

But it doesn't look like Ally can live with it. It looks like it's tearing her apart.

"Sometimes I wonder what it would be like to die the way she died. To know what she was feeling in those final moments."

The therapist stiffens. Ally doesn't notice. Her eyes are still fixed on the ceiling.

"She did it to end her pain. That much I understand," Ally whispers. She laughs but it's a sad, choked sound. "I *completely* understand."

I feel a hand on my waist. A cold, hard hand, and it pulls me backward.

"No," I say. I try to shrug off the hand, but it won't let go. "No, I want to hear this."

But my will alone isn't enough to keep me in the therapist's office. I'm jerked away from its intimacy. Away from Ally. Away from the time and place where she struggles to survive.

The scenery changes for a final time.

I'm on a battlefield. It's the smell of blood and ash that brings the scene into sharp focus. Embers rise into a blazing sky. The clouds are as red as blood, with liquid pink and orange bleeding out behind them.

I can't tell if the sun is rising or falling. Maybe both at once.

Gabriel stands beside me in beautiful armor. He has a sword, black to the hilt with blood and smoldering. His hands and cheek are smudged with ash.

"You're going too far," he says. "You'll lose your way if you don't go back."

I can't speak. I'm choking on the smell of corpses. If I open my mouth, I'm sure I'll vomit on myself. My stomach turns violently.

"I thought Michael was doing this to me, showing me these things."

"No," Gabriel says. "You're doing this to yourself. And he's letting you. He would know more of your heart."

My heart.

"Let me lead you back," he says, reaching for me.

I don't say anything. I try to remember who I am and how I came to be here. There is a name on my lips, a name I keep repeating over and over in my mind.

But I can't quite remember who it belongs to. Because the truth is, it's not really her name either. It is only a location. A moniker for a finite segment of time, for a temporal being that flickers like a candle flame, with every threat of blowing out.

"What is this place?" I whisper. I shift my foot and the body under me cracks. I look down and see a wing. A black wing as slick as oil, snapping like bird bones underfoot.

"You believed us into reality," Gabriel whispers. "You gave us names. You gave us powers. You declared that good shall triumph over evil. You think that everything happened before you came to be. But it was after. We walked from your dreams into this reality. And we can disappear into it as well. That is what Michael fears."

We created the angels? And God? With our stories and our beliefs...and if we forget you?

I don't know if I say it. But Gabriel nods his head.

"He doesn't believe the power of creation should be yours. That you should make us here one moment, and unmake us the next."

"And what am I in all this?" I whisper, looking at the rotting bodies at the edge of a city of glass. I can hear a sea, but can't smell it over the corpses. The only salt I smell is what I see on sweating skin.

Gabriel takes ahold of me.

An army of beasts emerge from the ashy smog. Hooves or paws or claws pound the earth. Skulls are crushed underneath. Skeletons crack. A wall of howling forms keep coming until I can see their reptilian eyes. They're almost upon me. I do not move. I watch them come. I want them to come and to overtake me.

"Am I a destroyer or a creator?" I whisper.

"Can't you be both?" he asks and pulls me into the sky.

I open my eyes. I'm on my back in the snow. The sky swirls blue around me.

Jesse, Gabriel calls. He sounds as if he is calling from a great distance, his voice a mere whisper on the wind. *Jesse*.

I can feel that other place calling me again. The gate with its sea, its salt and storm full of angels who want to tear the world apart. We all have visions...all have dreams, fighting to occupy this same space and time. Whose dreams should win while others die?

I cling to it as Gabriel begs me to get up.

But I'm so tired. I've never been so tired in my life.

And all I see when I close my eyes is her blood on my hands. Her blood soaking into my clothes. Her blood drowning all thoughts from my mind like a relentless river whispering, *your life is shit. Your life doesn't mean anything. She is all that is good and kind and true in this world, and you let them take her away.*

"Was that the past or the future, Gabriel?" I ask. My lips feel chapped and swollen. "All the things I just saw..."

A shadow passes overhead. Something black and great as one of those monsters from Gabriel's battlefield. A bird large enough to blot out the sun.

I can hear its thunderous, unforgiving wings.

It's come for me.

"Was it the past or future?" I ask again. "Because I can no longer tell."

"Get out! Everyone get out!" Gloria screams from her hospital bed. The monitor attached to her wrist wails until she yanks it off with one furious pull. The whole machine slams onto the floor.

"Now settle down, Ms. Jackson," Dr. Gray says. High color flushes her cheeks, and I can tell by the thin strain in her voice that she is on the verge of losing all her patience. If Gloria wasn't so broken, crushed by a boulder in the desert the day Georgia escaped with Maisie, I don't think she would have tolerated this much insolence. And there is the matter of Jeremiah's obvious fondness for her.

I never understood it. Did he feel akin to her because of the visions? Gloria wouldn't call herself a prophet. She blames all of her ability—the drawing and the remote viewing—on the tortuous program that came from her time in the military. It was her successful transformation that made the military turn its attention on her brother. They assumed that genetics played a role in the body's ability to adapt. So her brother was also recruited to undergo multiple procedures.

I don't think she ever forgave herself for that. And when Micah joined Caldwell, I think she blamed herself even more.

Since Micah is dead now, killed by her own hands, she will have to live with that, too.

"Please give Captain Jackson the privacy and peace she deserves," Jeremiah says, fidgeting with the knot of his tie as if preparing for a date.

They obey him without question, of course. Until it is only the three of us left and the remains of the buzzing machine that's been dashed against the floor.

"Get me paper, pens," Gloria demands. I don't know if she's talking to me or him.

"Alice, would you go to the service desk and tell Jan—"

"No," Gloria hisses. "You. Go and get them for me."

Jeremiah looks ready to protest.

"Please," she adds.

He opens and closes his mouth twice with his own shade of high color bleeding in. I see sweat standing out on the back of his neck.

"You just woke up," he says patiently, once he fixes that horrible smile back on his face. "You've sustained many injuries. I'm not sure you even have the use of your hand."

She lifts her right hand three inches off the baby blue coverlet tucked in around her legs and flips him her middle finger. She keeps her eyes locked dead on his. "My hand is working well enough. Paper. *Pens*."

"There's plenty in our sleeping pod, in our belongings." This is true because I brought her belongings from the hospital. "I'll go get it."

"No, he will," she says, without taking her eyes off of him.

When it is abundantly clear she will not say more until he leaves, Jeremiah gives in. "I'll be back." He casts me a severe look. "Try to keep her quiet, and restful. She will irreparably hurt herself if she tries to do anything strenuous before she's ready."

"I am right here," she says. "And last I checked, I still possess agency over my own body. If I want to throw the damn thing off a cliff, I will."

Jeremiah's thin lips press together until they lose all their color. Then he is out of the room in a heavy stride, leather shoes slapping at the tile.

"That man," Gloria says, falling back against her pillow. Her eyes roll to the ceiling.

"You've woken up in quite the mood," I say, coming to sit on the end of her bed. "Of course, I don't blame you. The last time we were under his command, he tried to keep Jesse in a medically-induced coma. Glad to see he hasn't done the same to you."

"I've not been under any man's *command* since I was discharged from the LDRVP in 2003."

I nod, accepting the correction. "Do you see something? Is that why you want to draw?"

"Yes."

I never know what to say here, if it's a matter of present or past tense. Does she see it in her mind now? Presently? Or did it come to her like a dream that she tries to remember? I've always been curious about it, about how she draws and what that experience must be like for her. But she's never opened up to me about it.

"Jesse has lost her mind," she says quietly.

I feel like someone has kicked me in the stomach. "What?"

"Michael is tearing apart her timeline. He's drowning her in all that could have been or will be. I suppose it's all the power in her. Gabriel was her transistor, but Michael has wounded him, separated them. She can't control the power on her own."

Gloria looks on the verge of tears. As if I needed to be any more frightened, the woman who I believe is the strongest, most fearless person in the world is on the verge of tears.

"If we don't get to her soon—"

Dr. Gray walks into the room holding the sketchbook and pack of pencils taped to the back of its thick cardboard folio. I was the one who added that tape, terrified I'd lose her pencils if I didn't attach them to the folio.

"Where is Jeremiah?" I ask as Gloria takes the book from her and flips it open in her lap with a stiff arm.

"He sent her on his errand." Gloria hisses in pain as she tries to adjust her position, but given all the casting and bandages, doesn't get far. I don't miss her press of the morphine drip. Twice. The lines in her face soften—either from actual relief or just the promise of it. "He ran up to control so he could see if he could listen to all this." Her eyes flick up to the black dome camera in the ceiling. "Didn't you, Tate?"

I unzip the pencil case taped to the back of the sketchbook and fish out a pencil for her.

"It's not a pen—" I begin, recalling her exact request.

She waves me off. "It's fine."

I help slip it between her two trembling fingers. Her movements are jerky and her hands shake. But she looks undeterred by this. Whatever she needs to draw, she intends to draw it.

She presses the lead to the page.

"You can see yourself out," Gloria says, casting a cool look at the doctor.

Instead of leaving, the doctor offers Gloria a hand. "I'm Doctor Evelyn Gray."

Gloria doesn't even look up.

"May I please check a few things before you dismiss me?" Dr. Gray says, with as much tolerance as she gave Nikki earlier. I catch myself tracing the curve of her brow and strong chin. Her bright, quick eyes. She has a kind face, but a voice that says she won't take nonsense from anyone.

"Just do enough to keep me conscious," Gloria says. "I'm going to see this through."

Dr. Gray's hard stare softens, looking a little surprised. I guess she was expecting more of a fight.

But the only thing Gloria is fighting is the pencil, trying to get the lead pressed to the page.

I slide up beside her and angle the book for her. "Here. I'll hold it. Just move the pencil."

She scowls at me. "Easy for you to say."

The three of us are silent for a long time with only the sound of Gloria's pencil slowly dragging across the page. It moves faster and faster as time stretches on, until there is a moment when I look up and see that Gloria's eyes are wide, vacant and unseeing.

No, not unseeing. More like fixed on a point far off in the distance that neither the doctor nor I can see.

Dr. Gray's face freezes in fear.

"This is normal," I whisper, as if raising my voice will frighten Gloria out of her stupor. "She will come out of it when she is finished."

Dr. Gray only stares for a moment and then says. "Right. Well, she is doing better than I think she has any right to be. She is healing remarkably well. Her contusions are horrendous. I don't need to tell you that. But the swelling is down, and her blood pressure and all other vitals have returned to manageable ranges. She could do with a month of sleep, but I won't ask for what I won't get."

"Please be patient with her," I say, casting her a sympathetic a look. "You can't possibly understand what she's been through."

I expect Gloria to tell me never to make an apology for

her—that nothing she has done deserves an apology—yet I can't help but feel that winning over one doctor to Gloria's side might be worth the effort. After all, I can't be everywhere all the time. I need good people in every corner. Whether or not Dr. Gray is willing to defy Jeremiah on Gloria's behalf is yet to be seen. But this is the first step.

Dr. Gray's face remains absolutely unreadable. Then her lips twitch into a smile. "I don't mind women who refuse to suffer fools. I don't suffer them myself."

An immense relief lightens my chest. "Thank you."

Dr. Gray leaves us alone.

I note the clock again. The urgent sense of time pressing in on me. I need to see my brother and Maisie at least one more time before I leave. And it wouldn't hurt to get a message to Gideon. But I don't dare leave Gloria's side until she's finished drawing whatever it is she needs me to see.

At one point, Gloria takes the sketchbook and moves it closer to her face. It seems like a subconscious movement, as if she is unaware that I was holding the book at all. I let it go. She doesn't stop drawing, and her eye never strays from the page.

Instead I tug Gloria's socks back down toward her ankles to make sure she is warm enough. Then I settle into the chair and wait.

And wait.

And I think too much about Jesse and what she must be doing now. I find my mind going over the usual concerns. Has she eaten? Is she cold? Has she slept at all in days?

Jesse has lost her mind.

I think of Rachel in her final hours. The Rachel who lost her mind and tried to kill me. Rachel who tried to kill Maisie. Is this what Gloria means when she says that Michael is tearing her apart? Should I expect a fight when I arrive?

I can still see the fire in Rachel's eyes as power raged through her.

And now Jesse has more power than all of them.

She seemed lucid—if a little confused—when I saw her in the hospital. But she hadn't stayed very long, had she? And even addicts can hold it together for minutes, can't they? They deceive family and friends all the time.

The truth is, I have no idea how Jesse is.

She barely knows who she is or where she is. And what if that is true. What if I get down to Antarctica and she doesn't even know who I am?

I picture walking across the ice toward her and seeing that vacant expression of unrecognition. It will be like walking into her Nashville office all over again. I was happy to find her alive. Thrilled. Beyond ecstatic. But facing the fact that she had no idea who I was after all we'd been through—I won't lie—it hurt.

And if she has forgotten me again? If this unimaginable power has blown through her mind and taken every memory of me away...every trace of the woman I love...what then?

I don't care.

I don't care if we meet on the ice as strangers.

I don't care if her only desire in that moment is to kill me.

I'll do what I did in Nashville. I'll stay anyway. I'll do what I can to help her. And with time...with time, maybe it'll all be okay again.

You don't have any more time, that cruel voice whispers.

The pencil falters on the page. The sudden snap of the lead pulls me from my dark thoughts. I realize Dr. Gray has left and Gloria's eyes are open. She's looking down at the page, and scowling.

"What is it?" I whisper. For no reason, my heart starts pounding in my chest.

Gloria doesn't say anything. She goes on staring at the

picture, each side of the sketchbook, gripping the edge so hard the color seeps from her fingers.

"Let me see," I say. The chair scrapes across the floor as I stand to look over the picture.

The page has been quartered, each corner of the page offering a different event around an enormous centerpiece image.

The drawings aren't her best. She usually renders her visions in such painstaking detail, but now...I just see the pain. The restricted movements of her fingers and the agony she must be feeling, even in her fingertips. Drawing this couldn't have been easy.

In the top right, there is a seat...the back of a seat. Car seat? Airplane seat? It's too close to be sure and the focus seems to be on what is under the seat.

In the bottom right frame, there is Maisie running down a hallway with Nikki. The two of them looking as if they are running for their lives—hair streaming out behind them—and further down the hall, I think that's me and Gideon close behind, but we are less defined, more shadow than anything.

In the top right frame, I'm yelling at Jeremiah. My face screwed up in unmistakable anger. Someone is behind me, twisting my arms behind my back. But that person isn't in the frame, so I can't be sure if it is Nikki holding me back or someone else.

And in the last frame, the bottom right panel, Gideon flies a plane, giant earmuffs fixed over his head.

I note and process each of these in turn. But my eyes keep coming back to the center picture, the one that each picture bleeds into.

It's Jesse. She stands in the shadowed landscape lacking definition. She could be anywhere. A plume of bright light envelops her, pouring through her—or from her—in all directions. It doesn't even look like her feet are touching the ground as she hangs airborne in this shaft of light, her head thrown back, her arms extended. She looks like a body suspended under water.

"What does it mean?" I ask. Because I can't interpret these on my own, though it isn't for lack of trying. My eyes keep roving over each, looking for clues that I may have missed at first glance.

When I meet Gloria's eyes, they're full of tears.

"What?" I ask her, taken aback.

"I have no right to ask you." Her lip quivers and she pinches her eyes closed.

"It's okay," I tell her. I don't even know what I'm saying is okay, but it doesn't stop me from saying it again. "It's okay."

"You will die if you go," she says. "You *will* die."

My vision darkens, and all I'm left with is the sound of my breath in my ears and the blood pounding in my temples.

"But if you stay, we all die."

No, *you might die*. No, *it's very dangerous*.

"I knew there was a risk," I tell her, but my voice sounds dreamy, spoken like a sleepwalker.

"I'm sorry," she says. And she does look sorry. The thick black circles under her puffy eyes. The tears standing in their corners, eyes bright and shining. The tremble to her voice... all of it together conveys her regret. "I would never ask you to go, but she needs you. She'll never survive this if she has to go it alone."

"But she might not even know who I am," I say. It isn't a question.

Gloria lets the sketchbook fall across her legs, her head hitting her pillow again. Her despair makes my heart hurt. If my throat were any tighter, I don't think I could speak.

"I want to go," I whisper. And it's true. "I don't want her to suffer alone."

"Even though it will kill you," Gloria whispers.

"Even if it kills me." Because losing her again will kill me, too. I've learned the hard way that dying isn't always when the heart stops. Often it is everything that happens after. There is such a thing as a slow and painful death, and it has nothing to do with the body or health. I have no interest in experiencing that again. I've lived in the world without Jesse Sullivan. And it isn't a world I want.

I'm nodding as if she's spoken. "We're leaving tonight. I'll be with her soon."

"That's too late."

I look up to see if she is serious.

"You need to go *now*," she adds. "Before Michael changes Jeremiah's mind. And...and there is something wrong with the plane."

"What do you mean there is something wrong with the plane?"

She shakes her head. Her face screws up with irritation. "He's blocking me. The fucking angel."

I flinch at her swear. "Gabriel?"

"No," she says. "The other one. The one who is trying to get you killed before you can get to her. I think he is the one sending Tate's visions."

More talk of angels. More things I don't understand.

"But I'm certain that you have to go now. If you wait any longer, she won't make it."

"Gloria, I can't fly a plane!" I hiss. "I can't just steal one. I'd also have to steal a pilot."

"Nikki will take you."

My words falter. "You saw Nikki in the plane?"

I want to say more. Clearly there are parts of this vision that she understands that I can't discern simply by looking at the picture. I open my mouth to beg for an explanation, but the breath leaves me in a *whoosh*. I feel electricity race along my skin, wringing every morsel of air from my lungs. My back bows, and I cry out as sparks ignite in my veins.

I'm going to be blown apart. My skin is sliding off my bones.

It's like when I stepped off the elevator with Nikki and Jesse's power overtook me...but this is much *much* worse.

"Go now," Gloria whispers. Her eyes wide and showing far too much white. "It's already begun."

CHAPTER EIGHTEEN

Jesse

Helicopters cut across the sky. Only they aren't helicopters. They're also angels with enormous wings sent to tear this world apart.

You thought you won, but you didn't, my father whispers in my head.

The father who hunted me. The father who tortured and killed me. The father who manipulated me into killing.

You thought you could come in and destroy this world that I built, he says. That voice echoes through my mind as it has so often.

"You're supposed to be dead. I cut off your head with my own hands."

I sit up. I turn in every direction of the beach.

Gabriel, Michael, and the angels are gone.

The house is destroyed, what is left of it is broken boards and shattered windows. A wave slams into me, tumbling me along the sand. I pull myself to standing and find that I'm up to my waist in ocean water. The tide sucks at my legs, eroding the sand beneath my feet.

The water isn't blue-grey anymore.

It's red. It's red with blood.

Footsteps sound, and I turn expecting to find someone—something—creeping up behind me.

Caldwell is here. His green eyes bright. His freckles darker than they had ever been in life. He looks more like the man I knew as a child: Eric Sullivan, the mechanic, the man with a young daughter, married to Danica and living paycheck to paycheck. Before he died. Before he became a monster.

But it's a monster in those fiery eyes I see...no matter which of his faces he wears.

"Did you really think you'd gotten rid of me so easily?" he asks. His voice is perfectly clear despite the storm kicking up around us. "I'm inside you now. Your power is my power. I'll never leave you."

I feel something brush my leg in the bloody water. I look down and see blond hair floating along the surface, a bleached, silky seaweed.

A face rolling over, wet skin bobbing to the surface.

Flat, lifeless brown eyes. Ally's face. Her white teeth bared in a grimace of agony. The bloody water settling into the grooves between her teeth.

Something inside me erupts.

A force rips through me and tears me in two.

I PULL A HELICOPTER FROM THE SKY. HELICOPTER AFTER helicopter. It isn't the beach they crash into, black smoke rising. It's the tundra. I'm not sure when I shifted back. I'm not even sure they are two separate places anymore: the gate and the convergence place.

All I know is that my father's words are pulsing into my mind, and the more I use my power the stronger his voice gets.

But my shield is back. And it ripples around me, warping against an impact.

The nearest helicopter is firing bullets. They ricochet across the face of the glowing force field and zip across the tundra. Shards of ice splinter from the landscape.

I throw a firebomb, and it catches the right side of the aircraft. Yellow-red flames leap from the windows. The glass explodes, and black smoke escapes. It drops, circling like a dragonfly with one wing ripped from its back.

There are four more helicopters. No. I blink to clear my eyes and count again. Five, six...eight. A whole fleet has come for me. They are my father's men. I know this because I reach out with my mind and touch theirs. Their love and loyalty and the confusion surrounding those affections oozing from their cracked minds like pus from a festering sore.

Circle back. We need to know her range.

What can be done about the shield.

Holy fucking god we're all gonna die—

—what am I even doing here.

Jesse—Jesse, my god, what the hell happened to you?

That last voice...

Where do I know that last voice from?

It doesn't matter. These people are working under my father's orders.

I bring them all down. I reach out with the gift that was Rachel's, and I seize the blades, I seize the engines. I start to peel them apart like skins from oranges.

They spark. They flame. They spiral to the ice in rivers of exploding glass and billowing smoke.

The ones who reach the ground start running toward me. Men with large guns held across their chest as they close the distance between us.

I find that gift in me that used to belong to a boy named

Jake. The earth responds. It rumbles like a giant awakening from slumber. It stirs, and the earth quivers.

The men stop running. They're looking at the snow-covered plain under their black boots like they've never seen it before.

Then it starts to split open, and they split themselves. Half run to the left, the others to the right. Scattered like roaches confronted by the light.

As the ice divides, deepening to a full-blown chasm, one of the collapsed flaming helicopters is swallowed up by its great, thirsty mouth.

Some of my father's more determined servants are still coming toward me. They don't find a little earthquake or flames to be enough of a deterrent.

I wait until they're close. I wait until I can see the whites of their eyes, and then I unleash Georgia's gift.

Death ribbons slide over their bodies like velvet. Their knees buckle. Their eyes roll up into their skulls. They topple, dropping dead.

The breath is gone from their bodies before their backs or knees even hit the ground. They fall like toy soldiers blown over by a strong breeze.

Then there is nothing. Nothing moves in the sky. Nothing moves on the ground.

That isn't quite right. I see one man in the distance, running full tilt away from me. I consider chasing him down and finishing him off. I don't want to leave any survivors that may take up my father's cause again. But when I brush this one's mind, I don't feel any loyalty, any intention to carry on in Caldwell's name.

There aren't even complete thoughts in this one's head. There's only crushing sadness. And fear. Fear drips from every fiber of his being.

I let him go.

I watch his form grow smaller through the shimmering heat of flames. I inhale deep the smell of blood and smoke and charred flesh.

Are you having fun? A whisper licks the inside of my ear.

Michael stands on the beach, a good ten feet away. I'm not concerned about this latest shift from ice to waves.

I'm concerned about Michael. He has blood on his hands up to his shoulder. My father looked like that once when he plunged his hand through Liza's chest and took her power from her. Whose chest has Michael been tearing open?

Yours, he says.

I look down and see that he's right. Blood pours down the front of my body.

"I don't have a heart," I say.

He smiles.

"My heart is gone. Where is it?"

"Where is it?" he mimics, cruelly.

Lies and illusions, Gabriel whispers. And it is his voice, loud and clear, though I can't see him. I keep turning my head, catching him in the corner of my eye, but never seeing him fully. It's only Michael and me on the beach—and those ever-circling angels who keep waiting for something.

Waiting for the gate to open.

Waiting to inherit the world.

Black feathers raining down in front of my eyes. The smell of rain grows so strong I expect to feel droplets on my face at any moment.

The time has come, Michael says. He's right in front of me now.

He reaches up and places one hand in my hair. His hand is warm and sticky with my blood.

"You have no enemies left. It's just me and you, for as long as I can keep your troublesome pet at bay. So let's hurry this along, shall we?"

My limbs grow heavy and weak. My knees buckle, and Michael catches me, his arm pressing into the small of my back, crushing me against his stone chest. His lips are danger-ously close to my face. So close I can smell his breath. He smells like carrion. Rotten meat and roadkill. The metallic tang of fresh blood.

I try to buck him off, but it's like moving underwater. The power is draining from me. *I used it all up*, I think. *I'm all used up*.

"No," he says, slipping his tongue into the crevices of my ear. "Let me show you what you can do."

CHAPTER NINETEEN

Ally

I'm trying to keep a casual pace as I walk through the labyrinth of hallways to the sleeping pods. I notice a slight tremor in my hand as I push the elevator button to go down to level three. Whatever is happening to Jesse, I can feel it.

Whatever is going on with her, I've run out of time. I have to go now. Even if Gloria hadn't given me some dire warning about using Jeremiah's plane, I can't wait.

A sick foreboding makes my stomach sour and limbs heavy.

I reach pod 333 and use the watch on my wrist to open the door.

It's empty except for the pug on the bed. Winston lets out a little yip of surprise the way he does when anyone knocks on the door, but then his cinnamon bun tail only wags. I spare him a weak hello and his tail sags.

Maisie's not in here and neither is Eli.

I try not to let dread send me into a full-blown frenzy. I go to the next room and knock on my brother's pod.

Again, only silence. No patter of feet. No one climbing out of a bunk and moving to answer the door. No voices.

I decide to check the rec hall before I panic. After all, knowing my brother, he would find the rec room to be a better place for getting to know a girl he's just met. The intimacy of the pod would probably make Maisie feel too vulnerable. My brother is very conscious of space like that, particularly about how he occupies space when he is around women. I've always loved that about him.

Somehow, I make it up to the rec room despite my unsteady legs trembling with that unseen electricity. When I step off the elevator, relief washes over me.

My brother is volleying a ping pong ball across the table to Maisie. It pops up and hits her in the chin and she laughs. *She's okay. They're okay.*

I take a deep breath and force calm into my voice. "Getting along?" I know this room is bugged, and so I can't simply shriek, *I'm going to steal a plane now! Wish me luck!*

And there is this issue with the pins and needles electricity that makes me feel as though my flesh is trying to crawl off my bones.

I sit on the sofa closest to the table. My brother catches the ball that Maisie serves without really looking at it. He's frowning at me. "Are you okay?"

"I'm a little winded," I say.

"Your breathing is fine," he says, immediately challenging me like only an older brother can. "You look like you're in pain."

"Come here," I whisper to both of them and I force a smile. "I need to tell you something."

They drop their paddles onto the tabletop at once and come sit beside me on the sofa.

"Gloria is awake," I say in a quick, hushed voice. "She says

I need to leave and get Jesse now. *Right* now. Not later. Not tomorrow."

"How are you going to do that?"

"I don't know," I say. "I need to find Nikki. And I need to get a message to Gideon, because I don't think I can wait until he gets here." I meet my brother's eyes. "And I need you to help me because…because I'm not feeling 100%."

But I am beginning to feel better.

That raw, itching power is pulling back, leaving me cold.

"But what about me and Winston?" Maisie asks, her brow knit in concern, blue eyes wide and searching mine.

"Eli will look after you."

"Why not you?" she demands.

"He's promised to help you get settled with Gloria. Just like you want." I'm hoping these words will comfort her, but her face remains pinched.

"Why not *you*? Or Jesse? What did Gloria say?"

When the rapid fire questions stop, I can only smile at her. "It's going to be okay."

I exchange a look with my brother, and the color rises in his cheeks. But he says nothing. He lets his working jaw say it all.

"Now, help me," I plead and offer them both a hand to pull me up.

"I thought we agreed that you would go when I could spare the plane," a voice calls.

I pivot in my seat and find Jeremiah standing there with three armed guards. I don't know any of these people. My one ally, Nikki, is nowhere in sight. This is definitely a bad sign, as bad as the fact that he's here with armed guards.

Gloria was obviously right. Jeremiah must have heard our conversation about the drawing. And he must have decided to detain me almost immediately after, if he was able to get three guards and arrive here so quickly.

I slip my hand in my pocket and search for the intercom. I feel the snail-shell coil of one side. I press it and nothing happens. I turn it over and mash the red emergency button. At least I hope I do.

"I was under the impression my sister could come and go as she pleases," my brother says, that hint of fury searing his words. "Is she a prisoner here? I wasn't aware that she has broken any law or that you had the authority to arrest her."

Maisie entwines her arm with mine.

I push the intercom button again.

"Don't get involved in this," I whisper into Maisie's ear.

"Too late for that," she says.

"Take them all," Jeremiah says, one hand on his hip as if he's disappointed in us.

The three figures in full black tactical gear descend on us. My brother starts to resist, but I shake my head. "Don't."

I cut my eyes to Maisie. I don't want her to hurt any more than she has already. So instead, when they surround us, I do my best to relax and put on a brave face.

"Does Nikki know you're detaining me?" I ask politely.

They don't answer. Instead, we are seized by the upper arms and ushered toward the elevator.

From there, we are taken to the 22nd floor. Yet another floor that I didn't know existed. We step off the elevator and take only five steps into a circular room. It's windowless, padded.

And Gideon is inside, crouched against one wall with his hands on his knees.

"This is for your own safety," Jeremiah says. "If you try to escape, I will have to use force."

"On whose authority?" my brother says.

Jeremiah doesn't say anything. He only pulls the door shut. I hear three bolts slide home, locking the door in place. And because the inside of the door looks exactly like the other padded panels lining the wall, I'm not even sure which one is the door now.

"Hello, Alice," Gideon says with his crisp British accent. "And here I was hoping that you would rescue me. Darling, if you're going to play the hero, you can't be captured unless it's part of the plan. Was this part of the plan?"

I shake my head.

"Of course not," he sighs and kicks his legs out in front of him.

My brother casts him a look.

"Gideon is a friend," I tell him by way of introduction.

"Do you think Gloria will figure out we are in here and break us out?" Maisie asks, hopefully. "God, of course not. She's in, like, a full-body cast. Stupid. And what about Winston! I left him sleeping in the pod! If we don't get out of here, he is going to starve. He's probably only got enough food and water for a day in there."

"Let's not panic," I say. "I paged Nikki before we were taken. Hopefully, she'll get to us. Soon."

I open and close my fists, trying to ease some of the electricity.

Gideon snorts. "You are ever the optimist, my dear. I've been in here for three hours. There is no bathroom, by the way. If I'd known I was going to be caught and imprisoned, I wouldn't have had that fourth mojito."

"Three hours?" I ask, stunned.

"Yes. And *four* mojitos."

If Gideon has been imprisoned for three hours, then Jeremiah was lying to me. Or at the very least, he misled me into believing that Gideon wasn't here yet.

I pull the intercom out of my pocket and mash it with my thumb again. The blue light didn't even come on. Did its battery die? Or did I break it?

"Did you check the room for weaknesses?" my brother asks.

"Of course," Gideon tells him. "I have skills, you know. Even though they took all my gadgets and there is no network access in here. I think this room was designed for someone like me."

"A spy?" Maisie asks.

"A troublemaker," he says and winks at her. The flirt.

He points at the seamless, padded walls.

"I can't really work with this. I ripped off part of the padding to see what's underneath, but it's only concrete. You can see where I tore up that bit there and the stuffing is coming out. I suspect we are being monitored, so I will not get very far trying to tear off the walls before they send someone to stop me, anyway. They've been rather civil about it so far. I'd hate to see what happens once they've lost their temper."

"Hopefully, he's just preparing the plane and the team," I say. But I can't get Gloria's warning out of my head. *Go now. It's already begun.*

If Jeremiah doesn't let us out soon, we're in big trouble. Then again, I can breathe almost normally now. Maybe the danger has passed.

Gloria can't rescue us. Nor can Jesse. And what if Nikki knows about this? What if Nikki didn't come with Jeremiah, not because I've been detained behind her back without her knowing, but because she didn't have the heart to look me in the eye while Jeremiah did it?

"Someone will come," Maisie whispers. She's looking at something in the corner. Something I can't see. Or maybe someone.

And I can't even bat an eyelash at that now, can I?

"Yes," I say. "Nikki will come."

Only she doesn't, and for a very long time all I can do is

replay Gloria's warning in my head while my agitation thickens the air around me.

I pace. I lean against the wall only to start walking again.

I hope that everyone in the room just sees it as symptoms of anxiety. No one needs to worry about that strange connection between Jesse, Gabriel, and I.

I'm not the only one acting anxious anyway.

My brother keeps repeating mindless laws and codes and meaningless phrases like *a violation of personal liberty* as if it means anything in here.

How do I tell him the rules don't apply in this world? In the world run by men like Caldwell, men like Jeremiah, who wear a good man's face half the time and a villain's the other —in this world, personal liberty is a privilege that is often revoked, on a whim without warning.

Maisie seems to be the only one taking it in stride.

She's adopted a stillness that I would have said is impossible in anyone so young. But I keep forgetting who she is and where she comes from. She's far from ordinary. She says, "I hate being trapped in rooms without doors."

"But these cream-colored walls are great for your complexion, love. You're positively glowing." Gideon keeps flicking the plastic hospital bracelet bound to his left wrist.

Maisie graces him with a smile.

He wears Rachel's asylum bracelet like a bangle. He plays with it until he catches me watching, and then like a little boy who's been reprimanded, he covers it protectively with his hand. "What?"

"Nothing," I say, and keep pacing. Then I say, "What did you see in her?"

His face flushes red. The color rises in his golden-brown cheeks and his eyes flash, hateful. But instead of yelling at me, he bursts out laughing.

"What did I *see* in her? Except the fact that she was a heartbreakingly beautiful, mad, bewitching little creature?"

The laughter rolls out of him until I think he's going to hyperventilate. I catch Maisie staring at him out of the corner of her eye.

"True, it was a brief, catastrophic affair. No matter what, that's how it would've been. Even without all of this." He gestures at the room, at all of us. "That's just how she was. I wouldn't have changed a minute of it."

He meets Maisie's eyes, and she looks away. He asks me, "Can you say the same?"

My brother cuts his eyes to mine. He's waiting for me to answer. They all are.

"What do you see in Jesse?" Gideon presses. "Come on now, we're live on Big Brother 6, the four of us trapped in this little room. The audience is waiting. They want to know your darkest secrets, love. Your most desperate regrets."

As if I could make such a list on command. But I'm already composing it.

I see her bravery.

I see her unwillingness to take herself too seriously.

I see her smile and laugh and fierce loyalty to the people she loves.

I see how desperate she is to say anything, do anything to make someone laugh.

I see her utter fearlessness in the face of challenge.

I see her sweet tenderness when she thinks no one is watching...

"If you could just bow out of all of this, would you?" Gideon says. His voice is soft now and a little tighter than before.

"No." And I say it with absolutely honesty. "Do you regret Brinkley dragging you into this? If he hadn't asked you to protect Jesse and Rachel, would you have come anyway?"

Gideon laughs again. But it's high and tight and much less good-natured than before.

"I was very angry, to be sure," he says. He slips his finger under the plastic bracelet again. "You can't imagine what it was like, watching this man, who was like my own father, refuse to protect himself. I wanted him to use them, Rachel or Jesse, I didn't care who. Either one would have replaced him just fine. But he wouldn't do it. He said Caldwell would use it as an opportunity to murder one or the other."

"He would," Maisie agrees.

"It was his right to choose," I say, my voice barely above a whisper.

"Let's see Jesse choose death, and I doubt you'll be so magnanimous. So *evolved*."

I know he's right, but his cold bitterness still stings.

"At the time, it seemed like he was giving up," Gideon adds, scraping at that plastic bracelet with his thumbnail. "And I hated him for it. I thought *how dare you give up on me? How dare you give up your life for hers and leave me here to deal with all of this alone?*"

He runs his fingers through his hair.

I slide down the padded wall and pull my coat around my shoulders a little tighter. I snuggle into my jacket. I don't know if my fear is making me cold, or if it is the room. No one else seems affected.

"Do you forgive him?" I ask.

"Oh, shut up," he says, but there is no venom in it. "Of course I do. Can we stop sharing our feelings now? It's bloody awful."

Maisie frowns at me, and I can hear the *are you okay* on the tip of her tongue. I close my eyes, hoping that this is a clear dismissal.

I almost fall asleep like that, exhaustion washing over me at long last. But a shadow moves in the corner of my eye, and my head snaps toward it. At first, I think I'm looking at Jeremiah. That he has some pathetic excuse for our detainment, not doubt for our own safety, but all is well now, etc., etc.

But it isn't Jeremiah. It's Gabriel.

He stands there, in all his glory, black swan wings stretched out on either side of him. Maisie makes a small sound beside me, and I turn, seeing her mouth has dropped open too, her eyes wide with surprise.

"Is she dead?" I ask him. I have no idea why this is the first thing I ask.

"I'm sure she's fine," Maisie says, giving me a sharp look.

My brother Eli looks at me with a quizzical brow.

"Jesse's tough," she adds. But it's Maisie's face that reminds me of the perils of this double vision.

Is she alright? I ask Gabriel, but only with my mind this time.

No. She can't push him out, and I can't get back in. He has placed his army between us. I must defeat them if I am to reach her. And the gate is open...the gate is open....

I want to ask what that means. I assume, of course that it is a metaphoric gate, not a literal gate. But still, a gate to what? To what purpose? Gates are opened so that things may pass through them. What in the world is going to pass through?

Before I can ask, three bolts slide back, and one of the panels unhinges. It swings into the room, separating from the wall. A siren is wailing so loud that I reach up to cover my ears against it. The padding covering the walls must have been soundproof.

Nikki steps around the door, appearing in full tactical gear, all black from the neck down and guns on her hips. Her hair in a high, severe ponytail. Her eyes sweep the room, noting each occupant until falling on me.

"You want to get out of here?" she asks by way of introduction.

"Yes," I breathe, and I'm already up and rushing for the door.

"Good. Because this offer expires immediately."

THE FIVE OF US RUN DOWN THE HALLWAY, FEET POUNDING thunderously. We must sound like a stampede. Nikki doesn't take us to the elevator. She leads us to a stairwell that is unmarked and easy to overlook. My chest is aching by the time we scramble through the narrow concrete space.

We step into the hangar, and the siren is deafening. One half turn, and I recognize where I am from my walk to the conference room earlier today. Gideon doesn't seem to care about orienting himself. He runs toward a sleek black plane with dark windows which sits in the shadows. He touches it lovingly, as if reunited with a long, lost friend.

He finds a ladder leaning against an adjacent wall and carries it over his head to the craft.

"Is that your plane?" Nikki asks. She shifts the guns strapped across her hips.

"No, darling, this belongs to a very good friend. And if I so much as *scratch* it, he will shave me, tar me, feather me, and dump what is left of me off the coast of Tripoli after a couple of his hyenas nibble off my most cherished..." He meets Maisie's eyes. "*Parts*."

"They will have removed one or both of the ignitor plugs," she says. She says this gently, the way one might say a beloved pet isn't going to survive the surgery.

His face screws up. "Bloody bastards."

"What does that do?" I shout over the roaring siren.

"Grounds the plane," she says. "We'll have to take one of Jeremiah's planes."

Gideon descends the ladder cursing, while Eli, Maisie, and I follow Nikki out of the hangar and onto the tarmac.

It's dark out here and almost completely empty. Only one plane sits on the tarmac, its nose pointed toward the dusty runaway stretching ahead. I guess Jeremiah wasn't kidding about not having a plane to spare.

"So many options," Gideon quips.

"What about Winston?" Maisie skids to a screeching halt. "We left Winston and Gloria in there!"

"We can't go back," Nikki says.

"Why?" I ask. Now that the shock of the sirens and the adrenaline of possible escape dips, I'm able to see the situation more clearly—I'm not asking enough questions.

"I directly disobeyed him. And I had half my soldiers detain him. He's the one who initiated lockdown." She turns her wristwatch in the moonlight, and its green face blinks to life. "We have two minutes to get off the base, or we aren't getting off at all."

I face Maisie, catching her wide, fearful eyes. I have to shout over the sound of that damned siren. "You should stay, Maisie," I say. I brace myself for her refusal. "Gloria and Winston need someone here to advocate for them. Someone to make sure Jeremiah doesn't take any...liberties."

But it's more than that. I don't want to take a teenager or my brother who is expecting a child onto a plane.

Maisie straightens her spine. "I can do that."

"I'll stay, too," my brother says, volunteering just as I expect him to. His eyes are like burning coals in the light. "I'll do everything I can."

"I know you will." I throw my arms around his neck and squeeze him hard. His return hug is just as fierce. And when our eyes meet, I know with absolute certainty that we are thinking the same thing: *I'm never going to see you again.*

"Good luck." His face tightens.

"You too."

He shakes his head as if clearing a thought and says, "Do what you have to do."

"I love you," I tell him, without reserve. Then I throw my arm around Maisie's neck and kiss her temple. "And I love you too."

Tears stand out in the girl's eyes. I think she's going to pull away from me and run toward the jet that Gideon is already firing up, but at the last second she leans forward and presses her mouth to my ear.

"Azrael says that you have to make her remember. Make her remember who she is. And tell Jesse I love her. Tell her that I'm proud to call her my sister."

Her lip trembles furiously."

So many questions. So many things left to say. To my brother, to Maisie, and even Gloria. I don't think I've even thanked her for all that she's done for us.

"We need to move!" Nikki screams, she's hanging out the side of the plane.

"I love you both," I say again, and I turn, running to the plane before I burst into tears.

Nikki helps me up into the aircraft with one strong pull of her arm.

"They'll be okay," Nikki assures me as she shuts the door, air-locking it behind me. "Jeremiah has a soft spot for Gloria, and if Maisie really needed to, she could go public and bring hell down on his head. She *is* Maisie Caldwell, after all."

I say a silent prayer for Maisie. That she finds her own strength. That she uses it to protect herself in the days ahead.

"I'm just glad she remembered the bloody dog," Gideon says from the copilot seat. He's already reading gauges and punching buttons. "For a moment, I thought you were actually going to bring her on this suicide mission."

Nikki gives us both stern looks. "No one is going to die."

"Sweetheart, if I don't nearly die at least twice, it hasn't been a good day." He flashes me one of his bright, roguish smiles. As charming as it may be, I don't miss the slight mania in his eyes.

"You're a little crazy," I blurt. It isn't meant as an insult, yet I realize how it must sound.

I blush.

Gideon only laughs and accelerates the plane down the long dark road ahead.

"Oh, darling. You have *no* idea."

CHAPTER TWENTY

Jesse

I walk down a street.

There is a line three blocks long extending out of the soup kitchen on the corner. Across the street, there are whole families who clutch their possessions in bags. All their possessions from their old lives in plastic sacks. Army jets zoom overhead. Police with dogs walk up and down the streets, trying to maintain order.

They thought they could live above the system, Michael whispers in my ear. I turn and see him beside me. Tall and handsome with long, blond hair and brown eyes. He reminds me of someone, but I can't quite place who. Did he look like this before? Or have his cheeks rounded, his eyes softened?

It seems so hard to hold a thought in my head for more than a minute or two.

They were born within an ecological system. A perfect check and balance equilibrium meant to breed prosperity and abundance. But their ambition, their carelessness led them to overreach.

I look at the woman holding an infant against her chest. She looks so tired. So alone.

You don't follow your own protocols. When an animal outgrows its ecosystem, when an imbalance is struck between predators and prey, your governments issue permits for a hunt. They cull the offending population to restore balance and harmony. And yet they can't impose the same order on their own species? They can't manage their own resources properly. They take too much and when you weaken your base, the top will fall.

You can restore the balance to the earth. You can make it a peaceful place of prosperity again.

The woman's eyes bore into mine.

"Please," she whispers, clutching her baby close. "*Please.*"

End her suffering, Jesse. End yours.

I count the bodies in the street, my eyes finally falling on a bare foot, protruding from the end of tattered jeans. A fly dances on the toes, rubbing its crystalline wings together in the smog-filled light.

You can do this for them, Michael whispers.

Be their savior.

Be their second coming.

The baby in her arms stops breathing. And I understand all that lies ahead for her is misery and death.

"I can do this for them," I whisper.

Yes.

"I can set them free."

CHAPTER TWENTY-ONE

Ally

*P*ain rockets through my body. Red starbursts erupt behind my eyes. My head splits in two. I throw my head back on the leather seat and scream.

I'm dying.

Oh my god, I'm dying.

Someone is yelling my name.

But I can't answer. Pain bows my back and hollows out my throat.

In the throes of it, I see Jesse clearly. I *feel* her, like a freezing cold hand on the back of my neck. The power ripping through me is her power. Someone is pulling it out of her, out of me. Someone is twisting it, polluting it, and it's his fingers that slip into my brain like ice.

"Alice," a voice whispers. And I become aware of the rush of wings. I'm enveloped in darkness, cut off from Jesse and drowning in the scent of rain. "Breathe."

I try. I really try, but there is so much pressure in my chest I can't get any air into my lungs.

"I can't breathe," I cry. "I can't breathe."

Someone releases my seatbelt and I slump.

Then the power ceases. I drop. I slide out of the seat, my hands and knees hit the ground, and I'm sucking air into my lungs with great hungry gulps. Tears stream down my face.

"Jesus Christ," Nikki pants beside me. "Are you okay?"

"No," I say. I'm aware of the snot and tears all over my face. The agonizing burning in my throat.

First, I just lay here, on the floor, with a rubber mat pressed against my cheek until I can stand to lift my head. The balled muscles in my back unclench. The world around me stops spinning, and someone is hauling me up into the leather seat again. I collapse against it, every inch of me sore and throbbing.

"Fucking Christ," Nikki says again and collapses into the seat across from me. "You scared the shit out of me. What happened?"

I lick my lips and say, "I don't know." My voice is hoarse from screaming. It comes out like a croak.

"Jesus."

And she looks like someone who's just been terrorized within an inch of her life. Her face is pale, and a thin sheen of sweat stands out along her temple. She runs her hands over her face as if to collect herself. I try to adjust myself in my seat but my muscles aren't working right.

"Can I have some water?" I ask. "Or a wet rag."

I'm in too much pain to really be embarrassed by what must be my mess of a face. Not to mention my terror for Jesse. I try to piece together what I just saw.

"Michael is manipulating her," I say to no one in particular, trying to understand what I just saw, the bits and fragments. "He's wielding her like a weapon."

"I thought you were dying," Nikki says. She hands me a bottle of water and a t-shirt. She opens the bottle, cracking the plastic cap with one twist, and wets the shirt. I drag it down my face and then drink the rest of the water in slow, steady gulps. I take long, deep breaths between swallows.

Nikki's still talking. "I thought I was watching you die."

She settles back against the seat.

And I thought I was dying until Gabriel stepped in and shielded me from the onslaught of power.

Gideon tries to look around the seat to see me with his own eyes. "All right back there? Or is Tamsin talking your ear off?"

I don't have an answer.

"I'm sure Alice wasn't trying to scare the devil out of you. Perhaps you can quit accusing her."

"No," Nikki says, her spine straightening. "I didn't mean it like that."

Gideon glances over his shoulder again and meets my eyes. "It was rather terrifying, love. I won't lie."

"I'm sorry," I say. "It was rather painful."

"It was rather painful," Gideon snorts. "You have a gift for understatement, darling."

And the aircraft suddenly feels wobbly and myself wobbly in it. I turn and vomit onto the floor between the seats. All the water and everything else—which is mostly burning acid bile—comes up. It hits the rubber mat.

Nikki holds back my hair.

"You don't have to apologize," Nikki says. But the way she turns her own face away and presses her lips together makes her look like she's going to be sick, too.

When I collapse against the seat, she throws a white sheet over the mess, as if giving it some decency. But now the whole plane smells like vomit.

I would be horrified if I didn't feel my pulse rabbiting in my throat and temples. My limbs are shaking and my voice nearly gone. I put the cold cloth over my face and breathe.

The plane dips suddenly, and I snatch hold of my seatbelt

at the last moment, securing it around me. The plane swerves again and then levels out.

"Are you trying to make me puke again?" I ask, pressing the cold cloth into my eyes.

"What is that?" Nikki asks as she climbs into the copilot seat.

"I suspect that's what she felt," Gideon says.

I pull the cold cloth from my face and find the world is basking in a soft, purple glow.

"What is that?" My voice cracks.

"Three guesses, darling, and they're all that damnable woman you love."

We watch the horizon, dumbfounded as purple light shimmers across the sky. It seems to be radiating from a central plume in the distance while lightning crackles overhead.

"Is that going to bring down the plane?" I ask, tightening my seatbelt across my hips.

"No. I lowered our altitude. But there goes our navigation instruments," Gideon says with an exasperated hiss.

Nikki pulls my face toward her. She forces me to look at her. "Jesus, your eyes are completely dilated."

"I'm okay," I say. "Or I will be if you can keep this plane in the sky."

She looks like she wants to kiss me. I can actually see her considering it, and that's just gross. I can taste the vomit in my mouth and that fuzzy sheen along my teeth. I turn my face away, trying to catch my breath again.

What's happening to me?

I have blocked the connection between you, Gabriel whispers.

I understand that this is a giant favor, considering that same power almost tore me apart just now.

I won't be able to close it off forever... when you get closer...

His voice is lost in a string of swear words pouring from Nikki's mouth. But I catch enough.

I understand, I tell him.

"Lucky for you," Gideon says, still talking about the navigation system. "I know how to fly blind. At this altitude, we won't run into any commercial traffic."

"You spoke too soon." Nikki's voice thins and is lost in the roar of the engine.

I lean forward just in time to see a 747 Boeing nose dive toward the earth, its left engine engulfed in flames. It hits the ocean and breaks apart like a child's toy dashed against concrete.

"I suppose something could fall from the sky and crash into us," he amends. "That would knock us from the sky. Once we get past Rio, air traffic will be almost non-existent."

"How far are we from Rio?" I ask. I can't be sure how long we've been flying. I remember Nikki pointing out the Caribbean and making a joke about taking me to Antigua when this is all over. But how long ago was that? How long after that had the surprise bolt of power ripped through me?

"We are a hundred miles from Rio," he says. "Fingers crossed, we'll be over the South Atlantic any moment now."

It seems like we all hold our breath for this.

Suddenly, I'm so tired. I catch my eyes drooping. The soft purple light permeating the cabin isn't helping. I feel like it's lulling me to sleep with its glow.

When my head slips off my hand for the third time, Nikki says, "Why don't you lay down? I think you need it."

And every part of my body agrees with her. So I place my head on my folded arm and close my eyes. I sleep without dreaming. I can hear the rustle of wings, and the scent of rain never leaves me. It seems to be in my hair and clothes, all around me. It's better than that bitter taste lingering in my mouth.

I doze, but don't fully enter unconsciousness. Part of me surveys the cabin and the soft conversation exchanged between Nikki and Gideon. Requests for flight adjustments. A couple gallows humor jokes from Gideon. Stone silence from Nikki.

Then I hear something click on. It's so loud, so noticeable because of its difference.

I sit up in my seat, coming straight out of my dozing.

"You're up," Nikki says. Her eyes are violet in the light emanating from the horizon. "How do you feel?"

Seeing Jesse's light like that, cast over everything, makes my heart sink again. I overlooked the sound for a moment, as I flirted with the edge of a dream.

Now that I'm awake, I have this horrible reminder that no matter what I do, whatever is coming next, is coming.

"I hear something," I say.

"The engine is riding a little rough," Gideon says. "I think the magnetism is affecting the parts—"

"No." I finger the seam along the leather seats.

"It's probably just wind shear," Nikki says.

"No," I say. How can I explain that I shouldn't hear it at all? I'm hearing it because Gabriel wants me to hear it.

The image of Gloria's drawing flashes in my mind, clear and bright. I see the thick powdery lead on the unforgiving white page. It was a seat. The back of a seat.

I unsnap the buckle on my safety belt, and I drop to the floor.

On the ground, the sound is louder, that strange mechanical *beep* clear as a bell.

I stick my hand under the seat and feel around.

"What are you doing?" Nikki asks. Her amused expression hardens.

I wrap my fingers around the cold plastic and slide the

box from under the seat. It's a cardboard box with something heavy inside.

I peel back one cardboard flap. Then the other.

For a moment, I just stare at the black face inside and watch the red light blink on and off periodically.

"Is this…?" I begin. But I can't even finish.

Nikki sees it. Her jaw clenches and she slams a fist into the dash covering the control panel.

"Oy! Easy there. Don't damage the merchandise." Gideon does a double-take at our faces and then cranes around in his seat.

"I think this is…" I try again, but get no further than I did the first time.

"That's a bomb," Gideon cries out. "That's a bloody bomb! Let me see it."

The plane dips suddenly as Nikki drops her controls and clambers over the seat.

I'm standing up, about to hand Gideon the box when Nikki starts screaming.

"No, no, no!" she says. "Stop! Don't move!"

She forces the box back flat on the plane floor. After taking a breath and seemingly collecting herself, she slips her hands into the box and turns it gently up on one side to show me the wires running from the back of the plastic casing into the darkness beneath Gideon's seat.

"It's wired to the engine. It must've turned on when the engine turned on, and it will explode when the engine turns off. He knew we would have to land the plane rather than fly over because of the shield. He was counting on us landing the plane within range of her."

"Fucking brilliant engineering," Gideon hisses. Gideon pulls a gun and shoves one end against the side of Nikki's head. "You don't look nearly surprised enough by this. Did you know about the bomb?

Nikki looks down at her lap.

My heart kicks. "Nick?"

But before she even speaks, it all makes sense to me now. Jeremiah's sudden offer to let me go to Antarctica. His suggestion that I shouldn't tell Nikki because she didn't want me to go. His insistence that I go in *his* plane, with *his* crew.

I voice my suspicions aloud. "Jeremiah believes I'm the only one she would lower her shield for. We fly in. She realizes it's me and lowers her shield, and as soon as we park the plane and turn off the engine, the bomb would go off, and that would be the end of it."

Nikki's face is blood red with her fury. "I told him *no* a hundred times."

"He didn't listen," I say simply. I think of their fights. Of Nikki's cold response to him and the quiet fury. I think of his talk of bombs at the international meeting. If they found evidence of a bomb in Antarctica now, he already had a cover, didn't he? He already had a person to pin the explosion on. Any device wouldn't be blamed on Jeremiah now. It would be Jesse who takes the fall.

"How long has he been planning to use me to betray Jesse? Since we came to the base? Since Chicago?" I ask her.

Nikki doesn't have an answer. Gideon shoves his gun against her forehead.

"Tell me why I shouldn't blow your brains all over this seat," he says, seething.

"Gideon!" I hiss.

"I think it's awfully convenient that my plane was disabled and the only other one on the tarmac was this one. All loaded up and ready to go—with a *bomb* on board."

"I didn't know," she says. She's looking at me. "Al, you know I wouldn't have let you get aboard this plane if I thought it had a bomb on it."

"Did you really defy him? Did you really stage a coup at all?" Gideon chides.

"Just let me explain," she begs.

Gideon thumbs off the safety instead.

I reach out and clamp down on his wrist. "Don't! Give her a chance!"

For a second, no one moves or speaks. There is just a lot of heavy breathing and furious, wide-eyed stares.

Nikki breaks the silence with a flood of words. "Yes. Jeremiah proposed that we send you to Antarctica with a bomb on board to try to neutralize Jesse. He first brought this up right after the meeting with the ambassadors."

"I remember the fight."

"Yes, well, I thought he'd dropped it. But then I suspected he hadn't when he cornered you in the medical ward and wanted to speak to you alone."

And that seems true for me too. He'd offered up a plane while we sat in the dimly lit medical bay. So he had planned to send me to Jesse—but with a bomb that would kill us both.

"But then something happened," Nikki says. "He had me running all over the base doing stupid shit. I got your page and confronted him, but he said you were fine, that you were still in the medical bay. He knew I'd go check and by the time I realized you weren't there, he'd already have the base locked down."

"So what happened?"

"I went to the medical bay. I checked Gloria's room because Dr. Gray told me she was awake. But when I got to Gloria, she told me that you'd been taken into custody. Then your distress call made all the sense in the world."

"I don't believe for a moment he would simply let you go," Gideon hisses.

"He didn't. I had to get my soldiers to restrain him long enough for us to get out before the base was sealed. He ranted. He raved. He told me that if I took you off this base and got you to Antarctica, that we'd all be dead."

I frown. "Then why did you do it?"

"Because of what Jackson said. Jackson said not to trust Jeremiah's vision. That he was being manipulated by another angel, Michael, to do whatever it took to keep you on the base, but that keeping you on the base meant we'd all die."

"And you believed her?" I ask.

She nods, the barrel of the gun sliding along her forehead.

"She didn't tell you there was a problem with the plane?" I ask her.

Her lip trembles. "She did. I assumed she meant Gideon's."

Gideon laughs derisively. The gun trembles in his hand. "So it's Jackson we can thank for this little surprise."

"She must've had her reasons," I say.

Gideon finally lowers the gun. "She always has her reasons. Damn her."

All the tension goes out of the plane just like that.

No one speaks for a long time.

"We can't land," I say. "If we land, it will go off."

"How many parachutes are on board?" Gideon asks, sparing a glance at the open sky and correcting course with his left hand

Nikki sucks in a deep breath. "One."

"Again, bloody convenient. I bet it even comes in your size."

Nikki turns the box over in her hand, looking at the wires.

"Can you disable the bomb?" I ask.

"No. If I try, it will explode."

"But it'll also explode when we land," I say.

"Or we run out of gas," she says. "Gideon?"

"I don't need to tell you that we'll be cutting it close, do I?

Even if we turned back now, I don't think we'd get farther than a hundred miles."

And what would be the point of that? I think. Jeremiah knows we won't parachute over the Atlantic for no good reason, with no hope of rescue. Not with that.

I look at the purple light pulsing through the sky, and a horrible sense of foreboding overtakes me. That's Jesse's light. Some way, somehow, that is Jesse's power, radiating in every direction as far as the eye can see.

Gideon's and Nikki's voices escalate until they're shouting over one another.

"Stop it!" I scream. "Both of you stop it! Nikki didn't plant the bomb on this plane. Jeremiah screwed her as much as he screwed us."

"Don't tell me you believe her story, just like that."

"I do."

"What about the parachute?" Gideon hisses. "The *one* parachute?"

It wouldn't have been Jeremiah. Jeremiah knew Nikki too well. He knew she would have to fly the plane. He knew it would be on the ice when it landed. And he knew that even if she discovered the bomb in time, she wouldn't jump without me.

They were told to take them all, Gabriel whispers. His voice is a rainy breeze through my mind. *But one was loyal to her. One left it for her escape.*

"It's more likely that whoever was instructed to inspect the plane, put one here for her." And it's true enough. There isn't a single person under Nick's command that doesn't respect her. She would die for any one of them, and they know it.

"Or Jeremiah himself," Nikki says with a low growl. "That way if I refuse to save myself, it is my own fault, not his. That is how he would see it."

"Charming man," Gideon says. "I'm certainly going to put a bullet through his brain the next time I see him."

Nikki gives him a stony look.

"Oh shut up," Gideon says. "He put you on a plane with a bomb on it. If you still call him a friend, then you're more deluded than I thought, Tamsin."

She doesn't make any retort to this. She only grips the controls harder.

"Just fly the plane," Gideon grumbles. "I want to have a looksee at my executioner."

Gideon clambers over the arm of the chair and crumples onto the floor with the bomb still nestled at my feet. He takes it in his hand as delicately as one might take the queen's china. He tilts it one way, then the other, inspecting the wires that disappear under the seat and that flashing red light.

"Isn't this a beautiful piece of bloody work?" he says with a huff. He sits it down and runs a hand through his hair. And we sit like that, hands on our knees, defeated as the minutes stretch by.

No one speaks for a long time.

We just sit there, each of us lost in our thoughts. Finally, Nikki says, "We're ten minutes away."

She says this gently as one might speak to a restless horse.

"I'm going to fly the plane, and you're going to jump tandem with her," she says.

"No," I say.

"Al. This is happening." A flat, but firm refusal. "And this is better anyway. Jesse might explode the moment she sees me. That's usually how she reacts to seeing me."

"*No*," I say again, pushing aside her joke.

"I'll call for help," she says, accepting that she can't laugh her way out of this. "Maybe someone will reach me in time."

She's saying this to calm me. She doesn't believe it for a second. Her face is a mask of surrender.

"No. We still have eight minutes. We'll think of a better plan."

"The sooner you jump, the more fuel I'll have," she says, simply.

She punches some controls on the plane and it levels out. "At least the autopilot still works."

Gideon picks up the parachute and begins inspecting it. "It's packed well."

The purple light in the sky intensifies suddenly. Nikki scrambles to lower the altitude so that we aren't quite so blinded by its glow. When she does, I see the source of the light at last. It shoots straight up in a beam of light so intense that it is constantly shifting.

"How in god's name are we going to get close enough?" Gideon says.

On foot, Gabriel whispers in my mind.

"On foot," I repeat. "I'll have to walk right up to her."

"You should go now. You'll have a mile," Nikki says. She's squeezing my hand. Gideon is already slipping on his jacket and winter gear. He's throwing things at my feet. A heavy coat. A face mask. Something that looks like goggles. I can barely see them through the tears filling my eyes.

Nikki is forcing me into the coat.

"Nick," I say. My voice breaks.

"I know this isn't your preferred method of exiting an aircraft," she says with a lopsided smile. "But please use the parachute."

She's trying to make a joke.

I catch Gideon's eye, and he turns politely away, busying himself with the chute and the layers of protective clothing that he's putting on his body.

Nikki puts her lips right against my ear and speaks, barely audible over the engine of the plane. "Before we made love the first time, I made you a promise."

My throat tightens so hard, my breath catches.

"I promised I would help you protect Jesse. I promised I would do whatever I needed to do to make sure you didn't lose her again."

Tears spill down my cheeks.

"It looks like I'll be keeping that promise, whether I want to or not."

I pinch my eyes shut against fresh, hot tears. I pull back and search her face. "Make me a new promise. Promise that you're going to call for help the second we jump."

She gives me a sad smile. "As soon as you're clear of the plane, I'm going to drive this as fast as I can make sure it doesn't explode over your heads. Then I'll make the call. I promise."

Our heads. Oh god, she's going to fly off with a bomb on a plane.

"If I fly east, I'll end up back over the station, and there will be more casualties. And who knows what will happen if this plane goes off so close to her. The energy wafting off her might make it explode early, or worse, give it extra power."

She says all of this while putting a harness on over my coat. I hear all the clicks and snaps, but I can't stop looking at her. This is a dream. This is a horrible, terrible dream.

"Two minutes," Gideon says.

Our eyes fall on the horizon.

Nikki nods, acknowledging Gideon. But she doesn't look at him. Her eyes remain fixed on mine. She's soaking me in, memorizing every line of my face.

"There's so much I want to say," she whispers. She laces her hands under my hair and clasps them at the back of my neck. "I had big dreams for us."

She kisses me. Her mouth is hot and feverish on mine. I feel her quivering jaw against mine. She pulls back and stares into my eyes, running one thumb over my cheek and lower lip. All I can think is that the last kiss I'll ever share with Nicole Tamsin must taste like vomit.

I hear the plane door open. Feel it's freezing suction on my back. Gideon's arms slip around my waist.

Nikki takes a deep breath, gives me another sweet, brief kiss, "I'll be rooting for you."

I open my mouth to say something. Tell her I love her. Tell her I appreciate every kindness. Tell her that there is no better soul than her in the world. But before I can speak, I'm pulled from the plane, into the wide, endless sky.

CHAPTER TWENTY-TWO

Jesse

I feel the door open inside me. And it is *the* door. A door I've carried around since I died on the floor of a barn. A door that bridges my present and past and future. A door that connects the intangible of my mind to the tangible world where my heart beats. All I ever dreamed lies on one side of the door. And somehow, by the magic of time and will, it passes through and manifests on the living plane, where billions of souls live out their lives.

I understand that now, with a clarity that I never had before. It was my desire to matter. My desire to be more than someone's play thing that had called Gabriel to me. And I had wanted someone to save me, an angel to swoop in and take it all away. To make the absuse seem small and insignificant. Gabriel gave me all of that and more.

But it has never been his power. Sure, I used their gifts to defeat my father and become the apex. But there is a power that has always been mine, that ability to manifest anything, anything I can dream up, here on this plane.

The power of dreaming.

The power of creation.

And it is through this door—this *gate*—that Michael wants to bring something from the intangible world, from his *when* and *where*, into this time and place.

You can make this better, Michael whispers into my ear as the power pours from my mouth, my hands, my mind. I feel it surge up into the sky. All of me goes limp with it, yet Michael holds me up. It's his arms I'm sagging in. *Don't you want to eliminate the darkness forever?*

Darkness... Dead children. Murdered wives. Cruelty. Pain. Hopelessness. Degradation. Fear. Above all, *fear.* Like a stench in the air, putrefying.

The shift in his voice cools the flame coursing through me.

One minute, I'm looking through the gate. I'm feeling all the power run from that other side, washing me in that unquenchable euphoria. Then there's his cold breath, like teeth in the back of my neck.

He's manipulating you.

Michael's grip tightens on my body, nearly crushing me against him.

He's using your fear to make you believe this is the reality. But it isn't. This is the lens of terror, and you're letting him hold it over your eyes.

I know this voice. I know it from somewhere...

My eyes flutter open and see the monster holding me.

He wears a face I know all too well. Those round, soft cheeks. That smooth jaw. Bright brown eyes that sparkle in the purple light pulsing all around me. Like a tornado's funnel, it shoots up into the sky, myself caught in the eye of its cyclone. We are a foot, maybe two off of the ground.

All that beautiful, blond hair floating in the breeze. That soft, hesitant smile—I'm not fooled. It's the eyes. There is a cold fire in those eyes.

"You're not her," I say. "Show me your real face. Show me who you are."

And it looks like the monster will refuse me. So I start to funnel some of that power into it—

power and my desire to know the truth, to see the world clearly for once. No more encryption. No more lies and manipulations.

In a furious rage, it slams my back into the snow. A hand closing over my throat. The face bleeds from Ally's to Caldwell's.

"I could have made this pleasant for you," Caldwell hisses. His dress shirt is open at the collar. His brown hair falls into his eyes. Veins in his forehead bulge as he squeezes all the air out of me. He's crushing my throat.

The face changes again. The hairline recedes. The jowls fatten and sag. A thin mustache forms over the lip, and when he smiles, one front tooth is blackened and crooked. It's Eddie, staunch potbelly and black shark eyes staring down at me. Sweat stands out on his pockmarked skin. "But if you prefer it the hard way."

Without thinking, I call forth the flames that I've carried in my heart ever since that night in the barn. I burst into fire. Only it isn't just me that burns now. The entire cyclonic funnel of power catches and fire rumbles up its pillar and into the sky.

The sky is burning.

The *whole* world is burning.

My god, what have I done?

CHAPTER TWENTY-THREE

"There, there," Gideon says. "It'll be all right. I'd wager your budding general was always looking for a way to play hero for you. She'll thrive on that dose of chivalry for decades. I'm sure of it."

"She's going to die up there," I scream. Tears stream freely down my face. I try to crane my neck to see the plane, to get a sense of where it has gone and if it's all right. But I can't see above the orange and white chute canopied overhead.

"Ah, give her some credit. Soldiers like that rarely die so easily."

He's trying to reassure me, but it isn't working. My heart aches as badly as my head.

"What the fuck!" Gideon cries. His mouth falls open in horror and surprise.

"What?" I try to turn around and see what he is seeing, but the way my harness is latched to his, I can't quite crane my neck fully in that direction.

"Put your legs together and bend them!" he screams.

"What? What's happening?"

"Hold on!" He wraps one arm around my torso, pinning me to his chest.

I see a wall of fire only a second before it tears through the parachute.

We drop, screaming for ten or twenty feet.

Then Gideon yanks a cord, and another chute explodes from his pack. I bite my tongue when it catches the wind and I'm jerked upward.

"Bless the bloody soul who thought two parachutes were better than one." All the air leaves him in a heavy sigh.

I'd forgotten that chutes are often packed with two should the first fail. But why did ours fail? Why did we pinwheel out of control for those terrifying thirty seconds?

I don't need to ask Gideon. The wind shifts, and I'm turned more directly in Jesse's direction.

I cry out in surprise at the shocking sight.

The sky is on fire. The purple light that was covering the ice shelf and giving it an enchanted look now burns with an orange glow. Flames lick the sky for as far as the eye can see, swirling like a mushroom cloud of destruction in every cardinal direction.

"Nikki!" I scream, squirming against Gideon's chest.

"She will lower the altitude in time," Gideon says, but he isn't even trying to convince me now. No jokes. No playfulness. It sounds like a prayer.

I hear a rumble, and I'm certain that it's the plane exploding, somewhere in the distance.

"Is that an earthquake?" Gideon asks. "It's an earthquake, look."

He points at a mound of ice in the distance. I can't tell if it's an iceberg in the ocean or if it's protruding from the earth itself at this vantage point. But I do see its side crumble and slide off.

"Bend your knees," he reminds me again, and I look down

to see the ice and snow rushing up to greet me. "We will actually hit this time."

We hit hard, and I pitch forward. I'm certain I'm going to hit the ground face first, and that Gideon will grind me into the snow after. But his long legs stumble and catch at the last minute, long before mine, given the difference in our heights. And he has the buckles of the parachute undone before we can be pulled down with it.

Two snaps of my harness and my dangling boots hit the earth.

He takes a moment to adjust the face mask, coat, and gloves protecting his skin. I do the same, searching for the cold that's seeping into the collar. It takes a minute, but I manage to seal the air out again.

"You'll warm up when we start walking. We have about a kilometer. Maybe less."

We start marching toward the light, toward that center plume of blazing fire. But the ground shakes under our feet, and the march is slow going. But what else can we do? I will walk to Jesse if I have to. I didn't come all this way to turn back now.

"Which snow queen do I have to seduce to get a snowmobile?" Gideon asks, groaning beside me. "I hate walking in snow."

"Careful," I tell him. "Our legs might freeze and fall off. Then you won't be walking at all."

I can't decide what I'm supposed to be looking at. The sky...? Searching every ripple of flame for a hint of a plane. For wreckage raining down into the distant ocean.

"Excellent point, love." Gideon catches me searching the sky. "You can't see Tamsin from here. Not with all this fire in the sky."

I force a strained smile. "True." But even as my anxiety for Nikki rises, and I hope against hope that she will survive, I keep looking toward the fiery plume. Toward Jesse.

Is that Jesse?

How in the world can Jesse be standing in the center of a blazing spire? Inside her shield?

Gideon is still watching me with that even gaze—or at least I think it is. It's hard to identify his exact line of sight beneath those large black goggles.

"What is the plan, darling?" he asks. "Are we simply going to walk up and say, 'All right now. You've had your fun. Time to stop destroying the world.'"

I snort. But it's tight and strained. There's no humor in it at all. The silence stretches between us.

"No, really," he says at last. "What do you intend to do once you get there?"

I have nothing to tell him but the truth. "Talk to her, I suppose."

He stops walking. "Talk to her. You *suppose*?"

I turn and face him. "What else can I do?"

"I don't know. Have you considered putting her in a sleeper hold?"

"Do you think she's going to *let* me put her in a sleeper hold, Gideon?"

He starts walking again. Snow and ice crunch under his boots like muffled Styrofoam.

His silence only expands all of my fears. I don't know what to say to Jesse. Gloria and Maisie both warned me that she might be out of her mind. And it isn't like I didn't have time to prepare for this. Months ago, Caldwell had trapped Jesse in the church with no windows or doors. And when she had a chance to kill Caldwell and take all of his power then, I had stopped her. I stopped her because I understood that when the power overtook her, the woman I loved might cease to be the woman I love at all.

It was more than that, my mind tsks. Haven't I been afraid of madness even before that? Back when Jesse was death replacing and every death meant one more step toward this fate? Okay, not a fiery plume in the middle of a tundra, true, but madness. Yes. Jesse was always afraid of madness. And so was I—because it was another way of losing her.

But how does one prepare for the inevitable? I might have always known this moment was coming, but even as I walk toward it, I don't feel prepared.

I have no right to ask you, Gloria had said. *You will die if you go. You will die.*

And I suppose if I have no better plan than to walk into the flames for her, then yes, I will die. But I don't want to die a pointless death. Would I die for Jesse? Without question. But dying just for death's sake? I need to do better than that.

"What would you do?" I ask Gideon.

He turns toward me. He yanks down the black mask covering the lower half of his face. "What would I do for what?"

"If it was Rachel in there. If Rachel was in the center of that fire, and you needed to convince her not to destroy the world, what would you say?"

He considers me a moment, his eyes hidden behind those dark glasses. I expect some joke, perhaps roguish flirting. But he surprises me with his seriousness.

"Well, we'd be fucked, wouldn't we? Rachel didn't give a damn for anything I said."

"But you'd try."

"Of course I'd bloody try. My behavior may suggest otherwise, but I don't actually *want* to perish in flames, Alice."

"So what would you say, if you were trying to convince her not to kill us all."

"Rachel and Jesse aren't the same person."

But even as he says it, both he and I know better. "Close enough."

Silence continues stretching between us as we walk. The fire grows brighter and brighter as we advance. I don't even know if I'll be able to see once I get much closer—*if* I can get that close.

"I would tell her that she gave everything in the room color," Gideon says finally. I can barely hear him over the crunching snow and the howling wind. "That seeing her face was like looking upon a Matisse that no one had ever seen. I would tell her that she was the greatest thrill I ever had. She terrified me, my every waking moment, but I loved—I'd tell her I—well, I'd tell her everything that I wish I'd told her."

My chest aches from the labor of walking in this climate, and the devastating heartache in Gideon's melodious voice.

"If we're all going to die anyway, I'd want to die knowing I said everything I wanted to," I say.

"Well, here's your chance," he replies. "What's that?"

He points at the horizon, and at first, I don't see anything. But after a few more steps, I see the black smudge on the ground. The outline of a body. My heart pounds.

We run, or *try* to run. When we reach him, Gideon turns him over and lifts his mask.

I recognize him immediately. "Lane?"

"Who?"

"Lane. Lane Handel." When he peers at me questioningly, I add, "Long story."

He bends an ear to Lane's mouth. "His breathing is shallow. If we don't get him out of here, I don't think he'll make it."

He turns Lane on his side, and we see the rod sticking out of his back. It looks like a piece of flying shrapnel got him on his lower left side.

"You'll have to take him to the base," I say. "Can you carry him?"

"Yes, but what about you?"

Hurry, Gabriel whispers. *We are almost out of time.*

I turn toward the fire and see the shimmering shape of a man, liquid heat rolling off him.

"I have to keep going." I give Gideon my bravest smile. Immense gratitude swells in my chest. "Thank you for seeing me this far, Gideon."

"You've got guts of steel, love. You're an amazing woman."

I laugh, surprised.

This seems to delight him. Then, with a nod. He stands, hefting Lane up onto his shoulders as if he is only a child. I never realized he was so strong. He positions him with his back to the sky as to not disturb the rod.

"Godspeed, Alice," he says, giving me a final smile. "Good luck."

"Good luck to you too. I hope you get your friend's plane back. But I hear Tripoli is nice this time of year."

He laughs. A low, melodious sound.

Sadness hangs between us for a moment, then he turns and walks away without another word.

I watch them head toward the station until their figures grow small. When I feel another nudge against the wall of my mind, I know Gabriel is urging me on.

It's time to go.

Without another thought, I march into the firestorm.

CHAPTER TWENTY-FOUR

Jesse

I'm on the beach. To my right is the A-frame house, flames dancing in its dark windows. On my left is the ocean, the storm so torrential that waves slam against the shore. The surf washes all the way up the back of my calves with each splash. And I have the clear sense that the water is rising. The tide is coming in.

Michael stands in front of me, his smile wide and defiant. Behind him, a hundred angels stand at the ready.

"You've made the way for me," he says with a wolfish grin. "Now you need only let me pass."

At first, I'm not sure where he wants to *pass* to. I cast one nervous glance over my shoulder and see it. A bright, shimmering door has appeared on the sand about ten feet behind me. It's more like a vortex of light than an actual door. At least five feet high, three feet wide, it sparkles like a star in the night sky.

I understand what I'm looking at. It's the bridge between Earth and this in-between place. Somehow, I've opened it, or it opened itself, and now Michael and his army intend to go through me and seize control of my time and place.

"Surrender, and I'll make sure you do not suffer."

I snort. "Promises, promises. Besides, you're too late for that. I've already suffered plenty."

He takes a step toward me.

We are coming, Gabriel whispers. I can feel him and his scent of rain. *Hold on.*

I need to buy time. "Did I tell you about the time my dog ate my finger while I was dead, and then I had to wait until he pooped it out so we could sew it back on?"

Michael stops advancing, a look of puzzlement on his face. Or maybe that's disgust.

"I'm just saying, if you were trying to save me some trouble, you should've come around *years* ago."

"You will let me pass," Michael says.

"I *won't*," I say.

He hurls one of his shafts of light. If I had stayed where I was, it would have run me through, splitting my chest wide open. But at the last moment, I duck and roll and come up gasping and sputtering in the surf. Salt water stings my eyes.

For a dreamscape, this place is awfully real.

Your power makes it real.

I shift my body so that I'm standing between the sparkling vortex and the advancing angel army again. But I'm closer now. He's overtaking the beach.

Michael grins, realizing his advantage, and throws another bolt.

I keep backing up, throwing death ribbons, which he deflects.

I try to call up the sea and drown him with it. He jumps over the waves as if they're nothing at all.

I try to use Rachel's telekinesis to push the angels back. This works for a moment, their limbs going stiff at their sides, but then they break free of this.

I cast light, fire, and even try to rumble the earth.

Michael parries each blow effortlessly.

As a last ditch effort, I reach into his mind with mine and try to stop him in his tracks. My father did this to countless men and women, controlling them from within.

He reached right into their heads and seized control of their bodies.

Michael screams furiously and buries a shaft of light through my shoulder. He pins my body against the sand, driving it right through me. Hot blood—my blood—pours out of the wound onto the sand, and a crashing waves sucks it greedily out to sea.

Another wave pounds my face and neck. I choke and sputter. When water washes into the open wound, I howl, writhing against the pain.

But I can't move. I can't get up.

And I'm so close to the vortex now. The light sparkles in my eyes, leaving dancing dots in its wake.

"Stop resisting. Let me pass, and all the pain will vanish. You'll have the satisfaction of knowing that I've cleansed the world for you. I will make it into a paradise. An absolute paradise better than you can imagine."

The pain twists my mind. I'm trying to pull myself together, but I can't focus on anything but my throbbing, burning shoulder.

He leans over me, adding weight to the blade. I'm screaming. I'm screaming until I taste blood in the back of my throat. Another wave of ocean water slams into my face, setting my shoulder on fire and choking me. I open my mouth to cough and suck in more freezing, salty water.

I'm drowning. And I'm bleeding to death on this beach. I can tell by the way my mind is going fuzzy around the edges that it is only a matter of time before I lose complete consciousness.

Then what will happen? What happens if I die in my own mind? I can only assume the worst.

The water recedes, and I suck in a desperate, ragged breath. A fresh bout of coughing ripples through me, and my shoulder tears more.

That's me screaming, I think. That horrible, horrible sound—that's me screaming.

"Jesse!"

I try to stop howling long enough to breathe. I just need to get some air into my lungs. But my limbs are so heavy that I can do little more than float in the surf.

"Jesse!"

I try to turn my head to see who is calling my name. I know that voice. It's so far away, like a voice carried on a wind through an open summer field, but I know it.

"Jesse, can you hear me! It's me, Ally. Oh, Jess. Look at me. Please!"

For an instant, I see her. A glowing face against a back drop of fire. A purple shield shimmers around her, warring with the flames for the same space.

I see those beautiful brown eyes and those glistening tears.

The world comes into sharp focus.

Despite the pain and unforgiving force of the waves trying to suck me out to sea, for one lightning-fast instant, I know who I am and where I am.

When I blink and find myself on the beach again, Michael's eyes are wide and fearful, but his lips are pulled back in a hissing grimace.

"You will give me back my power!"

He doesn't mean the blade of light in my shoulder. He means the power Gabriel stole from him, the power I'm using to protect Earth now.

"You want your power back?" I latch onto the shaft of

light, preventing him from withdrawing it. Before he can think to let go and run, I unleash all of my fury on him. "Take it."

Great waves of light and fire erupt from me. Not just death ribbons or that all-consuming smoke. Not just piercing electricity, or endless light. Not just fire and motion.

Power. Raw, relentless power blasts through me like an atomic bomb. It knocks the waves back with its force. Michael is thrown off his feet. His blade of light is cast into the water and disappears under a rolling, black wave. The angels evaporate into ash, nothing more than tumbling soot on the sand until the next crashing wave overtakes it.

I'm alone on the beach at last, my legs and arms shaking.

Then there's Gabriel.

He appears on the shore, looking windswept and beaten. He's bloody. His clothes shredded and skin slashed. That's what kept the angels busy, I realize. A hundred against one.

But here he is—victorious—standing in the same thigh-deep waves as me, his wing tips trailing the surf. His eyes bright and the color of midnight waters.

"You cast them out," he says. It sounds like praise.

"Jesse!" Ally screams. "For god's sake answer me!"

I turn toward the swirling light vortex, sparkling like infinity. The waves are so high now. They're lapping at the bottom of the house steps. And I think if I wait any longer, they will overtake the house completely.

"Seal the gate," Gabriel calls over the roar. He gestures to that beckoning star. He makes me follow him to its edge until most of his face is lost in its brilliance. I think he's going to pass through it and leave me here. But he pauses halfway through and offers me his hand. He waits for me to take it.

"It's not over?" I ask, and as soon as I say it, I realize what a stupid question it is.

Of course, it's not over.

I place my wet, shaking hand in his.

I take a deep breath, and he pulls me through.

CHAPTER TWENTY-FIVE

Ally

She's dead. I'm too late, and now she's dead. Her body is limp in my arms.

"Jesse!" I scream for what seems like the thousandth time. "Damn it, Jesse, answer me!"

Her eyes flutter.

Without considering what I'm doing, I want to take her into my arms and shake her until all this manic energy leaves me. I go to plant a thousand kisses on her cheeks and lips and hair.

But I can't. I can't get close enough to really touch her.

The shield keeps a minimal barrier between us, which I realize is for my benefit not hers, because that endless, flaming power hasn't stopped pouring from her. We are in the eye of the storm, but the world still burns.

She seems immune, the flames standing about three inches off her own body. But if this shield should fail suddenly, I imagine I'll burn away like grease in a pan. That's what happened to the mask I tore off my face. The winter gear that I shrugged off once I reached her had melted the instant I threw them away. All that's left of them is a bubbling smudge on the ice.

She pulls herself up to a sitting position, her hands traveling over her body as if she can't quite be sure she is really here.

She looks at me as if she's never seen me before. My stomach drops.

"It's me," I say, my throat tight.

"I know who you are."

"I came to get you." I feel so stupid saying this, but I'm immensely relieved. More relieved than I should be, trapped in a ring of fire. "Obviously."

"You shouldn't be here!"

"I had to come anyway."

"You're crazy!"

"You're one to talk." I gesture at the chaos enveloping us. "Can you turn this off?"

She looks around, her eyes reflecting all the dancing firelight.

"I know what this is…" she says. Her jaw sets.

"Great, then turn it off."

"I can't. I have to die to do that. This is a swirling vortex between the planes. This…" She gestures around herself. "This is like the giant death drain I see during a replacement."

I wish you could see it, she's said to me countless times.

Be careful what you wish for.

"There's only one way to close it. I have to die. This is one big replacement, and I have to die."

"Then die," I say. "Die, and I'll be here when you wake up."

There will be no returning from this, Gabriel says. He stands as a watery figure among the flames. In the firelight, he looks more like a demon than an angel. But considering where we've arrived, maybe he's been a demon all along.

I stare at him, trying to process what I am hearing—my worst fear.

"Take her away! Take her far away, and then I'll close it," Jesse screams. She's looking at Gabriel's vaporous form.

In order to seal the gate, all *of you must pass through*, Gabriel says. And there is some tenderness in his voice that causes me to search Jesse's face. Something passes between them.

"This is what he meant by sacrificing my heart?" She spits the words out.

Tears stream down her face.

"Gabriel, I can't kill her! You can't ask me to kill her."

She is part of you.

"No! I mean, yes, she is, but no! She's not going to die here!"

I see her rising panic, watch the flames whip around her, the vortex spiraling wildly.

She's going to lose control, I realize. She's going to destroy the world out of fear.

"Fuck you, Gabriel! Fuck you! You knew all along! You knew this would kill her! Every time you told me that I could protect her, you were lying to me!"

The power begins pulsing, throbbing like a heartbeat. The crack in the earth deepens. I have to calm her before she loses any more control.

"Jesse, look at me." I try to turn her head to look at me, but the shield won't let me. "Jesse, please!"

"Why aren't you pissed?" she screams over the pulsing flames. Fire dances in her eyes. "He led you here to die!"

"I came because I wanted to be here."

"Bullshit!"

I flinch, and for some reason this makes her crumple more than anything.

"I came because there is nowhere else I want to be. Do you think I can bear to lose you again?"

She clasps her hands at the back of her neck and screams.

I try to ignore this even as the ice under my feet shifts again—or is that the earth trembling? "What kind of life do you think I'll have without you?"

"A long one!"

"No," I say with certainty. "I've been in a world without you. I don't want that. Asking me to live without you is far crueler than ending my life and saving billions of people. And if we have to go through some vortex, death drain, whatever, in order to save our world, then I'm coming with you. I'm coming with you to the other side."

She screams. "There is no other side! When I die, there's nothing!"

"Then there's death," I tell her. "Then we die. Together. Because you're not leaving me here."

Tears spill over my cheeks.

"You're not leaving me here again."

Her face crumples. She covers her face with her hands.

Gideon's words come back to me. *I'd tell her...*

The words start pouring out of me. "I've been in love with you since I was fifteen, Jesse Sullivan. I love every smile, every smirk, every sarcastic eye roll that's ever graced your beautiful face. I love looking across the kitchen table and seeing you there. I love your laugh. I love the way my stomach twists up every time I hear it. I love the way I feel when you kiss me. When you wrap your arms around my neck, and look into my eyes..."

"Stop it," she begs, jaw working.

I take a ragged breath, my throat so tight I can barely breathe.

"The whole world stops. I love every kiss, every time you've put your hand in mine."

"That's enough!"

She looks ready to attack me, but I don't stop. "Every time you stood up for me and defended me... Waking up beside you. I love the way you feel in my arms when I curl into your back, when I kiss your neck..."

Tears stream down her face. "Please. Just—please."

I don't let her pull away from me. "I love listening to your breath as we lay together in the dark."

"Shut up, or I'll make you shut up!"

"Even when you're an asshole, I love you!" I scream at her. "So if you think you're going to leave this planet without me, you're out of your damn mind!"

"If you're going to die," she says, looking over the rim of her hands. "They'll all die."

Her eyes burn with her hate.

"There's nothing worth saving. You're the only good thing in this world," she says and the dark and hungry power in her eyes terrifies me. "If you're going to die, then let them burn."

"No. There are good people here. They deserve their chance."

"Why? Because you got yours? Because here we are with *our* happily ever after? There is no happily ever after for us."

I think of that silly book that Jesse loved when we were kids. The one resting on Maisie's bed a million miles away. I want her to live. I want her to read that book and go to school and live with Gloria.

"Do you remember *The Way Home*?" I ask.

She blinks back angry tears that shimmer in the firelight.

"Picture the beach house."

"How did you—"

"Picture the quiet, perfect beach. An island in the middle of a sea. The two of us on the back deck drinking iced tea with lemon. Picture Maisie and Winston and Gloria, happy and alive. Better than alive. *Thriving*. Picture Maisie in school. Picture Maisie with her friends. Picture Gideon in some posh palace, stuffing jewels in his pockets and charming the pants off some heiress."

Nikki... I picture her smiling face. Her laugh. I can't bring myself to ask Jesse to picture good things for her, but I'll do it for her. I'll imagine the perfect woman. One that will love her as fiercely as I love Jesse.

"I can't hold on any longer!" Jesse cries, her back bowing.

"Do you see them?" I ask her, trying to keep the calm in my voice despite my galloping heart, despite the fear strangling me. I inch closer to her. "Do you see the house and the ocean? Do you see the people we love? Picture them happy. Picture them safe..."

She's screaming, head thrown back, mouth open. Her body begins to lift off the ground. I wrap my arms around her. I still can't touch her because of the shield, but I clasp my hands behind her back.

"They're happy, Jesse," I say, feeling my lip tremble. "They'll have long and happy lives because of you. Do you see it?"

Firelight glimmers on her tear-stained cheeks.

Now! Gabriel commands, and without thinking, I tighten my hold on her.

The shield is gone. The purple light vanishes.

I expect fire, immense and terrible pain.

Instead, I feel cold black water rush up to greet us. We hit the surface hard, and all the air leaves me.

We are sinking through an inky black. I clutch Jesse, limp in my arms. She starts to slip away from me. I hold on harder.

I don't care if this black, salty ocean, these eternal, night-time waters, swallow me whole.

I give myself completely to the waiting darkness, but I refuse to let her go.

EPILOGUE

Nashville, Six Months After

Gloria sits back in her metal folding chair and pinches the bridge of her nose. Given only darkness, her eyes begin to search every time, every place. What emerges from the darkness first: sand, very close and textured. Only hues of black and white and gray until the color shifts forward. The view widens. Sand becomes a beach. A beach becomes a shoreline. A shore gives to rolling, gentle waves, pink with the approaching dawn. And the dawn itself, blinking awake over the horizon.

At last, the sound, felt first in her chest as a vibration, then as pressure in her mind, until she realizes what she is hearing.

A laugh.

Brinkley's laugh, the sight of his leather jacket turning toward her. It's been too long since she's heard that rich vibrato. Tears spring to the corners of her eyes unbidden.

She expects the vision to falter then, fade to black.

Why shouldn't her gift diminish now that the war against

Caldwell and the angels is over? What other purpose could she possibly have now that the danger has passed?

Why should you be the last one standing? Her bitter heart asks.

But six months have passed since Jesse cast her shield around the earth, giving them a new lease on life, and Gloria's gift hasn't diminished at all. In fact, some mornings she wakes with visions so clear in her mind that she can't be sure she's ever had such clarity.

Maybe this is what her gift is really like, now that there aren't angels around turning her head this way or that. Now that she doesn't have a target that narrows her vision and blinds her to possibility, perhaps she will finally experience it, her power in all of its intended glory.

Gloria lifts her hand, feeling the pencil roll between her tender knuckles. These tiny, wooden ridges are enough to make her finger bones ache. Yet she presses the lead to a page she can't see, perhaps only imagining the first brush of graphite dust falling onto the cream-colored page.

She doesn't *need* to see her hand, the paper, or the pencil. She need only concentrate on Brinkley's laugh, on the sound of his boots shifting in the sand, and follow its beckoning into the dark.

She never knows how long she is gone when she *views*. And this time is no different.

As with all previous attempts to see around the corners of time and space, she must first enter the darkness. She lets it wash over her like a cold, black wave until everything freezes around her and she finds herself suspended. A water droplet hanging in mid-air between faucet and basin.

That momentary pause of deafening eternity is the extent of her experience.

Then she returns. The droplet hits the basin, and she swims to the surface of consciousness.

Feeling finds her limbs first. Gathered heat begins to leave her, and she trembles. Falling adrenaline, chattering teeth, sweeping cold, and tight muscles. All of this serves as confirmation that she has returned to her time, her place, and to the body that holds her.

The weight of her settles into the chair. *I'm depressurizing,* she thinks. *Too fast now and I'll get the bends.*

She sits in her metal chair and listens. A lawnmower runs outside. A car horn blats further down the block. Children are laughing, screaming, but not in the way they sometimes scream in her dreams.

Basement pipes gurgle overhead, babbling their watery speech over metal teeth.

When she feels she can bear it, she opens her eyes.

The long work table in front of her shifts into view, the blurred double vision recombining, settling into a single shape. The overhead bulb gives the three sheets of paper a buttery hue. The lead shines like silver dust in its beams.

She's completed three sketches, she realizes, with the corrugated remains of a jagged edge along each side.

She leans forward to better inspect her handiwork. Her whole body responds to the movement. Her tight muscles groan. Sharp pains radiate through her chest and pelvis. The muscles along her spine clench and loosen, only to clench again. She hisses through her teeth.

It took fourteen surgeries to make her whole again. Over a hundred screws and pins hold her shattered bones in place. She has five months of physical therapy behind her, and perhaps five years ahead.

She drops the pencil, and it rattles onto the tabletop. It rolls off the edge and clatters to the floor. A high, musical sound.

She decides to pull the sketches to her, instead.

One is of Jeremiah Tate—or what is left of him. He's face up in the drawing, eyes staring at empty space somewhere over the viewer's right shoulder. His teeth showing between parted lips.

A single bullet hole sits in the middle of his forehead, a pool of blood runs from the back of his head, spreading on what looks like black and white checkered tiles.

His glasses sit askew on the bridge of his nose. Gloria taps a finger against the collar of his white dress shirt and it smudges. If she closes her eyes, she can see the blood soaking into those white fibers.

Upon seeing the drawing more closely comes the last piece of Gloria's gift.

The knowing.

Seeing him rendered in her own hand gives her that. She knows that it's Gideon who makes the final killing blow, using a Barrett M82 from a Chicago high rise blocks away. But she also knows Gideon is only granted this revenge because Tamsin couldn't follow through.

Gloria didn't draw it. So she can't be sure.

But she sees Tamsin there, standing like an Amazonian, laying her accusations of betrayal against her former boss. Sees...Tamsin press the barrel of her own gun to his forehead, maybe even to the same spot where Gideon's bullet found home. But she didn't pull the trigger.

She punched him in the nose instead. It broke. But there is no sign of that here. No swelling of the nose or bruising beneath the eyes. So Gideon's assassination will come at least two or three weeks after Tamsin's assault.

So many little clues, she thinks, her eyes flitting along the page.

The second drawing is Maisie—not Maisie, *Maya*, she reminds herself. Maya Jackson. A foster kid from Chicago, adopted this summer by retired Captain Gloria Jackson. Hair and eyebrows dyed black, making those baby blues stand out like a frozen pond in winter. Maya kneeling at a grave marker in Mt. Olivet's cemetery. Placing flowers on two headstones, while Gloria herself places flowers on a third.

Jesse Sullivan. Alice Gallagher.

The single slab of stone bears their names. But it's a symbolic marker, meant to comfort the living rather than enshrine the dead. There was nothing to bury. They found the destroyed helicopters and bodies—but no trace of either woman.

Nearly every agency of authority searched the frozen continent for evidence. They found remains of the soldiers that Jesse left in her wake. But no trace of either woman was recovered. No remnants of their clothing. No DNA on a scrap of cloth or blood or hair. There was nothing. Absolutely nothing.

It's as if they were never there at all.

Lane was found at the research facility, but despite being questioned by the authorities, he couldn't provide any information about what happened leading up to the event. Either stubborn willfulness, loyalty to Jesse's memory, or his head injury made that account impossible. Or so he says.

In this second drawing, to the left of the stone marker holding their place in this world, sits Brinkley's tombstone.

She hears that laugh again and the sound of ice hitting a glass.

I'll visit soon, she promises and moves the sketch aside.

And the third picture...

The backdoor slams and the overhead bulb swings wildly, casting the images in and out of whirling darkness.

Sneakers squeak across linoleum. They're followed by the scurry-click of nails.

"Gloria?" a girl calls out.

A dog's snout inserts itself beneath the crack of the door at the top of the basement stairs and sniffs. A snort and sneeze follow. The girl mumbles something in her high-pitched I'm-speaking-to-a-dog voice and then the basement door swings open.

"Gloria? Are you down there?" Maisie calls out.

"Yes," Gloria says, unable to keep the hint of a smile out of her voice. She manages a half turn in her rickety metal seat with the help of her cane.

Feet pound the battered wooden steps.

Then Maisie—Maya—is standing before her, grass stuck to her cheek, a thin sheen of sweat shining across her brow. Her black hair in a messy bun on the topmost part of her head.

"I got the front and back done," Maisie says. "I was wondering if you have a weed eater or one of those trim-y things." She makes a motion with her hand and a sound with her pursed lips that can be mistaken for a machine gun. Gloria does have an Ultimax 100 upstairs, under the floorboards of her bedroom, but she is certain that would not count as a *trim-y thing*.

"The weed eater and hedge trimmer are in the garage," Gloria says. But she also thinks they are likely so old they might not start at all. While her guns are always ready for use, the same cannot be said of her lawn care equipment. "Don't you have something better to do with your Sunday? Don't kids go to the movies or something?"

She's told Maisie this no less than five times today. But she couldn't deny that the girl seemed to actually enjoy herself. For the five months she's lived here, she's cooked, cleaned, and completed the yard work with enthusiasm. She seems as happy in the grocery store as she is in the mall.

Gloria has no experience with teenaged girls, so she is not entirely sure if this qualifies as normal behavior.

She redecorated the spare room upstairs, and at least that is recognizably the epitome of *teen girl*, complete with an unmade bed, clothes on the floor, and a stereo that plays a tad too loudly.

Gloria wouldn't have it any other way.

"Are you kidding?" Maisie snorts. "I've been waiting my whole life for someone to trust me with power tools."

"Maisie," Gloria says. But she feels so tired suddenly. Her head swims. The darkness presses in on the side of her vision, tunneling it. *Maya*, she thinks. *I've really got to start calling her Maya. Even when we're alone.*

All strength leaves her body. She feels herself slump, hears Maisie's frantic cry. There are more pounding footsteps, rattling stairs, a dog yips, but it all sounds so far away. Like Gloria is hearing this commotion at the end of a long hallway. Just on the other side of a closed door. All she can do is swim in that infinite darkness—that warm place where anything and everything exists in the same moment, where anything could rise to the surface of that inky black and become the *now*.

Something cold hits her teeth.

Someone is begging her to drink.

She obeys, opening her lips on reflex. She inhales and coughs. Something cracks against the floor and skitters into the dark.

Ice. Ice in Coke.

Gloria gets her eyes open again at last and sees the girl near tears.

"I'm sorry," Maisie says. She steps back, still holding the plastic tumbler full of soda. "I didn't realize you were drawing. I wouldn't have talked your ears off like that."

Gloria licks the soda off her lips and reaches for the tumbler. "It's okay."

Maisie hands it over with a frown.

I've scared her, Gloria thinks. *I'll have to try harder not to do that after everything she's been through. This child has had enough scares to fill a lifetime.*

"I'm so stupid. I mean, of course you were drawing. No one just sits down here in a dark, deep, basement for fun, you know? I'm so sorry."

Gloria's face cools with each swallow.

"Don't apologize. I've lived with this a long time," Gloria tells the girl, forcing a smile she doesn't feel. "You can't take any of it personally."

"It was still really stupid," Maisie says. "And now you've also got all this." Maisie sweeps a hand over Gloria's body, pausing longer at the cane.

All this.

A broken body to go with my broken mind.

Maisie stoops and grabs up the fallen cane, tilting the black polished wood toward her. It looks golden in the overhead light, the wood shining.

"Should I drive you to the ER?" she asks. And she could do it.

In just four weeks, she'll be eligible to trade in her learner's permit for a full license.

"No, I just need a minute," Gloria tells her, voice tight. She feels the sweat roll down her temple and under her chin.

Her gaze slides down the black cane to the sketches that've fallen on the floor.

Gloria thinks she must've knocked them off the table when she slumped. And not just the three fresh ones, but the whole book. When its spine hit the concrete, it must've vomited its contents on the cold floor.

Maisie follows her gaze. "Oh, I'll get them."

She bends down to gather up the drawings at once. She peels back the top flat and sweeps the pictures into the book with her other hand.

Gloria realizes she's still talking. "I was thinking after I finish up the yard and take a shower, I'll make lunch."

"You have school tomorrow. I'm sure you can think of better things to do with your last summer Sunday. Do you want to drive to school tomorrow? We can use my handicap sticker to get a good spot."

Maisie pauses. "Actually, Gideon texted me to say that he wants to take me to school. He wants to see us before he goes to Europe. He says it'll probably be a long time before we see him again."

Not long enough.

"I told him he could. Is that okay?" Maisie asks.

Gloria can only shrug. "What time is he supposed to arrive?"

Maisie doesn't answer. She's still hunkered on the floor, staring at one of the sketches.

Slowly, she stands and turns a picture toward Gloria. Gloria's eye only glances at the page before she meets those bright, blue eyes again.

"Promise me this isn't going to happen," Maisie says, her girlish voice tight with anger.

"I drew that months ago. Almost a year. Before I had you."

"Promise me." Maisie shakes the picture at her.

Gloria is forced to consider the drawing again, the only drawing she's ever done where she herself was the subject. She sits at this very table, in this very basement. Only it isn't drawings that litter the tabletop. It's her blood and brains. A smoking gun lays on the concrete floor, inches from her open hand.

Gloria thought that would be her ending for a long time. After all, what else was left for her?

Ever since Caldwell walked into their lives eleven years ago, she didn't think she would survive.

But then her brother died, and she didn't. Her best friend died, and she didn't. And so many others were dead—and she wasn't.

She hunted Caldwell, and he was dead. But so was almost everyone she loved.

After that much heartache, all she wanted was peace.

Maisie kneels down and places one hand on Gloria's knee. "I know you're in a lot of pain, and I know you lost a lot of people you love, but I did, too."

Her lip trembles.

"And I know that all that FBRD stuff has probably got you worried about work or having enough money…"

Gloria recalls the way Maisie looked three months prior, sitting at her little folding card table in her yellow kitchen. They'd ordered pizza, which Maisie had covered in parmesan and red pepper flakes, and they ate mostly in silence while a news program played on the television in the other room.

Following the administration's order to immediately dismantle the FBRD and permanently terminate all aspects of the death replacement industry, affected providers have been given notice. "Those with pending replacements will be allowed to complete the service they have paid for," Lieutenant Harris Baldwin told a NWRTV reporter. "But no future screenings will be offered going forward."

Due to this announcement, major upheaval has been seen in the medical, emergency, and law enforcement fields who were most closely linked to the death replacement industry.

"It will be an adjustment for all of us," Vice President Franklin Murphy says during the official news conference this week. "But it will be better in the long run. We cannot continue to publicly endorse a system that recruits and emboldens terrorists."

When asked what the nearly half a million active death replacement agents and thousands of A.M.Ps. were expected to do for work upon the termination of the program, Baldwin says, "They'll be free to pursue whatever occupation or course of study they desire—just like the rest of us."

That was the story. Jesse became an unstable terrorist due to the number of deaths that she had endured. Continuing to ask other death replacement agents to inflict damage on their minds was the same as creating and releasing mentally unstable individuals into the general population.

We exploited their abilities, the Massachusetts Governor had said. *And here is the retribution.*

"Everything's breaking apart," Maisie had said to that.

And Gloria had known what she was referring to. The Church also released a statement earlier in the summer, not long after the death of Caldwell and his wife Georgia—Maisie's parents, Gloria reminded herself—that the North American branch and their three worldwide partners were considering a sharp redistribution of power now that their leader was gone.

"It might be better for all of us if we look ahead, rather than behind, as we forge our future," a solemn man had said to the camera. He was meant to serve as Caldwell's replacement, but one look at the squat, balding man had put Gloria's mind at ease. Those two could not be more different.

Gloria had expected this. Without Caldwell there to control their minds, the Church was free to forge its own path. Gloria always suspected that Caldwell was behind the unification of The Church. He likely used it as a means to further his own power, and without him, it would dissolve.

Financially, Gloria's life remained uncertain.

She could live on what she'd saved. She would never be rich. But she was far from starving.

"People kill themselves over money all the time, but you don't have to worry about that. There's my money," Maisie says hastily.

Gloria clucks her tongue. "Don't you dare bring that up again."

They'd already fought over it twice. The portion of Maisie's funds which she was able to acquire with Eli's help was a fortune by any standard. But it was only a fraction of the Caldwell estate.

Just as well. Less of a paper trail should someone come looking.

"I'm just saying, if it's about the money—"

How did Gloria explain to a child, a seventeen-year-old child, that it wasn't money or pain or grief or loss that made her consider her own death in that way. It was just about being done. *Finished.*

She had a job, and she finished it.

"You're all I've got left," Maisie says. "You and Winnie Pug. So don't you dare quit on me!"

She considers the girl's face for a long time. She thinks, I have a new job now. Or perhaps it isn't even a new job, but a mere extension of her original quest.

Eleven years ago a little girl went missing, and Gloria searched for her. And searched and searched, because all she wanted was to make sure that little girl was safe.

Here she is. She isn't little anymore. But she is here, and Gloria can do what she can to keep her safe—for as long as she's is able.

Gloria places one hand on the girl's head and smiles. She plucks a blade of grass from her cheek. "I won't quit on you."

"Promise?"

"Promise." She sets the Coca-Cola tumbler down on the tabletop.

"I remember you, you know," Maisie says quietly. "The nice lady who fed me strawberries and let me watch *Wheel of Fortune.* You have the same afghan. And you smell the same. Like Coca-cola and lemon drops."

Caldwell had used her affection for the girl only twice. Apparently, his own enemies had gotten too close, or Georgia perhaps was too unstable. But either way, he'd delivered his daughter to her in the dead of night, swaddled in a cotton blanket, clutching a stuffed cow. And Gloria had simply taken her.

"Do you remember?" Maisie asks, those blue eyes searching hers.

"I remember."

She doesn't say all that she could. About how she hasn't ever quit looking for her. Since that day Caldwell—Eric Sullivan—took her from her adoptive parents...she's never quit looking. That there is a box of sketches, perhaps a hundred deep, under her bed right this instant, in a box marked *M*. Evidence of all the years she searched and searched for this child. And here she is. All grown up *and pretty as a peach* as her mother would say.

A new job, indeed.

Maisie kisses the back of Gloria's hand and sighs. Her knees pop when she stands and wipes her eyes. A weight settles against Gloria's leg, and she looks down to find a flattened pug face staring up into her own.

She hadn't been thrilled about the dog, but it was here now. For better or worse.

"What about this one?" Maisie asks, turning another sketch toward her. It was the one left on the tabletop.

The third sketch...

Gloria takes it between two fingers. Her other hand still rests on the polished, wooden grip of her cane, a cane she would likely need for the rest of her life.

"They look happy, don't they?" Gloria whispers at last, running one finger over their smiling faces.

"Is it heaven?" Maisie asks.

"Heaven? No," Gloria laughs, a short, bitter sound. "Well…"

Gloria regards the four figures: Brinkley in his James Dean leather jacket. Jesse in jeans and a black sweater, the sleeves pulled down over her hands. Rachel in a gorgeous mauve dress and petticoat that Gloria can still see so vividly when she closes her eyes. And Ally, too—blond hair wild in the ocean breeze.

They sit together on the porch of a house, a gorgeous A-frame with large looming windows.

They drink and laugh.

Gloria hands her the sketch. "I suppose this is as good a heaven as any."

MAISIE STARES AT THE ONE-STORY, BRICK BUILDING WITH A mixture of horror and excitement. Kids with backpacks stream through the double glass doors in twos and threes. Others linger under clusters of maple trees, talking and laughing. Or by the bike rack at the edge of the sidewalk where it meets the circle drive.

"High school," she whispers in fascination.

"*Public* high school," a crisp British voice echoes, but with scorn and remorse.

Gideon leans across the console of his Ferrari 458 and takes her hand.

"You don't have to go in, you know. I can have us in Paris by dinnertime. There's more art and learning in that city than you'll ever achieve in this hovel. Give me three months, and I'll give you *quite* the education."

She snorts. "Stop flirting."

She expected this. When he turned up on Gloria's stoop at 7:15 in the morning with Starbucks and his best grin, offering to take her to her first day of real school, she thought he might try to pull something like this.

She thinks of Gloria's face, of that horrible picture where she blew out her own brains, and Maisie knows she wouldn't leave Nashville for all the money in the world. And certainly not something as alluring as a beautiful boy with a nice car.

I love him. But he doesn't love me.

She forces a grin. It comes out awkward and nervous.

She wants to reach across the console and drag a thumb across his stubble. She wonders if he knows what she's thinking. There's mischief sparkling behind those black-rimmed glasses. It's the glasses that are undoing her, and he seems to know it.

"Can't you smell *le baguette,* darling?"

"No. Baguettes can't compete," she forces out.

"Baguettes can't compete?" he scoffs. Throwing himself against the driver's side door as if to get away from her. "Can't compete with what?"

"Gym shorts and crappy hot lunch and riding a bus that smells like corn chips. Sorry, macarons and patisseries just aren't on the same level."

He laughs at her as if she's just made the best joke in the world. "Darling, they aren't in the same league."

She rolls her eyes.

"And I suppose after this, it'll be college," he says, relaxing into the seat. "You'll be some cute sorority girl who studies something adorable like veterinary medicine."

"You know me too well." She's looking at the building again, at the thinning crowd, and knows she's running out of time.

The silence grows thick in the car between them. Maisie's head starts to feel swimmy. She doesn't know if it's the rich smell of leather, the cherry-scented air fresher, or her nerves.

Perhaps all three.

Gideon breaks the silence first. "We're not part of this world."

He rubs a thumb over her bare knuckles.

"I know," she says. She doesn't even argue. "But I've got to try anyway."

How many years did she spend dreaming of this? About going to school and making friends? The kind of kids she'd go to the mall with to browse H&M racks and eat oily pretzels from the food court.

Dates. And drama—but the innocent, annoying kind. Not the murdered-in-your-sleep kind.

Meeting boys like Sam... Her throat tightens.

Here is her chance.

A chance at a real school. A chance to make real friends.

She'll figure out how to live with the constant fear that someone will recognize her and bring the world down on her head. She can see her own name in the headlines: *Daughter of Murdered Zealots Found. Sole Witness of Their Final Hours.*

And there are other reasons she doesn't want to be found.

Ever since Jesse used her own breathing gift to wake her from death, Maisie's been...different. She isn't sure how, but she's certain she can still feel that power inside her—some *other* gift given to her when Jesse gave her back her life.

A new gift.

She supposes only time will tell. She's certain she will discover it the same way she discovered her breathing gift— in a time of need.

You were always meant to be special, Azrael had said. It was one of the very last things she'd said before disappearing.

When the gate closes, I'll be sealed on the other side.

But I need you!

Azrael had laughed at that.

Yet...she fought for this life. She *fought* for this. For the friends. For the homework and prom. For Gloria and Winston.

So she's going to live the dream, damn it.

Gideon lets go of her hand. "Go on then, love. You don't want to be late. First impressions and all that. I'll check back around graduation. Your public school Rumspringa will be over, and you'll be *legal*."

He smirks flirtatiously.

Before her nerves fail her, she leans across the console and plants a kiss on Gideon's mouth. It's hot and tastes like coffee. She feels his stubble scrape her cheeks and chin.

Then she's stepping out of the car and onto the sidewalk before he can say anything about it.

She doesn't expect more. She isn't even sure she *wants* more. He might have taken the plastic asylum bracelet off his wrist, but he isn't over Rachel. If Maisie is being honest with herself, he probably never will be. But she had to know what it was like to kiss Gideon Bale. Just once.

Life is too short to spend wondering.

On the sidewalk, a gaggle of girls stare at the cherry-red Ferrari and its handsome driver with unabashed curiosity. Realizing they must've seen the kiss, Maisie blushes harder.

She makes it only three steps away from the car before he's calling after her. "Maya, darling?"

The girls passing Maisie on the walk perk up at the sound of that melodic, British accent. One walks right into the back of the girl in front of her.

Maisie completely understands. "What do you want now, Gideon?"

"Call me if you change your mind about Paris, will you? The offer is good anytime." He gives her a devilish wink, and pulls away from the curb.

The first bell rings, and the last few kids dawdling on the sidewalk hurry in.

"Is that guy your boyfriend?" one of the girl asks, a pretty blonde with glossed lips. The others fall into step beside her.

Maisie takes a deep breath and smiles. "In his dreams."

JESSE

Somewhere, Sometime

I sit up. The comforter falls away from my chest. Its soft, feathery weight lays across my legs as I look around. I'm alone in this king-sized bed. To my right is nothing but an enormous window overlooking an endless ocean. The water is blue-gray with foamy white waves lapping at the shore.

I take it all in. The enormous bed. A hundred fluffy pillows laying against the polished, gray headboard that looks like some kind of reclaimed wood. Hell, it could've washed up on this very shore. Matching side tables with glass lamps and white shades. The door to the right is closed except for a thin crack. A white, silk robe hangs on a silver hook. And this breathtaking ocean view.

"I'm dead," I say.

No one confirms this.

"Oh shit. I'm *really* dead."

Still no answer.

"Gabriel?" I call out his name. Then I remember Ally. Ally holding onto me as the power ripped me apart. The soft feel of her hair across my face.

"Ally?"

Nothing. My voice echoes in the bedchamber. But no footfall rings through the house. No one comes running.

"Ally!"

I throw back the covers, and realize I'm in a gray tank top and black boxer shorts. Interesting, considering I can't remember how I got here, let alone who dressed me and put me in bed.

I step into the hallway. My feet settle against the cool, wood floor. To the right seems to be a bathroom. It's huge with white subway tile and double sinks. A white tub big enough for two grown men sits under another enormous, picturesque window, this one overlooking a sandy dune. There's also a shower with two waterfall shower heads against the adjacent wall and a linen closet full of fluffy white towels.

Toothpaste. Toothbrushes. Two of everything.

I catch my reflection in the mirror. Nope. Not two heads —in fact, I look exactly the same.

I give myself a good hard look in the vanity mirror. I look the same as always. Long chestnut hair. Bangs a tad too long. Green eyes and splatter of freckles across my nose. I open my mouth just to make sure I haven't grown fangs or anything. I don't know, maybe you need two toothbrushes for fangs.

Nada.

So who the hell is all this other stuff for?

I creep down the hallway, admiring the high ceilings, and find myself in a living room. It's spacious with a vaulted ceiling giving me a clear sense of the A-frame shape of the house. Windows run all the way up, and wooden beams cross overhead. To the right, there's a kitchen big enough to cater a family of twelve in.

"Someone has nice taste," I mumble. "Ally? Gabriel?"

Still no answer.

I swear, if someone comes popping out of a closet...

I open the back door and see only sand stretching out to a dense treeline. I can smell the salt and sun and hear the branches rustling in the soft and constant breeze. I close the door and cross the living room to the large windows facing the ocean, or what I consider the front of the house.

Someone stands on the shore, looking out over the sea.

Before I fully know what I'm doing, I throw open the

door, step out onto the deck, and clamber down the steps. I'm running across the sand at full tilt.

The woman in the white, silk robe stands with her bare feet in the surf.

"Ally!" I scream.

She turns, and smiles. It's radiant. She pulls blond hair away from her face. "Good morning."

The next instant, my arms are around her. I'm clinging to her the way a drowning man clings to flotsam.

"Fucking hell."

She wraps her arms around me.

"Are you okay? Are we okay?"

I'm aware that it's mostly gibberish falling out of my mouth.

"It's the beach house from *The Way Home*," she says, pushing the hair out of my eyes. She nods toward the house.

I only glance at it, but then I look again. The landscape is different now. Not the torrential battlefield with Michael and his angels. The storm has passed. It's only sunshine shimmering on the water as far as the eye can see. And the windows are no longer dark and insectile. Instead, they reflect the dancing light.

"Did you make this place? When we—"

"I don't know and don't care," I say. "I just want to kiss you."

So I do.

I kiss her about a thousand times. I kiss her until she sags in my arms, laughing and begging me to stop.

"I still have to breathe!" she says, laughing. Her eyes shine.

"Do you?" I ask, flabbergasted. "I don't know. I think we're dead."

Ally stiffens beside me, startled, and I have just an instant to think—*of course. Of course this isn't over. I'm going to turn*

*around and find out that Michael is right there, ready to kill me
again. And again, and he'll throw in Ally this time for good measure
because just killing me was getting boring...*

But I turn and see Gabriel. He's stark in this landscape of
light, with his black suit and wings.

I let go of Ally slowly, making sure she's regained her
footing.

"What the hell happened?" I cross to him and stare up
into his face to make sure it's really him. Hadn't Michael
changed faces on me there at the end? It's all a jumbled-up
blur now, but I'm pretty sure that happened.

But it's Gabriel, all right. And his placid green eyes.

"You saved them," he says.

"And we're dead," I say.

"Are you?" he asks with a sheepish smile.

"Really? *Really* Gabriel? After all we've been through
together? I would have thought that double-speak was behind
us now. We've shared... so much."

"You are inside the gate," he says, as if this is supposed to
answer all my questions.

"The gate where evil shit tries to come through and eat
the planet? The little in-between place where Earth meets...
meets whatever." I'm resorting to crude hand gestures.

"Yes."

I consider this. "Well...we must've gotten a great deal on
the house. Interdimensional beach front property can't be
cheap! What's the resale value, you think?"

He doesn't laugh at my joke. Save the world and can't even
get a guy to smile.

"Did I put a shield around the Earth or blow it up? Is
there even an Earth on the other side of the gate, because I'm
not going to lie, it was all a clusterfuck there at the end. I
didn't know which way was up or down."

"You cast the shield. They are safe to progress in their time."

"Until they destroy each other."

He says nothing.

"Is Michael going to come back?"

"My kind can only enter the gate through a mindscape, like the one you've created here. And they cannot enter any sanctum where your heart lives."

"And Ally is my heart."

"Yes. Evil cannot enter where the heart resides," Gabriel says. He casts a look over my shoulder. He's giving Ally the eyes.

"Hey now." I snap my fingers in front of his face. "Don't make eyes at my girlfriend. You misled me! You made me feel like I could keep her out of it, but the whole time you planned to get her in...here."

"I am sorry."

"You're sorry? She's dead because of you!"

"Jess." Ally slips her arms around my waist and puts her chin on my shoulder. "We have a house on the beach. We're safe. No more fighting. No more war."

I consider this. Then, to make sure I understand, I say, "My punishment for almost destroying the world is I have to live in a beachside paradise with the woman I love for all eternity?"

Never growing old. Never getting sick. Never losing her to someone else...

"And I never have to watch you die again," Ally adds.

She is so cute. I kiss the tip of her nose.

"Okay, maybe I forgive you," I say, turning back to Gabriel. "And what about you? Are you going back to Planet Angel? Is there a Planet Angel?"

But Gabriel isn't there. There's nothing but beach.

"Hey!" I exclaim. "Not even a decent goodbye? Aren't you

going to miss me? Even a little?"

I am never far. I will always be here if you need me, he whispers through my mind. But he doesn't appear again.

I sigh. "So dramatic."

Ally slips her hand into mine.

"How do I know this isn't a dream?" I ask, staring into Ally's beautiful, brown eyes. "I could be crispy toast on the tundra and someone could be scraping me up with a spatula right now. Or I'm just straight up hallucinating all this in an asylum. Is that mashed bananas I taste?"

Ally clasps her hands on the back of my neck and smiles up at me. Then she kisses me. It's a good kiss, lots of lower lip and jaw action going on.

When she's finished with me, she asks, "Do I feel like a dream?"

"Yes." I can't keep the grin off my face. "I don't know. Maybe. You should do that again so I can be sure."

She obliges.

I start to suspect that maybe we *don't* need to breathe anymore.

"You're going to get tired of kissing me," I say, squeezing her tight.

"Never."

"Don't say that! You want to jinx us?"

She laughs and runs a hand through my hair.

"You might get tired of me," she says.

"Are you kidding? My imagination is endless." I gesture at the ocean, the sky, the house. "You don't think I can keep things interesting?"

She laughs. "Of *that* I have no doubt."

"None?"

"None." She kisses the tip of my nose. "I've never doubted you, Jesse Sullivan."

"You must be into long shots." I snort. "Don't tell me this is the happy ending you wanted."

She pulls back so she can look into my eyes. "You're all I've ever wanted."

"And now you have me."

I hold her against me. I bury my face in her hair and smell the sunshine and the salt collected there.

"What about you? Did you get what you wanted?" She presses her warm cheek against mine.

A wave of gratitude washes over me. Gratitude for all the people who carried me through the darkest hours. Comrades like Gabriel. Gloria. Brinkley. Rachel. Gideon. Maisie. Winston. Even old friends like Kyra. Umbri. Kirk. Lane. Cindy.

Maybe I'll even count Sasquatch, for protecting Ally when I couldn't.

I take a moment to thank them all. Everyone who got me here.

But most of all, I'm grateful for the woman in my arms, for her endless love. For her boundless faith in me and her unwavering willingness to follow me to the ends of the earth —and beyond...

"I got what I wanted," I whisper into her ear and hold her tighter. "I got far more than I deserve."

Did you enjoy this book? You can make a BIG difference.

I don't have the same power as big New York publishers who can buy full spread ads in magazines and you won't see my covers on the side of a bus anytime soon, but what I *do* have are wonderful readers like you.

And honest reviews from readers garner more attention for my books and help my career more than anything else I could possibly do—and I can't get a review without **you!**

So if you would be so kind, I'd be very grateful if you would post a review. It only takes a minute or so of your time and yet you can't imagine how much it helps me.

It can be as short as you like and yes, I cherish every. single. one.

So please go to your preferred retailer and leave a review for this book today.

Eternally grateful,

Kory

Get Your Three Free Stories Today

Thank you so much for reading *Dying Day*. I hope you're enjoying Jesse's story. If you'd like more, I have a free, exclusive Jesse Sullivan story for you. See Ally survive her first death replacement gig, during her first week as Jesse's assistant. You'll also see how the lovable Winston came to be Jesse's loyal companion.

You can only read this story for free by signing up for my newsletter. If you would like this story, you can get your copy by visiting **www.korymshrum.com/jessenewsletteroffer**

I will also send you free stories from the other series that I write. If you've signed up for my newsletter already, no need to sign up again. You should have already received this story from me. Check your email! Can't find it? ➔ Email me at **kory@korymshrum.com** and I'll take care of it.

As to the newsletter itself, I send out 2-3 a month and host a monthly giveaway exclusive to my subscribers. The prizes are usually signed books or other freebies that I think you'll enjoy. I also share information about my current projects, and personal anecdotes.

If you want these free stories and access to the giveaways, you can sign up for the newsletter at ➔ **www.korymshrum.com/jessenewsletteroffer**

If this is not your cup of tea (I love tea), you can follow me on Facebook at **www.facebook.com/korymshrum** in order to be notified of my new releases.

You have just finished *Dying Day*, the final novel in the Dying for a Living series. Keep reading for a special preview of *Shadows in the Water,* the first Lou Thorne Thriller.

"*N*o, no, no." Her daughter's hand shot out and seized Courtney's slacks. "Don't leave me."

"Jesus Christ." She tugged her pants from Louie's dripping grip and shoved her back into the tub by her shoulders. "What is it with you and water? It isn't going to kill you. You won't drown! And I have to finish dinner before your father gets home."

Louie's chest collapsed with sobs. "Please. *Please* don't go."

"Stop crying. You're too old to be crying like this."

Louie recoiled like a kicked dog, her body hunching into a C-curve.

God almighty, Courtney thought as shame flooded her. *What am I supposed to do with her?*

The illogical nature of your daughter's fear doesn't negate the fact her fear is very real, the therapist had said. Dr. Loveless must have repeated this a hundred times, but it didn't make these episodes any easier. The fat-knuckled know-it-all had never been present for bath time.

Most ten-year-old girls could bathe on their own. No handholding. No hysterics. No goddamn therapy sessions once a week. And somehow this was supposed to be *her* fault? Why exactly? Because she'd gotten pregnant at eighteen?

No. She did everything right. She married Jack, despite her reservations. He was too young, uneducated, and a dreamer. Triple threat, her Republican father called it.

She read all the pregnancy books. She quit her managerial position at the insurance company and stayed home with Louie, practically giving the girl her undivided attention for the first five years of her life. If she was guilty of anything, it was over-attentiveness.

But Courtney didn't believe for a second this was her fault.

It was *Jack's.*

Jack was the one who insisted on renovating the upstairs bath and then insisted his friend do the renovations. Three years. *Three years* it sat unfinished and oh no they couldn't go to another builder because Jack *promised* Gary the job. Jack and his misplaced loyalties. What did it get them? Bum friends who always borrowed money and *three years* with only the clawfoot bathtub to share between them.

Things worth having are worth waiting for, Jack had said.

This philosophy worked for a DEA agent like Jack, someone who had to track criminals for months or years, but Courtney had never been good at waiting. She preferred what her alcoholic father had called *immediate gratification.*

Within a week of switching from the shower to the clawfoot tub, Louie's episodes began. After three *long* years, Courtney felt she'd had more than enough. God, it would be wonderful to shove a valium down the girl's throat and be done with this. She wanted to. *God almighty*, she wanted to. But Jack had been firm about pills. Courtney loved Jack, but goddamn his self-righteous "drugs are drugs" bullshit. Any half-wit knew the difference between valium and heroin.

You will have to be patient with her, Mrs. Thorne, if you want her to get through this without any lasting psychological damage.

Apparently, the therapist didn't know a damn thing. The damage had *already* begun to show. Louie not only feared water now but dirt also. The child who used to come in at night covered head to toe in grass stains and palms powdered with pastel sidewalk chalk, now crept around as if playing a constant game of The Floor is Hot Lava. This morning, Louie had burst into tears when Courtney asked her to pull weeds from the hosta bed. Even after putting her in coveralls and peony pink garden gloves, the girl had whimpered through the task, ridiculous tears streaming down her cheeks.

Now, hands on hips, Courtney stared down at her hunched, shaking daughter. She could count the vertebrae protruding through her skin. She'd grown so thin lately.

It could be worse, she told herself. She could have a child with quadriplegic cerebral palsy like her book club buddy Beth Rankin. Would she rather have a kid who screamed in the bathtub three or four times a week, or a man-child who had to be pushed in a stroller everywhere and his shitty diapers changed and drooling chin wiped?

Courtney forced a slow exhale through flared nostrils and pried apart her clenched teeth.

"Okay," she said in a soft, practiced tone. "Okay, I'm here. I'm right here."

She knelt beside the tub and grabbed a slick blue bottle of shampoo off a shelf above the toilet. As she squeezed the gel into her palm, Louie still cowered like a beaten dog, head and eyes down.

"I'm sorry," Courtney said, her cheeks flushing hotly. "But it's hard for me to understand this fear of yours."

The girl's teeth chattered, but she said nothing. Only one of her eyes was visible from the slate of black hair slicked against her head.

Courtney massaged the soap into her hair. Thick white bubbles foamed between her knotty fingers, her skin turning red from the pressure and steam. Her gentle massaging did nothing to relax the girl.

"Isn't this nice?" Courtney asked. "I'd love it if someone washed *my* hair."

Louie said nothing, her arms wrapped tightly around her knees.

"You have to lean back now." She trailed her fingers through the gray water. "So we can rinse."

Louie seized her mother's arms.

"I know." Courtney tried to add a sweet lilt to her voice, but only managed indifference. Better than angry at least. "I'm right here. Come on, lie back, baby."

She thought *baby* was a nice touch. Wasn't it?

But Louie's chest started to heave again as her head tipped back toward the soapy gray water.

"Breathe, *baby*. The sooner we do this, the sooner you can get out of the tub." Courtney hoped the girl wouldn't hyperventilate. That would be the fucking icing on the cake. Dragging her wet body out of the tub would be hell on her back, and she'd already had her valium for the night. She'd risk taking another, but she knew Jack counted them.

As the back of Louie's hair dipped into the water, her golden eyes widened. Her fingers raked down Courtney's arms as she clung tighter. All right. It only stung a little, and it would be something to show Jack later when she complained about his lateness.

It was your turn for bath night and look what happened. She might even get away with a second glass of wine at dinner sans lecturing if the marks were red enough.

This made her smile.

With one arm completely submerged under Louie's back, buoying the girl, she could use her free hand to rinse Louie's hair. Thick clumps of soap melted into the water with each swipe of her fingers.

"There."

Louie's muscles went soft, her nails retracting.

"Not so bad, is it?" Courtney cooed with genuine affection now. "I love baths. I find them very relaxing."

Louie even managed a small smile.

Then the oven dinged.

"My ham!" Courtney clambered to her feet.

"No, no, no!" Louie frantically wiped water from her eyes and tried to pull herself into an upright position. "Don't! Please!"

And just like that, the hysterics were in full swing again. *Fucking Jack. I'm going to kill you.* "Breathe, baby."

Shaking suds off her arms, Courtney jogged toward her glazed ham and caramelized Brussels sprouts three rooms away. The sweet, roasted smell met her halfway. "The door is open, *baby*. Keep talking so I can hear you."

"Mom!" Louie screamed. "Mommy! It's happening!"

"I'm right here." She slipped a quilted oven mitt over each hand. "Talk to me. I'm listening."

The girl's escalating hysteria cut off mid-scream. For a moment, there was only a buzzing silence.

Courtney's heart skipped a beat. Her body froze instinctually. Her reptilian brain registering *danger* entered a mimicked catatonia. For several heartbeats, she could only stand there before her electric range, in her gloved hands, the oven mitts spaced equidistantly as if still holding the casserole dish between them.

Her eyes were fixed on a spaghetti sauce splatter to the right of the stove, above a ceramic canister holding rice. She stared without seeing.

Then a chill shuddered up the woman's spine, reactivating her systems. As her muscles cramped, she thought, *fear trumps valium*. She yanked off the oven mitts, throwing them down beside the casserole dish steaming on the stove-top. She jogged back to the bathroom, the silence growing palpable.

"Louie?"

The tub was empty. No shadows beneath the soapy gray water.

In a ridiculous impulse, she looked behind the bathroom door and then inside the small cabinet beneath the sink, knowing full well Louie couldn't fit into either space.

The bathroom was empty. "Louie?"

She ran to the girl's bedroom.

It was empty too. And the wood floor tracing the entire length of the house was bone dry. Louie's soft Mickey Mouse towel, the one they bought on their trip to Disney World two years ago, still hung from the hook by the tub.

She searched every inch of their house, and when she couldn't find her, she called Jack. When he didn't answer, she called again and left a frantic message.

He arrived twenty minutes later.

They searched again. They called everyone. They spoke to every neighbor and the police. If Courtney thought Dr. Loveless was a ruthless interrogator with his second chin and swollen knuckles, she found the authorities much worse.

"I didn't kill her!" she said for the thousandth time. "Jack, do something! These are *your* friends!"

For three nights, they had no peace. Courtney doubled the wine and valium, but it wasn't enough currency to buy sleep.

In the early morning hours, she would find herself wandering their house, wearing down a path between the clawfoot tub and Louie's empty bed. Sitting on the firm twin mattress, she would pull back the Ninja Turtle comforter hoping to find her underneath.

In her mind, she apologized for every frustration, every cruel thought. *I'll do anything—anything. Bring her home.*

The call came on the fourth day.

Sixty miles east of the Thorne's home in St. Louis, Jacob Foxton was interviewed many times by the police, but his story never changed.

His nieces were coming down from Minnesota for the Memorial Day weekend, and he and his wife were very excited to see them. They'd changed the sheets on the spare bed and stocked the fridge with root beer and Klondike bars. The pool was uncovered and cleaned, and the heater turned on. All that was left to do before their arrival was mow the yard.

*I was cutting my grass, and she…*appeared.

As the police tried to pin the abduction on the man, the lack of evidence made it impossible. Foxton had no priors, and a neighbor confirmed Foxton's rendition.

Billie Hodges had been washing her Chevy Tahoe with a clear view of the Foxton family pool. Like Foxton, Hodges swore the girl simply appeared.

As if from thin air.

After thirty-six fruitless hours, the Perry County Sheriff's Department was forced to believe Jacob Foxton had merely cut a left around his rudbeckia bushes with his squat red push mower and found Louie Thorne standing there, on the top step of his pool.

Naked. Soaking wet. Her dark hair stuck to her pale back like an oil slick. Foxton released the lawnmower's safety bar, killing the engine.

"Hey! Hey you!" He rushed toward her, clumps of fresh cut grass clinging to his bare ankles.

The girl turned toward the sound of his voice, and his scolding lecture died on his lips. It wasn't only her fear that stopped him.

It was the blood.

So much that a cloud of pink swirled toward the drain in his pool.

The girl's body was covered in lacerations, the kind he got on his arms and legs as a kid, hiking through the woods. A great many of them stretched across her stomach and legs and a particularly nasty one across her cheek.

She must have run through the forests of hell, he thought.

But it wasn't the scratches that frightened him.

A ring of punctures encircled the girl's right shoulder. A ragged halo from neck to bicep. Like some hungry beast larger than the girl had grabbed ahold of her with its teeth. Long rivulets of blood streamed down her pale limbs, beading on her skin.

"Honey." Jacob pulled off his T-shirt and yanked it down over the child's head. If she cared about the sweaty condition of the shirt, the grass stains, or Jacob's hairy belly, she didn't show it. "Are you all right?"

"Is it still on me?" she whispered. She turned her face toward Jacob, but her eyes didn't focus. His mother called that *a thousand-yard stare.*

"Who did this to you, honey?" Jacob asked. He took her hands in his. The hairs on his arms rose at the sight of blood pooled beneath her nails.

"Jacob?" Called Billie from across the stretch of lawn between their two yards. "Is everything all right?"

"Call an ambulance," Jacob yelled. He saw the girl's mouth move. "What was that, honey?"

"Is it still on me?" she whispered again. "Is it?"

And that was the last thing she said before collapsing into his arms.

Fourteen years later

*L*ou unfolded the tourist map and eyed a man over the rim of the creased paper. A boxy man with a crooked nose and a single bushy brow stood on the harbor dock, smoking a cigarette. He draped an arm around a woman's shoulder while he joked with another guy twice his size, a hairy bear as wide as he was tall. The woman was a little more than a caricature to Lou. Big hair and a big mouth, made bigger by the annoying smack of bubblegum between her magenta lips. Her clothes were too tight in some places and nonexistent in others. *A Jersey girl*, Aunt Lucy would've called her.

Lou scowled at the tourist map, pretending to read about the seaport's attractions, and wondered if the girl under Angelo Martinelli's arm would feel half as cozy if she knew what a monster he was.

If Bubblegum Barbie was observant, she might have noticed Martinelli's penchant for leather, Dunhill cigarettes, and pointy shoes. Maybe Barbie even suspected the Martinelli family was responsible for fueling the heroin problem in Baltimore. Hell, she probably tolerated this after-shave-soaked prick *for* the heroin.

Whatever Barbie thought she knew of the Italian draped over her, Lou knew a hell of a lot more.

She should. She'd been hunting Angelo since she was fourteen.

Lou looked away as if to read the street sign, her heart fluttering with anticipation. A steady pulse throbbed in the side of her neck and in her hands. She was thankful her dark shades and windblown hair hid her excitement. And grateful that Martinelli was too nearsighted to see the map tremble in her sweaty grip.

Her mind kept turning toward the future, when he'd receive a shipment at Pier C and insist on counting everything himself. Better yet, because he'd want to be discreet as to how much dope he imported, his security detail would be thinner. He'd invite enough muscle to get the job done. No more.

Lou wouldn't get him entirely alone. A man like Angelo was *never* alone. He didn't even fuck without an audience. She knew this because she'd considered the possibility of going O-Ren Ishii on his ass. Before fully exploring this option, Lou realized she'd forsake her vow of revenge and blow her own brains out long before trying to seduce a Martinelli.

Tonight there would be guns, of course. And the ones chosen for this evening's mission would be fighters. Perhaps a few even better than Lou herself.

And there was the water to consider. The harbor sparkled in the late afternoon sun. Looking at it made Lou's skin itch.

Angelo ran a thick hand through his oiled hair and tossed his Dunhill butt on the ground. He smashed it out with a twist of his boot and hooked an arm around Barbie's waist.

Tonight, she thought, as a swarm of tourists swelled on the pier. *I'm going to kill you and love every minute of it.*

Her sunglasses hitched higher on her face as she grinned.

Before Angelo could turn toward her and spot a familiar ghost in the crowd, Lou did what she did best.

She disappeared, not returning until well after dark.

By 2:00 A.M., all the tourists were in bed with dreams of the next day.

Lou, on the other hand, wasn't sure she had another day in her. That was okay. She didn't need to see another sunrise as long as Angelo Martinelli didn't either.

Lying on top of one of the shipping containers, Lou had a great view of the docks below. Her forearms and body were covered in leather and Kevlar, but her palms were bare. The metal container serving as her lookout was warm under her palms, sun-soaked from the day. She was small enough to fit into the grooves in the top of the container, making her invisible to those below. Unless of course, Angelo arrived by helicopter.

Her body squirmed. Despite the pleasant breeze rolling off the deep harbor, sweat was starting to pool at the back of her neck beneath her hairline. Her feet twitched with excitement.

Death by waiting, she thought.

She was desperate to swing at something. She imagined certain animals felt this way during the full moon. Hungry, unsettled, itching all over.

Do it already, her mind begged. *Slip*. A heartbeat later she'd be standing behind Angelo. So close she could run her hands through his greased hair.

Boo, motherfucker.

Not motherfucker, she thought. Mother *killer*.

True, Courtney Thorne was hard to love. Her compulsive and domineering behavior, her impatience. Her tendency to chide and scorn rather than praise. Her face a perpetual pout rather than a smile.

But Louie also remembered how hard her mother had hugged her the day after she was found in Ohio. Louie had sat in the sheriff's office for hours, wrapped in a scratchy wool blanket consuming all the soda and peanut butter cups she could stomach until her parents arrived.

Louie! Her mother had cried the moment she stepped through the station's glass doors. Louie had only managed to put down her soda can and slide out of the chair before her mother fell on her, seizing and squeezing her half to death. She smelled like makeup powder and rose water. Like the old woman she would never become.

Courtney wasn't her favorite parent, but she didn't deserve to die either.

Louie's fists clenched at her side.

Angelo's men stirred on the pier. To anyone else, it seemed as if an innocuous few stood around, smoking, and talking. Apart from the hour, nothing suspicious there. But Lou glimpsed blades catching moonlight and saw the bulging outlines of guns under jackets.

Jackets in this heat were clue enough.

Cops stopped patrolling the harbor at midnight. Lou wondered if that could be blamed on budget cuts, ignorance, or money from Angelo's own pockets. *A little of each*, she thought.

She'd almost succumbed to drumming her fingers on the shipping container when a car pulled into view.

The black sedan was like so many others Angelo had rented in cities where he'd done business before: Chicago. San Francisco, New York, Atlanta and now Baltimore.

As soon as she saw the car, she started to slip. Bleeding through this side of the world. *No. Not yet*, she scolded herself. *Don't fuck this up.*

She'd only have one good shot. One chance to catch him off guard.

Tonight she would finish what her father started so many years ago.

Someone opened the back door, and Angelo stepped out. He adjusted the lapels of his leather jacket. She took a deep breath and let it out slowly. Again. Because the sight of him was enough to make her heart hammer.

Angelo called out to someone in Italian, then pointed at the boat. "Ho due cagne in calore che mi aspettano ed un grammo di neve con il mio nome scritto sopra."

Louie only understood a little Italian and caught the words *two whores* and *waiting*. Enough to get the gist of his harsh tone and thrusting hips, and comprehend why the men leered. One whistled through his teeth.

Angelo cupped his hands around a fresh Dunhill. A flame sparked, illuminating his face. With a wave, Angelo led his entourage to the pier where the boat sat tied to the dock. The boat rocked in the waves, straining against its rope, like a tied horse ready to run.

As soon as Angelo placed one foot on the boat, then dipping his head to enter the cabin, Lou let go.

She bled through. One moment she lay on top of the ship-ping container, the next, she stood in the shadows beneath the cabin's stairs. Her eyes leveled with Angelo's heels. It was hot in the unventilated room.

Angelo Martinelli descended the stairs with a man in front and one behind him. Lou smelled the leather of his boots and the smoke from his cigarette. *I can grab him now*, she thought. *Reach between the steps and seize his ankle like in a horror movie.*

Someone turned on the overhead light, and the interior of the boat burned yellow in the glow of the 40-watt bulb. Lou jumped back into the corner without thinking. An honest reaction to the sudden influx of light.

But her shoulder blades connected with a solid wall.

Heads snapped up at the sound of Lou searching for an exit that had been there only a moment before but was now gone.

She had only a second to decide.

She drew her gun, one fluid and practiced movement, and shot the overhead light. The 40-watt bulb burst, exploding in a shower of sparks. It was enough to throw them back into darkness and provide Lou with her exit. She slipped behind the stairs, then emerged from a narrow pathway between two shipping containers. Gunfire erupted inside the boat behind her. The ship strained against its rope again, and the wooden docks creaked.

More men came running, guns drawn.

She cursed and slammed her fist into the shipping container. So much for the surprise.

The chance to grab Martinelli and slip away undetected was gone. As her target emerged from the boat, gun at the ready, the weight of her mistake intensified.

He was spooked. Now he looked like the horse ready to run.

He inhaled sharp breaths of salty air as he hurried toward his car in short, quick strides. Fifty steps. Thirty-five. Twenty and he'll be gone.

It was now or never.

Fifteen steps.

Ten.

The thick tint of Angelo's car might work to her advantage, but her timing had to be perfect. Her blood whistled in her ears as she counted his last steps.

3....2...1...

She stepped from the edge of the shipping container into the backseat of Angelo's car. The leather seat rushed up to greet her, bending her legs into place.

But it was her hands that mattered. And she had plenty of time to position them.

Angelo turned away from her, pulling the car door shut. She pressed her gun to his temple the second the door clicked into place.

The driver began to turn, pulling his weapon up from his lap but he was too slow. Louie lifted a second pistol from her hip and shoved it to the back of his neck, to the smooth nape. His neck tensed under the barrel, shifting the gun metal against her fingers.

"Don't," she said. Her eyes were fixed on Angelo. "I have a better idea."

"You were not in the car when I opened the door," Angelo said. His tobacco breath stung her nose. "I'm certain of this."

"Imagine how quick I am with a gun." It was a bold bluff given her predicament. His men were abandoning the boat. Some were moving the heroin. Others were lumbering toward other vehicles. If even *one* of them got into this car, she was screwed.

She could produce a third gun, sure. But not a third hand to hold it.

"You were also on the boat." Angelo's eyes shined in the dark, reflecting light like the black sea in front of them. "Or one like you."

"That would put me in two places at once," she said. She arched an eyebrow. "Impossible."

The driver remained very still, his hands at the ten and two positions on the wheel. Lou didn't recognize him, but she doubted that she'd ever forget the thick stench of Old Spice turned sour with sweat. It made her head swim.

If he was new, he was probably uninterested in doing anything that would cost him his life. She'd have to test this theory.

"What do you want?" Angelo asked. He shifted uncomfortably. Lou had found her silence made men nervous. Or maybe it was her gun. Difficult to tell. "Money? The drugs?"

"Driver?" she said.

The driver didn't turn toward her or even make a small sound of acknowledgment.

"Do you see the pier?" she went on, eyes still on Angelo. One of his greased curls fell across his forehead, and one corner of his lip curled in a partial sneer. His cheek muscles twitched. "Beside the pier is a space between the guardrails. Do you see it?"

The driver remained mute. His shoulders remained hunched, eyes forward. It was as if he'd had guns pressed to his head before and had since learned how to keep even a single muscle from twitching.

Lou saw all this in her perfect peripheral vision, not daring to look away from the man she wanted most.

Angelo Martinelli. This close he was smaller than she'd imagined.

She smiled at him, the taste of victory on her lips. "Drive into the bay."

When the driver didn't move, she smacked the gun against his occipital bone. "If you don't do it, then you're useless to me, and I think you understand what happens to useless people."

If he refused to drive, she'd shoot them both. It would be messier. Riskier. But if she couldn't get Martinelli into the water, she wasn't going to let this opportunity escape.

Yes. If Lou had to, she'd shoot them both and drive the car into the bay herself.

"Make your choice, Martinelli," she said. His eyes were pools of ink shining in the lamplight.

The confused pinch of his brow smoothed out. The curling sneer pulled into a tight grin.

"Drive," he said.

Without hesitation, the driver put the car into motion, and the sedan rolled forward.

"Faster," Lou said, grinning wider.

"Faster," Angelo agreed. A small chuckle rumbled in his throat. He slapped the back of the driver's seat like this was a game. "*Faster.*"

The driver punched the accelerator, and the car lurched forward. As it blasted past the men on the docks, shouts pinged off the windows. Angelo's laugh grew more robust, pleasing belly laugh.

He's high as hell, she realized. *High as hell without any idea of what's happening to him.*

They hit a bump when flying past the guardrails and onto the pier. The wooden slats clunked under the car's tires.

In the wake of Angelo's mania, Lou couldn't help but smile herself. She didn't lower the gun. "You're crazy."

This proclamation only made him laugh harder, clutching at his belly. His laugh warped into a wheezing whine.

The thrum of the wooden slats disappeared as the car launched itself off the pier. The sharp stench of fish wafted up to greet them as they floated suspended above the ocean. Her stomach dropped as the nose of the car tipped forward and the windshield filled with black Atlantic water.

There was a moment of weightlessness, of being lifted out of her seat and then the car hit the water's surface. Her aim faltered on impact, but she'd righted herself before either man could.

Cold water rushed in through the windows, trickling first through the corners, filling the car slowly as they slid deeper into the darkness. It seeped through the laces of her boots.

"Now what?" Angelo asked. He seemed genuinely thrilled. As if this was the most exciting experience of his life.

"We wait," she said.

"She's going to shoot us and leave our bodies in the

water." The driver's voice surprised her, higher and more childish than she imagined. No wonder he'd kept his mouth shut.

The driver could open the door and swim away for all she cared. "I don't—"

The driver couldn't wait for any reassurance. He whirled, lifting his gun.

Without a thought, she fired two shots into his skull, a quick double tap. His head rocked back as if punched. The brains splattered across the windows like Pollock's paint thrown onto a canvas.

She was glad she'd decided on the suppressor. Her ears would be bleeding from the noise if she hadn't. The smell of blood bloomed in the car. Bright and metallic. It was followed by the smell of piss.

Angelo's humor left him. "Is it my turn now, ragazzina?"

Water gurgled around the windows as the car sank deeper into the dark bay.

"No," she said, her eyes reflecting the dark water around them. "I have something else for you."

ill you do it?

The question looped in King's mind. *Will you do it, Robbie?*

At the corner of St. Peter and Bourbon, Robert King paused beneath a neon bar sign. Thudding bass blared through the open door, hitting him in the chest. The doorman motioned him forward. King waved him off. He was done drinking for the night. Not only because the hurricane was getting acquainted with the pickle chips he'd eaten earlier, but because the case file under his arms wasn't going to examine itself.

Despite the riot in his stomach, he hoped the booze would help him sleep. He was overdue a good night. A night without crushing darkness and concrete blocks pinning him down on all sides. A night where he didn't wake up at least twice with the taste of plaster dust on his lips. Leaving the bedside light on helped, but sometimes even that wasn't enough to keep the nightmares away.

Drunk revelers stumbled out of the bar laughing, and a woman down the street busked with her violin case open at her feet. The violin's whine floated toward him but was swallowed by the bass from the bar.

King paused to inspect his reflection in the front window. He smoothed his shaggy hair with a slick palm. He could barely see the scar. A bullet had cut a ten-degree angle across his cheekbone before blasting a wedge off his ear. The ear folded in on itself when it grew back together, giving him an elfish look.

A whole building collapsed on him, and it hadn't left a single mark. One bullet and...well, he supposed that was how the world worked.

Calamity didn't kill you. What finished you was the shot you never saw coming.

He straightened and smiled at the man in the glass.

Good.

Now that he didn't *look* like a drunk, it was time to make sure he didn't *smell* like one. He pinned the file against his body with a clenched elbow and dug into his pocket for mints. He popped two mints out of the red tin and into his mouth, rolling them back and forth with his tongue as if to erase all the evidence. Satisfied, he continued his slow progress toward home.

The central streets of the French Quarter were never dark, even after the shops closed and all that remained were the human fleas feeding in the red light of Bourbon Street. The city didn't want a bunch of drunks searching for their hotels in the dark, nor did they care to provide cover for the petty pickpockets who preyed on them. There were plenty of both in this ecosystem.

At the corner of Royal and St. Peter, King paused beneath a metal sign swinging in the breeze rolling in off Lake Pontchartrain and wiped his boots on the curb. Gum. Vomit. Dog shit. A pedestrian could pick up all sorts of discarded waste on these streets. He balanced his unsteady body by placing one hand on a metal post, cane height and topped with a horse's head. The pointed ears pressed into his palm as he struggled to balance himself.

A fire engine red building stood waiting for him to clean his feet. Black iron railings crowned the place, with ferns lining the balcony. Hunter green shutters framed oversized windows overlooking both Royal and St. Peter.

The market across the street was still open. King considered ducking in and buying a bento box, but one acidic pickle belch changed his mind. He rubbed his nose, suppressing a sneeze.

Best to go to bed early and think about all that Brasso had told him. Sleep on it. Perhaps literally with the photographs and testimony of one Paula Venetti under his pillow for safe keeping.

And with his gun too, should someone come in during the night and press a blade to his throat in search of information. It wouldn't be the first time.

Will you do it?

King supposed if he thought this case was hot enough to warrant a knifing in the night, he should've said *no*. He should remind his old partner he's retired. Brasso should find some young buck full of piss and vinegar. Not a man pushing sixty who can't have two cocktails without getting acid reflux severe enough to be mistaken for a heart attack.

The case file sat heavy in his hand. Heavier than it had been when he'd first accepted it. He clutched the folder tighter and crossed the threshold into Mel's shop, the lights flickered, and a ghostly moan vibrated the shelves.

A gaggle of girls looked up from their cell phones wide-eyed. Then they burst into laughter. One with braces snorted, and the laughter began anew.

Mel's sales tactics may not be old hat to them, but King

found the 10,000[th] fake moan less thrilling than the first. Funny how it had been the same with his ex-wife.

It's all about theatrics with these folk, Mel had said when she forced him to help install the unconventional door chime. *They come to N'awlins for the witchy voodoo stuff, and if you want to keep renting my room upstairs, Mr. King, you best clip these two wires here together. My old fingers don't bend the way they used to.*

And he did want to keep renting the large one-bedroom apartment upstairs, so he offered no further resistance to her schemes.

The store was smoky with incense. Ylang ylang. Despite the open door and late breeze, a visible cloud hung in the air, haloing the bookshelves and trinket displays full of sugar skulls, candles, statues of saints, and porcelain figurines. The fact that he recognized the scent spoke of Mel's influence on him these past months. If someone had bet him he would know the difference between ylang ylang and geranium two years ago, he would have lost the shirt off his back.

Apart from the four girls clustered by a wall of talismans, only one other patron was in the store. A rail-thin man with a rainbow tank top and cut-off jean shorts showing the bottom of his ass cheeks plucked a *Revenge is Love* candle from a wooden shelf. He read the label with one hand on his hip. When he scratched his ash blond hair, glitter rained onto the floor.

King's heart sank. Despite Mel's endless tactics, business was still slow. At ten o'clock on a Friday, this place should be packed wall-to-wall with tourists, ravers, or even drunks. Five customers did not an income make.

Behind the counter, a twenty-two-year-old girl with a white pixie cut took one look at the falling glitter and her nostrils flared.

Piper wore a sleeveless tank top with deep arm holes revealing her black sports bra beneath. A diamond cat earring sat curled in the upper curve of her ear and sparkled in the light of the cathedral chandelier overhead. A hemp necklace with three glass beads hung around her neck. Every finger had a silver ring, and a crow in flight was tattooed on her inner wrist. She managed to mask her irritation before Booty Shorts reached the counter with his purchase.

"$6.99." Piper slipped the candle into a paper bag with the *Madame Melandra's Fortunes and Fixes* logo stamped on the front.

Booty Shorts thanked her and sashayed out into the night. A glow stick around his neck burned magenta in the dark.

"I don't see what a candle can do that a hitman can't." Piper blew her long bangs out of her face.

"Why would you have someone else fight your battles for you?"

"I don't hit girls." Piper scoffed in mock indignation. "Anyway, my point is it's a waste of time sitting up all night with a candle praying to some goddess who doesn't give two shits about my sex life. Don't cry about your sour milk! Go get another fish! A cute, kissable fish who'll let you unsnap her bra after a couple tequila shots."

"Be grateful for the candle-burning crybabies," King adjusted the folder under his arms. "Unless you want to be a shop girl somewhere else."

Her nostrils flared. "*Apprentice*. I'm learning how to read fortunes. Sometimes I set up a table in Jackson Square and make shit up. People *pay* me! It's unbelievable."

"The Quarter is a dicey place for a young woman to be alone."

"*Awww*. I've always wanted a concerned father figure." She pressed her hands to her heart. Then she rolled her eyes. "Who said I was alone?"

"Were you with Tiffany?"

"Tanya," she corrected. "And *no*. We broke up weeks ago."

King rubbed the back of his head, leaning heavily against the glass case. "That's right. You left her for Amy."

"Amanda," she said. "Keep up, man."

He'd never been great with names. Now faces—he never forgot a face. "I'm sorry. How's Amanda?"

"She's—"

A teenage girl burst from behind the curtain, clutching her palm as if it'd been burned. Fat tears slid down her cheeks, glistening in the light until her friends enfolded her in their arms.

The velvety curtain with its spiraling gold tassels was pulled back again and hung on a hook to one side of the door frame. From the shadows, a voluptuous black woman with considerable hips emerged. Mel's kohl-rimmed eyes burned and an off-the-shoulders patchwork dress hugged her curvy frame. Gold bangles jangled against her wrist as she adjusted the purple shawl around her.

"Bad news?" Piper arched a brow, and King realized she'd begun to mimic Mel's dramatic eye makeup.

Mel crossed the small shop, and King straightened again. He hoped his eyes weren't glassy, and the mints had done the trick.

Mel stopped short of the counter and put one hand on her hip.

"Crushing hearts?" Piper asked, and she sounded excited about it.

Mel rolled her eyes. "I only suggested a book."

Piper frowned. "What book?"

Mel puckered her lips. "*He's Just Not That Into You.*"

Piper's grin deepened. "You're so cruel. Do you want me to talk to her? I'm *really* good with damsels."

"They're release tears. They're good for the soul. She'll wake up tomorrow and feel like the sun is shining, the baby bluebirds are singing, and—"

"—she'll be $80 lighter for it," Piper muttered.

"She'll be fine." Mel tapped her long purple nails on the checkout counter and turned her dark eyes on King. "You, on the other hand, you're in trouble. *Big* trouble."

King felt the sweat beading under his collar. He resisted the urge to reach up and pull at it. It was the chandelier overhead, beating down on him. Or he could blame the muggy night. New Orleans was hot as hell in June. Sweating didn't mean a damn thing.

"You're awfully quiet tonight, Mr. King."

He shrugged.

Mel stopped tapping her fingers on the glass countertops. King noticed reflective gems had been glued to the end of her index fingernails. "I see a woman in your future. She's someone from your past. Pretty little white thing. Blonde. Big blue eyes. And she needs your help."

His ex-wife Fiona had brown eyes, and no one would have called her *a pretty little white thing."* She'd been nearly six feet tall with the body of a rugby player.

Lucy.

"Is this a real fortune, Mel?" he asked his tongue heavy in his mouth.

Mel wrinkled her nose. "As real as the booze on your breath, Mr. King."

He adjusted the file under his arm. "It's mouthwash."

"I've done told you when you signed your lease, I wouldn't let no drunk man in my house again."

King found it amusing when Mel's southern accent thickened with her anger. Amusing, but he didn't dare smile. Mel hadn't wanted to rent her spare apartment to anyone, let alone a man. It had taken two weeks of wooing and reference checking to convince the fortune teller an ex-DEA agent was an asset rather than a liability.

"At least he's not an angry drunk." Piper tried to pull the

file free from King's underarm. She bit her lip as she tried to peel the flaps apart and glimpse the contents within.

He slapped her hand lightly. "I'm not even buzzed."

Mel's eyes flicked to the case file then met his again. She arched an eyebrow.

King didn't believe in palm reading or fortune telling. Ghosts only existed in the mind, and he would be the first to admit he had a menagerie of malevolent spirits haunting him.

But despite what his mother called a healthy dose of skepticism, he believed in intuition. Intuition was knowledge the frontal lobe had yet to process. He trusted his instinct and he respected the instinct of others. No one person could see every angle. Shooters on the roof. Boots on the ground. You had to rely on someone else's eyes, and this was no different.

Did Mel sense something about the case Brasso brought him? About a witness on the run and the man hunting her? And this mysterious woman from his past...

Mel spoke to the gaggle of girls. "Who's next?"

Three hands shot up. Someone cried, "Me!"

Clearly, they were eager to have their hearts broken.

"Wait." King touched her shoulder, and she turned. "Were you serious about the woman?"

"I don't need to be a fortune teller to know there's a woman, Mr. King." Mel tucked one of the girls behind the curtain and met his eyes again. She looked at him through long, painted lashes. Candle flames danced on the walls behind her. "She's in your apartment."

"You let a woman into my apartment?" His heart took off. "There's a woman in my apartment? *Now?*"

Mel grinned and dropped the burgundy curtain.

"Good luck with your ex-girlfriend." Piper swiped at the floor with a corn husk broom, doing no more than smearing the glitter. "Hope you have better luck than I do with mine."

"I'll be okay." King stood at the base of the stairs, looking up at his dark door. "Probably."

Did you enjoy this excerpt from *Shadows in the Water*? You can find and purchase the book at your favorite retailer or learn more at www.korymshrum.com.

ACKNOWLEDGMENTS

A round of applause to my critique group, The Horsemen of the Bookocalypse: Angela Roquet, Monica La Porta, and Katie Pendleton for your hard work on this book and being the first to call me on my bullshit! They're always the first to approve—or veto the story. Lucky for y'all.

Thanks to my ever-eager proofers and early reviewers: For this book we have: Wendy Nelson, Rachel Menzies, Cindy Bailey, Catherine Longi, Amy Morga, Kristina Hawley, Andrea Cook, Christina Wheeler, Trisha Gushue, Barbara Solzberg Lukin, Claudette Bouchard, Fiona Agnew, Tami McClain, Betsi O'Hara, Judy Johnson, Ashley Ferguson, Misty Neal, Lisa Morris, Alli March, Jennifer Wadlington, Marix Barrow, Rosemary Kenny, Linda Longo, Tammy Baker, Katja van der Heijde, and Heather Williams.

Eternal gratitude to John K. Addis for the special edition cover for #7. And thanks to Christian Bentulan for brand new *Dying for a Living* covers for all seven books

Thank you to Hollie Jackson who will narrate the audiobook. Thank you to everyone who reviews it and ensures its mutual success by telling everyone they know to go buy it.

And last but far from least, thank you to my wife, Kimberly Anne. We just celebrated our first year of marriage together and every passing day I feel more and more blessed to have you in my life.

Winning your love is my greatest achievement. In the words of Jesse Sullivan, with you, "I got far more than I deserve."

ABOUT THE AUTHOR

Kory M. Shrum is author of the bestselling *Shadows in the Water* and *Dying for a Living* series, as well as several other novels. She has loved books and words all her life. She reads almost every genre you can think of, but when she writes, she writes science fiction, fantasy, and thrillers, or often something that's all of the above.

In 2020, she launched a true crime podcast "Who Killed My Mother?" sharing the true story of her mother's tragic death. You can listen for free on YouTube or your favorite podcast app.

When not writing or producing her show, she can usually be found under thick blankets with snacks. The kettle is almost always on. When she's not eating, reading, writing, or indulging in her true calling as a stay-at-home dog mom, she loves to plan her next adventure. (Travel.)

She lives in Michigan with her equally bookish wife, Kim, and their rescue pug, Charley.

She'd love to hear from you!
www.korymshrum.com

ALSO BY KORY M. SHRUM

Dying for a Living series

Dying for a Living

Dying by the Hour

Dying for Her: A Companion Novel

Dying Light

Worth Dying For

Dying Breath

Dying Day

Shadows in the Water: Lou Thorne Thrillers

Shadows in the Water

Under the Bones

Danse Macabre

Carnival

Devil's Luck

Design Your Destiny Castle Cove series

Welcome to Castle Cove

Night Tide

The City: the 2603 novels

The City Below

The City Within

Learn more about Kory's work at: www.korymshrum.com